Hugh Thomas was educated at Sherborne, Queen's College, Cambridge and the Sorbonne. He wrote two books about Hispanic revolutionary experience: *The Spanish Civil War* (1961), for which he received the Somerset Maugham Prize, and *Cuba, or the Pursuit of Freedom* (1971). His other books include *Goya's 'Third of May', 1808* and a biography of John Strachey. His *An Unfinished History of the World* was published in 1979 and won the Arts Council Prize for history in 1980. *Armed Truce*, a history of the beginning of the Cold War, followed in 1986.

Hugh Thomas was Professor of History at the University of Reading from 1966 to 1976, and has been Chairman of the Centre of Policy Studies since 1979. He has been a member of the House of Lords since 1981, sitting as Lord Thomas of Swynnerton.

Besides *Klara*, his novels include *The World's Game* (1957) and *Havannah* (1984).

GW00712357

HUGH THOMAS

KLARA

AN ABACUS BOOK

First published in Great Britain
by Hamish Hamilton Ltd 1988
Published by Sphere Books Ltd in Abacus 1990

Copyright © Hugh Thomas 1988

All rights reserved.
No part of this publication may be reproduced,
stored in a retrieval system, or transmitted, in any
form or by any means without the prior
permission in writing of the publisher, nor be
otherwise circulated in any form of binding or
cover other than that in which it is published and
without a similar condition including this
condition being imposed on the subsequent
purchaser.

Printed and bound in Great Britain by
Richard Clay Ltd, Bungay, Suffolk

ISBN 0 349 50130 2

Sphere Books Ltd
A Division of
Macdonald & Co. (Publishers) Ltd
27 Wrights Lane, London W8 5TZ
A member of Maxwell Pergamon Publishing Corporation plc

This book is dedicated to the memory of
Sam Spiegel
1904–1986.

PART 1

APRIL–MAY
1945

I

*I*N THE SPRING OF 1945, A GROUP OF GIRLS, FRIENDS AND cousins from Dobling and Heiligenstadt, decided to go up past the Cobenzl hill to greet the Russian liberators whom they had heard would that morning be coming down towards Vienna.

These girls who, despite their youth, had been working for the Red Cross, thought that they would protect themselves from the consequences of any misunderstanding by carrying a home-made red cross on a white sheet. There was, presumably, safety in numbers. A girl alone could come to all sorts of trouble: ten or twelve girls would constitute a chaperonage.

In the group was Klara von Acht. She was a sparkling girl, full of life, an excellent actress, a Greek scholar, good at the piano, a person of promise. Everyone liked her. At seventeen, she was not strictly beautiful, perhaps, but charming to look at. Perhaps her chin was a little too strong for beauty. She had a humorous personality and, although high-minded, like most of the Achts, she teased her socialist father Alois for his "r-r-revolutionary" views. She was the eldest child, her two brothers, Karl and Poldo being fifteen and thirteen. Two other friends, Anna von Velden and Maria Gasner, both artistic and intelligent, were staying in the big house in Heiligenstadt. They too went along with Klara on the road to the Wienerwald, laughing and talking, as they usually did.

They planned to greet the Russians at a curve just before the path starts to climb into the woods. You can walk from there to the Wienerwald by a charming way which leads up to the main ridge overlooking Vienna. The path is through beech trees so tall that you can hardly see their tops. In spring these trees are so green that each year you believe that you have never seen such a colour before. Ladies who search China for jade of the "right green" recognise in the Wienerwald that they have been going about the matter the wrong way. Underfoot, wild garlic flowers were coming up, but they did not yet have that heavy scent which makes a walk a month later quite tiresome to the delicate nostril. Here Klimt as a child loved to look on Vienna, and learned of colour.

Afterwards, there was discussion as to the exact spot where the girls stopped. It seems that it was beyond the Cobenzl but not as far as the point known as Bei der Kreuzen. They had flowers to throw to the gallant Russian liberators,. and a large red cross to wave.

They were sitting beside the road discussing things when suddenly a colossal noise – artillery, bombs, thunder, a tree cracking and falling? – was heard in the wood just above them. A moment before all had been quiet. There was noise too of shouting and even, so someone said later, music. Two or three men in German military uniform came running down the path at a tremendous pace and disappeared into the trees like smoke without a glance to either side. Then two other men came running down, not so fast, since they were older. One of them stopped and shouted at the girls. They could not hear him. But he pointed backwards. They understood him to say that something large was coming. He then turned to follow his companion down into Grinzing. The girls did nothing. Of course, they were frightened, but as a group they could not admit what they would have confessed to one another singly. The noise in the woods grew more and more powerful.

A big Russian tank rumbled out of the Wienerwald. It kept to the path as a disciplined machine should, but was too large for it and so created havoc in the bushes. A second tank followed and then others. The girls stood up, formed a line, raised their flag and their flowers and the tanks began to fire. They were rooted to the spot in terror, for a second. Then the chaperonage scattered into the woodland, and into the hillside. The firing continued. The tanks rumbled on.

The fate of the twelve girls who had stood so bravely, expectantly looking towards the future, optimistic about the nature of the world, was various. Anna von Velden found herself lifted up by a friendly Russian and rode into Grinzing waving flowers past the Heuriger restaurants, on the top of the tank. Maria Gasner was shot in the neck, the shoulder and the leg, spent many months in hospital, but recovered. Two girls named Vera Huba and Mizzi Reichenau were killed. Four girls ran home without stopping, one of whom, Antoinette Messner, never recovered her reason. Klara von Acht disappeared. No one knew what had happened. No one saw. She simply vanished.

Later that day other Russian forces reached the Danube canal. Vienna had fallen. The war was over. Several months followed during which one could only hold on to one's watch by hanging it on a long string within one's trouser.

Shuddering explosions shook Vienna. The Opera House, Kärtner-strasse, and the Ring were in ruins. Avenues which had given their names to operettas became clogged with metal and bodies, parks suddenly became battlefields. Only a few weeks before, the Opera had been going. There had been dinner parties. Of course, there had been shortages but nothing like those of 1918. Now the land of smiles was an inferno.

The German armies were falling back into Austria. The extraordinary logistical arrangements which had taken millions of men in field grey to the Caucasus and the Pyrenees, the gates of Cairo and those of Moscow, were now being concentrated on obscure triangles based on the Salzkammergut. Göttweig, Melk, and St Florian would perhaps soon be as famous in real history – that of the pursuit of power – as Monte Cassino, Coventry and Rotterdam. Along roads where Schubert's and Mozart's tracks had so often been followed by lovers of music, prisoners, of all nations, stumbled towards sanctuary: French prisoners of Germans; German prisoners of Americans; Englishmen made prisoners by Germans but lately in Russian hands; Russians kidnapped in Germany to work in the Reich – all blinked, on foot, at the dawn of the new age. Encamped near the reeds of the Neusiedlersee, among the storks of Rust, the remains of a Hungarian army precariously bivouacked. On the Drau, near Lienz, fifty thousand Cossacks, survivors of a new White Russian war against the Bolsheviks, were establishing a settlement for their wives, children, horses, cattle and chickens as well as for themselves. Thirty years before, the smiling Austrian foreign minister had stood smoking a cigarette outside Sacher's hotel in Vienna, while the crowds cheered his ultimatum to Serbia. Austria had brought down Europe: now Europe was apparently emptying itself into Austria. Austria had become the last sink of the old world.

II

WESTBAHNHOF, VIENNA. GREAT CARAVANSERAI THROUGH which Viennese for a century have passed on their way to the intellectual conquest of the West. Always ugly, now badly damaged but still working. The noise of fighting could be heard from other parts of the city: noise of artillery, even of rifle-fire, apparently close. Aircraft appeared fitfully overhead through grey clouds. Fires appeared to burn indiscriminately in the inner city.

A small group of resistance leaders assembled in Alois von Acht's office. Around a brown table, they planned the recovery of the country. It would be an Austria radical in character; a people's Austria; an Austria free from the troubles of the past.

For Alois von Acht – black sheep of the extraordinary family with that name – it seemed right that this meeting, of such importance for the future of suffering humanity as well as for Austria, should be in the Westbahnhof. Socialism for Alois had always had the spirit of a railway. If great trains could be assembled, despatched all over Europe at speed, reaching not only Melk, and Linz, but Munich and Paris at preordained moments, human beings too could surely be organised, in all sorts of endeavours, working together, to timetables. What began with railways could be extended to all departments of life. Railways had already united countries. Soon they would unite continents. The brotherhood of socialism would keep man on the rails.

There was something deeply satisfying in the nice timings of express trains. To see the stationmaster stand with baton and watch in hand, as the Schubert Express shot past a small station – Purkersdorf, say – at 11.27 exactly, is surely to observe a triumph of the species.

It was a triumph with which he, Alois von Acht, had had much to do since, for four years, throughout nearly all the war, since indeed he had left the concentration camp at Dachau for reasons of bad health – yes, such concessions were possible if one had influence outside – he had worked on timetables at the Westbahnhof. His task had been to co-ordinate the movements of long-distance trains in those south-east *gaue* of the Third Reich which would now, in 1945, thanks to the Red Army, soon again be Austria. In this capacity, Alois had risen in the railway service to a position of command, being now in 1945 responsible for thousands of trains. Alois had trained as a mathematician. He had already brought to the timetables a real sense of the beauties of arithmetic – for the first time, he believed. He hoped next to bring to socialism the discipline of the train. His socialism, in short, was *Bahnhöflich*: his word.

Alois was a revolutionary socialist, thanks to the Red Army, not a communist. The distinction was important. He stood for the old socialism of the years before 1934. He would never desert old comrades and cross over to join the supremely tactical, and still devious communists as Comrade Fritz had done – Fritz who, even now with his back to the door, in the office, was talking with energy, his blue cap on his head, moving his hands to emphasise a point. Fritz Toblach had made his transition in 1934. It was method, though, not aim, which set Alois apart from the communists. And where would Austria be, where would Europe be, without the Red Army, now, as Alois knew, already in the Wienerwald, perhaps almost in Grinzing, perhaps being greeted with flowers even in his own Heiligenstadt, city of Beethoven as of the Karlmarxhof? One could not avoid elation!

He had incidentally once tried to call himself plain Alois Acht, without the "von", but, though that particule was only three generations old, few in the railway service had liked the dignified renunciation and Alois now used the old style without apology. One day soon, of course, all such things would vanish.

'We need a declaration,' Alois heard himself saying.

'But we already have a declaration, Comrade,' said Toblach. 'The communist party already has a text.'

Toblach fished out of the pocket of his worn light brown leather jacket some lines of script typed on paper the colour of porridge. Alois, with Franz Demangeon, a fellow socialist, and Leopold Moser, a dapper conservative resistance leader – all in ties and dark suits – leant over the desk, pushing aside trays full of correspondence (including a letter from the station master at Linz complaining that some socialist railwaymen were saboteurs) in order to read harsh words which said the right things, though scarcely in the German of Goethe: now that the nazi hyenas had been expelled by the valiant Red Army, the people of Austria should assert their independence: the first country to be conquered by the nazis would be the first to rise again; in a People's Austria, the old class structure would vanish; and so on.

All signed: even Poldi Moser, whose support before the war for the idea of union (*Anschluss*) with Germany had been enthusiastic. He seemed to have been purged of such feelings by his work in the resistance in the Burgenland. Even so, the act of signature was a turning point. Perhaps even Poldi, up till then, had not realised how far he had gone in accepting an alliance with communists, for the re-making of his country. It would be all hands, really, to the pump!

Alois's 'moment of understanding' about Austria's future association with Germany had been long ago, well, nearly a year ago, in 1944, when, secretly, a Prussian colonel had come to his brother's house in the country, Besselberg. The colonel was party to a plot against Hitler – was it *the* plot? Alois did not know – which, the colonel insisted, was backed by every field marshal in the German army. Like most socialists Alois had once thought that Austria could not survive as an independent economy. He and Poldi Moser had seen eye to eye in 1938 on that, though they would not have admitted it.

'What would your conditions of peace then be?' Alois had asked, as he and the Prussian colonel paced beneath the chestnuts then in marvellous colour.

'Oh, the frontiers of October 1938,' the Prussian colonel had said airily, 'we would need the Sudetenland. We wouldn't want to store up more trouble ahead. And we should, of course, give the Austrian Germans every right to be part of Germany. Though, mind you,' said the colonel, as they reached the white gate leading to the orchard, 'we should have to give Vienna a special place. The nazis have mismanaged Vienna. To make it a provincial capital: what an error!' The colonel sighed. If only the Third Reich had been directed by people like himself. They would have won the war, made friends with England, and ruled the world. World power! What an adventure!

Talking to the colonel from Prussia, neat, handsome and tall, with a complexion almost like that of an Englishman, it had suddenly come to Alois, almost as if it had been a revelation, that the idea of Anschluss could not be maintained. The Germans – the nazis – had behaved towards Austria in such a way as to make the idea of further union out of the question. Even Austrian nazis such as Alois's brother Gottfried had agreed.

After the momentous signature of the People's Pact in the West-bahnhof, some railway officials came into the office. Vienna might be in flames, the Westbahnhof might be close to ruin, and the service to Lower Austria entirely halted (the line between Hüttledorf–Hacking and St Pölten was only usable on a single track). That was no reason to cancel the meeting which Alois always had on Tuesdays, at 10.45 a.m. precisely, with Fritz Worgl, Karl Wolf and Max Flisch, the sub-directors of communications of the main regions. After all, the long-distance trains, from Stuttgart, Zurich and Munich had arrived that morning. Not really very late. Alois over the years had grown to feel affection for these workers' leaders. He knew that they were communists. They knew that he was still a socialist. But there had always been an understanding

14

between them. It was mutual respect based, as Alois realised, on the timetable. *They* knew that, even in the war, Alois had been able to modernise it. *He* knew that, even with the bombs falling, the modernisation had been carried through. That had meant that Germany had been able to carry, up to the very last minute, millions of men, and hundreds of thousands of ammunition wagons, to the East. These communist railwaymen were proud of their lines, even though they naturally welcomed the liberators.

On this morning they came in, as usual together; having had a preliminary meeting in Worgl's office beforehand, as always. If they were surprised to see their old famous comrade, Fritz Toblach, they showed no sign of it. Each gave him a salute with a clenched fist and withdrew silently to the window; grey NCOs of the international communist army, ready for anything: obedience or insurrection; collaboration with the bourgeoisie or with the nazis: it was a matter of emphasis or tactics. There was nothing which might not constitute, in certain circumstances, a step forward for the cause.

Toblach went over to them. He shook each of them by the shoulder, slapped them on the back, with that special smile which all leaders, kings and commissars alike, keep for such occasions. It was a great moment for these men to see Toblach, Alois thought, since Comrade Fritz in his way, in the party way, was a legend: a hero of 1934, at the Karlmarxhof and elsewhere. He had been in Schuschnigg's gaols. He had of course been in Spain in the civil war – though no one dared ask what he had done there – and most of the world war he had been in Moscow, with all the other grand old men of the communist parties, in the Hotel Lux, the glorious hospice of revolution. People talked of the decline of religion. But where there were modern saints such as Toblach to inspire them, did it matter? Toblach's jaw, his profile, smile, were well-known throughout the torture houses of nazi Europe since he had been on the posters for wanted men. Toblach had, so Alois heard, dropped by parachute in 1944 into Croatia and directed a group of Austrian communists in a series of guerrilla actions – against the Cossacks and some of Mihailovic's Chetniks. Then, last week, Toblach had led two thousand tried, tough, party men, into Austria, through the woodland paths near the Drau, liberating the Laibacher Moos and the quicksilver mines of Idria, shooting the SS and the local nazis, and "breaking into Vienna" a few days ahead of the Red Army. Toblach and he might differ in politics. Alois still maintained that democratic socialism was just possible and knew that the Communist party's democratic centralism left little room for that. But the two could understand each other. The communists had proved themselves in the war, Alois conceded, their unsentimental martyrs had been more numerous than those of any other party, they had still men for every occasion!

Franz Demangeon, his French surname indicating a descent from one of Napoleon's soldiers, drew Alois aside. Franz and Alois had been bitter enemies in the past. Bitter as only the relations between a right-wing working class socialist and a left-wing intellectual can be. Demangeon lived by his hands. He had been one of those engineers who had been kept during the war in Vienna for special building projects – too valuable to send to the front.

'Toblach wants to make a list of "democratic" policemen to take over Vienna when the Germans are beaten. He's got a list of thirty. Predictably. We had better have some names if we want to avoid a communist police in this city.' Demangeon was worried.

Afterwards Alois would remember his reply: 'Oh I don't think that's necessary. Communists make good policemen.'

Such was the innocence then. Demangeon shook his head. There was no time to dwell on such doubts. A message was passed saying that half the big maintenance shop at Amstetten station had that morning been destroyed by an Allied bomb. Apparently, a British bomb. The sub-station had also gone. Only three tracks at the marshalling yards were passable. The trains were getting through to St. Valentin, it was true. The fact that they were still carrying munitions, new guns, new men for the fronts, was irrelevant. The Austrian train service was still showing strength in adversity.

All over Vienna, large posters on walls signed by Baldur von Schirach, the nazi Gauleiter – and "the best nazi" most people knew – had told non-combatants to leave the city. How? By train! How else? Alois and his colleagues had laid on extra services to Salzburg, Innsbruck, Linz. The only part of the Reich which was still working well was the railway service. That was *bahnhöflich* socialism in action.

III

MAX VON ACHT, ALOIS'S UNCLE, AT EIGHTY-TWO, WAS A grand survivor. He walked round the Ringstrasse every morning before breakfast. People set their clocks by him – just as, as he liked to remember, the citizens of Königsberg had once done by Kant. Although Max no longer carried out this walk in an hour exactly, he never took longer than an hour and a quarter. He had done this regularly for fifty years since the time that his first *feuilleton* had been published in the *Neue Freie Presse* (when Theodore Herzl had still been *feuilleton* editor). He alone of the generation of Mahler and Berg, Freud and Schonberg, Herzl and Kraus, was still both alive and in Vienna. He had known those great ones, had been friends of some, enemies of others. Tall, stiff as a ramrod, unbending in spirit and stance, he continued to live in Vienna at the lower end of Johannesgasse throughout the war. He expected to go on doing so. 'The situation is hopeless but not serious': he repeated the old Viennese saying to himself almost every day, though he did not yet claim to have invented it.

The reasons for his survival were various. First, the Achts, whatever their origin – some said they had originally been Italian – were not Jewish – as the successful men of Max's youth had been. Second, he had written a book in 1912 which guaranteed his survival under the nazis. It had been called *Endlösung* – final solution.

The book was not anti-semitic. It argued that the problems of the Habsburg Empire could be solved only by a new form of polity: Germans, Czechs, Hungarians, Croats, Jews, should each be governed, within the Empire, on a cantonal basis, in the Swiss style, with the qualification that the cantons would be decided not on a territorial basis, but on the basis of blood. The German canton would thus have its zones everywhere from Romania to Bohemia, the Czechs in Vienna would be subject to Czech laws. A child of intermarriage would choose his canton at twenty-one, but be able to change later. Wives would take the cantonal designation of their husbands, widows would be able to return, if they wished, to their own canton after their husband's death. Governments would be formed by designation of the Emperor, but the upper house of the parliament would, like the US Senate, take two members elected by each canton, however small. Even the Wends would have two senators. The lower house would be elected from the people on the usual territorial basis.

The book had been short, slight, well-written. It had created a furore. The Archduke Franz Ferdinand, serious, stiff, icy, as was his custom, had been photographed with it in hand, at the Sudbahnhof: useful propaganda for both Max Acht and his publisher, Professor Kippenberg, of Insel Verlag. Perhaps the Archduke would have made Max his adviser for national problems, and the 'prisonhouse of free peoples' might have become a confederation. Looking back at the book, Max Acht thought that he had little of which to be ashamed. Not that he was ever ashamed of anything. The trouble was the title.

He did not know when the nazis had seized on the phrase. Surely before 1933. They confined it to the Jewish problem, as they saw it: whereas Max had sought a solution for all the races. Final Solution! Well, one could be sure that, of all his books, that would be the most difficult to reprint now.

That was obvious even if, at that time, in 1945, nobody knew for certain quite how the nazis had behaved. One had learned to distrust everything one heard. Everything was rumour. Particularly, in Max's case, when they derived from one's wife.

Berta, Max's wife, was wellborn: born indeed a Papenlohe. She had vitality, and a sense of gossip second to none. Her life had never recovered its momentum since, after 1919, and the creation of 'Yugoslavia', she had had to abandon going every summer to Abbazia, where her family had owned the Villa Iris. Both her sons were now prisoners of war; Otto, of the Americans; Jakob, of the Russians. Yet even in the changed circumstances, she still thought it important to imply, in every sentence, that she knew that the key to so-and-so's character was that, though formally a Liechtenstein, he was really a child of the late Prince Lichnowsky. She herself had talked, when young, to the infamous Countess Larisch, who had assured her that she had papers which showed that the Archduke Rudolf had not died by his own hand, but in consequence of a conspiracy. It was to her that one would turn for confirmation of the tale that Alban Berg's beautiful wife really was a daughter of Franz Josef. It was the same with the reports that she brought to her husband about the events of the war. She had known, for example, in 1940 that Hitler had avoided an attack on England, since he had prepared his *putsch* there: why waste men on an invasion when the same result could be achieved by guile? Her knowledge of the court of Stalin was equally sound. Stalin had been an agent of the British since the civil war, in the Caucasus. And so on. Thus, when she told Max that the Jews of Austria were being systematically murdered in Poland, not 'resettled' there, as the newspapers said, he heard the news with his customary reservation. Max Acht just did not know what was happening at Oświeçim, a Polish town in what had been not long ago Austrian Galicia three hundred kilometres to the north of Vienna.

Max was walking round the Ring as usual. It was now a grim walk. Not only the Opera had been destroyed. So had the Burgtheater, the Albertina, the Schwarzenbergpalais, and Hartmann's restaurant. Most of the bridges over the canal had been ruined, though there was traffic on the Salztorbrücke. Unfortunately, Max thought, the old ministry of war in the Stubenring, the ugliest building in Europe, whence Field Marshal Conrad von Hötzendorf had in 1914 sent out so many troops on such hopeless missions, was still there. So, more happily, was the statue of Johann Strauss, his moustache twirling forever in stone, in the centre of the Stadt park near the Kursalon. Just beyond, three members of the Austrian resistance, officers in the German army who had tried to betray their command post to the Russians, were still hanging, dead, head downwards on a gibbet. People walked by without looking. Max recalled how, in a French eighteenth-century novel, whose name he had forgotten, a traveller is wrecked on what he takes to be a desert island. He finds a gibbet. What a relief! He has reached civilisation.

This fine crisp morning, there was so much artillery fire going on that Max von Acht seemed to be the only civilian about. But after fifty years he was determined that his walk would not be interrupted. The walk was an instruction, after all.

In the Stadtpark that morning Max halted by the statue to the painter Schindler. He liked it: that left hand lying idle! That firm gaze! He was then approached by Prince Papenlohe, a second cousin of his wife's, in agitation: on this occasion, Max sensed, there was just a possibility that he was not going to speculate, as was his wont, as to whether the Archduke Rudolf had passed 'a certain disease' to the Princess Stephanie. It was indeed uncertain whether anything would be mentioned at all. A small group of men in SS uniform ran into the park from the Parkring, firing in the direction of the Landstrasse, shouting to the two elderly gentlemen to lie down, to hide under a bench, even to vanish.

The Prince and Max Acht were ready to hide under a bench – particularly if they thought that now Metternich's allegation was being proved more right than ever and Asia itself really was in the Landstrasse. 'A little different from Beethoven's remark to Goethe on this spot,' squeaked Prince Papenlohe. (This was exactly where Goethe complained of being cheered by the crowd: to which Beethoven answered: 'Do not let that trouble Your Excellency; the greetings are intended for me.')

The firing continued and it became evident that enemy troops were driving up from the Grossmarktstrasse. Above the shooting, Max could hear the cry of a peacock, an old friend who, since it was the mating season, was accustomed to cry from the roof of the Kursalon.

Prince Papenlohe crawled closer to Max under the bench.

'I've got something embarrassing to say to you,' he said confidentially.

An art historian known throughout Europe and America, a man said to have 'gossiped for Austria' (as his Oxford friends had said of him in 1900) and so a fit cousin for Berta, an exquisite bachelor, but also kind and in certain ways strong, Prince Papenlohe had lived for as long as anyone could remember in a beautiful house in the Herrengasse surrounded by interesting pictures, fine objects and relics, including a lock of Beethoven's hair and a suspect Giorgione. During the war, he had assisted the Director of the Kunsthistorisches Museum to evacuate its treasures to the Salzkammergut. He had himself hidden during the war a hundred 'U boats' – that is, Jews or other condemned people, who had no papers and no food rations. Sometimes, he said, he was tempted to confuse things and wondered if he had hidden people in the caverns in the Salzkammergut and works of art in recesses of his house in the Herrengasse.

'In case anything happens to me,' Prince Papenlohe squeaked, in an embarrassed tone, 'I must tell you that in the Herrengasse under my bed, in a hat box, I have the Crown of Charles V.'

'Really?'

'Really,' went on Prince Papenlohe, winking. 'There are two hatboxes. One has the Crown. One has my diaries. The pre-1939 ones are in Salzburg,' he added, winking and smiling once more.

Max Acht could not believe his ears. Here, under one of those park benches which meant so much to Vienna's history but were now labelled with swastikas 'Only for Aryans', he was hearing an extraordinary story.

After a few minutes, the firing died down, as inexplicably as it had begun, the SS men disappeared, and the two old men got up, and shook hands. Max continued to walk on, at his usual speed. Prince Papenlohe disappeared into the inner city. There was no one else to be seen. The firing, now that Max was in the Opernring, had ceased. War seemed like tropical weather: one minute violent, the next calm. Max reached the Goethe statue on the corner of the Burggarten. A small man ran out of the Goethegasse.

'Max von Acht! You've got it coming to you, you know. You're responsible for all this. And much more! You and your "final solution"! Curses on you! You'll be on a lamp post before you know what's happening.'

Max Acht did not answer. Better, in such circumstances, to say nothing.

But the man persisted:

'I know your sort. Murderer! Beast! You're going to be killed, you know. I'll be there to watch!'

Since the artillery had begun again in both south and north, Max's answer was easy:

'It looks as if we both might be killed,' he said, 'but thank you for warning me, all the same.'

He hurried on, and did not look round.

Just beyond the Burgtheater, by Landtmann's Kaffeehaus, which seemed not only to be opening its doors as usual, but to be full, an SS officer came up to him, saluted and said politely, 'Herr von Acht. It is dangerous to be walking this morning. We recommend you to remain inside these days when the destiny of our people is being decided. The population of Vienna was ordered to leave. You have not found it possible to obey that order. A person of your eminence has his priorities. But please, Herr von Acht, at least stay at home!'

What a pleasant young man! thought Max. So good-looking, and he certainly knew how to talk in a most appealing way.

'I always walk,' said Max von Acht.

'Yes, yes, of course, and the Führer wishes you to go on walking. But in order to do that for many years more, you must stop walking here today. I can tell you that, if you persist, you will not get any further than the Schottenring. There are barriers which prevent all movement. Those barriers affect the pavements. Not all barriers affect the pavements, Herr von Acht, but those do!'

Max might have challenged this and walked on until stopped physically from doing so, had it not been for the appearance of a boy whom he knew: it was Willy Svoboda, son of the Czech tailor who lived in Bauermarkt, just near the Stefansdom, next to Max's own flat in Johannesgasse. Why was he not in the Army? He must be at least seventeen. Max supposed that his clever Czech father must have managed something.

'Quick, Herr von Acht, the Stefansdom's on fire and your place is in danger. My father and many people have gone into the cellars. You must come, Herr von Acht, you must come now.'

Max went with him. What could he do, what should he do if the Stefansdom were ablaze? Of course, he must do something. They rushed back towards the centre of the city.

Willy Svoboda had had an interesting war. Until last year, he had lived in the heart of Vienna. His family, despite its Czech name, was Germanised. When the bombing of Vienna had begun, the children were evacuated. He had been sent, with thousands of others, to Hungary which, until the end of 1944, had been an oasis of peace. He joined the colony of German settlers, descendants of colonists of Maria Theresia's time, who had since maintained their sober culture there without interruption. When the war had drawn closer to Hungary, he had been sent back to Vienna. He should have gone away again to the country to avoid what was now happening in the capital. But he had stayed to work with his father. In the last few days, following Schirach's instructions for all non-combatants to leave, he had been among the gangs of boys who had chalked up on the walls "Wir Bleiben Hier", we stay where we are, an action which had incurred the death penalty on at least one occasion.

Max and Willy, an incongruous pair but one typical of the old Vienna if not of the new, the man of letters and the assimilated Czech immigrant, turned into the city along Bankgasse, then walked down the Herrengasse where the old Klonser Hotel had stood, and in which Colonel Redl had killed himself before the First World War. As they walked into the city, there was nobody to be seen save firemen and policemen. A few ambulances careered past at a speed which surely threatened the lives of the patients inside. One or two bodies lay in the street untended. Strange, Max thought, how one gets used to the macabre. From the end of the Graben, they could see that the great cathedral was indeed on fire. Sheets of flame came from the roof. Many firemen were there and, despite the barriers, a crowd of onlookers was gathering from nowhere. Disaster usually attracts observers. It turned out later that the roof had been set on fire by *German* artillery who were seeking to destroy an Austrian resistance group in the Inner City.

Max turned into his street by Petersplatz. When he got there, he found it in flames too. He had left, an hour before, the flat in which he had lived a lifetime. Now there was nothing but a ruin, with firemen unable to get close to the remains because of the heat. Max von Acht observed the end of his possessions and his neighbourhood as if in a dream. He was dazed.

'My street is all right, Herr von Acht,' said Willy, 'won't you come there? My father would give you coffee. He always has coffee. People sometimes pay him in coffee, that's why.'

Thus the man who had coined the phrase 'the final solution', passed the end of the war in a Czech tailor's cellar in the Bauermarkt. What he would miss the most, Max told Willy dreamily, were the splinters of the boards from the stage of the old Burgtheater which he had taken himself the night the place had closed, following the last concert played by the Rosé quartet.

IV

*D*URING THESE EXTRAORDINARY DAYS, THE ARMIES OF THE Americans, the French and the English as well as that of the Russians from the east were pressing into Austria from the north-west, the west and the south respectively.

The nazi Gauleiter in Upper Austria was August Eigruber: a thirty-eight-year-old Styrian, party member since 1928 and once a worker in the Steyr gas works. He had been Gauleiter since 1938. He had been the genius behind the conversion of the monastery of St Florian into a musical "gymnasium". He was a model nazi who believed in work, authority, good administration and the deterrent power of good punishment. In Linz, he had a court martial which did much deterrent work in the last days of the war. He had, for example, the Viennese Landesbauen-führer Mayzerzedt, a friend, hanged because he had left the capital without permission. There was no reason at all, Eigruber believed, to hold back on shooting people because they were friends. Many Allied prisoners were also prevented from playing any part in the Second World Peace by Eigruber's dedication to duty.

Eigruber's greatest achievement was in the world of art.

In certain salt mines near Alt Aussee in the Salzkammergut, the nazis had established the finest pinakothek in history. The best works from the Kunsthistorisches museum in Vienna, the National Museum in Berlin, the Alte Pinakothek in Munich and the Louvre had been concentrated there. The treasures of the Prado, the Hermitage and the National Gallery could not yet be added, but, a war or two later, that deficiency could doubtless be made up. The collection could admittedly not be visited, since the pictures were held in beautifully made wooden boxes, in beautifully finished caves: yet who, before the nazis, ever heard of caves with oak doors? Someone, perhaps Prince Papenlohe from Vienna, had arranged that each cave had been proclaimed "cultural property", in four languages (French, English, Russian as well as German). Whoever inspired those notices had providently wanted to insure against everything: even presumably a Russian defeat by France.

Everyone knows Alt Aussee. It is beautiful. There are waters to be taken. On the Erzherzog Franz Karl Promenade in Alt Aussee, Mahler conceived the Schönbühel Overture. The salt mines used also to be much visited.

Gauleiter Eigruber gave orders to his staff that the salt mines were to be blown up, in the eventuality – itself inconceivable in Eigruber's view, even in April 1945 – of Allied troops reaching them. Dynamite was laid.

Sometime in April 1945, the Führer showed how even heroes age by telling Eigruber that this implied method of commemorating the Third Reich was too extreme: in his hot youth, no doubt, Hitler would have positively enjoyed the prospect of the destruction of a hundred Titians. Heinrich Stoppack, under-Gauleiter in Vienna, risked his historic reputation as a man of iron to ring Eigruber to tell him to remove the dynamite. To no avail: Eigruber had given his orders. Nazis were not flexible in defeat: that was the point of national socialism. One had to think of history, or at least of the next generation.

In the far west of Austria, a French army, led by General Leclerc, was attempting to ensure, by winning last-minute victories, a seat for its government at the great world conferences which lay ahead. To be sure, within the Great Alliance, Leclerc's army was not as Napoleon's but every department of state in Paris was represented in it. There was even a colonel in charge of artistic matters, *un colonel des beaux arts*, Jean Georges Marchais.

This officer, an *inspecteur des finances* employed at the Louvre, had a mission to find out where the Germans had taken the works of art captured in France and to recover them.

Colonel Marchais had been working on a *catalogue raisonné* of the works of Goya. This reserved occupation enabled him to live in the Impasse de la Visitation No. 5 *bis*, throughout the war. He had had nothing to do with the Resistance, de Gaulle, Giraud, the English, Petain. He had daily walked to the Louvre and back, and seen few people. Now, however, the curtains of the liberation were drawing back for him.

The French staff were at the Hotel Elephant in Bregenz. A first step, no doubt, towards the reconstruction of French influence in Central Europe. General Leclerc sent for Colonel Marchais.

There was disquieting news: '*Nous avons bien reçus de nos amis en Autriche centrale* the news that our pictures are under threat. In chaos anything can happen. My experience of war is that when anything can happen, it does. German resistance is at an end. But there may be a fanatical redoubt here in Austria. The Werewolf Plan is to establish a nucleus of resistance in the Austrian Alps even after the formal surrender:

on guerrilla lines.' General Leclerc sighed. 'If we are not careful, it will come, this werewolf movement, in the very zone of Austria allocated to us by the gentlemen of Yalta, where France is to be responsible. Most inconvenient.' The General lit a cigarette.

'We know from our aerial survey that the road from here to Innsbruck is now free of organised German army movement. Innsbruck has already liberated herself. She awaits the Americans. Today, tomorrow, who knows? Colonel, take two men and a driver and go there.' The General stabbed a map. 'There, there are the treasures of the French nation. Recover them. Remain till we can withdraw them. Telephone me when you reach your destination. General de Gaulle takes a special interest. It would be strange if he did not. A patriot has an instinctive sense of artistic proprieties. Leave at dawn, colonel.'

The colonel did so. He had four men with him, not three, and two cars: two old Peugeots. The Colonel took with him his secretary, Madame Charpentier, whose charms were well-known in the Louvre. She was plain, well-dressed and amusing. The tricolore flew from both cars. The journey was, to begin with, simple. From Bregenz to Innsbruck there is only one road. In none of the small villages through which they passed was there any activity. No flags, no people, no traffic. Innsbruck heaved with a vast number of men and women wearing red-and-white armbands to proclaim their support for the Austrian resistance which, in the last stages of the war, had been successfully invented in the Tyrol. The sight of the *cortège* of French cars inspired extraordinary enthusiasm.

'I had no idea that France was so popular,' remarked Colonel Marchais.

'Hein, it is the popularity of neurosis,' said Madame Charpentier, waving to the crowds as if she were a Queen. Nearly every woman seemed to be wearing a dirndl. There were not many men of marriageable age but those that were there were mostly dressed in rather crushed green linen suits or lederhosen.

After two hours, the *cortège* of France escaped from Innsbruck. The road was full of pedestrians and carts. Refugees from east Europe were to be seen with bundles. Both lanes of the road were full.

'An agricultural revolution, hein?' said Madame Charpentier when the Colonel told her that many were probably Volksdeutsche, peasants from the Balkans.

'You could put it so.'

'Let us hope that they will not reach France,' Madame Charpentier remarked, 'their methods of rotation are unlikely to be ours.'

They drove on against the tide of refugees which seemed ever more impoverished.

'Are you sure that this is not the end of the Thirty Years War?'

Madame Charpentier had an acute sense of history, if not of humans.

'*A* thirty years war, perhaps.'

The journey continued. There was no sign of fighting. Even the flow of refugees suddenly ceased.

'Perhaps the armistice has been signed after all,' commented the Colonel.

'Surely they would have told you.'

'They are very bureaucratic in regular armies. Such information is distributed on a "need to know" basis.'

'Yet the French army is a new army?'

'It is in new institutions that bureaucracies establish themselves the deepest.'

The chauffeur drove in a straight line, past romantic lakes, and through beautiful valleys. The French mission saw fine waterfalls, avenues of oaks, mountain villages, and extraordinary castles on hillsides. They noticed fine summer villas, anxious cows, and, from time to time, fields full of disarmed soldiers. After many hours, they met a road block, an American flag, and four American soldiers with helmets like pudding basins. They were then only a few hundred yards from the salt mines above Aussee.

The Americans were friendly. A black soldier offered coffee to the French while their papers were examined. They accepted.

'This is tea,' declared Madame Charpentier in charming English.

'No, no, madam, it is coffee. American coffee.'

An officer came towards them from the Goldener Kreuz, a small Gasthof now copiously decked with the stars and stripes. The officer, who proclaimed himself to be Captain Norbert Stern of the 4th US Cavalry, was apologetic. He was unable to let anyone through to the salt mines. It might seem an insult, injustice, mistake, but those were his orders. There were urgent international reasons.

Colonel Marchais knew the language of the empire. 'In preventing a French officer from proceeding in a French road vehicle to deal with French national interests, you are, though you may not realise it, insulting the French flag and therefore France. My orders are to proceed unless physically stopped. I shall order my chauffeur to drive on at a speed normal for this stretch of road. Any physical interruption of this journey will be your responsibility, Major –'

'Stern.'

'Major Stern. The last soldier of that name whom I had the privilege to meet was part of the German occuping army in Paris. Subsequently we heard that he had been killed on the Russian front. Murdered by partisans horribly. So. We continue.' Colonel Marchais returned to his car and talked to the chauffeur.

Major Stern looked at the barrier across the road. It was thin, it was

26

wood, it would not survive any kind of assault. He walked over to Colonel Marchais.

'I shall telephone my commanding officer. May I ask you to wait?'

'I have already waited longer than my own commanding officer would have expected.'

'Would you wait ten minutes?'

'Does not the richest country in the world have a way to enable officers of your seniority to speak to their superiors more speedily than ten minutes? Very well, we shall wait.'

Colonel Marchais got out of his car again, looked at his watch and walked slowly towards a waterwheel standing in a stream and apparently working. He inspected with care this survival from an age when Louisiana was still French.

He returned after ten minutes.

'*Alors*, we must start,' Colonel Marchais, a cigarette in his lips hanging down like early pictures of Malraux returned to the car. 'We must start. But I confess I do not know how we shall end.'

Major Stern came out of the Goldener Kreuz. Two or three American soldiers, lazily playing with their rifles, watched him as he walked up to the French car.

'Colonel, I have information for you.'

'Well?'

'The situation is not as you suspect it. We are faced with a delicate state of affairs. Round the next corner there is the entry to the salt mines of Aussee.'

'My map says the same,' said Colonel Marchais.

'Precisely. As you know, those caves contain certain objects.'

'I was aware of it.'

'The caves are guarded by an SS detachment.'

'Well? The United Nations have presumably taken the appropriate means to deal with this rump of a dictatorship at the end of a war which, in conjunction with France, they have won.'

'Colonel, listen to me. The commander of the SS has orders from his commanding officer.'

'So it would seem, have we all,' the gleam of a smirk flickered over Colonel Marchais' sallow features.

Major Stern, sweating, leant into the window of the car.

'No, no, Colonel, he has orders to dynamite the mine if we approach. He seems determined.'

'Hein.' Perhaps that did alter things. Colonel Marchais told his chauffeur to stop the engine.

'Why didn't you tell me before? Your commanding officer told you not to? Who is the SS commanding officer?'

'He answers to the name of Gauleiter Eigruber, Gauleiter of Upper Austria.'

'Where is he?'

'We shot him yesterday in Linz.'

'Ah, that could turn out a rather expensive act of justice.' Colonel Marchais had ceased to be impatient. He was thinking. 'In the circumstances it might be helpful if I were to look at the site.'

'Certainly. I have orders to allow you through. But –'

'Only one car and only myself and a chauffeur. I read your thoughts. Madame Charpentier, our driver needs refreshment after the long drive. Would you take the wheel? Edouard, follow the Major to the Goldener Kreuz and eat? The Major will afford you that facility. Now Major, shall we go ahead? It is possible that France will have some ideas.'

They set off, following Major Stern's car to the mouth of the cave. It was a beautiful short drive. The Romantic movement might have been devised at this spot.

Colonel Marchais was impressed that the collections assembled by French kings had passed the war in such surroundings.

He and Major Stern walked towards the mouth of the cave. It resembled a railway station set into the hillside. A large oak door, half open, showed the entrance to the mine.

'Fifty yards down there you will find a hundred kegs of dynamite, Colonel,' Major Stern sought to make up for his previous lack of welcome by a desire to explain everything. 'In front, there is an SS officer to light them if he detects the presence of any Frenchman, American, Russian, or Englishman. It's delicate, I can tell you.'

'Looks as if patience is the only policy. Patience without publicity.'

'They have considered that. They have food there, enough to keep a platoon of men for two years. The air is good. For men as for paintings.'

There was firing.

'The SS men are having pistol practice,' said Major Stern. It was not a reassuring sound.

Colonel Livingstone of the British army artistic department heard the firing as he sat fuming in his staff car at the crossroads below the salt mines in Alt Aussee. He, too, had been held up by Major Stern's men. He was looking at a crumpled, coffee-stained, but still legible paper which ran, 'It is the duty of Military government staffs and detachments to collect information about works of art and other cultural materials which have been plundered by the Axis powers; to locate and secure them for eventual restitution; and to collect information about the personnel who have been responsible for such plundering . . .' After the words "Axis powers" the words, "or their allies" had been carefully written in, in secretarial long-hand.

The document also listed a number of Austrian cities which were not to be bombed, according to categories. The list began with the remark "There are no Austrian towns which fall into category A of this paper." Category B included the Inner City of Vienna, Salzburg, Melk and Göttweig. Someone had scribbled in pencil: "Category A is a category to be confined exclusively to places of the standing of Oxford, but not Cambridge, which is considered Category B."

Colonel Livingstone had been in Vienna in 1934: 'I was "out" in '34' he would say, making a deliberate confusion with those who would have said they were "out" in the 1745, because of being in support of Prince Charles.

What he had done in Vienna in 1934 was never clear. It had been however, a "seminal" experience for him. He talked nostalgically of that time, as if it had been one of *douceur de vivre* instead of a ghastly political failure, particularly for those whom he admired. An admirer of Dollfuss or Starhemberg might just have been able to look back on 1934 as a golden age. But to talk with rapture of it, as the Colonel affected, as a socialist, was odd.

Presented with the paradox, Livingstone would admit the unexpected-ness of it all. But he never explained. Did his enthusiasm derive from artistic appreciation of the "dream cities" for workers, the *Gemeinde Häuser* established strategically, as well as healthily, on the edge of the city? Surely an Anglo–Celtic art historian with any sense of humour could not go so far – particularly one who lived in a pretty flat in Chelsea and never saw council houses. Nor surely could the firing on council houses, by artillery of the state, be a matter for enthusiasm. Perhaps he had enjoyed the international camaraderie, akin to love, in favour of the defeated socialists. People of many nationalities gathered in tiny rooms, telephones rang incessantly, there was the distant mutter of guns, there were mysterious meetings at cafés in the Wienerwald with couriers from Moscow, the singing of the Internationale had been interwoven with *Ach, du lieber Augustin*! What days they had been! And what nights! That was the time when Livingstone made a break with the comfortable stan-dards of golf, gin and sporting prints among which he had been brought up. There, somewhere in the Josefstadt, perhaps, the spirit of socialism had come to Livingstone in the way that it had come to so many Eng-lishmen of his kind, so curiously anxious for discipline, as for commit-ment; it had come as spirits often come, in rather a vague manner.

Yet here in 1945, Colonel – as he temporarily was – Livingstone was being held up by Americans. He had instructions similar to those of

Colonel Marchais. He was an impatient man, just as Colonel Marchais was. He had not thought it possible to be prevented by an American from doing anything, much less one's clear duty. If being held up by Americans was what the postwar world was going to be like, he, Livingstone, was going to re-examine his loyalties. If one were going to be obstructed, better by the Russians, who had had a long history of so doing. The trouble with the Americans, Livingstone had decided, was that they had nothing to teach him.

A group of Austrians, with red-white-red armbands, presented themselves at the mouth of the mine. They had avoided the fate of Colonel Livingstone, even the experiences of Colonel Marchais, by coming up on foot by one of those *wanderwegen* marked in red on maps that the people of Attersee culture get to know well. They proclaimed themselves to Major Stern as the Austrian resistance of the neighbourhood.

Major Stern did not know how to deal with these men who looked appealing in traditional Austrian dress and hats with feathers. Elegant, no doubt, but impractical. But, on Colonel Marchais' suggestion, he explained to them the *damnosa inheritas* of Gauleiter Eigruber: as soon as any member of the Allies challenged him, the SS captain would blow up the caves and everything within them. He, Major Stern, believed that the threat would be carried out.

'But in that case *we* can bring a solution!' exclaimed Karl Reinhardt, the handsome and friendly leader of the Salzkammergut Resistance, 'we alone have the key.'

Major Stern did not understand.

'He means,' said Colonel Marchais, 'that, though the Allies can trigger the explosion, the Austrians are not certain to do so.'

'We are not included in Gauleiter Eigruber's prohibition,' pointed out Karl Reinhardt.

Major Stern admitted it. With reluctance, he allowed Karl Reinhardt to go to the mouth of the cave, enter it, and disappear behind the oak door within it.

Five minutes passed.

'Just so did Sancho Panza and the Knight wait while Don Quixote descended to the cave of Montesinos,' reflected Colonel Marchais.

'The Colonel sees something Spanish in improbable occurrences,' commented Madame Charpentier.

'Do we know anything of this man?' asked Colonel Marchais.

Major Stern admitted he did not.

'Yet you have allowed him into the caves where the treasures of France are held. Was that not a neglect of your responsibilities? You held me up, the accredited representative of General Leclerc, while permitting the entry of a person of no antecedents and no papers! Indeed, I do not know that you even asked for this gentleman's papers.'

'We have his men as a guarantee.'

'Who are they? Ten men who, now the war is over, have declared themselves the Resistance. They might merely be the Aussee tennis club who decided they had better negotiate themselves into a better world?'

Major Stern was silent. Another five minutes ticked away. The sweat stood out on his forehead, dark patches were appearing on the neat military jacket.

'I also have the English colonel waiting at the barrier down there,' he unwisely said to Colonel Marchais.

'Hein?'

'Perhaps you would feel better if he were brought up to accompany you?'

'What reason could you suggest for such an absurdity?'

'It would promote the solidarity of the Allies.'

'I see what you mean, Major. If things go wrong, as they might, it would be desirable to spread the responsibility. Of course, the real fault would remain yours. But a British, as well as a French, presence would have certain benefits for public relations.'

'What is your decision?'

'Oh, so you have decided to pass the authority to France? A suggestion which would have saved trouble had it been made earlier. My decision is in the negative. I cannot imagine circumstances in which any artistic proceedings could be assisted by the presence of a British officer.'

Major Stern gulped. He had not realised that patriotism went so deep.

Karl Reinhardt had now been in the salt mine twenty-five minutes. Colonel Livingstone had been waiting at the barrier for an hour. Major Stern said he thought that he should see what had happened. Colonel Marchais restrained him.

After an hour of disappearance, Karl Reinhardt came up and, with a smile at Major Stern, ordered his followers to join him in the caves. By this time, Colonel Marchais pointed out, it looked 'as if Austria had resumed authority.'

Ten minutes later, there was a modest commotion in the cave: shouts and orders. Five SS men, smartly dressed, came up, their hands clasped on their heads. They were followed by two blonde SS women, handsome and well-turned-out, also with their hands over their heads. Karl Reinhardt followed them.

'I have, as you see, secured the surrender of the detachment. But I gave conditions. These men and women are free. They must be permitted to return to their homes. By this offer, and by pointing out that Gauleiter Eigruber did not provide for the eventuality of the mines being liberated by Austrians, the Austrian resistance has liberated the mine. I hope that the production of salt can begin once again as soon as what has been illegally stored there is removed. You, gentlemen, may be interested in the works of art. We Austrians are concerned with the salt.'

Colonel Marchais found it hard to reply.

'Perhaps the time has now come to invite the English colleague to share our success,' he muttered to Major Stern, who telephoned down to the barrier where Colonel Livingstone had been waiting. Too late: that aesthetic individual had turned round and, making for Bad Aussee, had established himself at the Erzherzog Johann Hotel in Kurhausplatz. He was on the telephone to *The Times* office in Verona explaining how British policy was being frustrated by the United States.

Major Stern permitted the safe departure of the SS detachment without consulting his commanding officer. For this neglect, he was reprimanded, but his career suffered no impediment.

Colonel Marchais followed Karl Reinhardt into the mine. A veritable cathedral had been constructed there, complete with side aisles and side chapels, each carefully labelled in four languages, each describing what was, and what was not, to be found. Within minutes of the SS surrender, other Austrian officials (or were they German? What did it matter, they were lovers of art if not of mankind?) had appeared and were busy explaining how they had been instrumental in securing the right humidity in the caves. They admitted that they had become nazis: they had made that sacrifice to preserve the culture of Europe.

Colonel Marchais found his way to the aisle where the French treasures were held. He settled down to three days of successful cataloguing. Austrian, German, Russian and British "experts" also arrived, including Colonel Livingstone. The mine seemed for a time an international congress of art historians such as would years later be held in peace, a few miles away, in Ischl, under the auspices of learned foundations. The experts found nearly all the important items. But they were surprised to discover that the much-loved Crown of Charles V was not to be found, although a special place had been allocated to it. The special place was empty.

'The important thing is to say nothing about this in public,' said Dr Schmiedenberg, the expert on the Schatzkammer, 'once news like this gets out it can reach the international press quickly.' His colleagues heartily agreed, nodding sagely. None of them looked forward with pleasure to the revival of a free press. They were liberty-loving men for whom the end of the war promised good things. But a free press! The thing would in time have to be borne. The search for the last Crown of the Emperor Charles V was at least able to begin in secrecy.

V

THE ELDEST OF ALOIS VON ACHT'S BROTHERS, OTTO, LIVED AT Besselberg, a family property in the Wachau not far from the Danube. He was fond of saying that he lived just outside the boundaries of the old Roman Empire. That, however, would not have been noticed by the casual visitor to his house, since it was a triumph of a later Roman imperium, the baroque one whose dimensions were much larger than those of Trajan. One drove into a big courtyard, with three chestnut trees in the centre. The arches of the courtyard were white. The cloister-like passages around it had been painted blue and had a faded look. The house was full of interesting things. Although Otto had gone to Vienna to make money, the maintenance of Besselberg was his life's work.

The estate was not large: about five hundred hectares, chiefly vineyards and woodland. The Besselberg wines were excellent. They deserved a better reputation than they had had before the war. Max von Acht had often said that, if the Austrians only had the application of the Germans, their wine would do twice as well. Otto's wine if marketed would never be as good as when drunk from an open carafe on the terraces of the Danube. But it could make money.

Though over fifty, Otto had been called up in 1940. He went to the Russian front as an officer and was wounded in the siege of Leningrad. He had been a liaison officer there to the Spaniards of the Blue Division. Due to his wife, half Spanish, half German – although known as Betty – Otto spoke good Spanish. He had returned in 1943. He had then set about learning Russian seriously. 'It may be useful. You never know, it could be very useful,' he would say. When drawn out further, he would say, 'This war will be won when the Germans reach Vladivostock or when the Russians get to Paris. And, you know, Besselberg's on the road to Paris.'

During 1944, it had become obvious that the second of Otto's eventualities was the more likely. The Russians were in Hungary. Hungarians were fleeing across the border into Austria. An estate such as Besselberg was an obvious attraction. Betty had many distant cousins from Hungary. By Christmas 1944, the house was full of Cirakys, Konopys and Nadasys.

'Well, they all look pretty, the little refugees,' said Otto on Christmas Day, 'but why on earth do they think Besselberg is safe? Much too far east. Practically the Orient. People had better start to realise that Asia will now begin in the Boulevard Michel.'

With that, he returned to his Russian lessons, in the dark comfortable library, dominated by globes, atlases and a special clock which told the time, as if in a shipping office, in San Francisco, New York, London, Hong Kong, as well as Vienna though not in Moscow.

The news from Hungary was unpleasant. Not just of the fighting which was bad enough. But the consequences: one of the Cirakys arrived on New Year's Day.

'If any woman in Budapest says she's not been raped by a Russian, she's lying,' he declared to the bridge-players in the drawing room. 'Of course, one only believes half what is said by a Hungarian. Even so –'

By February, the Hungarians had left. They went west. Heaven knows where. The beautiful young Countess Malevolti, born Hungarian, but married recently to one of the Italian Austrians in Carinthia, came in for a night, described the pleasure of killing Russians, and left for Salzburg.

Her ravishing looks, her turbulent temper, her beautiful clothes, and her violent memories made an extraordinary impression on all who saw her. The sixteen-year-old Jean Marie von Acht wrote many letters to her during the next few weeks. None was answered.

'Is Austria big enough for the Hungarians? Surely not,' remarked Otto, 'but perhaps, in one of those empty countries, like Venezuela, there could be room. Most of them will probably die of malaria. The survivors will become millionaires and fly in Hungarian violinists from New York to distract them from their second marriages.'

Otto expected the Russian army to arrive in the spring. He made preparations to receive them. He spent every spare moment with his Russian grammar and irregular verbs. By the end of March 1945, he talked the language well enough to engage in arguments.

One day his daughter interrupted these studies.

'Papi, the soldiers have come. Franzie is holding them as long as he can.'

'Franzie?'

Otto and Betty had four children. In addition to Jean Marie, there was Franzie aged fifteen, Hansie aged thirteen and Theresia eleven. Otto went to the window from which he could see the entrance of the house. Franzie was at the top of the steps with a toy rifle. Below, beyond the stables, he saw a cavalcade of men and horses. The time for which Otto had trained himself had arrived. He told Betty to gather the family in the dining room. Such servants as remained, with their families, were to assemble too. He went down to greet the guests. He told Franzie to go in. Otto walked alone across the courtyard. A Russian corporal looked at him curiously.

'Take me to your commanding officer.' The fluent Russian worked wonders. The corporal nodded in the direction of the lodge, where a car had come to a halt. Otto made a salute, in the Russian style. A general rolled down the window.

'*Da.*'

'Welcome to Besselberg. We were expecting you. I hope your men will find accommodation in the stables. We could take three hundred men there with ease. You, General, and your staff must stay in the house. Some rooms have been prepared. But if you would prefer others, you have only to ask. Would you like to be shown them now?'

The general, a slow, heavy individual, with the face of a boxer, was unprepared for such courtesy. He grunted to a major sitting next to him, who asked another officer, sitting in front, a question which Otto did not hear. It was the major in the end who answered Otto and said 'General Krivoshein wishes to be received on the steps of the castle. What is your name?'

Otto gave his name. The major grunted.

All turned out as Otto had planned. The general and his staff were established in the main bedrooms. Otto and his family withdrew to an under-decorated wing, where he had prepared everything required to survive in happiness. The soldiers were in the stables. Otto asked the general if he would dine with himself and his family. The general declined but said that he would be glad to do so when his wife arrived from Moscow, an eventuality which would occur when the war was finally over. Otto thus learned that General Krivoshein expected his stay to be a long one.

The Russian soldiers in the stables conducted themselves impeccably, the general and his staff (which included the cooks) behaved like princes. Of course, the soldiers sang loudly as they drank Otto's wine, but Otto had himself shown them the cellars. The Army of Liberty needed its comforts.

VI

AUNT THEKLA, THE TALL, FINE, UNMARRIED, ELDER SISTER OF Max von Acht, was at that time a young eighty-five. She lived in a flat behind the Karlskirche with a bumptious maid, Gisela. Everyone had sought to persuade her to leave Vienna: to stay with the Papenlohes in Salzburg or other relations in the Tyrol. Like her brother Max, she had refused. She wanted to know what was going to happen.

'I know the beginning of the story. I must know the end.'

'But Aunt Thekla' – her name was never abbreviated –

'There are no "buts" about it. I don't believe in hearsay. There have to be witnesses. Look at what happened in Budapest.'

'Exactly, look at what happened in Budapest.'

'I don't know who there is to trust about Budapest.'

'You may not be alive to tell the tale.'

'I grant that. You may be right. But I want to take the risk.'

Nearly everyone else in the large apartment block in Gusshausstrasse had left Vienna "on some excuse", said Aunt Thekla scornfully, and the streets seemed empty.

The bombing, the fires, and the attack on the city followed. Russian tanks thundered along the streets. Thousands of people were taken to hospital because they had spent too long in the smoke.

Drunken Russian soldiers staggered about, embraced everyone whom they could see, including each other, broke shop windows, burst into houses, made fires of Biedermeier furniture, vomited out of balconies into the streets, and assaulted elderly and young women alike. Four Russian soldiers rang the bell of Aunt Thekla's apartment block. The concierge had left "on essential family business" for the Vorarlberg. The Russians broke the lock. While occupied with this task, two Viennese gentlemen passed. The Russians relieved them of their wallets, wrist-watches and fountain pens. Fired by that triumph, they forgot the door and adjourned to the gardens of the Schwarzenbergpalais, wrecked as they were, where they had a much-needed sleep.

Half an hour later, Aunt Thekla's maid announced that there were two new Russians outside wanting something. Gisela, by birth a Croat, brought her little boy to work with her. She could not have left him at home: her husband was at the war.

'Show them in,' said Aunt Thekla imperiously, as if they were distant relations. 'Bring them cake.'

'There is no cake.'

'Then bring them wine. They all like wine.'

Aunt Thekla spent most of her life reading. Usually after breakfast, she would settle down to a French novel. She preferred reading French to any other language. She thought it silly to read German: 'One may as well learn while one reads', she used to say.

The first Russian came, in, smiled broadly and started to rub his bottom, then point to it. For a moment, Aunt Thekla thought that he was asking to be beaten for some misdeed. Fortunately she did not act on that misunderstanding. He pointed to the sofa on which cushions lay piled in a comfortable heap. He wants to lie down, thought Aunt Thekla. No, no, it was not that. In broken German, the Russian explained. He had driven from Kiev on his motor bike. His bottom was sore. He needed a cushion. Aunt Thekla offered him one which her own aunt Thekla, after whom she had been named, had embroidered during, it was said, the revolution of 1848. Grateful, the Russian departed, after refusing even a glass of wine.

The other Russian, more boisterous, had been in some argument with Gisela in the anteroom. He talked some Serbo-Croat. Gisela came in to see Aunt Thekla with him.

'He wants to buy Hansie,' said Gisela. Hansie was her son. 'His own little boy was killed in Russia and he can't understand why I won't sell Hansie for two thousand marks.'

'Tell him it doesn't seem enough,' said Aunt Thekla. 'Have you tried offering him a drink?'

'Yes, he doesn't want one. He wants Hansie.'

The Russian lurched about.

'Give him a cushion.'

'A cushion?'

'Try it, his friend was more than satisfied.'

He waved the cushion away. But he pointed to a fine Empire clock. He got it. He pointed to a portrait of Aunt Thekla's mother, studied it more closely and then shook his head, picked up four silver boxes which he found on a velvet-covered table, and then pulled the velvet off the table. Gisela watched horrified, while he swept everything he could see into it, and made to go.

'You've forgotten this,' Aunt Thekla said, handing him an ivory paper knife.

The Russian left with it in his teeth.

Many such visits took place in the city at that time. Precisely what happened is obscure. Best to say that, while the Viennese were the poorer for five hundred thousand watches, the Russian sense of timeliness did not improve while anything between two hundred thousand and one hundred rapes took place. Accuracy in such matters is not a feature of the twentieth century. Many men were injured, and some killed, often while attempting to protect women from what a Russian colonel, a cultivated officer named Alexei Voronov, smilingly described to the chief medical inspector of Vienna as "a law of nature".

VII

*B*RIGADIER GENERAL BROOKS SHEAY III, OF THE UNITED STATES
Third Army, was experiencing a cruel spring. He came from Upper
New York State. Along the Hudson River, the Sheays were as well-
known as their neighbours the Roosevelts, the Craigs and the Heaven-
bridges. Brooks Sheay's father, Brooks Sheay II, had been a childhood
friend of Franklin Roosevelt, had bicycled with him in the Black Forest,
had stayed with the Roosevelt parents at Lord Ripon's shoot in Yorkshire.
The Sheays had started going to Austria well before the First War. That
was, to begin with, because Ruthy (Brooks Sheay III's mother) was musical. They stayed in a villa on the Traunsee in 1911 and at Altaussee in
1913. Next year, Brooks Sheay II had been at Dr Schreiber's Kur-Anstalt
Alpenheim on the road between Aussee and Altaussee when the news
came of the assassination of the Archduke.

Brooks Sheay III wanted to follow the family tradition. The Sheays
were, after all, old-fashioned. No son felt it necessary to rebel against his
father. Brooks Sheay III had been a proper young man. He just missed
the war in 1918 and went to Europe in 1920. He went to Paris, sat around
the Coupole and the Select, finding the great men of the lost generation,
and, after leaving Harvard in 1921, went to Vienna. He remained a year.
He was standing in the Kärtnerstrasse when the windows of Vienna were
swathed in black and purple for the Emperor Karl's funeral in the spring
of 1922. He learned German and had a Viennese accent. He became a
real Austrophil – unusual for an Ivy League American. He irritated
people in New York, and also in Vienna, by his uncritical defence of
everything Austrian: if one admired the satirist Karl Kraus, as Sheay did,
it was surely perverse to admire the society which Kraus was attacking.

In New York in the "twenties" people thought that Sheay would marry
one of the Kuttenbergs, Papenlohes or Janowitzes of whom he talked so
much. That was not so. He married Penelope Gates from Poughkeepsie.
His visits to Austria tailed off. He was in Salzburg in 1934 for the
festival, however, with Penelope. Both returned, talking enthusiastically:
'We had Klemperer, Bruno Walter, Fürtwängler. We shall never hear
better music.' But Salzburg was also full of nazis, dressed in lederhosen,

white socks, and swastikas. Thereafter, Austria ceased to be a proper subject of obsession for a responsible American. Sheay devoted his time to the stocktrading firm of Whitehead, Rifkind and Lohan. He did well. He made money and, by the time that his friend, Jim Smithson, got him into the War Department in 1941, was well off.

Sheay quickly became one of the best-known characters in General Patton's army. He was promoted quickly. As the Americans swept into Bohemia in April 1945, he was, people said, the man of whom the General used to ask the way. 'Sheay, where's the Danube now?' As they drove through Passau, Patton asked, 'Sheay, where's the Inn?' Sheay identified exactly where, on Count Arco's estate, the Germans had quartered the Lippizaner horses. With his knowledge of horses (gained on the Papenlohes' estates before the war) Sheay convinced Patton that the only way to round them up was to send in tanks. Sheay's brigade was easy to lead: it was a brigade of mechanics, all of whom, men and officers, looked on themselves not as soldiers but mobilised civilians.

Disagreeable things began to happen to Sheay in April 1945. First, there was the liberation of Braunau-am-Inn, the Fuhrer's birthplace. The crowds cheering the Americans who arrived in open cars were overwhelming. It was moving to all Sheay's colleagues. Not to Sheay. He knew how, at the time of the Anschluss, the crowds then had been the same. By the time that Sheay got to Braunau, the Austrian resistance, in red and white armlets, were controlling the administration. The nazi bürgermeister had been bundled into the town gaol and other local nazi leaders had fled. A new bürgermeister, Dr Eckert, was dispensing news, confidence, and red and white armlets, as if he had opposed the nazis since 1933. Sheay was disgusted.

'Hey, Brigadier, don't you want to see the house where Hitler was born?' asked an enthusiastic member of his staff.

'Nope. I've seen it before. The sooner you blow it up the better.'

'Well then, what about having a word with the new bürgermeister?'

'I don't think I will. I'm going on to Eferding.'

'Say, Eferding's right off the route. Why are you going there? Got family there?'

'Let's say I'm going to where Kriemhilde passed the night on her journey to Hungary.'

'What's that, Brigadier Sheay?'

'That's the *Nibelungenlied*, Captain. So long. See you in Linz tomorrow.'

Sheay drove on. What was this new Austria which he did not know? Would anything of the past that he remembered still be there?

Next day, Sheay and his brigade had the task of driving from Linz down the north shore of the Danube to meet the Russians. It was fine weather. The Danube riverside villages came out to meet and greet them.

'They're enthusiastic, Brigadier,' said Sheay's ADC.

'They're pleased to see us and not the Russians. It's quite a near thing actually,' Shea answered drily. They drove on.

'A fine body of men,' said the captain approvingly as he saluted yet another well-organised Resistance group in red and white armlets.

'Where were they on March 12 1938?' growled Sheay, 'or, come to that, on March 12 1945?'

'Come again, Brigadier?'

'Nothing. I was entertaining myself to an historical reflection. It's dangerous in a soldier. Particularly at the moment of victory.'

'Brigadier, they say there's a concentration camp just above the next village.'

'Yeah. What's it called?'

'Eichenwald.'

'I've heard of it. We'll go up there.'

The small detachment turned off the main road and climbed along a narrow lane which soon began to offer spectacular views of the Danube. Sheay heard his first cuckoo of 1945. The Captain heard it too.

'Summer already here, Brigadier,' he said with his usual agreeable desire for small talk.

Round the next corner, behind a long farmhouse, they observed the walls of what looked like a small, if dilapidated, castle. Grey walls. A tall chimney.

'Pretty site for a place like this.'

Sheay nodded. It was a good site. He was almost sure that Eichenwald was mentioned in the *Nibelungenlied*. Even if it had not been, Kriemhilde and the Burgundians would both certainly have passed through it.

The gate of the prison of Eichenwald was open, and there were three American cars parked outside. Major John Fish of the intelligence corps from Bethesda, Maryland, stood in front of the gate. Sheay's driver drew to a halt in front of him. Sheay got out. Fish saluted, and Sheay saw an extraordinary thing: tears were streaming down the major's cheeks. Major Fish was a hearty, strong man with no claim to be an intellectual. At home he had been in insurance. But there was no doubt about it: he was crying.

'Well, Major Fish?'

'Brigadier. If you go in there you'll see a sight which will be with you all your life. How could they? Brigadier. You go in there and you'll find out why we've fought this war.'

Sheay did go in, and he never did forget his sight of Eichenwald concentration camp.

Sheay drove off down the hill. The site was beautiful. The wild flowers were wonderful. He was not surprised to hear, as his driver braked just short of the village, the sound of the town band playing the *Radetzky March*. That was in honour of the liberation and the Americans. It was Eichenwald's good fortune that had brought them General Patton's army, not Marshal Tolbukhin's. The Austrians were still lucky.

A day later Sheay found himself at St Florian's. The calm of the marvellous church inspired him, as it had done before. It gave him a sense of serenity which he had never encountered in America: not even in his brother's sail boat at Vineyard Haven on a calm day. It reminded him of the nobility of old Austria. He was not the only one to be confused in the spring of 1945.

VIII

ABOUT THIS TIME, CHARLIE GREW, SECOND LIEUTENANT IN THE 10th Lancers, but attached to one of those secret agencies so amply developed in the region of London's Victoria Street, dropped by parachute into the woods north west of the resort town of Baden-bei-Wien.

He had flown in a Liberator bomber up from an airfield in northern Italy, which had the code name "Darkwater". Previous to that he had been sitting out in Rome, waiting, going to parties in old palaces given by Italian aristocrats. These Italians were "spending their way back to respectability", making friends of English and American officers, where they could, in case their many years of courteous connivance with Fascism should be a difficulty in the new world of peace. 'Under the white gloves of those footmen,' Charlie would remark of their hosts' servants, 'you can find the hands of murderers, or the fingers of thieves.' Meantime, the music had gone on and on, and the Englishmen – and the few English girls – present would forget for a few hours not only that the Italians had till a short time ago been enemies, but that the war was still on.

While approaching the dropping area, Charlie noticed that his leg-bag did not fit properly. In this, there was his wireless set, signal plan, food, compass, ammunition, and clean underwear. Neither he nor his "dispatch" could fit it on. This should not matter much, the "dispatch" explained. Charlie jumped with it loose.

The jump was one of those things for which Eton had prepared him.

'Now then,' said the dispatch, 'at the count of zero, the hatch will open and down you go. Happy landings! Take that deep breath now, Sir, and God speed! Ten, nine, eight –'

Charlie had been carefully trained for this moment. He had a reputation of being the school joker, the laughing scholar, the boy who could keep more easily hot coals in his mouth than a good remark, but at this moment no play on words came to him. This was seriousness, at last. Then the count came: "two, one, zero". Out he fell, at one with so many other parachutists of the war, a new order of human beings who have known the air as others have known the sea, caught between exhilaration and fear, but moved at this moment by an appreciation of the beauty of the earth for which Eton had not prepared him. A successful night parachute drop into enemy territory has no equivalent.

'Weather and visibility excellent,' Charlie Grew giggled to himself, in the words of the report which he would presumably some day write, 'and I landed right on target.' Why "on target"? Surely it should be "at" target. Well, he would see how he could polish up military English, now that he was a lieutenant.

To Englishmen who recall walks in the Vienna Woods, the spot where Lieutenant Grew landed is familiar: "*Auf dem Hohen Lindkogel (Eisernes Tor, 847m), den höchsten Berg der Umgebung, von Baden in 3 Stunden lohnend*". Thus Baedeker. There is a meadow on the top of the hill, and a restaurant, open in summer, in peacetime. The Lieutenant spent half an hour in this meadow looking for the leg bag. Not finding it, he hid his parachute and flying suit under beech leaves and, at four in the morning, began to walk to Baden-bei-Wien. The walk along the wooded path was cold. The air promised snow. A few deer stood in a meadow near a deserted café called *der Jägerhaus*, the hunting lodge. There were fine views of remote valleys, beech trees of great height, a wind sometimes so fierce that once the Lieutenant imagined himself to be near a great road. For a section only the path needed more of a scramble than a walk. He was in Baden not in the three hours predicted by the Guide, but two: at six o'clock. He reached the Erzherzogin Isabellastrasse, his destination on the outskirts of the town, without difficulty, without romance, and without being observed. The low Biedermeier houses retain the charm of a different age. It still seemed that those who lived there might have nothing to complain of more serious than Beethoven's bad debts. Baden breathed the tranquility of a great spa.

Tranquility, however, was not a word which one could use about Dr Primorius and his wife, the "contact" at Baden to whom the Lieutenant had been recommended. They were elderly with four sons in the army: one was a prisoner in Russia, of another they had had no news since before Christmas. One was in a hospital in Berlin, another believed to be on leave in Salzburg. The Primoriuses were social democrats. But even the Lieutenant, whose knowledge of Austrian politics was negligible, could sense that they were on the extreme right of that elastic movement. Dr Primorius said that he was half Jewish and could not understand why he had been left free by the nazis. Inefficiency, he presumed. He had lived throughout the war in Baden with no interruptions. Now, however, he was terrified. He expected the German army to fall back from Wiener Neustadt to Baden and the Russian army to come in. There! Was not that the sound of artillery in the south? Dr Primorius did not himself mind death. But what would happen to his wife, his books, his pictures, his ivories? He had had an opportunity earlier in the war to send those treasures to a safe place in the mountains. He had turned it down. He had thought that there would be fighting there at the end of the war. Now what was to be done? There! Dr Primorius pointed out, it had begun to snow. On top of everything! Snow in April!

Lieutenant Grew explained his propositions. His mission was to assist the Allied advance by leading a socialist underground: to attack Gestapo headquarters; to kill nazis; to blow up bridges. Where was the Baden underground? How could he establish relations with it?

'The socialist underground in Baden,' said Dr Primorius, in a voice of agitation, 'is not what it was. Some of us were arrested only a few weeks ago. Others, whom the Gestapo thought might be socialists, but against whom they had nothing, were recruited at Christmas time into the Volkstürm and sent, we believe, to Slovakia.' It became clear to Charlie that there was nothing in Baden on which he could build.

While they talked, a maid brought coffee and boiling milk in silver jugs. The Lieutenant expressed surprise at the doctor having such supplies after five years of war. Dr Primorius said that his brother, who had gone to Brazil, regularly sent him coffee: 'The post survived; I have survived. Up till now. But listen – surely that is artillery?'

After drinking the coffee, and some random conversation chiefly about Baden (Beethoven's stay there in 1822, Mozart's in 1791, the Emperor Karl's in 1917, the "fatal year"), Dr Primorius calmed down and became helpful. He no longer had much to do with the socialist underground, he said. Of course, he would be a socialist till his dying day. One could not desert a movement within which one had lived for so long. But in Baden the socialist party pursued its own political ideals, and refused to compromise its position cooperating with other movements. By this, Dr Primorius meant to allude politely to the communists. He believed that the best thing for the Lieutenant would be to go to Vienna, to those whose address he would give him. The right way to go was through the Wienerwald. There were good paths. The Lieutenant should realise that the Wienerwald covered agricultural land and villages, as well as woodland and hills. It was perfect cover. Dr Primorius gave him a map. Baden was twenty-seven kilometres from the centre of Vienna by a direct route. Say thirty-five through the hills. Eight hours' walk. Perhaps less. That would be better than waiting for death in Baden.

The Lieutenant set off for Vienna at lunchtime, having been fed by the Doctor, who continued to believe that the Russians were about to arrive. The Lieutenant said that that could only be welcomed because it would bring the end of the war. Would it, Dr Primorius asked? Or would it not bring the beginning of another war? In Budapest, the Russians had shot every male they could see between sixteen and sixty and raped all the women. If the Russians approached Baden, he and his wife would take to the hills.

Lieutenant Grew left Baden with no real indication that war was near, though the thunder in the south had become louder. He was prepared to accept that it might be artillery. He reached Vienna, by walking fast, in seven hours. The snow did not persist. In another hour he was at his appointed rendezvous: the house of the socialist leader Alois von Acht in Heiligenstadt.

The remains of a German army fell back through Baden that evening. The Russians came in the following dawn. The street lamps were hung with the bodies of members of the local SS, Dr Primorius's house was taken over as the residence of a Soviet colonel. Baden became the headquarters of the Soviet high command. Dr Primorius and his wife were both shot in his library, for reasons which were never clear. The maid became the mistress of the colonel and gave him good coffee with no interruption of her usual routine.

IX

RÜDIGER VON ACHT, ALOIS'S YOUNGEST BROTHER, WAS A romantic. It was because of that that he had become so attached to General von Pannwitz. The Pannwitzes had been landowners in Silesia and, important for a romantic, were related to the poet Kleist, whose mother was a Pannwitz, and whose sister married another one. General von Pannwitz had even been appointed by a kinsman, Field Marshal von Kleist, to command the regiment of Cossacks from the Kuban which had volunteered in 1942 to fight the Bolshevik usurpers. Von Kleist asked Rüdiger, a cavalry officer, to help him re-train these regiments for twentieth century war, and afterwards to take a command within them. Rüdiger accepted with enthusiasm. These opportunities constituted a good way out of a war for which he had felt decreasing enthusiasm.

At the beginning, it had been different. Rüdiger, before the war, had been attached to the Heimwehr, the right wing para-military operation. In the 1930s, he would find himself in the middle of family arguments centring on the personality of Starhemberg, the Austrian fascist, whom he admired. Unlike Alois, with whom he quarrelled, Rüdiger thought that there was much to be said for the Dollfuss-Schuschnigg experience of authoritarian government in 1934. When pressed by his left-wing relations, he would say triumphantly:

'And Karl Kraus agrees with me!'

It was true: that satirist in old age had said that he considered authoritarianism to be the only answer for a country with a nazi neighbour.

Rüdiger had been in the Heldplatz in March 1938 when Hitler had made his famous speech, but he had gone as a spectator, with a million others. That did not mean support for Hitler. Had he cheered? Well, perhaps, he had. But it was easy to be carried away: "Emotion is epidemic."

Rüdiger was one of the first Austrians to be commissioned into the German Army after that. As a second lieutenant, he had taken part in the invasion of France. That aroused in him complicated emotions. He knew France well, he loved it and even carried in his pocket a volume of Jacques Bainville, whom he regarded as the greatest modern French writer. All the same, the excitement of taking part in a successful invasion of a great country was overwhelming. Even afterwards, he could not help a *frisson* of pleasure when he thought of the swiftness of the victory, the efficiency of the German army, the grandeur of being in an army which, unlike the Kaiser's, reached as far into France as Napoleon had into Austria.

At first, the Russian front had been much the same. As the troops crossed the frontier, singing *Kleine Monika*, there had been just the same excitement. The liberation of Russia! What an intoxication! At the front, there was always, while advancing, an extraordinary pleasure. How could one deny it? Conquest is a great adventure. The defeat of Bolshevism was a great cause. But the savagery behind the lines sickened many people. They overlooked it, or tried to. Rüdiger heard excuses that the blame for the barbarism lay with the Russian partisans. But that could not excuse the Germans. It was a matter of breeding. The Germans whom they sent to administer Russia had been such low grade people. Dentists' assistants from Schleswig were becoming gauleiters. How could such men be expected to run an empire? The English, now, would never have made that kind of mistake.

Of course, there had been some marvellous moments later on the Russian front. Rüdiger had read Verlaine aloud to his men outside Stavropol. That had been something! Imagine if the Führer had heard of it!

Pannwitz's men were taken to Yugoslavia to fight Tito's partisans. Rüdiger would have liked these old Russians to have been given a chance to fight against the new ones, as they themselves burned to do, but that happened only briefly, when, for a time, they found themselves in 1945 pitted against the 133rd Soviet Infantry Division. Otherwise, the fighting had been in the valleys of northern Slovenia. Rüdiger had to admit that there, though there were losses, he had enjoyed himself. The country was glorious, the air good and, for a time, it seemed again as if war were still just hunting carried on by other means.

Rüdiger's corps was withdrawn into Austria at the end of the war, across the border at Lavamünd, on the Drava: a river which there turned into the more friendly-sounding Drau. The commander-in-chief ordered the surrender of all troops under his command, to the Allies. General von Pannwitz was determined to surrender to the British, whom he knew had come up from Italy to Klagenfurt. He knew what would happen to his men and himself if he were to surrender either to the Russians, not far away up the road at Judenburg, or to the Yugoslavs or Bulgarians: a swift death was the very best one could hope for.

The British were at Klagenfurt. Pannwitz was lunching in a farmhouse between Wolfsberg and Völkermarkt, with Rüdiger and several other officers, when a British major arrived by car. This gentleman was tall, pale, but courteous and correct. He introduced himself.

'I am Major St Vincent. In the name of General Whitelegge, I have the honour to ask for your surrender.'

It was the end of a chapter in German history. Perhaps it was the end of German history. No, surely not, the battle between Teuton and Slav would one day begin again, with different results.

General von Pannwitz said: 'I am agreeable subject to certain conditions.'

'I am under orders to offer no conditions,' returned Major St Vincent.

'Not even the condition that none of us should be surrendered to the Red Army?'

'Not even that.'

Major St Vincent looked at General von Pannwitz quizzically. The glance was returned. General von Pannwitz added:

'Major, you seem to have forgotten where we last met. It was with the Kuttenbergs at Pottendorf.'

Major St Vincent smiled, though not very warmly. It was the watery smile of the victor. 'I thought that we had met before. All the same,' he added, 'I have to insist on no conditions. Also,' he added, 'Pottendorf is in ruins.'

General von Pannwitz asked the major to be seated and offered him lunch. He refused.

General von Pannwitz conferred hurriedly with his officers. Several were against this conditionless abnegation. But there was little choice, surrender he must. The British could anyway be counted upon. Rüdiger was among the group of officers who supported him.

The Cossack corps was next day escorted by Major St Vincent as far as St Veit an der Glan. They were ordered by General von Pannwitz to give up their arms. Rüdiger was on duty in a meadow as several thousand Cossacks, dressed in traditional clothes, their *chapkas* on their heads, rode up, saluted, and flung their arms down in piles. Most of the troops were then allowed to bivouac in St Veit and the villages nearby. The General was asked to make his headquarters a few miles north of St Veit at Althofen in a dilapidated Schloss which had once belonged to the Tanzenberg family. Here the proud staff of General von Pannwitz, half of it German, half of it Russian, sat about for several days, looked after by the old servants, playing cards and entertaining themselves with thoughts as to where they would be sent by their British captors: Argentina? South Africa? Australia?

'A war between the Americans and Russia is bound to begin soon and probably it will start here,' said Colonel von Teplitz, a large, handsome man with a loud voice, 'we shall be in the thick of it. Our experience will be invaluable. Let us benefit from these days of tranquility.'

'We shall be sent to Persia. The British need men like us to guard their oil wells,' said Captain Schwarzkopf.

'No, we will have to fight the Japanese,' insisted Colonel Weitz.

'I shall make for Argentina,' said the swashbuckling Major Reichenberg, 'they like men who understand horses there.'

General von Pannwitz said nothing. For him the war was over. He would return to his properties outside Breslau and cultivate his garden. Rüdiger also said nothing since, just before dinner, he had been told by one of the servants that the British had been handing over their prisoners to the Russians, the only exception being the Croats; who were being given to the Yugoslavs. The servant said that he had been told this by his sister who lived at Judenburg, where the Russian zone then began.

After dinner, von Pannwitz said that they had been asked to a meeting the following day at another Schloss, that of Hoch-Wahlenberg, outside Launsdorf, where General Whitelegge had set up his headquarters. Cars would be provided. All would attend.

Rüdiger told von Pannwitz the story that he had heard from the servant.

The General replied, 'It is natural in these circumstances for wild rumours to start. It is our responsibility as officers to see that they do not have any consequence on the morale of the men. Good night.'

Rüdiger believed Pannwitz had heard the same story as he had, but was putting on a brave face. He did not sleep much that night. His instincts were to vanish into the greenwood. He contemplated walking down the twenty miles or so down to the Worthersee where he had once spent a summer, in a house as enchanting in its position as it was ugly inside. Surely he could hide there? Or would it have been requisitioned by the invaders? At all events, it might constitute the first step to escape. Some castles on the Italian border might serve as staging points to South America. But he did not want to leave his companions. Above all, he could not abandon von Pannwitz unless ordered to. Rüdiger had read too much Kleist to be able to flee a decision.

Rüdiger's room looked over the valley. In the early morning, a mist was coming up. The sun was breaking through. He could hear, through the open window, the hen pheasants clucking in the bushes, birds proclaiming that spring had come. Though he lived in Vienna, he was at heart a countryman. This was his country, his Austria. Did his fate have to be decided by Englishmen? He breathed the good Austrian air deeply, went downstairs, breakfasted with Colonel von Teplitz, who told him yet another tale of fighting with the White armies in Russia in 1917, and drove off, two cars behind von Pannwitz, to the conference with the English general at Hoch-Wahlenberg.

This Schloss was thirty minutes or so from Althofen. Though Rüdiger knew the two officers who accompanied him well, none of them spoke. Apprehension about the future now possessed the command. The English driver, a corporal, said nothing either. Rüdiger sensed in him a distaste for driving German officers.

They arrived. Hoch-Wahlenberg was a romantic castle set high above a river. The column of cars drove up to the Victorian entrance, where many British soldiers were standing around at ease. They seemed short, untidy, and ill-disciplined to Rüdiger. He did not see much justice in their having been on the winning side of this war. Luck, of course, had usually helped England. Think of 1917!

Pannwitz and his party were ushered into a long room with a table in the centre of it. Portraits of wigged eighteenth century heads surrounded them. The gold and white of the decoration gave continuity to an unprecedented scene. Generations of Wahlenbergs had here dined, laughed, teased and delivered themselves of *ex-cathedra* statements from the days of the Turkish threat onwards.

The English general Whitelegge came in, followed by several staff officers in khaki with red tabs. He was still quite a young man, but self-confident, amused, intelligent.

'Gentlemen, please sit down,' he said in passable German. He glanced up and down the table. He had an English officer on either side of him. A bevy of young men stood behind him.

General Whitelegge's German stood up well. He must have studied it seriously. What a pleasant change! He spoke laconically.

'Gentlemen, I have asked you here to discuss the future. The war is over. You are my prisoners. So are your men. We are doing what we can to see that both you and they are looked after as well as possible. How long any of you can remain *my* prisoners is, however, a matter of doubt. As a result of decisions taken by the Allied governments, my colleague General Smith was yesterday instructed to hand over all Russian-born citizens in his control to the Soviet High Command. That has already begun. I have not yet received any such order. But I expect to. Probably by tomorrow at latest. I expect indeed to be ordered to begin transfers at Judenburg on Friday. The theme of our policies is: we shall hand over the Germans to SHAEF. We will deliver the Cossacks to the Russians. We will deliver Croats and Chetniks to the Jugs. That is, the Yugoslavs.'

'As to the officers of German or –' he coughed '– Austrian nationality in command of Russian-born troops: my colleague General Smith has had the specific order to include these officers among those handed over to the Russian High Command. He is fulfilling that order. If I receive it, I shall carry out its instructions. The Allied nations, are after all, *united* nations.

51

'I shall have to act by Friday at latest. Today, gentlemen, is Tuesday. Though you are prisoners of war, I personally tell you that my division will be celebrating the end of the war tomorrow, Wednesday, and the next day, Thursday. Can I leave you to draw your own conclusions?'

General Whitelegge stood up: 'Gentlemen, I have nothing more to say. I cannot enter into discussion. I am talking about a future whose details I do not know. I have taken the initiative to hold this meeting. I daresay – and as officers you will know the truth of this – that there are some who feel that a senior officer should not take such initiatives. As to that, I have no comment.'

General Whitelegge saluted von Pannwitz (who saluted him in return) and left the room. There was no time to talk before Rüdiger and his colleagues were put back into their cars and driven back to their Schloss by the same taciturn drivers whom they had had on the outward journey.

On their return, von Pannwitz and his staff sat in the drawing room to decide on their conduct. All agreed with the General that General Whitelegge's speech, and the information that his division would be celebrating the end of the war for the next few days, constituted a chivalrous invitation to escape. The instincts of most present were to accept what seemed a compassionate proposal.

Von Pannwitz did not see the matter so. The English General's offer had not been made to the men. They could expect years of imprisonment in labour camps. After all, Stalin sent even his best friends to such places. He would not hesitate to send people who had fought against him, even if he allowed them to live. He did not wish to prejudge the choices of his officers. He released them from their obligations. They were now free men. Doubtless even the Germans among them would be able to find their way to freedom through Austria. After all, he gave a wry smile, 'so far as I know, Austria at the moment is still part of the Reich'. But he, von Pannwitz, would accompany his men into imprisonment in Russia. After all, the Cossacks had honoured him, they had even made him Ataman, a rank which no foreigner had ever held before. He would not desert them.

'But won't the Germans be separated from the Cossacks once they are in the hands of the Bolsheviks?' Colonel Weitz asked.

'That is likely,' returned Pannwitz, 'but that doesn't alter the moral of the thing.'

The conversation in the Schloss Althofen went round and round: what was the right action? Under what circumstances could an officer desert his men? Were these the circumstances? Groups of men could be seen walking up and down the lawns, round the rose garden, in and out of the shrubberies, debating indeed the "moral of the thing". And, was it certain the Russians would send them to camps?

Rüdiger knew what he wanted: to vanish into the soft Austrian countryside, where every beech tree coming into leaf seemed a friend, every oak a guide to a new life. He recognised his duties to his family, to his wife Alice and their children. But how could he desert his heroic chief, if von Pannwitz refused to desert his men?

He sought out von Pannwitz in his room. Von Pannwitz listened gravely and simply said: 'The decision is yours. I cannot take it for you. You are now an Austrian again, not a German. There is likely to be a difference.'

'What does that mean, Herr General?' said Rüdiger a little sharply.

Could von Pannwitz be suggesting that standards of honour among Austrians were inferior to that among Prussians?

'It is something your generation will have to decide,' returned von Pannwitz. 'The Allies will create a new independent Austria, with the frontiers of 1919.'

Rüdiger returned to his room. He wrote a letter to Alice of stark simplicity:

'Dearest Treasure – though I am back here in our beloved Austria, the English will on Friday hand over our corps to the Russians as prisoners. You will see that I cannot abandon my men and my leader, von Pannwitz. This will mean that the end of the war will not bring our reunion as we both so much hoped. This decision is my decision and mine alone. It may'

he crossed out the word '*may*' and wrote instead '*will*'

'bring you even greater difficulties than we feared. Forgive me. It may be, however, that our imprisonment will not be long. God may be merciful to us. Give a kiss to Heini and to Anna. I should write to them but what can I say? They would not understand. I shall be with you again. Your beloved: RUDI. P.S. Du gefällst mir.

This last phrase, taken from Kleist's *Prince Friedrich of Homburg*, meant more to Rudi and Alice than "you please me", as is the translation; it had been those words of understatement which had led to their betrothal in 1934 – just as, in the play, Princess Nathalie pronounces them to the Prince: a simple, generous woman of the Prussian country nobility, even if talking to one sentenced to death.

After these words he added – with a line pointing to Heini and Anna – 'help them to build a new Austria'.

He read the letter through – a thing, being impulsive, he rarely did. He enclosed it in an envelope taken from the bureau in his bedroom and addressed it. He then sent for his groom, a young Georgian named Kamo, a tough boy of dexterity with horses and charm with men, and told him to take the letter by hand to his wife in Dietrichsteingasse in Vienna: 'tell her to look after you', he added nonchalantly, not realising that the plight of a Georgian groom in ruined Vienna might be difficult: even if, after two years in the service of an Austrian officer, the groom spoke German.

With these quixotic and, as he hoped, Kleistian gestures, Rüdiger von Acht, two days later, drove off with von Pannwitz, von Teplitz and some others to meet an uncertain destiny at Judenburg. Most of their fellow German or Austrian officers had vanished into the woods, making their journey to the new Austria rather shorter than Rüdiger's turned out to be. But when on a fine clear spring morning, the staff car drew into Judenburg, and drove across the Mur, to be welcomed by smirking officers of the Red Army, Rüdiger knew that he had done at last the kind of thing of which Kleist had dreamed.

X

LIEUTENANT GREW WAS OFFERED BY THE SOCIALISTS IN
Vienna one hundred and three young deserters from the Wehrmacht
who had been hiding in the Klosterneuberg part of the Wienerwald.
Charlie announced that he proposed to stage a raid on Gestapo headquarters in Vienna. With a voice which he did not recognise as his own, he
called for a 'campaign of open terror against all prominent members of
the nazi party'. His audience was enthusiastic. Such action, they thought,
would at least help them do something to end the war: perhaps would
establish for them some kind of status for the future. In the subsequent
days, desertion from the Wehrmacht by Austrians was occurring in ever
larger numbers. The deserters had some help from the population, which
gave them civilian clothing. They hid them in their cellars.

These were confusing days for Lieutenant Grew. Formally he was a
military officer assigned to help the Austrian resistance. In practice, he
was the coordinator of fifteen groups of seven or eight men each which,
well supplied as they soon became with tommy guns, hand grenades,
ammunition and "*Panzerfeuste*", attacked supply lorries on their way to
the hard-pressed German SS troops. The attack on Gestapo headquarters
never seemed to happen. Lieutenant Grew worked with a map of Vienna
torn from a Baedeker's *Oesterreich 1926*: to which certain amendments
had been made, due to the heavy bombing and destruction caused by
shelling. He wondered whether the map which he had lost in his jumps
would have the *character* of his present one, which marked the good
hotels.

One of the Lieutenant's friends fixed him up with a wireless trans-
mitter. He was able to send a message to London saying that, 'as a result
of our action, the front line of the enemy has been forced back as far as
Schlachthausgasse-Rennweg Barracks-Baumgasse'. The crispness defied
the reality. In fact, the resistance were concentrating on holding a few
uninhabited blocks till they were liberated by the advancing Russians.
The SS – the Germans who were still fighting were nearly all SS – took
some time to realise that they were being fired upon from the rear. They
then directed some furious counter-attacks against these tall, classical,

now rather dirty apartment blocks (built in the 1880s by the Czech workers for the Ringstrasse bourgeoisie) which served as foci of civil war between two branches of the German family: or, considering that the Resistance was composed of army deserters, between two branches of the Wehrmacht.

During these days, Charlie Grew saw very disagreeable things. In one of these blocks – it was Schimmelgasse 15 – the SS forced the front door and shot a boy of fifteen in front of his mother, the concierge. Grew's friends shot the murderer a few hours later. Lost dogs wandered wild, every doorway seemed full of old men or women who had been half asphyxiated by fire. During another attack, in Paulusplatz, Grew's position became so difficult that he decided to make his way to the Russian lines and ask the Red Army for help. He left the building by a back door, accompanied by an Austrian who spoke Russian. By crossing two courtyards, and scaling two walls, they reached the Schlachthausgasse. He shot a man in SS uniform who moved forward to stop them. This, his first successful shooting, passed almost without him noticing it. Firing was too heavy. While he and the Russian-speaking Austrian approached the abattoir at St Mark's, they were met by a shower of bullets. Grew had a piece of white cloth with him. He waved it several times. The firing stopped. Several heavily armed Russians appeared from nowhere. The Austrian explained who they were and what they needed. They were taken to their headquarters, in what had once been the manager's office in the abattoir.

Grew there repeated his request for help to an officer who spoke some English. To his surprise, the request was instantly granted. He was escorted back to his men in Paulusplatz by a unit of twenty large Russians with tommy guns. By then, most of the SS had fled. But there were a few whom the Russians claimed were trying to set fire to buildings. Most were shot soon after in a small courtyard.

Fighting of this indiscriminate character was still going on when Charlie Grew received an invitation to visit the Red Army divisional security section. There he was treated with courtesy, and interrogated so intelligently that he had completed his tale before he even realised an interrogation was going on. He gave the Russian colonel a message from the Austrian Social Democrat Party, welcoming the Red Army, thanking it for its help, and calling for the total destruction of Hitlerism.

Two days later, another disagreeable thing occurred. Charlie Grew had moved to an empty flat not far from the scene of this "operation" in Paulusplatz. The Lieutenant had been compiling his report of his activities and analysing Vienna at the moment of the Russian liberation.

He made recommendations to London about the lessons to be learned for comparable resistance movements in future wars. He completed a meticulous account of how he used the ten thousand reichsmarks and three hundred dollars which he had in his breast pocket when he dropped onto Eisernes Tor. He noted that he still had the gold ring with which he had also been equipped. (His organisation in London set a high store by gold "particularly in Balkan countries".)

'Considering the ridiculously high prices at which I am offered arms,' (wrote the Lieutenant) 'I have come to the conclusion that the funds were adequate for an agent to live on but too little to equip a resistance group. The clothes I wore,' (he added in conclusion) 'were, however, correct and I don't think I "showed up" from the rest of the population.'

The Lieutenant was folding the report when three plain-clothes agents of the *Staatspolizei* – Austrians – knocked on the door. An old lady who had previously seemed benign and who lived next door, showed them the Lieutenant's room. They asked for his registration papers. When he admitted that he had none, he was arrested as an "unregistered foreigner". This was under Article 61, Section 4, of the Criminal Code, as revised by the Law of 1883 (the "Law Lubben"). The information that Grew was there had reached the *Staatspolizei* by a tip-off from the janitor in a block next door, in Strohgasse. He protested. The city was free—he was one of the liberators. All the same, the police insisted that he accompany them to police headquarters in Elisabeth Promenade.

In the street, there were many more unregistered foreigners about in the shape of drunken Russian soldiers, including a number of officers, who were leaning against the wall of the Imperial Hotel, being sick quietly into the Kärtnerring, prior to resuming their duties in the restaurant. When the Lieutenant pointed out these further infractions of the "Law Lubben", he received a sharp twist of the elbow, such as he had not experienced since the lower forms of his private school. He decided to reserve such comments for the report which he would have to make on his release.

That report, he realised with alarm, would not be something to embark upon immediately. Despite the collapse of the nazi regime, and the inevitability of Russian military control, certain forms had to be complied with. The *Staatspolizei* in Vienna had had a history of procrastination in respect of innocent people who want to get out of gaols. So Charlie was held in Elisabeth Promenade in Vienna for an indefinite period as an "unregistered alien" and, to compound the indignity, was placed in a cell in which there were already three other gentlemen, all of whom were nazis.

These were Gottfried von Acht, Fritz Musschleger, and Heinrich Demmer.

Of the three, Gottfried had been an idealistic nazi of the early 'thirties;

Musschleger an opportunist of the late 'thirties now ready to serve a Red Austria in any way that it manifested itself or, indeed, a white or blue Austria, if that were necessary; while Heinrich Demmer had committed many crimes which he would no doubt perform again if permitted to. The character of each of these men was new for the Lieutenant: he had no knowledge of people such as Gottfried; Heinrich's crimes were on a scale that he could not have imagined; and Fritz was a character for which there was no precedent in England since the days of Queen Anne.

Gottfried von Acht was Alois's brother. Two years younger. As a young man, under Alois's influence, he had thought of himself as a socialist. But he had disliked the way that socialism offered itself as a world complete in itself, not just exclusive but self-consciously self-sufficient.

'Would you ever rejoin the SDP?' naively asked Gottfried's sister-in-law Lise, Alois's wife, one evening in 1932, while doing her needlework, in the tone of voice that she might have used if he would go again to the Restaurant Hartmann, having had there an underdone *tafelspitz*.

'It's the smell of the party workers which would prevent me. No, I don't mean their physical odour. What I cannot abide is their self-righteous drabness.'

'Even if they are poor?'

'Even if they are poor? But they – we – the German people must become prosperous. We could be the most prosperous people in the world. Twice as rich as England. Four times as rich as France. What is stopping us? Socialism. Exclusiveness of the workers. I agree with Alois in one thing. We are Germans. We have always been Germans. Austria has never existed. What's the point of trying to invent it?'

Gottfried in those days used to walk up and down when he talked, nervously smoothing his fair hair.

'Anyway I feel German. I don't feel Austrian. Definitely not Viennese. Not now. To be Viennese is to belong to a railway station. Vienna is just a big railway station. Hundreds of people milling about on platforms, wondering where, and when, to go. That's not a nation. Listen to the language you hear. It's ridiculous. We must become Germans. I do not care at all about purity of blood. But I do care about purity of speech.'

Gottfried joined the Austrian nazi movement in 1931. His high-mindedness, his soulful energy and upper-class mien made him useful to the party. Most early nazis in Austria were shopkeepers, clerks, barbers, hotel porters: there were few educated people. Gottfried stood out. His friends were impressed: "Gottfried's going to right our wrongs and save Germany" they murmured, not entirely frivolously, over their slivovitzes in the bar of the Grand Hotel.

It looked for a moment as if he just might. He busied himself in those years with philanthropy, founding weekend schools to study the common inheritance of German philosophy. He wrote obscure verse which the party published without enthusiasm.

After Dollfuss's murder in 1934, and the banning of the party, Gottfried had his first spell in prison, because he had supported Pfinder, the Gauleiter of Styria, who had wanted to establish a dictatorship there and then, led by himself. When he was released, Gottfried went to Germany. He did not much like the lack of freedom. But he admired the work of reconstruction and the mood of dedication. He was bowled over by the discipline which went into the great rallies. Once he met the Führer: he took Gottfried to a cinema – an ironical version of the making of the Treaty of Versailles, made by Leni Riefensthal. Hitler had laughed in an inane way. Gottfried had been upset by that. Decidedly, he did not like the way that Hitler laughed.

With the Anschluss, Gottfried began to be disillusioned. He was away in Italy when it happened, so, unlike his brother Rüdiger, he was not there to see Hitler in the Heldplatz. Nor did he have to see Jewish professors being made to climb into the trees in the Stadtpark to make animal noises for the enjoyment of the comrades. He would have opposed that. He did oppose the burning of books. He also opposed the changing of the names of operas, and of streets: Maximilianstrasse for Mahlerstrasse, for example. He opposed these things in party meetings. As early as April 1938, he told his uncle Max that the Anschluss had been a mistake, that he regretted it, and that the German nazis were treating the Austrian nazis as if they were servants. Yet he remained in the nazi party. He believed that he might be able to influence it: an old self-deception to which each generation surrenders.

By 1940, he knew that his life since 1931 had been a mistake. How to undo what he had done? How to do good? He could not see the way. Should he enlist as a simple soldier and be killed on the Russian front? An easy way out. Should he serve in a camp and save lives? It would not work. Remaining a member of the party, he served the nazi leaders in Vienna, trying to emphasise all things Viennese, and Austrian, in a regime which wanted to forget those labels. He had been quite effective. Gottfried helped to give the Vienna Philharmonic Orchestra relative freedom to play what it wanted. He helped to organise the 80th birthday festival of Richard Strauss. Yet here he was now, a bachelor only just over forty, in a prison run by communist police, certain to be tried, and probably condemned: just possibly, to death.

Gottfried still looked like the kind of German which would have been bred all over Europe if the nazis had won the war: tall, thin, handsome in an angular way, serious, with penetrating blue eyes. Fritz Musschleger, his companion in the cell, did not look like any of that. Short, frog-like in features, small-boned, thick-set, in normal times Musschleger would not have drawn attention to himself. He was a builder from Pöchlarn who had supported the Heimwehr. He had not joined the nazis till 1938. He was the perfect example of a political opportunist. He did not have deep feelings. His concern had been to survive. He had been given military assignments during the war – prefabricated huts for camps in Poland, for example – and, up till 1945, he had been prosperous. By this influence, he had enabled his sons to avoid conscription and to find reserved occupations for them. They went to Munich to study medicine. The thousand-year Reich would presumably still need physicians, however many diseases would have been conquered.

Then, at last, in 1945, troubles came fast. Both his sons in the end were called up and, though one had reappeared, exhausted, one was missing in Silesia. His wife, whose blameless life had been occupied by the children, had been killed in an air raid in Wiener Neustadt, where she had gone to see her mother. Finally the nazi party in Pöchlarn made Musschleger their leader just when it had become obvious, anyway to opportunists such as he, that the war was lost. Musschleger did not want this unexpected promotion but he had been too frightened to refuse. Illness? Flight? Both were complicated to arrange at short notice. Besides, what of his business? Thus Musschleger had made a preposterous speech predicting the "turn of the tide", the "recovery of our fortunes", the "transformation of the dice of destiny" on the very day that the Red Army crashed into Austria. From then on, Musschleger was doomed. His daughter declared herself an anti-nazi. That upset him. He was eventually arrested by two young plumbers in his own firm who had joined the Resistance. They pushed him into a van and drove him at high speed to Vienna, where they had handed him over to the Communists. At six in the morning, Baumeister Musschleger had been shaving in his own bathroom, examining his face for marks of disrepair; at twelve, he was in an interrogation room in Vienna being questioned by people who, the day before yesterday, might have been begging him for a job.

Musschleger assured Charlie Grew that, in a short time, everything would be cleared up, that he would be back in Pöchlarn, and that the new regime, even if it were communist, could count on his services. All governments needed builders, particularly communist ones, because, he supposed, new government departments would be needed, to run the economy; there would have to be new police stations, new interrogation centres and, perhaps, even new concentration camps: or at least the adaption of old ones. He, Musschleger, had heard that ten per cent of the Russian population was in camps. Musschleger insisted to Charlie that there was nothing which he would not do. He had, he said, no political principles. He was a professional, an Austrian professional, at the service of whatever authority was in power. Charlie Grew, whose education was now more complete than it had been two days before, believed him.

The fourth member of the cell in Elisabeth Promenade, Heinrich Demmer, was gross, hideous, heavy, with dull grey-brown eyes looking perpetually but opaquely into a middle distance which, in this case, led to the peephole in the door. He grunted, or dribbled, rather than talked. He had one habit, however, by which Lieutenant Grew could not but be fascinated: he would, out of the blue, hit his head hard against the wall, several times, as if some last, long-neglected, inner mechanism had told him that he could perhaps knock some sense into himself. Perhaps a flicker of decency could indeed be thus revived in his revolting personality which, already coarse when it had begun its melancholy journey through life thirty years before in the Tyrol, had been given much rein, when its owner had been a camp-warden in Poland, as to have made him, as he sat there in his corner, appear the personification of evil in retreat. He did not talk much but occasionally the Lieutenant observed that he winked – to himself – as if the memory of outrages had come back to him to ignite, however briefly, the sadistic humour which had marked his terrible career.

The one conversation which Charlie Grew had with Demmer was when the latter asked if Churchill really had been planning the extermination of the Germans. If not, why were there large factories for the manufacture of arsenic pills in and around London. That, Demmer explained, was why the bombing of London had been intense.

Fired by this repellent man, both the others asked the Lieutenant a number of interesting questions:

'Are the communists now the main party of opposition in England?' And, 'How many fellow Jews did Roosevelt bring into the government?' And, 'Is it true that the Japanese have conquered India? Will France be colonised by Australia? Will *Rule Britannia* continue as the English national anthem, even if the King has fled to Canada? Does the Lieutenant know that the Russians have exterminated not only the people, but even the animals, which they found in East Prussia – wild birds as well as cattle, cats, dogs, rats and squirrels? Does the Lieutenant know that Austria will soon be divided into three, between Yugoslavia, Czechoslovakia and Russia, with Vienna, in all probability, transported stone by stone to California?'

To all these unusual questions, the Lieutenant gave negative answers, but his incredulity merely fired his interlocutors. They were, though grown men, the children of myth-making on a scale not seen since the invention of printing. Even Gottfried, with his classical education, with Virgil still rattling about in his once fine brain, shared in these forlorn fantasies – though Gottfried believed himself partly responsible for all, lies as well as crime.

PART 2

SEPTEMBER 1945–
MARCH 1946

XI

*F*OUR MONTHS LATER, A CEREMONY TOOK PLACE IN THE Schwarzenbergplatz, in front of the palace of that name. It was to unveil a pillar a hundred feet high. This was to commemorate the deaths of the Russians in the liberation of Vienna. This Russian war memorial was intended to be one of the great monuments of the city. The Communists in Vienna were there with banners. Many other people turned out to cheer, to mourn or to look. Remembering the hundred thousand burning houses, the broken pianos, the lost heirlooms, the rapings, with even more clarity than the act of liberation, the Viennese described the figure of the soldier on the lofty summit as the "Unknown Plunderer". It was an expression of ingratitude which the Communists and Soviet generals considered tasteless.

One could not fail to be impressed by the speed with which this monument had been put up. Russia was able to show an achievement months before the decayed West would even have appointed the necessary committees. Perhaps the monument had been under construction in Siberia before the end of the war. The Viennese could by this triumph learn how the future would be. Things would happen fast. No red-tape, no bureaucracy; and if, for the moment, one had to add "no food, no fuel, clothes" as well, that was temporary. Lenin defined communism as Soviet power plus electricity. In Vienna, it could surely be described as military power plus architecture.

By this time, after certain conversations in Potsdam, of which the Austrians knew nothing, the Russians had said they would allow their democratic allies into Vienna. Aunt Thekla cheered up Alice Acht when she said that the British always won the last conflicts in their wars; so perhaps the same would be true of their peaces. Beethoven after all had used an English piano: a Broadwood. Austria was divided into four and Vienna was also split, though the city itself was inside the Russian zone. The Austrians understood that the Americans, the British and the Russians had to have their slices, but they did think the presence of France was unpleasantly surreal.

'I suppose if the Italians had deserted us a bit earlier, they'd have their zone of occupation too. I rather regret they don't.' Aunt Thekla frequently delivered remarks such as these to the Russian colonel who was now living in her flat and, so far as she could tell, with Gisela too.

This colonel was not a receptive audience, though Aunt Thekla thought that he could speak respectable German if he wanted to. The only other person to whom she talked in those days was Alice Acht. Someone had told someone else who had told a friend of Alice's that they had seen Rüdiger on a train going east in the Carpathians. Such information was not impossible to find since every day one had heard of someone who had jumped off just such a train in the night and walked home from Transylvania. Those people usually had one tale in particular: how helpful the Hungarian peasants had been, and how unhelpful the Czechs.

Alice too had Russians in her flat: a colonel and a major. They never spoke to her. They shared her kitchen. The colonel occupied her bedroom, leaving her to make do in a child's room. She was glad that she had stayed and not accompanied the children to Salzburg. All the same, she rarely saw others except when she went to the flat of Thekla – only two streets away. A visit to Lise and Alois in Heiligenstadt would have been unthinkable, because of the permissions needed to cross zonal lines. Anyway, she did not want to see Alois with his socialism, now so horribly in the saddle, while poor Lise, with the loss of her daughter, was believed to be deranged. Alice, like everyone else left in Vienna, worked from dawn to dusk trying to clear streets, collect bricks usable again and carry rubbish to a central point.

The parade at Schwarzenbergplatz was the first public occasion in postwar Vienna. Thekla and Alice went together. Later, the communist press made a fuss of saying how many thousands had been present but, if Thekla and Alice were representative, the crowd could not have been counted as enthusiasts. The two women walked quietly down Seilerstrasse. There were few people about and, as so often in those days in Vienna, half of those looked as if they were cripples. Everywhere there were red flags. Despite the presence of Britain, America and France, it seemed likely that the Viennese would end up as Russian subjects. What a fate after a thousand years of empire! If this were to come, what a pity their great-grandfathers had not accepted Napoleon! The vision of being part of a French empire instead of a Russian one made one very angry with the English who had prevented it.

As Thekla and Alice walked on, an extraordinary thing happened. Out of nowhere, a side street, an impasse, perhaps a hotel, a column of Americans emerged. It was, as it happened, one of the biggest bands of the American army – belonging to the 81st Armoured Division. The bandsmen were tall, crew-cut Americans, neatly clothed, but they seemed like happy warriors. They were playing *Don't sit under the Apple Tree with anyone else but me*.

Alice and Aunt Thekla had been brought up on music. Both their families had looked on it as a religion. Music was Austria's strength. But that was real music. They had mocked Johann Strauss and despised Lehar. But suddenly to hear this silly song, played by happy-go-lucky soldiers in ruined, half-communist Vienna, was a revelation. Even the stray dogs stopped. Thekla and Alice also stopped. They clapped, laughed and wept. Relief had come! The relief of Vienna. Like Starhemberg and Sobieski in 1683. *Don't sit under the Apple Tree*, a different song from any that they had liked before, became the anthem which enabled them to dream that they, and Austria, might one day yet be free.

They walked on to the Schwarzenbergplatz. The old palace of the Schwarzenbergs had been destroyed by bombs. The ruins lay untended. In front, an ugly new stone colonnade had been built. Red flags, with hammers and sickles, and banners were hanging everywhere. A red flag bigger than any other was draped over the monument itself. Behind, a dozen men in civilian clothes were holding onto strings which held down the flag. A Russian colonel-general in medals was inspecting a parade of Soviet soldiers. To the left behind the fountain, a happy survivor of other days even if it were not playing at that moment, stood the Allies' box. There were Americans, Englishmen and Frenchmen, as well as representatives of other nations – including the "Lublin Poles", who were popular with nobody and showed in their faces that they knew it.

Among the officers in the Allies' box stood General Whitelegge, Brigadier Sheay, Captain Grew, as he now was, Major Stern, Colonel Marchais and even Colonel Livingstone. All of these men were now attached to the Allied missions. Ladies were present: among them the new secretary to the French mission, Madame Charpentier. The Soviet band was playing but all the other Allies had bands ready too. The band which had played *The Apple Tree* had fallen in next to the Soviet military orchestra, as it was described on the programme.

The officers were in full dress. The Soviet ones looked the grandest. They were covered in gold braid. The medals of several seemed to reach their waists.

Speeches followed. From where they were standing, on the edge of the Ring, Aunt Thekla and Alice could hear the words "glory to the glorious Red Army for having liberated Vienna from the yoke of the nazi beast". These words, or something like them, also emanated from Austrian speakers. After six speeches, this seemed monotonous. At the end, a pistol shot was fired. The civilian assistants let go the strings. The red flag flew from the monument. Rockets were let off. Guns were fired. The fountain started to play. A colossal black Soviet soldier on a marble pedestal was left to stand glaring at the city. Several flights of pigeons flew off, startled, towards the inner city. Everyone stood to attention and saluted. The Soviet national anthem was thumped out by the bands. The Russian division, which had taken Vienna, marched past. All these Soviet soldiers were heavily armed. Aunt Thekla thought that they looked keen to go straight into battle again.

Such a reflection could not have been entertained of the British company which strolled by next. They were unarmed, in khaki shorts. What, Aunt Thekla asked Alice, did the British think Vienna was, some kind of lido? At least, the Russians knew what it was that they had conquered. The Americans and French, also unarmed, at least were in trousers. Next followed representatives of communist parties of Vienna, with red embroidered banners. These included old women, old men, and ten-year-old grandchildren. The generals and marshals had begun to be restless. It looked as if they were already giving interviews to newspaper correspondents. Probably, therefore, few of them saw, as Thekla did, the two old women who marched at the end of the parade giving, doubtless from absentmindedness, not the salute of the clenched fist of the communists, but the outstretched arm of the nazis.

Some too saw a banner which proclaimed this slogan: "Glory to the Red Army for saving Vienna from the atom bomb". It was not the last of the misunderstandings which the Viennese, having improvidently handed over their fortunes to an unsuccessful house painter, were now to endure.

XII

SOME WEEKS LATER, THE RUSSIANS GAVE A RECEPTION IN THE Hofburg. That historic building, with its innumerable courts and entrances, linked so formidably with the past of Europe, was festooned with red flags and with portraits of Lenin and Stalin. The Russian General Konev and his lady received the guests at the top of the main staircase, standing on the same spot that Franz Josef used to stand on. Konev was surrounded by major-generals. All, dressed in green, wore almost as many medals as even Goering had liked to sport. Within, a military band played marches, dances and overtures. People stood around waiting for a sign to move into the next room where, it was said, there would be food and drink. These guests were mostly "Allies" – smart Americans, wonderfully at ease in the Hofburg; Englishmen, now well turned out in contrast with their appearance in the Schwarzenbergplatz; a few dyspeptic Frenchmen; many Russians, overbearing but uncomfortable in their dress uniforms. They escorted girls, the paint on whose faces compensated in thickness for the lack of skill with which it was applied. There were also, *mirabile dictu*, Austrians: from the puppet Austrian coalition government, as the English and Americans thought it, set up by the Russians from a list of men whom they thought would keep the smell of Russian leather strong on the shores of Lake Constance and the Brenner Pass.

Among these Austrians there was Alois von Acht. He was the socialist Under-Secretary in the Ministry of Railways. His party, though recognising his talents, would have preferred a right-winger. But his left-wing history made the communists keen to support him. So Alois's appointment was agreed, just one among many arrangements between political parties which had come out into the open again. Everyone seemed satisfied: the communists, because they had a friend in a delicate position; and the socialists, because their leaders believed that Alois like many others had since April undergone a change of heart about communism. The only party hostile to Alois's appointment was the People's Party, the new conservatives, who could understand leaders of the working class, but disliked men of the *haute bourgeoisie* who had joined a party which, in theory, was concerned to destroy everything from which they came. Alois, good-looking, well-connected, sardonic, eloquent and educated, seemed the worst example of this treachery. The only thing that could be said of him, they thought, was that the Achts had always been so odd that anything was possible with them. They accepted him at the Ministry without enthusiasm as part of the deals of those days and hoped that all the decisions would be taken by their own nominee, his colleague, the People's Party man, Poldi Moser.

People had miscalculated. For after the atrocious events in the Wienerwald in April, Alois was not the same man as he had been at the university in 1927, in Karlmarxhof in 1934, in Dachau in 1940–42. All was changed. As he came up the grand staircase in the Hofburg where his father and grandfather would as schoolboys have bowed to Franz Josef, Alois only seemed the same as ever. He had that old contemptuous air which was one reason why he used to be so disliked: he stood apart at gatherings like this, drumming his fingers on a nearby cabinet or table. He also, as in the past, had the air of a man with a mission: an uncomfortable person to have at a party. But the mission was not the same as it had been six months before. Alois no longer dreamed of running countries as he had run trains. His mission, since the disappearance of his daughter, Klara, was to secure the removal of the Russians from Austria, the eclipse of the communists, and their ruin wherever possible.

He had embarked on this mission in a roundabout way, worthy of the communist party itself. He had not broken with his old friends. He had said nothing openly. His silences had scarcely been noticed. Too much happened in the months following the Soviet capture of Vienna for reticence to be remarked. With the collapse of the food supply, with the fouling of the city's water, with the impossibility of collecting rubbish because the few remaining municipal lorries had been "liberated" by the Russians (and had been sent to Kiev), with the daily thefts by Russian soldiers, it was easy not to notice a comrade's silence. Only Fritz Tolbach, Alois's old friend and now the communist Railway Minister, was too intelligent not to observe that something had happened. But he took Alois's imperturbability for stoicism. Tolbach remembered the Acht family's liking for Kleist. Ulrike von Kleist, sister of the poet, after all, had admired that quality above all else. Had not Ulrike loved a man, who, on hearing of his only son's death, continued to sit at the gaming board? When Tolbach heard of the tragedy in the Wienerwald, he had sought out Alois: they had been still in the Westbahnhof. He clasped his hand firmly for a long time, his eyes burning. There was nothing to say. The clasp of comrade Tolbach was equivalent to the eloquence of an advocate of the old days. Tolbach, as he now moved across to where Alois was standing in the ballroom of the Hofburg, did not know that his friend had given himself over to the idea of vengeance.

Vengeance! A primitive motive, inappropriate, it might be supposed, for a cultivated Viennese in the twentieth century. But Alois had ceased, for the time being, to be a man of the enlightenment.

His wife, Lise, had not reacted in the same way to the tragedy. Of course, when the terrible news had come she had broken down. Any moment she expected to have brought to her the news that the mangled body of Klara had been found. Lise also knew of her husband's change of heart, as she did of the new emotion which stirred him to the roots. She, who had come to share his pleasure in collaboration with the communists, did not participate in his relief at a decisive break with them. Nor could she gain any solace from her factory, as she had in the war. It had ceased production. So far as she knew, the machines and office equipment and even one or two technicians – the men in white coats whom she had been used to see shaking their heads in the passage – had been taken as "reparations" to Russia. (That fate had befallen most Viennese factories in those days, before the Western Allies had arrived. Many such had been placed on trains and left on sidings near the Russian border. To rust! As for the technicians, who could say?) But her loss of work did not mean that Lise was idle. Though her husband was now a minister she, like all other Viennese, had to scramble for food. In order to get food, one had to work, one had to work several hours, to help clear Vienna of rubble. Everyday, Lise, with thousands of other survivors, would bicycle into the centre of the city and, with her hands alone, shift stone and wood from places which had been bombed or shelled. Vienna had been bombed back into the age of the wheelbarrow. On her return from this work, Lise fed her family and went to bed – living by the sun. But as time passed, and nothing transpired about Klara, she became demented. The fact that the crime, as she supposed it to be, had been committed by the Russians, whom Alois had over many years educated her to suppose to be the bringers of light, drove her to imbecility. Alois tried to persuade her that the Achts normally were survivors. Look at Herr Doktor Max! When his house was destroyed, he had gone for a walk. He was alive. Probably Klara was alive. She was not the sort of person to be killed at seventeen. Lise could not be comforted. Indeed, only Alois tried to do so. No one else had had the time. All the Viennese then had their own troubles, a husband killed, a son crippled, or a prisoner of the Russians (to be a prisoner of the Americans did not seem likely to portend hardship), a relation accused of nazism, or another who had come out of a concentration camp with his health ruined – even a mother imprisoned as a German by the Czechs. Those were harsh days. One did not have time to sympathise with others.

In the ballroom of the Hofburg, meantime, the heterogenous gathering had been standing for a long time when a message arrived. How it was transmitted one could not be sure. Not by an announcement. It spread like a breeze among aspen trees in summer:

'In the Redoutensäle, there is food and drink! An unlimited supply! Incredible!' Instantly, the crowd began to move towards the staircase. By the time that Alois reached it, some people were running up the stairs, two at a time. The communist Minister of the Interior was moving almost at a sprint towards the buffet. What an especial sense of politeness these communists had, to show such enthusiasm for Soviet offerings! And surely those young men reaching for the food over the shoulders of others were from the French Mission? They knew that one had to take official banquets seriously. Alois noticed that the Soviet government was giving its first peacetime banquet in the room where Mozart had first conducted *The Marriage of Figaro*, and that there – in the centre of the room – was the leader of the People's Party, the good-hearted Dr Figl, a minister in the government, drinking vodka with General Konev.

The banquet was held in the Russian style: men and women stood awkwardly, and hungrily, with a glass of vodka or light Georgian wine balanced uneasily on plates. Nobody seemed at ease, not even the Russians. A secretary to the President, Dr Renner, told Alois that the Russian generals were drinking in separate rooms and were holding court in them – and at tables. Several Allied generals had been invited there. Alois looked into such a *séparé* to see General Krivoshein, whom he knew to have settled at his brother Otto's place at Besselberg, dispensing hospitality. An American general and some Frenchmen were toasting him in enthusiastic tones. Drink was flowing in General Krivoshein's *séparé*. There was even laughter. Peace had evidently returned!

As Alois stood on the edge of the room, he felt a hand on his shoulder. He turned to find an American senior officer whom he did not remember seeing before, and who addressed him in good German.

'Why don't we join them?'

'No,' Alois demurred, 'I'd rather not. I'm not one for toasts.'

That was true, even if it were not the only reason why he did not want to drink with the Russian general whom he believed to have been in command in April in the Wienerwald.

'You should. The gentlemen there need an Austrian to keep them company. But let me introduce myself. My name's Brooks Sheay of the American Mission here. And you?'

'Acht. I'm Under Secretary for Railways in the provisional government.'

'Very well met indeed. Did you say Acht? – like Max von Acht?'

'Yes. I'm his nephew.'

'Ah! But –'

'But of course I don't belong to his –' Alois was about to say his way of thinking. But why should he distance himself from Uncle Max who had lost all and was temporarily in exile from Vienna, as he put it, in Salzburg. So he ended lamely – 'his generation.'

'No, of course not.'

Sheay hesitated. He had been in Austria now for several weeks as a deputy in the American Mission but had not sought to renew old acquaintances. This reluctance was due to sensitivity, not a lack of curiosity, about the whereabouts of people whom he had once known. He had known Alois to be in the government and Gottfried to be in prison. Still, the time for the renewal had surely come, whatever his hesitations, and whatever this nephew of old friends had done in the war.

'I was here often before the war,' he said. 'I know several Achts. Thekla, for example.'

'My aunt.'

'Otto and Betty?'

'My brother and sister-in-law.'

'And you are again –?'

'Alois.'

Sheay did not remember meeting Alois. He had known that Otto had several brothers. Including a nazi.

'Yes, Alois,' he said nevertheless. 'I'm sure we met. I was sometimes at Besselberg in the old days.'

'I don't think we met before,' said Alois decisively, 'I was a revolutionary then. We didn't get on with one another in the family.' He smiled. 'We rejected the family. That is, I and my friends did. We had the greater family of international socialism. At least, that's how we looked at things.' He smiled self-deprecatingly.

Sheay looked at him with interest.

'And now?' he asked.

'And now? Well,' Alois said hesitantly. Then he continued, 'A lot has happened. I suppose the family is one of the things in Austria that has survived. Yes, there's been a revival there. Who would have thought that possible? In the 1920s we wanted to bury the idea. Still, there's been a counter revolution, as we'd have said in the past. That's about the only thing that counts now. The family. That and the country. That's new too. Austria.'

'The country?' Sheay was unable to keep the incredulity out of his voice.

'You're surprised?'

'Yes. I don't want to be rude. I love this country. But you're on your knees now. Everything's gone,' Sheay spoke excitedly, 'your buildings destroyed. Your reputation's gone; you have got four occupying powers. You've got Russians in the Hofburg. And you've even got Austrians toasting them. Look at that.'

73

They had walked back to the Redoutensäle. Sheay pointed out Dr Leopold Figl drinking yet another toast with yet another Colonel-General.

'Yes,' said Alois, 'it's true we're ruined. We are at the bottom. We've lost everything. Our reputation has gone. But still, Brigadier Sheay, we will recover. I sense it. We're better men than we were in 1919. Even though sometimes it may seem we're the same. The difference is that this time we know we're ruined and we know it's our fault. In 1919, we thought it was everyone's fault but our own. That's the difference. We've been through fire to get here. Come back in ten years, you'll be amazed.'

Sheay smiled.

'We've all had to suffer. Do you know –' Alois was about to speak intimately to this American but thought the better of it and concluded nonetheless powerfully, 'do you know where this government was formed?'

'The Soviet mission?'

'No. Dachau. Half the government was there. That's where this government was formed.' Alois was conscious of sounding like an editorial in the newspapers, but he continued, 'I was there. That's where the hatreds between socialists and Christian Socialists were overcome. In those camps. Yes, I assure you, we've changed.'

Sheay was interested, not convinced. He still had in his mind his visit to the concentration camp near Linz. Nor could he reject the memory of Austria before the war; that, after all, was his Austria.

'I hope we'll meet again, Herr von Acht,' he said, holding out his hand. It was the first time he had done so to an Austrian since the war.

A little after that, a new rumour spread through the party: dancing was beginning in the ballroom.

There followed the same surge downstairs that had marked the rush upstairs towards the food. Persons again ceased to be individuals and became a mass: appropriate no doubt for the hosts, but scarcely for the Hofburg. The grand ballroom had been turned into something resembling the Leningrad *palais de danse*: with a platform, streamers hanging from the chandeliers and flags over the pictures. Two heavy Russian orchestras played tunes of the pre-war West, one at each end of the ballroom. Songs merged into one another, the whole sounding as if a sponge had been laid over dance music between 1918 and 1939 and was now being squeezed to emit recognisable, if not well-syncopated, sounds. There was also a Russian jazz band, in a neighbouring room, where several English officers smugly recalled to each other the case of Dr Johnson and the female preacher.

The Austrians looked on the scene with mixed feelings. The Russians were enjoying themselves. The sight of these officers, in gold braid, boots, sea-green uniforms with red stripes, high epaulets, dancing with their painted ladies, was a cabaret in itself. It was the first time that

Austria had seen her liberators at ease. The English were also an interesting sight. What surprised Alois and his colleagues was that there seemed nearly as many English girls as Russian ones: interpreters, secretaries, no doubt, administrators in the British Mission. Or had they too felt it necessary to bring their 'children of pleasure', as Alois's companion Poldi Moser put it? Perhaps the English too had changed? Most other people had. National character did not seem a reliable concept in the mid-twentieth century. Yet the Americans and the French were, so far as the Austrians could judge, behaving predictably. One could easily tell who they were. The first had an air of well-being: temporary soldiers who soon would slough off uniforms. The French were standing in coteries on the edge, smoking gauloises cigarettes and deploring, by gestures, the nature of some action by their allies.

Alois and Poldi Moser found themselves standing next to two Englishmen. One was Colonel Livingstone, the other a shorter, square, curly-headed individual of thirty-five, who laughed drunkenly at everything that his comrade was saying.

Colonel Livingstone was telling his friend, who had come out from London from the Foreign Office, or some such agency, his version of what had occurred at Aussee:

'And then, I have to say, my dear,' said Livingstone, 'the most villainous American appeared and said that he could not allow anyone through. If that is the kind of person we shall have to look up to in the post-war world, God help us all. I wish you could have seen him. Of course, one has to accept all sorts of things in war, as I am perfectly aware, but does one expect obstruction from temporary officers from somewhere very far west of anywhere civilised in the United States? One does not. I subsequently discovered his name was "Stern". I suppose he was trying to live up to his name.'

'Jewish obviously,' said the curly-headed man.

'I hadn't thought of that,' said Livingstone, 'but of course you're right.'

Livingstone's companion shook with laughter, for no good reason, stubbed out his cigarette on the floor of the ballroom and lit up another. They were joined by a tall, fair English girl with blue eyes, and a beautiful smile.

'Well, Colonel,' she said in a *dégagé* manner, 'have you found anything nice to say about anything today?'

'Oh Pat, that's not fair! You make me out to be a complainer.'

'So you are.' The girl turned her eyes on his companion. 'I'm Pat Mackenzie. I run the interpreters' pool here. If you need any proverbs in Serbo-Croat, it's my job to find them. Who are you?'

Livingstone's companion stuttered with laughter.

Livingstone himself made the introductions, 'This is an old Oxford friend, Harry Mercer. Just out from London. Coming to our mission here. He'll keep us amused, won't you Harry,' he said, looking at the new arrival with apprehension and adoration.

'That's good. We're often in need of a laugh here,' said Pat. 'It's grim: the Austrians don't seem keen on trying to clear up their city. Can't blame them, poor darlings, it's tough, 'cos they don't get much food. They rely for that on the Russians, who won't give them more than their people are getting at home. There's no hot water. I haven't had a bath since I came here.'

'There isn't much food,' Livingstone conceded. 'Mind you, one doesn't know exactly what goes on. I take no Austrian at his face value. I'd say most of them get more than they say.'

'They're badly off,' insisted Pat. 'They really don't get enough to eat. God knows what the winter will be like.'

Alois, who understood English, listened as if in a dream. It was the first time he had heard his countrymen being talked of as if they were rare specimens: 'I take no Austrian at face value!' Indeed!

At this moment an unexpected thing occurred. The two Russian orchestras stopped playing and even the jazz band from Omsk could not be heard. Instead, on a balcony, which no one had previously noted, a Viennese orchestra began to play a waltz. Never mind that it was by Lehár, so frowned upon by people of Alois's circle, but so loved by most Austrians (rightly, since *The Merry Widow* had been for years Austria's chief source of foreign exchange). The Austrians were the first on the floor. Alois, aware that he risked a rebuff, and one which he would have interpreted sourly, asked the tall English girl to dance.

'Well,' she said, looking at him with interest, 'I really don't see why not.' The rules of the "non-fraternisation" which had marked the first months after the war in Austria had been amended: one could talk to Austrians in any public place, though *not* as yet in their own homes.

He took her arm.

'Who the hell's that, I wonder?' asked Colonel Livingstone.

'An Austrian, Colonel, just an Austrian,' said Alois, over his shoulder, 'not to be taken at his face value.'

Alois could not see Livingstone's reaction, since he was leading his partner through the steps of the waltz *Warum?* from *The Land of Smiles*.

The girl was friendly, easy and charming with an innocent camaraderie, that Alois found, from the complex depths of his own life, appealing.

'You talk very good English for –' she stopped and corrected herself, 'so far as I can see.'

'You were about to say "for an Austrian"!'

'Well, yes I was. But I didn't want to be rude. Of course, I know you are often clever; much cleverer than us. But the Austrians I deal with don't talk even very good German.'

'Who are they?'

'Maids and so on.'

'Probably Croats or Slovenes.'

'Possibly.'

By now they had waltzed round the room.

'My,' said Pat, 'you know, I have an office in Schönbrunn Palace. And now I've danced in the Hofburg. I do think I've done the right things. In three or four weeks too! Who are you, incidentally?'

'I'm in the Austrian government,' Alois smiled, 'I'm a socialist.'

'Like our government. I voted Labour this time. Well I don't know why I say "this time" because I've never voted before. I voted against all those solicitors with double-barrelled names who ran the country for the Conservatives. Of course, I loved Churchill. If I thought there was going to be another war, I'd vote for him again. But if not, we need a change. I'd love to know what you think. Whoops! We nearly hit the Russian general. Or rather he nearly hit us. You certainly waltz well, but then so you should, you're an Austrian. Do you see that divine little man over there? That's the top Frenchman. De Change or something like that. No, even that doesn't sound right. Anyway, that's him. And that big, ugly woman he's dancing with is his lady friend. *Not* his wife. She's very amusing.'

And so she went on, her conversation to Alois a charming mixture of nonsense and perception, delivered with enthusiasm. The waltz did not interfere with her flow of conversation. She could not dance well. But Alois liked her freshness, her clear white skin and her fair hair which swung across her face like a curtain when she turned her head. The Anglo-Saxons were sometimes rather a tonic, he admitted to himself.

'Who are your friends?'

'My friends? Well, do you mean in England? That's a big question. Oh, you mean those two pansies I was talking to? The tall one looks after artistic questions. He's rather sweet, though *very* silly. Knows everything about the baroque. He's written books about it. That's why he's here, one supposes. The other dirty little chap with curly hair I've just met for the first time but I've heard of him. Harry Mercer. He's supposed to be clever. Brilliant. Not that it shows. Very left, I suppose. All the clever ones are.'

The waltz was at an end. With just a little more reluctance than he had expected, Alois returned the tall girl to where he had found her. Livingstone and Mercer were still standing there talking, rather surprisingly, to Poldi Moser. They welcomed Pat back with mock astonishment that she had escaped from "the Austrian". They were determined to make a pleasantry out of Alois's pointed comment before the dance. They might be English but they were not pompous. They seemed to be talking to Poldi with animation.

'I'm new here,' Mercer said to Alois in excellent German, 'It would be interesting to know how things are going.' He dropped his voice. 'I know where you stand, of course. And of course, I agree. These are critical times. The national bourgeoisie here does not exist. We've got great opportunities.' He drew on his cigarette, smiled conspiratorially and put the stub out again against the floor: 'Listen, let's have lunch one of these days. I'd like it. Where can I find you?'

Alois, surprised, told him. He had not yet realised that the English invite one to lunch if they want to avoid a difficult conversation.

XIII

*I*N ANOTHER PART OF THE HOFBURG, COLONEL MARCHAIS, Madame Charpentier, and two Soviet officers were sitting at a large table. The Russians had no companions. They had been listening to the bands with nothing to drink. This abstinence, Colonel Marchais thought, showed that the two officers were in intelligence. The impression was confirmed when he realised they spoke good German. Despite their sobriety, they were talkative.

Colonel Marchais was a skilled talker in difficult circumstances and Madame Charpentier was attractive in the way that Parisians are when abroad: quick-witted, smartly dressed in a simple black dress, astute enough to know when and where not to take part in a conversation, and when to seem unobtrusive. She remained silent but made her presence felt by a lively interest.

'With a ball in the Hofburg, one really feels that the war is over,' said Colonel Marchais.

'It is true, yet the Emperor and the Tsar are missing,' commented Colonel Voronov, a thin, pale officer, slightly stooped, whom it would have been possible to picture among the latter's Preobrazhenski guards.

'The dancing would be superior to this and the women more refined,' added his grosser companion, Colonel Pavlov, 'our military occasions lack style.'

'Oh, but, now we live in a republican society,' said Colonel Marchais 'it is good to see all classes in the ballroom of the Hofburg. In this room we are seeing a veritable united nations.'

'At the Congress of Vienna,' said Colonel Voronov, 'Russia was represented by a young Tsar, handsome, with blue eyes. The favourite of the archduchesses. Now we have Marshal Konev and Colonel-General Zheltov. One really cannot make comparisons.'

'Nor is Stalin here,' put in Colonel Pavlov.

'Would it be better if he were?' asked Colonel Marchais.

'Of course. He is now the Tsar,' Colonel Pavlov said.

These comments confirmed Colonel Marchais in his supposition that these Russians were in intelligence. Only officers in that organisation would speak thus. He had encountered Russian intelligence men in Paris. They had been free of the hesitations of even senior generals who were normal members of the army.

'Stalin knows Vienna,' Colonel Pavlov was saying, 'he met Trotsky here in 1909. They did not get on well.' Both the Russian officers laughed heartily. An English couple passing looked round startled. The sight of a laughing Russian was not so common as to escape attention.

'Trotsky? I didn't know you allowed that he existed?' said Colonel Marchais.

Colonel Voronov gave him a look presumably intended to imply that fools might have to accept such things but they were not sitting at their table.

'Will Stalin return then to Vienna?' asked Colonel Marchais.

'Stalin will come back to Vienna when we have secured for him control of Austria,' said Colonel Voronov, with another of his remarks of devastating candour.

'When will that be?'

'When the fig is ripe. We will not need to do anything. The fig will drop off the tree into our hands. It will be like the fig trees in the Caucasus. Wait and see. Very interesting, Colonel Marchais. Besides, that will only be one new stage. There will be others. We will water our horses in the Seine one day. Wait and see.'

'And Paris?' asked Madame Charpentier, unable to remain silent.

'Tsar Alexander got to Paris, Madame. Comrade Stalin can do no less.'

Both colonels rose. They had obviously seen a comrade who had given them a message: time to make an end to candour for the moment. They bowed to their allies and left the room at a measured pace: Colonel Voronov, to the neat apartment of Alice von Acht, Rüdiger's wife, where he had pitched his tent for the time being; Colonel Pavlov to a place in the Inner City, close to the Graben. Colonel Marchais danced idly with Madame Charpentier but they too soon left. The colonel of the arts had learned something of Russia, but, he suddenly remembered on his way home, he had learned nothing of the whereabouts of the Crown of the Emperor Charles V, the loss of which now looked like becoming one of the *causes célèbres* of the era.

XIV

*A*MONG THOSE WHO WERE TO BE SEEN FOR THE FIRST TIME IN Vienna since 1938 at this unusual, to many Austrians horrible, gathering was Ludwig Börne, before the Anschluss, of Börne Verlag. Börne was a Jew who really did seem to belong to an international conspiracy. He had always operated on an international scale and his attitudes were those of a conspirator. Fortunately, he had had to leave Vienna for an appointment in Zurich on March 11, 1938, else, like other cousins of Christ (in his youth he used to explain to Frenchmen – parodying Mirabeau – '*Jesus Christ qui, en parenthèse, était mon cousin, a prêché l'égalité*'), he would have found himself washing the Graben with a dishcloth. Many stories were told of how he had escaped from Vienna on that day. The most elaborate myths were built about his appearing suddenly, on a train in Bregenz, as a conductor punching tickets.

These tales, which he did nothing to deny, formed the basis of his wartime reputation – as a broadcaster, as "friend of President Roosevelt", as "Austria's friend in New York": for there was no official Austrian presence of any sort in any Allied capital. Börne had been disconcerted by the appearance in Vienna, under Soviet patronage, of Dr Renner's provisional government: he had seen himself, in a similar role, under American protection. Now, however, he had installed himself in the Hotel Imperial. He was the only civilian with a room, much less a suite of rooms. Indeed, he was the only client in the hotel who was not a member of the Soviet forces of occupation. What was his game? What was he doing? The intelligence services of four countries fretted about him, listened to his telephone calls, interrogated the girls whom he took to dinner, but no one could discover his intentions, his loyalties, his source of foreign exchange, nor, indeed, much about his character. Perhaps there was nothing more to learn. The only certainty was that, whatever had happened during the war to his school friends in the Josefstadt, Börne was no more popular in the Vienna of 1945 than he had been in 1938.

Börne did not, as it happens, "look Jewish": rather, Tartar. He looked as if he might have been a cousin of Lenin, not of Christ. His eyes were the eyes not of the 'near' but of the central East. Now he was sitting with the British general, General Whitelegge, and telling that officer how he should conduct himself with the Russians.

'Remember, General, they are Slavs. They don't like hesitations. They don't like indecisions. They don't like weakness. Better say nothing than apologise. Don't laugh at them. They like strength because it's the only thing they know about. They are happier with people who stand up to them than those who give way. Their inclination is to kill those who flatter them. With those who resist them, they drink. You must not treat them as human beings. They are Slavs.'

'A racial theory?' commented General Whitelegge.

'Are there any other theories?' Dr Börne shrugged his shoulders, puffed his cigar, and permitted himself to smile.

'My colleagues have many theories,' said General Whitelegge. 'The ones in Whitehall send me a theory a week. Wrapped up in a "most secret" envelope, they try and tell me how to behave. How to treat the Austrians. Just as you tell me how to treat the Russians. Can't say I like theories. I'm a practical man.' He looked at Dr Börne through the smoke: 'Are you a practical man, Dr Boon?'

'Börne – as in Burn.'

'Quite so, Dr Boon. Are you a practical man? I should doubt it. A dreamer. That's what you are. Dangerous. Not for us. But for yourself. Nice to have talked to you.'

With these remarks, General Whitelegge woke up his ADC, Captain Hudson, in the chair next to him. Together they left the room, and returned to Schönbrunn where they now lived as if they had been doing it all their lives.

'There's no bore like a clever bore,' the General muttered, as they got into their Rolls-Royce, 'and when he's an American, it's worse.' For Börne, despite his political ambitions, travelled on an American passport.

Dr Börne, left alone, wondered on whom he should next inflict the benefit of his unique company. He looked round the room, as a bird of prey before identifying its victim. He saw General Clark, the American equivalent to Whitelegge and started towards him. But General Clark moved fast and, before Börne was within speaking distance, he had vanished. Brigadier Sheay was still there. He and Dr Börne did not see eye to eye. They had discussed the Austrian soul, to the satisfaction of neither, four times since the liberation of Vienna. But Dr Börne did not like the only Frenchman whom he knew in Vienna, Colonel Jean Georges Marchais, who anyway was talking to his general. Alternatively, there were a few Russians whom he might advise as to how to cope with the Americans: "Remember they are children. They know nothing. They have no experience. They are ignorant of how to behave. They will conduct themselves as children conduct themselves. Sometimes well, sometimes badly. They are strong children, though, remember, unlike the English who are not as strong as they seem.''

Dr Börne finally settled for an Austrian: Poldi Moser, the People's Party Under-Secretary at the Ministry of Railways.

'Dr Moser. How are we going to treat all these new friends of ours? The liberators. What an extraordinary thing for us to have to go through! Do you remember me telling you in 1936 that, unless we got rid of Schuschnigg we should be occupied by the Germans, the Russians and the Americans? In that order! I had, I admit, forgotten the others. But you know, the English are not as strong as they seem. And the French. A nation of art collectors! So, I think my prophecy was right. Napoleon said that, without him, all Europe would be either "*américanisée*" or "*bien cosaque*". I am bad at many things but at least I am a good prophet.'

Poldi Moser did not remember the conversation with Dr Börne before the war. He did, however, remember Dr Börne. As a small boy, he had been in the old restaurant in the Sudbahnhof, on the way to Graz, with his father. Dr Börne, looking the same age as he was now, had come in, with some overdressed and overpainted women, covered in furs and jewels, possibly Balkan, and had talked in a loud voice. A beggar had approached. The rich women had waved him away. Then Poldi's father had given him a thousand schilling note and had told Poldi: 'Those are the kind of people who make all the trouble.'

'Well,' said Dr Börne, 'how are we going to recreate our Austria? Shouldn't be too difficult if you remember all the interlopers are ignor-amuses. Ig-nor-amuses! It is not pleasant to have to say so. But I must. I have just been talking to the English general. Doesn't know the first thing. The American? A child. The French? A nation of art collectors.' He stopped, aware that he was repeating himself. 'Dr Moser. A lot depends on you. Not just your party. But on you. Remember that I am at your disposal. Good night.'

Dr Börne believed that he had done enough for one night for the recuperation of Europe and left for the Imperial Hotel, as the last dance of the first ball in Vienna since the war was beginning.

XV

SOME WEEKS AFTER THIS MUCH DISCUSSED OCCASION, THERE was a ring at four in the afternoon at the door of the apartment of Alice von Acht in the Gusshausstrasse. Colonel Voronov was in the salon, but Alice's other Russian lodger, Major Stefkov, was out. It would not have occurred to Colonel Voronov to open the door. That function had to be fulfilled by whoever of the liberated people happened to be available. Had there been no liberated person available, the Colonel would still not have risen from his papers. The bell would go on ringing. These instructions were written down in the Soviet manual for officers as to how they should conduct themselves in Germany and Austria. Though Colonel Voronov was not only in intelligence but intelligent, there was no chance of his acting differently. Besides, there was a question of convenience. Colonel Voronov was working. He read many papers "at home". If one were to get up whenever the bell rang, one would get nothing done. He had noticed that Frau von Acht had several friends who were people of no importance.

At five o'clock, Alice returned. She did not walk along Gusshausstrasse with a spring in her step. On the contrary, she looked at the ground. She had a basket in which were her rations and a copy of the *Oestereichische Zeitung*, the dull four-power official newspaper edited by a middle-of-the-road socialist. Hidden below the newspaper were two cups and saucers which had been given to her by her mother, whose tea set had survived the battle for Vienna better than Alice's. She entered the apartment house and walked up three storeys. Outside her door she saw a short young man – almost a boy – with an ugly face and an attractive smile. He was standing there, waiting, for her, as she supposed. Though Vienna was full of disagreeable intrusions, Alice had no sense of anxiety.

'Frau von Acht?' said he, still smiling.

'Yes.'

'I could see it was you, Frau von Acht. I knew it would be you. I am Kamo, the groom of Captain Rüdiger.'

'Rüdiger's groom? You don't sound as if German is your language.'

'Indeed not. I am from the Caucasus. From Georgia. The homeland of Djugashvili. Surely you know that? Captain Rüdiger would have written about it. Anyway, here is a new letter from him. I am sorry it is late. I have carried it here for you. It is late because I am cautious. I have walked here from Carinthia. It took me six months. I walked slowly. Mostly at night. See, here is the letter!'

Alice accepted the letter happily.

'But come in,' she said to Kamo. 'Don't let's stand outside. Do come in.' She unlocked the door and entered the apartment first. Kamo followed her into the kitchen.

'Frau von Acht,' a voice came from the salon.

'Forgive me, I had forgotten I have a guest. A Russian guest. A colonel in intelligence,' she whispered to Kamo. She put the letter on the kitchen table and went across the hall into the salon. The Colonel was sitting on a sofa, his back to the door. He did not rise as she came in.

'Frau Acht. The noise of bells ringing in the afternoons when I am working is irritating. Discourage your friends from ringing when I am here and you are out! Thank you. That is all.'

'I could try,' said Alice.

'Thank you. That is all.'

She returned to the kitchen. Kamo stood there, the bread knife in his hand.

'Why do you hold that knife in such a manner?'

'In case you returned with the Colonel. He might like me to return to Russia. It would be uncomfortable for me if I did. After all, I was with the German army. Grooms rarely fight. I did not fight. But all the same they might not ask about that. Not in Russia. So I thought I should take precautions.'

'I shall make you some cocoa. I have no coffee.'

Alice made a dull brew and sat down to read Rüdiger's letter. She wept. Kamo turned away, examined the broken kitchen window which had been partly sealed by cardboard, a portrait of a top-hatted boulevardier (Alice's grandfather), and the fire escape, and said: 'He was an excellent officer, Captain von Acht. So I will do what you want now. I shall await his return to Vienna. But always remembering that I cannot, will not, go back to Russia. It would not be convenient.'

Alice shut the door of the kitchen. She asked many questions about the last stage of the war in Yugoslavia where Rüdiger had been with the Cossacks, and then said:

'We must make plans for you. If you can't go back to Russia, where do you want to go? Can you stay here? Isn't it too dangerous?'

'Yes, it is dangerous. What I will eventually do is to go to America. I shall make a fortune. Afterwards I shall help my people in Georgia.' He smiled again that fine, exhilarating but at the same time rather frightening smile.

'Very idealistic and ambitious.'

'We Georgians are often both.'

'I do not think that you should ever mention being a Georgian. But if the Colonel comes in, who shall I say you are? I cannot say Georgian. He would arrest you.'

The dreary papers in those days had described how a Soviet repatriation mission was 'assisting the return home of displaced persons of Soviet origin'. That mission was to be found even in the British and American zones.

'Well,' Kamo considered, 'could you say I was American?'

'I don't think that would work.'

'I shall become an American.'

'I think there are rules you have to follow.'

'But they are not like those in the Soviet Union. Where are the children then?'

'In Salzburg.'

'I have promised Captain Rüdiger to embrace them.'

'You would be safer there than here.'

'Oh, you would advise me to go there?'

'No, not now. You can't possibly start your walks again. But eventually. Now you must avoid the Soviet army. This is the Russian zone of Vienna. You must live in the American zone for a start. There is the Russian colonel in my salon.'

'How long will he stay?'

'How should I know? Six months, six years?'

Kamo grunted.

'You must leave here now. Wait, I will give you an address. You will be safe there. I'll write a letter.'

She scribbled a note. Kamo watched, fascinated, the speed with which she wrote, as well as the legibility of the hand.

She had given him the address of Prince Papenlohe in the Herrengasse. She knew that the old man had helped the Jews. Why should he not now help Georgians?

She took Kamo to the door. As she was going, her other Russian "guest", Major Stefkov, clattered in. As always, he was correct. More so than Voronov. He stood back and let her pass to say goodbye to Kamo, which she did warmly. On her return, Major Stefkov said:

'Forgive me, Frau von Acht, but could you tell me who that charming young man was? He had such a smile!'

'Oh Major,' she said, 'he was the son of an old servant. He has just been released by the Americans. A charming man, as you say. He comes from Carinthia.'

XVI

CAPTAIN GREW HAD BEEN ASKED TO VISIT PRINCE PAPENLOHE and ask him how he fared. He was told by the head of his organisation in London: 'he has helped so many people. We want to know if he's in good shape.'

Charlie Grew went to the old house in the Herrengasse. That part of Vienna was disheartening. No one seemed to be doing much about it. Panelling, whole rooms, marble fireplaces, old mouldings, lay as they had crashed. When Charlie reached where the door of No. 10 had been, he found a few boards nailed together to close the opening. No one surely could be living there. But he knocked. He called. His voice echoed back at him from empty stone passages. He began to retreat when a window shifted and a face looked down.'

'British?' a voice asked.

'That is so!' said the Captain.

'Good. I envy you having a country to be proud of. Wait. I'll let you in.'

A long pause and Prince Papenlohe came down. There was another pause while he dismantled the door. Though it was cold, the Prince was wearing a suit in white linen that he might have worn at the Lido in Venice in 1937. Over it, he wore a floor-length, dark blue dressing gown with cord froggings.

'Sorry to be slow. But one can't be too careful,' he said, bracing the makeshift door from inside.

They walked through icy passages into a library. Prince Papenlohe pushed some books off a chair and they both sat down. Charlie gave him a letter of thanks from his chief and several from people whom he had saved. The Prince read these carefully, looking pleased. Charlie wondered who kept his thick white hair so well trimmed and his yellow suede shoes so well brushed. Having read the letter, the Prince said:

'Would you dine?'

'I should be honoured.'

Still sitting in the old cracked leather chair which revolved, the Prince opened a cupboard within reach and took out a spirit stove, which he lit.

He opened another cupboard which looked as if it had once housed manuscripts, found a tin, opened it and poured some peas into a saucepan. He added some water from a bottle, and some salami which he took from a drawer. He produced a half bottle of red wine from the bookshelf and some biscuits.

'Not a bad meal, what do you think?'

Charlie took out some chocolate he had with him and placed his flask of whisky on the table.

Prince Papenlohe asked several questions about England which Charlie could not answer: chiefly about art historians and galleries. He asked whether the Germans' bombing had destroyed the ugly buildings which the English had put up in the 1930s – 'a sign to me that your country had lost its way'. The Captain assured him that there were, unfortunately, a great many such buildings extant. Prince Papenlohe sighed and said: 'I prayed for an Allied victory throughout the war. That was why I helped to do what I could. The letter from your chief shows that I was not unappreciated. But now we learn that you, the Allies, destroyed Dresden, just as you bombed Monte Cassino. I cannot understand it.'

'We had to do it,' said Charlie, 'It helped us win. It saved lives.'

'A life is worth nothing in comparison with a masterpiece.'

'But you risked your life so often to save so many lives.'

'I hoped that one of them might produce something which would last longer than a life. Our lives are meaningless without works of art. In the pursuit of personal immortality all the artists have had their motive.'

'We were preserving civilisation.'

'Yes, but you destroyed a great deal when you bombed Dresden. What was the point, when the war was won?'

'The Germans would have used it as a place in which to rally. The war was far from won.'

'Do not be deceived. You have been conquered by the nazis in spirit if you allow yourself to use their weapons.'

Charlie did not agree: 'The nazis took a risk when they went to war. They had to lose some of their treasures.'

'They were not their treasures. They had none. Dresden belonged to civilisation. It certainly did not belong to Churchill, who, if he ordered the bombing, was showing himself as much a barbarian as his enemies.'

'Is that not too extreme?'

'It is moderation itself. I accept what the Allies did to the nazis. When the Russians got to Dresden, Gauleiter Mutschmann was driven naked on a cart through the city and beaten to death. In cold weather. That was all right. That is Russia. But the bombing. Is that English?' He looked at Grew. 'I see I shock you, but perhaps I have made you think in a new way. That's good. Come and see me again. I'm always here. I shan't move.'

Prince Papenlohe showed his guest out. They parted, warmly, on the doorstep, and Captain Grew heard the bolts being shoved and nails hammered in.

But what he did not hear was, just after he had done so, Prince Papenlohe's exclamation of surprise as he found himself facing a short, fair young man, with a disquieting smile, standing in his corridor.

'How did you get here?' asked Prince Papenlohe, without excessive anxiety.

'When you were saying goodbye to the officer. I was hidden behind the boards. I hope you don't mind, I have a message for you.' Kamo gave Alice's note to Prince Papenlohe.

'I'm too old to mind anything much,' said Papenlohe, 'and I am certainly too blind to read messages in the dark. Come with me.'

They returned to the library which the Prince had just left with Captain Grew.

The Prince read Alice's note: it read

'This is Rüdiger's groom. R. seems to have found him in Russia. He doesn't want to go back there. Help him please. Alice.'

The Prince looked at Kamo over the top of his spectacles.

'Where do you come from?'

'From Georgia.'

'Where precisely?'

'A village called Solbunovo, on the railway between Tibilisi and Yaroslav.'

'Tell me about your family. What is your father?'

'My father is a peasant, my mother is dead. I am one of seven children. Our father taught each of us different things. My sisters to cook, to launder and to sew, my eldest brother to grow vines, my second brother to care for sheep, and me to look after horses.'

'A good education. And how did you meet Rüdiger?'

'When the German army came, the village went to meet them. With their women and children. We were delighted to be done with the communists. As we thought.'

'And?'

'The Germans were kind. In many places, I know, they were not kind. They even killed people who had come to greet them with flowers. With us, they were good.'

'Perhaps they had learned how to be kind by the time that they got to you.'

'Probably. They gave us work. They gave us food. They told us that they would allow us to live in peace. The German general held a meeting in our market place. He said that Georgia would be a free country. He spoke in German. One of his officers translated into Georgian. It was a very nice speech.' Kamo sighed. 'Two days later, I was told that one of the officers needed a groom. I volunteered. There were three of us who tried for the job. We were all poor boys. Captain von Acht made us ride round the market place. First, we walked, then we trotted, then we cantered. Then we had to try and walk our horses sideways. I knew all about that. So I got the job.'

'Do you remember the general's name?'

'I believe it was von Kleist.'

'How is it that you speak such good German?'

'I learned it with Captain von Acht. I am good with languages. In Georgia one needs to know many. Georgian and Mingrelian, as well as Russian. There is also Ossete and Armenian. My father says that in our village fifteen languages used to be spoken. That was before the communists came.'

'What happened next?'

'The Germans didn't advance much more. We hoped they would move on to Baku to liberate the oil fields. If they had done that my father said they would have won the war. Instead, they captured the next two stations on the railway line, but nothing more. Then they – we – began to withdraw. The whole village wanted to withdraw with us. Not just our village, but all the villages. They knew the communists would shoot everyone who remained.'

'Did they?'

'I suppose so. We never stopped withdrawing. Then Captain Rüdiger transferred to the Cossack Corps. They were handed over to the Russians at Judenburg.'

'You escaped?'

'I walked out of the camp because I had a message for Captain Rüdiger's wife.'

'How did you come?'

'On foot.'

'Your route?' Prince Papenlohe had made a habit of not helping anyone unless he had the full story with no details omitted.

'I walked up the Mur as far as Bruck. I turned north at Bruck, to go to Mariazell. Then to Lilienfeld and St Pölten. At St Pölten, I began to go east towards the Wienerwald. I lived very well in the Wienerwald for a month or so. I came into Vienna from Wiedlingbach.'

'That's not much of a place to remember.'

'Two houses, I think. Then I came across the Wienerwald and down through Neuwaldegg.'

Prince Papenlohe looked at Kamo with satisfaction.

'Very well,' he said, 'you shall stay with me until I see the way to get you to Salzburg. I expect you are aiming for America?'

'How did you know?'

'Most of you aim for America, I've noticed.'

'But I must stay till Captain Rüdiger is back.'

'Then you may have to wait some time.'

'I am patient.'

So the young Georgian, with the charming smile, found himself living in the Papenlohepalais – or what was left of it – in the Herrengasse, in a room the size of a conference hall, but with neither windows, running water, food nor identity. Doubtless he would have overcome these inconveniences had not Prince Papenlohe collapsed two or three days later. He died, unattended except by Kamo. His last words were: 'Well, Marcus Aurelius died in Vienna.'

XVII

COLONEL MARCHAIS HAD TO TALK TO THE BRITISH ABOUT the disappearance of the Crown of Charles V. Other treasures had vanished in the war, often as a result of Goering's activities. But for Austria, the loss of this Crown, with its famous St Agatha pearl, was the most severe one. The loss had not yet reached the newspapers, but that was because the press was either controlled, or licensed, by the four Allies. Anything inconvenient to any of the four did not appear. The foreign press had also up to now been too busy talking about "human conditions" to be concerned with art treasures. But the Vienna correspondent of *Le Figaro* had been asking questions. Colonel Marchais could not put him off forever. But, what was the "Allied view"? Could there be an "Anglo-French front" on the matter?

Colonel Marchais lived at a noisy hotel in the Mariahilferstrasse. He drove the short distance to the Schloss Schönbrunn where the English were established. Schönbrunn had not been damaged, apart from a bomb or two in the gardens. The English had taken it over as their headquarters. It was the only outstanding building of Vienna, except for the Karls-kirche, which had not suffered any damage.

Colonel Marchais drove in to Schönbrunn in his tiny car, English soldiers saluting him on all sides, beneath a number of Union Jacks hanging from every possible summit.

The courtyard had been transformed by a few weeks of English occupa-tion. When the Western Allies arrived in Vienna, Colonel Marchais had been struck by its sad grandeur, neglected, shabby, its yellow paint peeling but giving an impression of historic aloofness. Napoleon's stay seemed an affair of yesterday. Now soldiers male and female were walking about as if in Piccadilly Circus, there was much cheerful whistling – Colonel Mar-chais could not abide that – and the whole place had a joyful if ramshackle air. That impression was still more pronounced inside. There was much clutter, subdividing and reorganising. The English, finding Schönbrunn melancholy, had made it cosy.

Sighing, Colonel Marchais told a pretty Scots girl at the reception that he was expected at a meeting in "Conference Room C".

'Och, that's the puir gold one on the mezza,' said the girl, 'wait, will yer, while,' and never, so it seemed to this French aesthete had the "h", in an English "while", been so emphasised, 'while I get the orderly.'

The orderly, who was six foot four inches, but formidably silent, escorted the Colonel up a once noble staircase, which now had posters along it announcing a concert by the entertaining institution, ENSA, in the Schloss theatre.

Colonel Marchais was ushered into a room which was indeed gold. An enormous rough table, perhaps made yesterday by the quartermaster's carpenter, had been placed in the middle to serve as a table for conferences. On it ashtrays, paper, pencils and blotting paper had been laid. Sitting at the table were several officers, of whom he recognised only one, the eccentric Colonel Livingstone. That individual was not, however, in the chair. The senior officer was General Whitelegge, who rose to introduce himself. Sitting on his left was a good-looking girl, in uniform, whom he presented as Tatiana Bezhukov: 'the first member of our auxiliary territorial service into Vienna,' said General Whitelegge, 'and don't worry about her Russian name. Her grandfather may have been General Bezhukov but *she*'s as English as the white cliffs of Dover.'

At that, several people in the room cheered, and Miss Bezhukov herself gave a pretty, proud smile. She was dark, her hair was parted in the middle and pulled back from her face, so as to emphasise her high cheekbones, more in keeping with her name than her uniform. Her function at the general's side was not instantly clear but, Colonel Marchais assumed, rightly, as it happened, that she was an interpreter: an unnecessary function, since he spoke good English. But King's Regulations specify that officers of the General's rank must have an interpreter at their service. Since Miss Bezhukov was attractive, Colonel Marchais felt that her presence had justification.

The General's chest was covered with medals. Colonel Marchais was aware of his good name as a combat soldier. Singapore? Burma? Crete? Dunkirk? Most of the recent defeats in English history, thought the Frenchman, had seen this General in action. But the General was not particularly interested in the Crown of Charles V; nor, indeed, well-informed. He talked as if anxious to get the business over so that he could attend to such urgent matters as the boundaries of the zone in which British officers could shoot roe deer.

'Well, then, gentlemen and Miss Bezhukov,' he said, 'we all know why we've come together today. We have a difficult matter to resolve. We need to do so as allies. This discussion between us is only a preliminary one to a discussion with our other allies on whose collaboration we count.'

With these remarks, the General sat back in his seat and, throughout the rest of the meeting, listened with a detached air.

Colonel Marchais then heard Colonel Livingstone describing how the Crown of Charles V had last been seen in August 1941, how it had been packed, immediately after that, for consignment to the caves in the Salzkammergut under the supervision of Prince Papenlohe, as much a friend of Britain as he had been of culture.

'The two are not necessarily exclusive,' agreed Colonel Marchais.

There was a silence for a split second and then, fortunately, the English officers, led by Miss Bezhukov, laughed. It was not clear whether the General understood the joke.

'Yet the place where the Crown should have been in the cave was empty. There was no sign even of a packing case,' Colonel Livingstone concluded.

'Have you asked Prince Papenlohe for his views?'

'He died last week.'

Colonel Marchais was able by a gesture to give the impression that this left the English in a weak position.

Tea was brought. Milk and sugar had been added. Colonel Marchais found it undrinkable.

'Excuse me.'

An officer at the end of the room expostulated. It was Charlie Grew.

'We – that is, I – saw him. On other matters. I did not raise this with him since I then knew nothing of it. An admirable man. A true patriot. Whatever he did would have been for the best.'

'Thank you, Captain Grew.' The General resumed control. 'Is there anything more to be said today?'

'We haven't precisely solved the problem, Sir,' said Colonel Livingstone.

'No, I suppose that's true.' The General considered carefully. 'I had the impression, however,' he said, 'that we were not getting far. In such circumstances, it is usually wise to bring discussions to an end. I speak, Colonel –' this to Colonel Marchais – 'I speak from considerable experience of inter-allied meetings. So I speak from the heart. Did you know, Colonel, that the King of Rome,' he paused to make an effect, 'the King of Rome died in this room? Concentrates the mind, does it not?'

'I did not know it.'

'Thank you, gentlemen.' the General rolled his eyes, and the artistic conference over which he had presided with neither success nor attention came to an end. He observed Colonel Livingstone and the French Colonel leaving together. They, he hoped, would sort things out. That was the point of meetings: to get people together afterwards. He motioned Captain Grew to his side.

'How are things going then, Charlie?'

'Well, Sir, conditions in Schönbrunn are far from ideal, Sir. The offices open into one another. There is a fire risk. The furniture is inadequate. We've got serious problems on our hands with the caretaker.'

'Who's that, Charlie?'

'He's a man who's run the building ever since the Emperor left. The Emperor Franz Josef, of course. Not Napoleon. Knows every stick and stone. Every board and tile, I should say. Served the Emperor. Worked for the Republic. Kept on with the Germans. An intelligent man – I've interviewed him. We ought to keep him on.'

'Well, why not?'

'He was a nazi, Sir.'

'Oh. I see. Well? Have you talked to him?'

'I have. Sir.'

'What kind of a nazi, Charlie?'

'A fair weather nazi, I'd say, Sir. I'd say he joined the nazis to keep his job.'

'I see. In that case –' General Whitelegge had a deserved reputation for taking decisions – 'in that case, keep him on temporarily. I'll talk to the Political Adviser. I'm sure it'll work.' General Whitelegge made a note on a pad in front of him. 'What else?'

'In what respect, Sir?'

'Life of the town, Charlie. Behaviour of the Russians. Morale of the Austrians.'

'Well, Sir, I think things have picked up a lot since we and the Americans came in.'

'Not forgetting the French.'

'Not forgetting the French.'

'The food position's bad. No one looks forward to the winter. The Austrians are not getting enough to eat to do a day's work. People spend a lot of time going into the country to try and get something extra. The rations are not enough.'

'I see. And the life, Charlie.'

'Well, Sir, the cafés have opened up. There are a lot of shops. I wouldn't know what they sell. You'd better ask Miss Bezhukov that.'

'Miss Bezhukov?'

'Yes Sir, she goes about a lot, sir.'

'I see. Sergeant!' This was addressed to the silent man who had taken Colonel Marchais upstairs.

'Sir?'

'Bring Miss Bezhukov will you?'

'Sir!' He left the room.

'What about the dancing places, what are they like?'

'Again, I should ask Miss Bezhukov, Sir, she's more experienced.'

'Very well. What about the new government? Any views?'

'I think it's a success, Sir. Even though the Russians invented it and we knew nothing of it till it was there and so have been agin' it.'

'Next month's elections?'

'Well, Sir, there are several views about that.'

'Tell me.'

'The Americans think the socialists will win but the communists will get a deciding vote. Our political people agree the communists will have the deciding vote but think the People's Party will win. Other people have a different view.'

'What do you think, Charlie?'

'Well, Sir, I think the People's Party will win and the communists will get very few votes.'

'Why so?'

'The people here were shocked by what happened when the Russians came in. They've had a civilised life here for centuries. Concerts, sewerage, trams. That sort of thing. Everything on time. Everything functioned. The Russians behaved like barbarians. The figures for raping may be exaggerated. They always are. All the same, it did happen. Thefts too. A lot of houses were plundered. Nothing left. The working class districts too. Even some of the socialist apartment blocks. People were horrified. I don't think there will be many votes there, for the communists.'

Miss Bezhukov had come in.

'Sit down, Miss Bezhukov. Tell me,' the General asked, 'about the shops.'

'Nothing in them,' said Tatiana decisively. 'Everything was taken by Russians. Everything. One can't get anything cleaned either. I have found a dressmaker, it's true – good and very cheap. And quick. She's a sort of cousin, though. My father had Austrian relations.'

'I thought you were a Russian, Miss Bezhukov?'

'I am. But not this sort of Russian. We were from a different breed of the human race, I hope. We all had Polish and Austrian connections.' She gave a tinkling burst of laughter. 'I say, General, could you do something about the hot water – no one has had a hot bath since they left home.'

'Miss Bezhukov, I've heard a lot about the hot water. Captain Grew tells me you go about quite a bit here in Vienna. Cafés. Music. That sort of thing. Is it so?'

'Well, Sir. I try to find as much contrast as I can in the harsh circumstances.'

'Quite so. Keep your eyes open. Come and talk to me regularly. Sergeant!'

'Sir?'

'See that Miss Bezhukov comes to lunch once a fortnight.'

'Sir.'

'And, Miss Bezhukov.'

'Yes, Sir?'

'There's a bath at your disposal when you come to lunch.'

'That really is –'

'Don't think of it. Charlie, there is a Mozart concert at the Musikverein tomorrow night. Take Miss Bezhukov. Here are tickets which were given to me. I can't use them. Don't understand. Anyway have to work. That will be all, thank you. And you know it wasn't in *this* room that the King of Rome died. It was upstairs. But I needed some ammunition. We couldn't have that frog talking to us as if we were dirt. One finds ammunition in strange places, does one not? I hadn't expected to fire a Bonaparte at a French colonel.'

XVIII

*A*LOIS AND HIS REMOTE COUSIN FATHER GEORGE WERE AT the deathbed of Uncle Max. Max had been to Salzburg and returned. Beatrice von Acht had remained there. Max lay in the bedroom of lodgings in which he had been living since the battle of Vienna. He had become attached to his landlords, the Svobodas, and they to him. He talked to them about the past and told many stories which were afterwards of use to them. Willy Svoboda had become Max Acht's confidant. He looked after the ailing man of letters whose demands in his last months became difficult. Once he told Willy that he wished to hear a record of *Küssen Ist Keine Sünd'*, the song from *Brüder Straubiger*, by Edmund Eysler: a demand which Willy had the devil to satisfy, since most people's gramophone records were in poor shape. Even Willy's gramophone, which he had treasured since his eighth birthday, had been stolen during the invasion: not, in his opinion, by Russian soldiers, but by the wife of the chemist who lived two storeys below. In the end, Willy had satisfied this request; he had borrowed the record from a friend of his from school who had been at the first night of Eysler's last operetta, *Die Goldene Meisterin*.

On another occasion, Max had sent Willy to see if Prince Papenlohe were still alive and to give a mysterious coded message, namely, that he, Max von Acht, remembered the story of the hatbox. He carried out this mission with difficulty since Prince Papenlohe's door never seemed to open except about once a week when the Prince let in an old servant who took in food and books. Prince Papenlohe had smiled, been friendly and patted Willy's shoulder. There were other such errands. Willy's parents at that time were busy in the ruins of Vienna, like all others, his father's task being to shovel rubble, his mother's to find yet more bricks which could be used again.

'Will he talk to us?' Alois asked, impatiently, striding up and down the tiny room in which the author of *The Final Solution* lay with his face to the wall.

'Not likely, I'm afraid, Herr Doktor,' said Willy, 'but I've told him you're here.'

'He might like to be told again that I am here,' said Father George, very pleasantly.

'I told him twice,' said Willy, 'but I'll tell him again.'

With that, he loudly but kindly passed the information. Max, wearing a mysterious headband round his bald head, presumably to keep sweat from dripping onto his face, signified that he would prefer to see Father George alone. Alois and Willy left them for a few minutes during which, presumably, the Father gave the last rites. On their return to the room, Max was sitting up. He became talkative.

'People keep telling me of a new Austria,' he said crossly, 'Alois, tell them not to. I don't believe in it.'

Who were these people who had been talking to Max so optimistically, Alois wondered. He said:

'Perhaps, Uncle Max, it will happen without our noticing?'

'Nonsense,' said Max, 'nothing comes save by design. And by craftmanship. Or effort. Things don't just happen. Look at what took place in my lifetime. All by design. Mark my words. Austria will not exist in the future. There will be a Western Austria, capital Salzburg. There will be an Eastern Austria, capital Vienna. Western Austria will join Germany. East Austria will be a Soviet dependency. It was the obvious solution before the Anschluss. That's the name of my next book incidentally: *The Obvious Solution*. Why should a country like ours stick together? Its mission, to give coherence to central Europe, no longer exists. The same collapse will soon come to England and France. They've lost their missions. So they will collapse. The only countries with a mission are Russia and America. The Russians know it. The Americans don't. All we can hope for is that the Americans will realise it before it's too late. Otherwise, the world state will be built by Stalin. Whether that will be better than Hitler's world state would have been, I don't know. I doubt it. The difference is that Stalin's will last. Hitler's, even if it had been achieved, could never last. Nothing lasts if it comes from the brain of someone who failed to get into the Academy of Art in Vienna. A boy whose family was from the Waldviertel. Nothing lasts if it comes from the Waldviertel. Hitler's family was typically Waldviertel. People say he was Jewish. Don't you believe it! No one who's Jewish makes so many mistakes.' He sighed.

'Aren't you tired, Herr von Acht?' asked the tireless Willy.

'Very. What I can't bear, though, is to think of all this' – he tapped his forehead – 'going to waste. I've accumulated too much knowledge,' he added and lay back in silence.

'Nothing is wasted in the eye of the Eternal Father,' said Father George, 'the soul will be comforted by memory in eternity.'

'Let us hope that it may be so,' said Max Acht, sitting up once more, this time violently, 'which reminds me, Alois. Go and ask Erich Papenlohe what he has done with his hatbox. Tell him I've been reading the papers to see if the hatbox has been opened up as it should have. Don't forget. The hatbox was under his bed. Ask him why he hasn't opened it. He shouldn't keep it. That is my last request to you.'

He lay back in bed and closed his eyes.

'I don't think I can be blamed for an expression,' he said dreamily, 'Anyone might have written a book called *The Final Solution*. Everyone used the expression when I was young. I wasn't to know that a failed painter from the Waldviertel would take to it, was I? It just wasn't predictable. I remember people saying that it was a good title. In the Café Eisvogel, Altenberg approved.'

Alois was wondering whether the church approved such a lively conversation after the giving of Extreme Unction. 'Of course, no one blames you, Uncle Max,' he said.

'I think you should leave him,' Willy said in a proprietary manner, 'He's become demonstrative.'

Father George had not taken part in these discussions. He was himself in those days just still a part of the Church. But his connection hung by a thread. A thin thread. He was there because he was a priest. Alois and Uncle Max saw him as a priest. But he was there on false pretences. *The Final Solution*: what worried Uncle Max perturbed him on different grounds. How could the benign Being who was ready to receive Uncle Max, have put it in the mind of the failed painter from the Waldviertel to do what he had done up in Poland? It was not comprehensible.

But Max was continuing.

'The only person who knows what the new Austria will be is Willy Svoboda,' he said. 'We Achts, Papenlohes, people of families known in the past, will have nothing to say. The new Austria will be anonymous. We are all of us, Achts, guilty of something. All the people of quality were Jewish. They've left. They're in New York or London. Or dead. They won't come back. Some may say they'll be back. But why should they?'

'Ludwig Börne's already back,' Alois said.

'Ludwig Börne!' Max Acht seemed to enter a profound reverie. Actually, he was not thinking so much of Börne as trying to remember the last time that he had been with him, in a group that included other survivors of the great days. Then he remembered that his photographs, and other archives, as well as his house had gone up in the smoke of April.

Willy Svoboda was taking over. With patience he was shepherding the cousins out of the tiny room. Both shook Max's hand when they left. He did not seem responsive. He was back in his memories. Ludwig Börne had published one of his books in, could it be, 1930? He had deserted his regular publisher to go to him, he remembered. The book had been about Fascism. Was it for it or against it? He could not recall. Perhaps it took no position. Yes, that had been its originality! On the cover, it had said "by the author of *The Final Solution*". Just as well there were no copies around of *that*. The second-hand bookshops might have it. Dietrich could get it, no doubt.

It was with dreams of second-hand bookshops, old friends, and works written by them, and attended by the spirit of a new Austria, that Max Acht painlessly breathed his last.

XIX

*A*LOIS AND GEORGE ACHT WERE WALKING DOWN WHAT HAD once been the Kohlmarkt. They did not know each other well. Their conversation was halting. Alois had to return to his Ministry, now in the Kruggasse, but he wanted to finish the conversation on friendly terms. Perhaps one day he might need the Church. George had already sensed something of this in Max's room. It put him in a difficult position. He himself had been released from all duties, after all, for a period of "reflection and meditation". The Cardinal had insisted that this should be as untroubled a time for him as possible.

George asked Alois if he had any news of his brother Gottfried.

'The news is not good,' Alois replied. 'He is still in prison, though, thank heavens, he has a cell to himself. A prison is like a hospital. It can be recuperative, provided it is accompanied by solitude.'

'Such faith in solitary confinement suggests you are still a man of the last century. Will they try him?'

'We do not know. If they do he will surely get a mild sentence. He did nothing himself. It is on his *words* that the case for the prosecution will rest. Well, he said some bad things. So did many people. So did we all. How do you account for it, George, that so much madness seized hold of us? I do not understand it.'

The question was seriously asked. Father George felt its urgency.

'It goes back even further. Think of the last ten years before the First War. Such excess! Such agitation.'

'But that was the golden age.'

'The golden age possibly, but people did not love each other. On the contrary. The greatest of them were egotists.'

'Do you think there is a connection then?'

'A close connection. Vienna at the beginning of the century was a place for questioning. There was no acceptance. Each year it became worse. No one believed in anything. In God, least of all. The agitation grew. Was it surprising that a Hitler should rise out of it? He was a consequence of the agitation. He saw it all and would have liked to have been a part of it. In the next street to where he lived there was Trotsky.

Beyond, there was Freud. Mahler was at the Opera House.'

'Poor Mahler, surely he did not contribute?'

'Yes, because he tried to discipline everyone. His audiences. Members of his orchestra. His wife. It was fatal. It was too late.' They walked out in silence, Father George rather shaken by giving voice to his theories. 'But how is Lise?', he asked, wanting to return to family questions.

'Lise has not recovered from the disappearance of Klara,' said Alois decisively, 'she is a shadow of her old self.'

'And you?'

'Well, George, I have to tell you the truth. When Klara vanished, something else vanished. I changed. I shall never forgive the Russians. I shall never trust them. I shall fight them. Always.' He smiled. 'As a man of God, you will disapprove of vengeance. But whatever happens, George, I mean to have it.'

George was shocked. He was about to remonstrate, when two cars passed and drew up by the pavement ahead of them at the bottom of the Herrengasse. One had a Tricolore on it, the other a Union Jack. That meant less trouble, thought George, than if either of them had had a hammer and sickle.

Two colonels descended from the two cars. They had reached the Papenlohepalais in the Herrengasse. One was short, scowling, smoking a cigarette: Colonel Jean Georges Marchais. The other was tall and waving languidly: Colonel Livingstone. Colonel Marchais hammered against the makeshift door while Colonel Livingstone leant on his stick and watched. The two Austrians observed too from a distance.

'That is the Papenlohe house,' said Alois. 'I wonder what they want there? It used to be full of Jews in the war. I've seen the Gestapo hammering outside just as that man is. *Autre temps, autre moeurs!*'

Eventually Colonel Marchais heard sounds and the boarding of a down-stairs window shifted slightly.

'Colonel Marchais and Colonel Livingstone,' the former announced to the crack in the windowboards, 'may we come in? We are from the *Département des Beaux Arts* of the French and British High Commissions.'

'Certainly,' said a voice, coming from whoever it was that had shifted the window, and then, by a swift action which Alois and George saw, but could not have explained, the two colonels disappeared into the house, while a fair youth jumped out of a ground floor window into the street, and shut and bolted the makeshift door after the colonels from the outside. He had a case with him.

'Never mind,' said the youth to Alois and George von Acht, who had by now reached the house, 'the main lights are on inside, and there's plenty to occupy them. By the way, would you mind if I accompanied you for about a hundred yards? One often feels lonely in an empty street.'

There was no one in sight. It was a sign of the effect that Kamo had on those with whom he came into contact that Alois and George didn't even question him about the scene that they had witnessed.

'You speak good German, yet one would say that there was a trace of a Baltic accent,' Alois said.

'I am not a Balt,' Kamo said decisively. 'Indeed, I sometimes forget who I am.'

He gave them both a smile, shifted the case he was carrying to his other hand and turned away from them down a tiny street on the left of the Herrengasse towards the Volksgarten. It was just as well since, two minutes later, a Russian patrol car passed the Achts and slowed down. Turning down the window, an officer within studied the two men, gave a long imperious look and then drove on. Whether he would have done only that had he been confronted by a stranger, as well as an Austrian, whom he recognised to be in the Government, and a priest, it is hard to say.

XX

*B*ROOKS SHEAY WAS TRYING TO SEE AS MANY AUSTRIANS AS he could in order to write a report about what was going on in the country. His contempt, fury and impatience had modified in these months. But they were still present. His was, no doubt, a case of love turned inside out, but it was not less strongly felt. All the same, Sheay, for all his independence of spirit, could not step out of line. He was a temporary officer, brigadier though he might be, and soon he expected to return to the firm which had made him rich. Further, Sheay, however shocked he was at what he learned, was incapable of shaking himself free from that optimism that characterised most Americans at that time. In the offices of the American Mission in Vienna, though they looked onto ruins, messengers were still whistling *Happy Days Are Here Again*. There was a buoyancy and an irresistible sense that everything was possible in the building.

One day he talked with Fritz Toblach. That tall communist, whose family came from the now lost South Tyrol, was still a minister: the cleverest of the communist ministers, he was the only leader of that party to take any trouble with western journalists. Sheay invited him to lunch at the Allied Officers' Club in the Kinskypalais. Full "fraternisation" for "social" purposes was still forbidden, but these could be termed official discussions. Nevertheless, Sheay was mildly surprised that Toblach made no suggestions for a more convenient site for their meeting. He arrived on time, made no attempt at disguising who he was, drank a dry martini before lunch with pleasure, and responded sympathetically when Sheay pointed out the empty frames on the walls where the Dürers used to be.

'What's your estimate, Herr Toblach, of your party's standing in the elections? Is that too delicate a question?'

'No, not delicate but difficult. We have good estimates for Vienna. Bad for everywhere else. We could have done better if it had not been for the behaviour of our Soviet friends in April and May. One must face facts. Soviet soldiers are like any other. They had fought a war. The moment of victory for them was a moment of indiscipline. They lost control. Actually *you* should be glad of that, in some ways. What happened showed to the world that the Soviets are human beings. Twenty-five years of communism hasn't changed the essential Russian.'

'That will have a real effect on how people vote?'

'Of course, Brigadier, of course. The Viennese have centuries of civilisation behind them. The workers will not vote for us if they think we are the friends of Russian soldiers. And it will be a free vote.'

'Herr Toblach, you are candid. Do you always talk in this way?'

'What is the point of refusing to see things as they are?'

'Many people see such a point. Including some of your comrades.'

'I don't always speak for my comrades. We will not do so badly. We should have enough votes to hold the balance. So we shall remain on the scene. I do not think we can be expected to be more. My children will vote for the People's Party. They are rebels, you see. They will not vote for parties which take politics seriously. They want a quiet time, with apolitical conservatives.'

'Perhaps it's understandable?'

'I find it most understandable.'

Fritz Toblach looked amused at Sheay's evident surprise. During the rest of lunch, they talked of the revival of the Salzburg Festival and the capacity of Austrians to avoid political categorisation. Yet Sheay knew the next evening Toblach would be in some famous square, or on the radio, calling for "a final heave to prevent the re-establishment of monopoly capitalism". There would be clenched fists, allusions to heroic days in the Karlmarxhof, and an expression of gratitude to the Red Army.

A week later, at the same table, in the same club, Sheay entertained Poldi Moser. He chose the same menu as did Toblach even to taking the same two spoonfuls of horseradish and apple sauce that Toblach had had with the *tafelspitz*.

Poldi Moser had, in a short time, filled out. It could not be said that he had fattened with power, since the then Chancellor had made a special point of never feeding his ministers till the cabinets were over. But he seemed a larger, easier man than when Sheay had first met him. He was one of the few right-wing Austrians with a genuine record of active hostility to the nazis. Perhaps that meant that he was at ease with himself. People thought of him as 'Dr Leopold Moser', not as 'Poldi' any more. A trace of pomposity had crept into his rotund sentences.

'I have to say it's difficult. To pretend to be a government where the supreme authority is held by four Allied generals is abnormal. It really is. And then the Russians put so many communists into the police. Thugs! Many with little experience even as communists! One or two ex-nazis. Several out-of-work trade unionists who joined the guerrillas at the last moment because they liked shooting. Or because they liked the open air. They often have no knowledge of the law which they are supposed to administer. Still, Brigadier, we shall not be downhearted. We will be patient.'

'The trouble is,' he went on, 'that the communists, including those in the police, behave as if they are the agents of an imperial power, not as Austrians. That is our difficulty. And once an Austrian goes into the Soviet security building, you know where I mean – that dark block between the Kunsthistoriches Museum and the old parliament – one never knows how long they will be kept. An hour? A week? A lifetime? Who can tell? But we keep our spirits up, Brigadier. To do so, we are inspired by you, by America. The old world can only now look to the new one. We have no choice. There is no one to look to in Europe.'

Sheay's third guest, some days later, was Alois. Alois did not have the same tastes, it seemed, as his coalition partners. So Sheay had, regretfully, to abandon the projected first sentence of his report which he had already half framed around the *tafelspitz*. At the next table, and unfortunately within listening distance, there sat the English official, Harry Mercer, eating messily, with his guests: one was Ludwig Börne, the other was a tall fair man of about forty with protruding blue eyes whom Alois recognised as Count Kurt Gmunden, a well-known friend of the nazis. He had assumed that Gmunden was either dead or in South America by that time and was disgusted to see him at the Officers' Club. It was impossible not to overhear their conversation.

'So long as we work sensibly with the Soviets,' Mercer was saying, mopping the gravy from his plate with bread and smacking his lips, 'we will have no difficulties. We *must* work with them. They are the paramount power in Europe, whatever we may think. They will dictate policy in this continent. The Americans' – he giggled – 'have no idea. They neither know how to run an empire nor do they want to. They want to get "the boys home". Isn't that so, Count?'

'That's quite true, Mr Mercer, I am pleased that we understand each other so well. We Austrians, you know, are realists. In the 1930s, I believed we had to have an accommodation with Hitler. Not out of enthusiasm, you understand.'

'Quite, quite.'

'But out of realism.'

'Quite, quite,' Mercer was cleaning his fingernails with his fork.

'Out of realism. Now we are in exactly the same conditions *vis-à-vis* the Soviets. We have to be sensible. The world is not our oyster. It once was. Not any more. We must take comfort where we can. So we must work with them. The Soviets, I mean. We must make things easy for them.'

'Quite.' Mercer obviously did not want anyone else to talk so much. 'What is very important,' Mercer said, 'is that we go on helping the Soviets over the Soviet-born persons whom we have here in Austria. There has been so much misunderstanding over this. Anything you can do from your position, Count, or yours, Herr Börne, will be appreciated by the British High Commission, as well as by the Russians. We must stick by our agreements. That's the only hope for world peace. We can't afford not to.'

'Excuse me. I don't understand.' Ludwig Börne was wearing a pale blue suit more suitable for a day in Florida than in Vienna.

'Of course you don't, Herr Börne, how clumsy of us. Why should you? The Count and I have discussed this several times. But the situation is this –'

And then Mercer explained how there were a multitude of Russians in Austria, some ex-prisoners of war, some brought back from Russia by the Germans to work in German factories as semi-slave labour, many of whom (foolishly, in Mercer's opinion) did not want to go back to the land of electricity and Soviet power, but wished (incredibly, said Mercer) to stay in the decadent *Mitteleuropa* or even make their way to the United States.

'Where, of course,' said Mercer, 'they are treated like coolies, worked to the bone in mines or brothels, and soon long for the peasant fields of the Ukraine which are by then unattainable.'

'Excuse me.' Brigadier Sheay had lost his temper and shouted across, unable to contain himself, 'You're talking drivel in a voice a little too high for it not to seem like a public statement. Please withdraw that last remark or I'll have you out of this club for good.'

Mercer had experienced this kind of reaction to his opinions previously. On many previous occasions perhaps.

'I withdraw them instantly, of course, if it upsets you so much. Though,' he said lightly, 'it's a little rude to interrupt someone else's conversation. Not quite what we're used to in Europe, dear boy.'

Sheay turned round and faced Alois. 'Excuse me for a moment,' he said, and went over to the desk where the head waiter was standing. In the meantime, Mercer was exchanging looks with his companions.

'American imperialism isn't slow to show its spots,' said he.

Count Gmunden and Ludwig Börne were becoming reluctant to stay involved and, as Alois noticed, were showing signs of embarrassment.

'All the same, Mr Mercer,' Count Gmunden said, 'we have to recognise that there is a US presence in Europe. It will not go away. Perhaps it is good that it will not go away. I do not know. Perhaps it assists the balance.' He was talking in the direction of Sheay's table. He could sense the way the wind was blowing.

'You know, Mr Mercer, I am an American citizen,' Ludwig Börne was saying. 'Of course, I am Austrian first and foremost, and always will be. But I am technically American. I say this: the Americans do not understand Russians. They could not, even if they devoted a lifetime to the study, as you have done, Mr Mercer. All the same, the Russians do not understand the Americans either. That also is important.'

After that, the conversation seemed to go into calmer waters. Sheay returned to his table. He said to Alois Acht:

'The man appears to be a British official. By the name of Mercer. Odd, don't you think? As for the tall, fair Austrian!'

'Count Gmunden.'

'That's right. You know him? Apparently he's been taken on by the British as superintendent of their game reserves. Ex-nazi.'

'Certainly.'

'Yes, well, many strange things are going on like that. We live in unexpected times.'

They ate for some time in silence.

'Tell me, Brigadier,' Alois said, 'how important is Austria to the United States?'

Sheay looked at him hard.

'I'd say, Alois, that's not a question which we have begun yet to think about, but it's not a question which we can avoid answering much longer. We certainly can't.'

The waiter was a short, fair, young man, with a disturbing smile. Was it his imagination, wondered Alois, but could he have seen him before?

'Wait,' he called, 'weren't you the boy I walked with not long ago in the Herrengasse?'

'The Herrengasse?' The young man looked puzzled and did not smile.

'No, perhaps I'm mistaken. Forgive me. A cousin of mine and I found ourselves walking with someone like you not long ago in the Herrengasse. It was dark. It is easy to make mistakes.'

'Of course, Sir.'

Alois Acht watched him until he left the dining room. That's certainly the boy, he thought. Why did he not admit it, he wondered. Then he thought, well, what does it matter? There are too many problems in Vienna for me to worry about that.

XXI

*I*N THE MUSIKVEREIN, NOTHING HAD CHANGED. AUNT THEKLA
sat with Alice, her niece, as she had done in the past, in one of the
boxes to the left of the stage. The chandeliers were lacking one or two
lights. There was dust. But otherwise the hall had changed less than
anything in Vienna. Thekla von Acht had been there nearly every week
of her life save for the days just after the Russians had arrived. Throughout the war, certainly. The day after the Anschluss, of course. Peoples
and provinces might become pawns in the game of power. What did that
matter in comparison with the part played by music?

Thekla was a symbol of continuity. Who else, she wondered, among
those there had been present, as she had been, on March 31, 1913, when
Schönberg's first symphony was played and there had been fighting in
the second gallery? Who remembered the booing, shouting and how the
philistines had stormed onto the platform in front of the terrified musicians? That had marked the real breakdown, Aunt Thekla had thought,
in European civilisation. As for the rest, the world wars and the nazis,
they were the consequence.

This present concert was of three separate pieces played by four
Hungarians – Alice Berszenyi, Toni and Ferenc Kiraly and Amadeo
Szasvaros. The conductor, Sandor Miko, was a Romanian, or at least so it
was believed. No one knew his nationality but it did not matter: he was a
conductor. He was not well-known, nor young, certainly not handsome.
He walked in an ungainly fashion, bending forwards too low for style or,
even, one must surely suppose, for comfort. But he had about him an air
of courtliness and of indifference to all but music – a fine independence,
which made him impervious to fashion as much as to politics. He was a
professional. One looked in vain for any explanation of his non-profes-
sional life in the brief biography, on the back of the programme: Royal
Hungarian Conservatory; Conservatoire de St Petersburg; the State Academy of Music at Salzburg. He was just Sandor Miko, musician. The
fact that, as some in the Musikverein recognised, the conductor came
from Transylvania, a once Austrian territory which, for the second time
since 1919, was at that very time being "transferred" from one nation to

another, gave poignance to the evening. Born Austro-Hungarian, Sandor Miko could look upon himself as a Transylvanian. But he could also think of himself as a citizen of the world.

The concert hall remained, like Sandor himself, a survival of an older order. Here, as not only Thekla remembered, there had been so much life before 1914. Mahler had stood often in the place where Sandor now stood, the Emperor had been in the box where Russian officers were now sprawled.

The concert was modest. There was, to begin with, the *Concerto Grosso in G minor*, Opus 6, Number 6, by Handel. A delicate piece, perhaps played too quietly. None of them had taken in what the Musikverein would be like with an audience which included so many foreigners. That gave the evening a new tone. There followed the delightful *Apollo Musagetes* by Stravinsky; elegant, and optimistic. It had been written in 1927. The quartet conveyed the spirit of that half-forgotten time of confidence before the fall of humanity into the hands of the nazis.

An interval ensued. There was no bar. People walked about. Thekla and Alice sat where they were. It was one of the first occasions when Austrians and liberators were together in the same public hall, and when Austrians, by the very fact of it being their hall, were able to feel comfortable, even superior.

Charlie Grew walked in the foyer with Tatiana Bezhukov. Several others of the British Mission joined them. Over the weeks all these people, none of them more than thirty, had developed a fine camaraderie. They had not been in Vienna more than a few months, but each of them felt that their stay there was a lifetime. Some were in the army: that entailed the showing of the Union Jack at special places on specific days, as well as certain police functions. It entailed help towards Austrian recovery, such as the rebuilding of bridges and gas and electricity lines. Some were translators. Some were political officers or embryo diplomats; some were in "intelligence", which already included "keeping an eye" on Russians as well as the pursuit of nazis. They all knew each other well. There were romances. But more important was the sense of friendship, temporary but ardent.

Tatiana Bezhukov was the only one on the English side who, through her relations, had anything of a link with Austria. In consequence, though she knew no German, she had visited old Princess Selztal, a friend – mistress, perhaps – of her grandfather's, and called on the Chorinskys and the Leopoldsteins, with whom she had a blood connection.

'But,' she firmly told Charlie, 'I'm not going to learn German. I'm going to learn the piano.'

They walked up and down the foyer talking about people whom they knew.

Charlie had by now recovered from the experience of imprisonment. In terms of his service, that imprisonment had been considered a benefit. His report on the character of the Austrian resistance was as esteemed as his notes on his time in prison. "They" in London were doing their best to persuade Charlie to stay on with "them" in peacetime. Charlie was considering the offer. He had no idea what the future would bring him. He had a vague sense that people like him were expected to go into public service and eventually to "rise" within it. The idea of commerce he never considered. Eton did not produce businessmen. His father was a general. None of the Grews had been "in trade". But what, he wondered, would become of England in the future? What would "public service" be in the age of nationalisation? Would the Empire last? Was he not too flippant for "service"?

They stopped to say good evening to Pat Mackenzie, who was accompanying a young American whom she introduced as Major Stern. This officer was much more happy than he had been at the gates of the Salzkammergut at the end of the war. He now seemed the essence of the young American officer, anxious to learn, polite, apologetic, inclined to listen rather than to address his Allied comrades.

His chief, Brigadier Sheay, who, in the absence in the US of his general was temporarily in command of the American mission, strolled by, benign for once, nodding to the members of his staff, apparently alone. For a few moments, he walked with his Russian colleague, Colonel-General Zheltov, carrying his customary burden of medals.

The French general had taken a party. This included Colonel Marchais and Madame Charpentier. Colonel Livingstone was also there, with his incessant companion, the gluttonous Mr Mercer, as usual making jokes against the United States. Even the Minister for Railways, Comrade Toblach, was present and, for the first time on that occasion, the world saw his "companion", the "Red Countess", Henrietta Huszar, who seemed, on examination, to be red of dress, lip and cheek, whatever her politics. Despite the recent death of Cousin Max, George von Acht had been able to satisfy his conscience that it was right to go to the concert. Father George was sitting in a box which he shared with Leopold Moser and his wife, the once beautiful Gertrud von Degenfeld, who was also in public for the first time. She had spent the last year of the war in prison in Vienna. Had she not been in a wing there which the nazis believed was riddled with typhus, she would have been marched off to be killed, as were many others, at Eisenerz.

The interval was nearing its end when Alice gave an exclamation of surprise and told Aunt Thekla that, in the grand box directly opposed to theirs, there was someone she recognised.

'Who is it?' asked Aunt Thekla peering through the opera glasses of which she had managed to keep hold during the early days of the Russian occupation by hiding them in the chimney along with her pearls and the diamond chain left her by her grandmother, Elisabeth Petzel-Perard.

'It's the boy who used to be Rüdiger's groom. I can't understand it, he looks so at home, he's so well-dressed.'

Then she told her aunt the story of Kamo's appearance, and her recommendation to him to go to Prince Papenlohe.

'Erich Papenlohe probably left him a fortune,' said Aunt Thekla, 'and,' she added, 'I know who he is with.'

'No, who?'

'It is the publisher Ludwig Börne,' said Aunt Thekla. 'I had heard that he had returned. What a strange combination, to be sure!'

Alice was about to comment when the lights were lowered and Sandor Miko walked onto the stage to prolonged cheers. The last item on the programme, Mozart's *Divertimento in D major* began.

The piece was one of Thekla's favourites. Mozart! To hear Mozart again! To be reminded of his unyielding youth! To recall through him another Austria untouched by the events of the past thirty years! Here surely was a resilient elegance reflecting true aristocracy. If Mozart could again be played, by performers who cared nothing for anything except music, this was a sign that there was hope. If that past could be re-articulated, there could be a broader future.

Between each of the movements, the silence was eloquent even if disturbed by the single hand clap by an enthusiast who could not restrain himself, or who believed that the end had been reached: a clap, whose author – was it Captain Grew? – received that contemptuous scowl at the amateur which is among the special products of the concert hall. The conclusion, reached after a brilliant *Rondo Allegro*, was a triumph. The little conductor had to come from the wings not once, not twice, but three times. There was an encore. There were two encores. Even that did not seem adequate. Sandor Miko believed, though, by then that his work was done. The performers gave a deep bow. Alice Berszenyi's curtsey was the deepest of her life. The applause was overwhelming. Aunt Thekla, who had experienced many stirring evenings in that hall, could not remember anything like it.

Thekla was moved: just as she had been when she heard the American band in Seilerstrasse the day of the unveiling of the Russian war memorial.

The audience walked down the much-loved staircases into the shabby Vienna of today, carrying with them the memory of better days. Aunt Thekla found herself beside a thick-set American senior officer in uniform. It was Brigadier Sheay. His face seemed familiar. He had not, after all, much changed since his stay in Austria the summer before the Anschluss.

'I think I know you,' she said to him in English, 'Isn't it Brooks Sheay?'

He, for his part, had recognised her before, but had hesitated. Should he claim acquaintance?

'You've put on weight, Brooks, and you look too prosperous,' she said strictly, 'but I know whom I'm talking to.'

They reached the foyer. 'Thekla, I should have visited you and your family. Circumstances have been against it.'

'My circumstances also prevent me from inviting you, Brooks. I'm eighty-five. This is Alice. Do you remember my nephew Rüdiger? Used to be making silly speeches in your day, I remember. Well, he's in Russia. Not as a tourist. This is Rüdiger's wife.'

Brooks Sheay shook hands. He remembered Alice perfectly, and Rüdiger too.

'Captain Adams, we'll give these friends of mine a lift home.' He turned to his ADC, who had been hovering at a distance.

Thekla hesitated. 'Is it allowed?'

Brooks Sheay smiled. 'Do you mean for me? Or for you?'

'Oh, I meant for you, General Sheay.'

'I think it is,' he said, decisive again. 'You see, Thekla, I make the rules.'

They drove Thekla home. Sheay walked with her to the door and kissed her hand on saying goodnight.

'I see you've lost none of your central European ways, Brooks,' said Thekla.

'I've forgotten some of them. But I still know how to say goodnight to a lady,' Sheay said.

'Americans are still gluttons for saying the obvious,' returned Thekla, stepping into the lift, 'even if they have won a war. Goodnight – and thank you.'

'I hope my Russians don't see us arrive,' said Alice when Sheay returned to the car.

'Why is that?'

'Well, I can't explain. It might make them unpleasant tomorrow,' Alice said.

'They are unpleasant?'

'No. Just silent. But I don't want them to start talking.'

Sheay laughed.

'No, no, one can't laugh. It's quite serious.'

'How often do you hear from Rudi?' he asked in a more serious tone.

'Hear from Rudi? Brigadier Sheay!'

'Brooks?'

'Brooks, you can't be serious. Surely you knew. One never hears from the prisoners of war in Russia. And as he was in command of Cossack troops, the odds must be that he's dead.' She spoke simply, without allowing emotion to enter her voice.

'Oh, I didn't know.' Then he added, to fill the silence, 'They should have surrendered to us.'

'Don't think they didn't try. They surrendered to the English. The English turned them over to the Russians.'

'We all have our troubles with England,' said Brooks, soothingly.

'I think they are just tired,' said Alice, 'Goodnight, Brooks, thank you for taking me home. I'm glad to meet you again, 'and I'm even gladder to have been able to tell you things you didn't know.'

She jumped out of the car. Before Brooks could manage his hand-kissing, she had gone, her door clashing behind her. Voronov was complaining that the pipes had burst, there was no water upstairs.

Two lively representatives of that allegedly tired England, Charlie Grew and Tatiana Bezhukov, were sitting in the Drei Hussaren, one of the only night clubs open in Vienna. A tall boy with a guitar boomed Russian folk songs in bad Russian. He followed with what he described as a song of Transylvania in German entitled *Deine Augen brennen heisser als Paprika*. The English couple drank glasses of *ersatz* orangeade.

'The Austrians are rather a tired people;' said Charlie, 'if this is the best they can do.'

In the end, a popular song *Wien kommt wieder* was produced by a girl described as the best Jewish singer in Austria. There was no definite evidence that she could sing.

'I rather wish,' said Tatiana Bezhukov, 'that we had gone straight home after the concert.' Tomorrow was her day for lunching with the General and she was not going to learn anything new in that depressing place. She was looking forward to having a good splash in the General's canvas bath. Better than a bad nightclub.

As they were going out, however, they met a Soviet officer coming in. He was alone. He stood back to allow them to pass. It was Colonel Voronov. 'Be careful, Miss Bezhukov,' he said, 'Russian emigrés should not stay too long in Central Europe.'

XXII

*A*LOIS VON ACHT WAS NOT AT THE FAMOUS CONCERT. THAT night, he was making a speech in Baden-bei-Wien, in the Casino. It had been turned into a place for public meetings during the election campaign. At first sight, little had changed to show that this charming town was the Russian headquarters, where they had their secret prisons, interrogation centres, even, as important, archives. There were few Russian soldiers in the streets. In the hotels there were coloured pictures of Marx, Lenin and Stalin, smiling under their moustaches. But one had become used to those in Vienna. The streets were shabbier than they used to be. The houses needed paint. Yet there seemed no damage. A number of citizens walked about with what seemed to be a lighter step than one would have seen in the capital.

The first sign of anything untoward occurred when Alois reached the Hotel Erzherzog Karl, in whose sumptuous saloons the socialist party had set up headquarters. As Alois and his chauffeur drove up, two Russian soldiers appeared from the shadows to check their papers. They must have had instructions to spend as long a time on this inspection as possible, to intimidate, or to irritate, impatient Austrians into "provocation". Alois dissuaded his more explosive driver from protest.

'To what good?' he murmured, as the driver seemed likely to object.

Eventually he was allowed to walk into the hotel. A group of Soviet officers stood at the hotel entrance at ease, with no purpose save to frighten by their presence. In Room 104, a group of young men and girls were busy preparing posters, checking lists, and shaking the telephone in the hope of making it work. One of them, Fritz Schwarz, who looked as if he were a student, welcomed Alois and introduced his colleagues. A few veterans came in and gave Alois the salute with a clenched fist. The party had decided not to use that salute during the election, so as to avoid the impression that they were allies of the communists. All the same, it was difficult to abandoned the habits of a lifetime.

The Casino was five minutes away. When the group came downstairs in the hotel, neither Alois's car nor his driver was to be seen. Alois made enquiries of the doorman, who looked at him blankly. He turned to ask the two men at the reception desk if they had seen the driver. Scared, they refused to speak. Fritz Schwarz insisted, in the interests of those who had already arrived, on going on foot: doubtless, the driver was having a drink in a bar nearby.

At the Casino they saw, as they approached, a file of patient people.

'What's going on?' Fritz Schwarz asked the people standing at the back.

'The Russians. They are asking for the names of everyone going to the meeting,' said a man at the back of the line.

'What's this, why is this necessary? It's an interference in the rights of citizens,' Alois insisted to the senior Russian present.

'Orders, orders,' he said, not disagreeably, but firmly sent Alois and Fritz and the others back down to the end of the line. They entered the hall of the Casino half an hour after the meeting itself had been due to begin.

The Russians thought perhaps that, by so behaving, they would frighten the Austrians into absenting themselves from such meetings. They made a mistake. The Casino was full. Five hundred people sat on gold chairs waiting for Alois. Tired people, but also determined. They had spent the day helping to repair their capital or the road and railway to it. It was a different kind of crowd from those whom Alois had addressed before 1934. They had wanted to be carried away by emotion. Now that had changed. The Austrians, socialists and conservatives alike, wanted reason, calm, and *dis*passion.

Fritz introduced Alois from a table at the end of the room. It was not raised higher than the rest of the audience. There was no microphone, yet it was the most attentive audience which he had addressed.

Alois's speech at Baden was a turning point of his career. Until that day, he had been seen as a middle-class intellectual who had remained close to his left-wing position of 1934. He was among those whom the middle class excoriated. But at Baden he surprised everyone, perhaps even himself.

He began with a sober description of what Austria now was: how since 1914, it had undergone every possible experience: empire, independent province, occupied nation. In the course of the occupation, something uniquely Austrian had been born. He was not among those who would say that everything done by the Germans was evil. They had, for instance, taught the Austrians much about the manufacture of wine. Perhaps this very year's vintage would show that (laughter and clapping). All the same, the best lesson taught by the Germans was that Austrians were Austrians. They could not be a province of Germany. Even von Schirach had been forced to see that.

The mention of the nazi Gauleiter was a risk for Alois, but it was successful. Everyone knew that Schirach, possibly against his own interests, had been forced to accept that there was something different about Austria in order to survive in Vienna.

So far, the speech had followed predictable lines. But then Alois turned to the present state of affairs.

'I am,' he said, 'of course, an international socialist. It would be impossible to imagine a socialist who did not believe in the brotherhood of man. Yet one has to make reservations. The brotherhood of man cannot be helped by guns. One cannot win a battle for the brotherhood of man in a military sense. We know in Austria that, when it comes to battles, even the armies of socialism can behave like animals. None of us can forget, for instance, much less condone, the conduct of the Red Army in Vienna, in Austria, in the first weeks after the late conflict. None of us can forgive the incomprehensible deaths of Eduard and Netty Primorius of this town, devoted socialists, devoted scholars, devoted enemies of the nazis.'

Brave stuff, thought the audience! Even to *think* thus in Baden was astonishing. Two hundred yards only from the Soviet headquarters! True, the Soviet army was not in the Casino. But they surely had their ears within it.

'Our experiences are there to remind us,' said Alois, 'that there can be both a democratic and a totalitarian socialism. Democratic socialism uses the methods of conciliation, of respect for the views of opponents. Of humanity. But we know that there is an alternative. Socialism through the voice of the bully. Socialism *via* the gun and the secret police – a secret police which is no less brutal, because it is dressed in red.'

Could this be Alois Acht speaking? Could this be the tribune of the people, whom so many even of that audience had loved to hate?

But, believe it or not, he was going on in the same vein.

'Whether you like it or not, a democratic socialist is a man who would prefer not to be in power if that means being there against the wishes of the people expressed in the ballot box. That is why we appeal to you to vote for us, not for the communist party! Of course, we all know the communist party of Austria. It is full of brave men, heroic individuals. In the struggle against nazism, it was in the first rank. But in the struggle for peace, it must fall back. Because it looks on human liberty as a tool to be used where appropriate, and then to be jettisoned – also when appropriate.'

The cheers at this were overpowering. The chairman, Fritz Schwarz, mopped his brow. He could see some of his pro-communist friends walking out. They were the eyes and ears of the Russians. Alois was now finishing '. . . and that is why, ladies and gentlemen, we ask you to vote for us in this election which we believe will determine the fate of Austria, perhaps of Europe, for our time. For our time!'

Tremendous cheering, clapping, people standing up. What an evening, thought Fritz Schwarz, carried away. He was only twenty-five, he had fought in the war, he thought just as Alois did. Up till now, he had never dared speak in such a way. But he would, in future! Alois had given a lead. That was what leadership was!

The crowds were streaming out of the hall, enthusiastic, smiling, taking no notice of the Russian soldiers in the hallway. Alois had taken them to a higher level of self-knowledge than they had expected. Real democratic socialism!

Alois walked back to the Erherzog Karl with Fritz Schwarz. As they walked, a man ran up to them out of the shadows.

'Herr von Acht! I am a waiter in the hotel. I heard about your car. Herr von Acht, I must tell you that your driver was forced to drive away by the Russians. They held a gun to him. They drove in the direction of their headquarters. Don't tell anyone I told you. But that's the truth. That's what happens in Baden nowadays. He's not the first to go that way. You'll never see him again, Herr von Acht.'

It was true that the driver and the car had vanished. In the morning, Alois registered a protest with the Soviet High Command. But there was no sign of either man or machine. Had the intemperate man become dragged into a quarrel in which there was no chance of survival? Did the Russians appropriate the car and driver because they wished to intimidate? The Communists explained that the man must have stolen the car and was driving to Paris.

A few weeks later, Poldi Moser's party came top in the elections. Alois and the socialists came second. The communists did badly. It had been as Charlie Grew predicted. The new government was still a coalition. But it was headed by Poldi's chief, Dr Figl. He and the socialists shared the seats in the government. The communists were given one minor post. Moser was the cabinet minister concerned with questions of security. Alois entered the new government as a Minister for Planning.

Comrade "Fritz" had to abandon the government. When he and his wife left the ministry for the last time, he talked to Alois: 'We were defeated by the memory of the Red Army's last action; and, of course, by your treachery,' he said in his usual amiable voice. 'In the end, people will forget the Red Army. But they will not forget your treachery. And this is only the first battle, Comrade. Let's see who'll win the last.'

His black car swirled away towards Leopoldstadt. It was the last time that he had a government chauffeur to drive him.

XXIII

*T*HAT SAME DAY, THE TRIAL BEGAN, IN VIENNA COURTROOM
Number 22, of Gottfried von Acht for having been a senior
member of the nazi party before 1938. Gottfried made a brief appearance, pleaded guilty to having been a nazi but innocent of the other
charges. He was driven back to the prison at Elisabeth Promenade.

Gottfried had not been at the Elisabeth Promenade prison continuously
since Charlie Grew had left it. He had spent months in a converted
concentration camp south-west of the capital. There, conditions had been
appalling. Save that the guards were Americans, and were not consistently
brutal, and save that no one was deliberately killed, it might still have
been a nazi camp. The huts were overcrowded, there was no electricity
and the food was minimal. The camp was filled with outraged men and
women, all of whom said that they had only followed orders, and that
they had had no choice but to do so, or to risk unpleasant punishments.

Among these was the merchant Musschleger, from Pöchlarn, who was
released at the time that Gottfried returned to Vienna. At the time of
Gottfried's trial, Musschleger was back, a respectable citizen of his town,
though he would not, for the time being, be able to play any part in
public life. 'So much the better,' his sister had said to him. 'You must
make money instead.' He forgot the promises of assistance which he had
made to Gottfried. Demmer, the third member of the cell in Elisabeth
Promenade, was in detention in Styria still waiting trial, in company with
other members of the SS who had served in concentration camps in
Poland.

Gottfried's state of mind in these months of imprisonment was marked
by a recognition of personal responsibility. The more terrible the news
about nazi atrocities in the course of the war, the more guilty he believed
himself to be. He was not conscious of ever having been exactly anti-
semitic, but he had often heard his friends speaking of Jews in a contemptuous fashion and he had not protested. He had passed on to another
subject, as if such prejudices were a tedious matter of a minor kind easily
disposed of. Schöner Karl, Gottfried thought, Karl Lueger, the mayor
of Vienna at the turn of the century, was the key to what had happened

in Austria: a brilliant personality who had shown Hitler how one could use anti-semitic demagoguery to rise to power.

Back in Elisabeth Promenade, Gottfried had a cell to himself, a bed, and light from a high window. The scrawled names on the woodwork reminded him, at every moment, that this cell had been the place of imprisonment of a long succession of Austrian democrats.

Two days after his first presentation in the court, an American orderly opened the door, and told Gottfried to follow him in order to see the General. The orderly was a man with a sense of the ridiculous. He made jokes which suggested that it was fortuitous that Gottfried should be in a cell and that he, an ignorant boy from South Carolina, should be an orderly. How easily the cards might have been dealt differently! Gottfried found the orderly an agreeable diversion from his soul-searching, and accompanied him with pleasure.

Gottfried was escorted along the passage by the orderly who did not trouble to handcuff him, as he believed that he should have. Gottfried was still golden-haired, tall and, though thin, did not appear to have suffered since that May morning a year before when he had been arrested in his own home in Rodaun. He walked with his head high, and with a stance very different from his internal feelings. He was as handsome now, in a Teutonic way, as in the 1930s. He was unconscious of it, as he had always been.

He was ushered into a waiting room. A clock in the city outside struck eleven. Two men in uniform came in from the next room. Gottfried stood up. One of these men was the governor of the prison. The other, a high ranking American officer, had a familiar face, which he could not immediately identify. The governor indicated an armchair to Gottfried and withdrew. The orderly stood at one side of the room, but the officer waved him away.

'I'm Brooks Sheay. You may not remember but we met ten years ago. I knew other members of your family better than I knew you. But we met. I remember a conversation about the music of Richard Strauss. We were sitting in one of those villages of the Wachau. Weisendorf? Weissenkirchen? I can't remember which. Do you?'

Gottfried considered. He remembered Sheay. An enthusiastic austrophile. The family used to make fun of him for being so. Well, at least the orderly would have a homely phrase for his and Sheay's present juxtaposition.

'Yes, General Sheay,' he said, 'I remember you. The talk about Strauss, I'm afraid I forgot. We often talked about Richard Strauss.'

'I'm only a brigadier.' Brooks smiled as warmly as he could manage. He had never liked Gottfried in the past. But now he had a specific mission. He tried to look at him kindly.

122

'How are your conditions? Cell, food, treatment by the military people?'

'Thank you. I appreciate your asking. I have nothing of which to complain.'

'Do you see people whom you want to see? Your brothers? Your relatives?'

'Thank you. I need no one. My brothers have paid calls since the beginning of my imprisonment.'

'Forgive me for asking. How do you see your future? After your trial, of course.'

'I do not see it, Brigadier. I have given no thought to it.'

'None?'

'None. I think that is normal. After all, my sentence could be severe, could it not?' Gottfried looked at Sheay and allowed a smile to play round his thin lips for a few minutes.

'But your family will stand by you?'

'Possibly. It would be pleasant to stay at Besselberg with Otto one day again. But I understand it's in the Soviet zone.'

'How do you see the Soviet threat?'

'We've brought it on ourselves. The Russians have been to Vienna before. We've never got to Moscow. Neither us nor the French. Doesn't look as if it'll happen now.'

'It doesn't.'

Sheay was finding the discussions more difficult than he'd expected. Gottfried was encased in a protective glass of his own.

'Cigarette?' he offered.

'No, I don't, thank you.'

Sheay took out a cheroot and then asked him:

'You seem disillusioned with the movement you were once proud of. How do you account for it, though, that it should be the German peoples' – that was Sheay's convenient expression for the German and the Austrians together – 'who succumbed in this way?'

'Sounds like a university essay for the future,' Gottfried smiled again.

'Well perhaps it is. All the same it's an interesting question.'

'But I can't answer it. You knew Austria in the past well. You can answer it better than I can. I'm just a part of the evidence. I can't be the analyst.'

Sheay tried another tactic.

'You're not concerned with your own future. You're not concerned with your past. How do you exercise your mind all day? You must be thinking about something.'

'Oh, I dream.'

'What about? Women? Drink? Music?'

'No, no, I just let my imagination wander. I think of the Wienerwald, certainly. I walk in my mind from Kahlenburg to Hermannskogel and then on to Sofienalp. I try and recall the walk along the Danube between Göttweig and Melk. I wonder how much damage the Russians did in coming into Vienna that way, for instance. A lot, I suppose. Then – but why do you want to know all this?'

'You could help us.'

'Us?'

'Us being the United States. We need people. Intelligent men. Agents, if you like. We've got to make ourselves a responsible power. A world power. The time has come. If it weren't for us, the Russians would be in Paris. Perhaps in Madrid and London. They have both the capacity and the will for empire. We must do something about it. We need intelligent friends throughout the world. A network of intelligent friends. You, Gottfried, could be one of them.'

'And how could I help you? I'm a dangerous ex-nazi waiting trial. Guarded by American soldiers, but due to be tried by Austrians.'

'Well, we could help you get out of here, for example.'

'How?'

'As you pointed out, we furnish the guards.'

'And suppose I got out? What then? Where would I go? What would you do to make me one of your intelligent friends?'

'We'd get you to Washington.'

Sheay was a man who thought that a visit to Washington was an achievement in itself. Once there, anything was possible for anyone. It was, he knew himself, a romantic view.

'What would I do about the courts in Austria?'

'We'd arrange it.'

'I find it difficult to believe. I thought I was a war criminal.'

'You are. But not a major one. I've read your papers. You've got little to answer for. People who were nazis before the Anschluss appear in the public eye to be the bad men. I've ceased to think that. It's the opportunists who joined later who committed the crimes. Men like your friend Demmer, for example.'

'You know about Demmer?'

'Yes, I read his papers too. They're horrible.'

'Are you making an offer to him too?'

'He will hang, Gottfried.'

'How long can I take to make up my mind?'

'You must decide now,' said Sheay. 'We haven't a minute to lose. Because you've already appeared before the court.'

'Are you making these offers to people other than nazis?'

'Yes.'

'How do you know that the Russians haven't made the same offer to me and the others?'

'We've studied that possibility.'

'Aren't you a little naive as a people to be a world power?'

'Probably, but the British teach us a lot.'

'If I have to decide now, I have to say "no".'

'You are sure?'

'Yes. I have to go through with the trial. I have to explain, in public, why it all happened as it did. I count on that exposure. It's important to me and I think it's important for Austria. I may have been wrong, but there were many like me. My trial is the trial of my generation. Does that sound sententious?'

'A little.'

'All the same, it is true. All the same, I'm grateful to you. Sorry if I seem bleak. But thank you. I am grateful to you.'

Gottfried stood and held out his hand. Sheay rose and shook it, feeling for the first time a tinge of respect for a man who had been a nazi.

'Good luck,' he said.

'Better luck with the others,' said Gottfried.

He was returned to his cell, conscious of having acted positively for the first time for years.

XXIV

*T*HANKS TO LUDWIG BÖRNE, WHO KNEW EVERYONE, KAMO secured a job with the Vienna State Opera. Following the destruction of the famous building, the opera was based at the much smaller Theater an der Wien. The theatre had become dilapidated. The caretaker had grown mushrooms on the stage during the war. The only other activity had been the wild running of rats in the auditorium.

Kamo, though technically only a stage-hand, made himself indispensable. It was he who, after the continued failure of the stage lighting, suggested linking the theatre to the cable which supplied the Russian Kommandatura. It was he who suggested borrowing the grand chairs from the Redoutensaal, placing them in the boxes, and selling at an increased cost to Russian officers who fancied themselves sitting on gold.

Kamo lived in a partially bombed out and therefore deserted apartment block in Gumpendorferstrasse, in the British zone, next door to the theatre. His now excellent German, the fact that Vienna was full of foreigners with accents even more mysterious than his, and the confusion of the time, prevented attention being paid to him. All the same, he became aware in the spring of 1946 that this benign neglect was coming to an end.

One day, he met Alice von Acht in the street. Her flat was not far from his home. She was with her two children, Heini and Anna, who now seemed mature, though they could not have been more than twelve and thirteen.

'You are rash to stay in Vienna,' she said to Kamo. 'Sooner or later they will find you. The Russians have a special commission to take home Soviet citizens whom they discover here.'

'Does your colonel talk to you about it?'

'My colonel still never talks. I heard it from Aunt Thekla, who also has a colonel now. He does talk. What's more, the Western Allies collaborate with Russia. You should ask your friend Börne to get you to America as soon as possible. If he can find you a job in Vienna now, especially at the Opera, he can do anything.'

'What I'm doing is important,' said Kamo, giving her his irresistible smile.

'That's what everyone says. Everyone thinks what they're doing is important. Not just for themselves. For Austria. For civilisation.'

'Perhaps with the Opera, it's true. The opera, being fantasy, is the only reality in Vienna.'

'How easily you have become a Viennese!' said Alice. 'I don't approve. Anyway, I've warned you. Now I have to take the children to their aunts. I'm late.' And she hurried off.

Kamo ran after her.

'Any news?' he asked.

She knew, of course, to what he referred.

'None,' she shook her head.

'I will wait till he returns.'

'Alas, poor Kamo, in that case you will have time to become very Viennese indeed.'

Two madmen used to stand chattering outside the Theater an der Wien during these days. One of them, like Hugo Wolf when *he* was mad, used to claim to be Director of the Opera House. The other sometimes claimed to be Jan Kiepura, sometimes Alfred Piccaver, both famous performers of the past. Kamo usually talked to them. At this moment, they wandered along the road towards him and Alice, talking enthusiastically to no one in particular, certainly not to each other.

'These are the happiest people in Vienna,' Kamo said, 'and they are mad.'

Alice considered this. 'What about you?'

'Well I am Georgian, so I don't count.' Throwing a brilliant if unnerving smile at her over his shoulder he joined the two men as they ambled down the street. Was it her imagination or did Alice see a black car draw up while she and Kamo talked and did it leave when he did? At that time, in Vienna, there were so many fancies that she could not be sure and, when she looked again, both car and Kamo had vanished round the corner. She was late and the children were complaining. They therefore walked firmly on, and in a short time were in the Opernring. The south side of this famous street was still in ruins, and no efforts were being made to repair it. There was no traffic and people walked down the middle of the road as if it had been a pavement. Alice and the children crossed and were about to turn down the Goethegasse when, and this time there was no imagining it, the same – or perhaps another – black car slid, purposefully, to a stop next to her. She was too frightened to walk on, though her son was tugging at her. She turned to smile, brightly, at the occupants of the car. One of them, obviously a Russian, one could tell that from his heavy flat face, had wound down his window. What could they want with her? Had they arrested Kamo? Would they arrest her?

The Russian was looking up at her and smiling. He then did a surprising thing. He raised his hand, extended his index finger and shook it chidingly at Alice as if she had been a naughty child. He shook it three times. Then he withdrew his hand, and wound up the window, and the car then slid quietly away while Alice leant, terrified, against the railing of the Burggarten.

'What did those men want?' asked Heini.

'He was a very silly man,' said her daughter Anna.

'It was just a Russian,' said Alice, recovering somewhat, 'Russians are like that.'

XXV

*T*HE FUNERAL MASS FOR MAX VON ACHT WAS IN THE
Karlskirche, the great Baroque church which stood out more sharply
than ever, since, though buildings near it had suffered in bombardment,
it was itself untouched. The noble dome, the beautiful gilding, the splendid organ, were as they had always been.

All, it seemed, gathered there on a spring morning in what for many
was the first public gathering since the war. Aristocrats and intellectuals,
soldiers and scholars, old survivors from the Emperor's day and even
children from school, assembled in their pews, turning their heads this
way and that to see "how stooped is poor Fritz", or "look, Uncle Franzie
has lost all his hair" or "Lord, what a *coup de vieux* Mari-Lou has had".
A few foreigners were there, including Tatiana Bezhukov, still with the
British mission, and Brooks Sheay, hiding behind frowns of angular dis-
content.

Max von Acht's widow, poor talkative Berta, had come back to Vienna
for this occasion from Salzburg. She had insisted on an empty seat
being left on either side of her to represent her sons: both prisoners of
war. Otto, a prisoner in the United States, would soon be coming home;
but Jakob was presumed a prisoner in Russia. She had only one scribbled
letter from him since his capture at Stalingrad three years before and did
not know if he was still alive.

All the surviving Achts who were able to be there were present except,
as everyone noticed, Lise and Alois.

'She's gone quite mad you know, poor Lise, since Klara. Won't speak
at all.'

'Not true, quite the contrary, she's violent. Poor Alois!'

'Is she really in the asylum at Klosterneuburg?'

At the front of the church, in a pew level with the one occupied by
Frau Max, but slightly to the side of the main altar, there was a young
man in morning dress. From time to time, he could be seen giving signals
to the ushers. It was obvious that he was in charge of arrangements. It
was Willy Svoboda.

'Of course his father's a tailor. That's how he's got that suit.'

'But how did he learn to *command*, a tailor's son?'

'He's illegitimate.'

'Of course. His mother was good looking, the tailor's wife.'

One had to admit that everything was beautifully done. What an accomplished boy this Willy Svoboda was: was he really only eighteen? One was going to hear more of him.

Noble music swelled the great church. The congregation allowed their memories of different times to envelop them. Nobody there could remember how sparkling the young Max had been when he first appeared on the Viennese literary scene in the late 1880s. But hundreds could recall his lectures at the turn of the century. A great many people had been old enough to read *The Final Solution* when it first came out.

'It's certainly the end of an age.'

'No doubt. What next, I wonder?'

What would come next? The age of Willy Svoboda? The Viennese have a method of adjusting to the times.

XXVI

*T*HE REASON WHY ALOIS HAD NOT BEEN AT UNCLE MAX'S funeral mass was that Lise had thrown herself into the Danube that morning. She had left a furious note to Alois saying that it was not Klara's disappearance itself which was distressing her but the circumstances which had made Klara's disappearance such a typical event. Unlike Alois, she could not shake off the socialist convictions of a lifetime easily. She did not believe in a "new Austria", because countries do not slough off old ways any more than people do. She hated the Americans as much as she did the Russians. A world divided between these powers was not civilisation. Lise wrote that she realised that her sons would grieve but, now that they were fourteen and fifteen, they could fend for themselves. A mother in her condition of despair was too heavy a burden for them: she would drag them down. Her spirit was dead already, she would allow the waters of the Danube to close over her body. The Danube had done so much in the past. Her soul would merge with other Danube souls and be purified. She had also been told that Alois had been seen with an interpreter from the British Mission – a secretary – which she regarded as the confirmation of his contemptible misbehaviour.

The two boys, Karl and Poldo, were still in Salzburg with their cousins, the Kotulskys. They had left when school closed for the holidays. Lise and Alois were to follow after Easter. Alois discovered the letter only that evening. He went to the Heiligenstadt police. They confirmed that the body of a woman aged about forty had been found in the river that day. Could he go with them to the mortuary in Vienna to identify her? He did so.

At midnight the morgue was a centre of action. Almost of life. Anyone who thinks a morgue a place of inactivity has plainly never visited one. Alois could not believe that so many had died that day in Vienna. Many had collapsed in the street and died there and then. The morgue itself had been saved from destruction in the war by the work, so the director said proudly, of firefighters who had devoted themselves to the building as if it had been a church.

'In some ways, this building is more than a church,' the director remarked dreamily. 'It is a place where one has to recognise the facts of death straightforwardly. You know,' he added to Alois confidentially, 'this is an extraordinary job, mine. You meet everyone here – Russians, Americans, Croats, officers, priests, whores and countesses – they all come either as corpses or to have a look. They need to know what's going on. You notice that fellow we just passed. He's the correspondent of *Il Tempo* of Milan. Interesting man, he's always here. Must like it, I shouldn't wonder. Now over there we have our first Russian visitors of the night. A lot of White Russian suicides, you know, because they all think they're going to be sent back to the labour camps. But take a look at those Soviets talking to my assistant. They've lost one of their fellows – drunk, not dead, I expect. Could be both, of course. Rather, first one then the other. Happens pretty often. But do you know what one of them said to me: "Never mind, there'll be plenty more of us!" Well, Herr Acht, it's been interesting talking to you, only sorry that what brings you here is such a sad occasion. But I do hope we'll meet again. Here, or elsewhere. And remember I'm always ready to answer your questions. *Wiedersehen*.'

Alois afterwards recalled the rambling self-confident voice of the director of the Vienna morgue almost more clearly than his last look at Lise which took place during his monologue.

Alois made his secretary arrange the details of the funeral. Since Lise had died by her own hand, it was impossible to have her buried with the other Achts in the Christian section of the cemetery in Vienna. But the director of the cemetery was as helpful as the director of the mortuary had been. Lise was buried on the edge of the civil section *in the shadow of the trees planted in the Christian section*. Such ingenuity has rarely been shown. The funeral was held with no one present other than Alois, Father George Acht and Lise's brother and sister-in-law, Fritz and Lily Weltheim. George Acht took the service.

On their way back to the city, George said, 'Alois, I've been meaning to tell you. I'm going to leave the church. I had intended to tell you this after Max's death. But there didn't seem time. But this will be my last service. I'm going to re-enter the world. The University has made me an offer and I'll be just Doctor von Acht, not Father. And, Alois, I'm going to become a socialist. Like you. A man needs a church of some sort. Socialism will help me, as it helped you.'

'George,' said Alois, 'we've come to the same crossroads, I can see that. But we're going in different directions. You are travelling away from one church and are looking for another. I had no idea of it. But I can understand. I, on the other hand, have left the church which you will now want to join. Of course, I'm still a democrat, George, but if the choice were to come between democracy and socialism, I'd choose the first. I don't believe that revolutionary socialism has anything to it any more. I'm not sure but I may even end up in the church in which I was born and which you are now leaving. Probably, though, despite Lise's death, I'll remain at the crossroads. But you can't count on me to help in the road down which you're travelling.'

They had reached the centre of the inner city. They were in the half ruined Graben. Volunteers were still carrying rubble in wheelbarrows. They resembled purposeful ants. Alois made his goodbyes to George. He wondered in what circumstances he would see his cousin again.

He turned home, walked there and prepared for the journey which he had to undertake to Salzburg in order to tell his sons what had happened. Until that was done, he felt unable to think of Lise's death as an event affecting himself. Afterwards he might be able to contemplate it. But death affects so many people, and has so many consequences, that it is its administration which seems overwhelming. The nature of the death insulated him from feeling remorse. A woman who kills herself reproaches for ever those who have known her well. Alois did not criticise himself, however. He was merely angry with Lise for her selfish action.

His sons took the news alarmingly philosophically. 'I expect she was driven to it,' said Karl.

XXVII

CHARLIE GREW WAS IN COMMAND OF THE BRITISH UNIT set up to deal with the search for the lost Crown of Charles V. The appointment infuriated Colonel Livingstone, who believed, with evidence in his favour, that everything to do with art in Vienna, so far as Britain was concerned, was for him to decide. The General pointed out that he was an aesthete, not a sleuth.

'But nowadays,' Colonel Livingstone insisted, 'art historians have to be sleuths. We must look for clues which will tell us whether a Giorgione is in fact such. We have to be detectives of the past.'

'A good reason why you should not be concerned with the present.'

'But my Soviet opposite number –'

'Belongs to the secret police. No, no, we know all about him. His name is Colonel Voronov. Must be senior. Otherwise I don't suppose he'd talk so indiscreetly.'

'General. I too must be frank. Captain Grew knows nothing of painting.'

'Since we are looking for jewels, that scarcely matters, Colonel.'

So Captain Grew assumed his new assignment. By this time, his character also had changed remarkably from the flippant one with which he had leapt into the Wienerwald in the weeks before the German collapse. It was not simply a matter of obtaining the rank of Captain, nor having a floor to himself in Schönbrunn with a batman which worked such wonders; nor was the company of the delightful Tatiana Bezhukov a determining factor, though these things exerted some influence. The Captain had also acquired a knowledge of human nature from his days in prison in company with the ignoble Demmer, the contemptible Musschleger and the idealistic Gottfried. It was not exactly that the Captain had acquired a sense of evil. But at least he had begun to have a sense of proportion. Very surprisingly, the well-known school on the Thames of which he had been such an ornament had had no classes in self-knowledge.

Charlie studied the history of the stones accumulated in the Crown. The so-called "Champagne Diamond" had passed to the Habsburgs through the marriage of one of the Dukes of Burgundy with the heiress of Thibaut of Champagne. The Pearl of Saint Agatha, the second of the large jewels, presented few problems historically, since it was one of the few examples of a big pearl apparently known in the early middle ages. By the end of a month, he could have given a lecture on the nature of the Crown, the provenance of its stones, the attitudes which Charles V and other monarchs had towards it, the occasions on which it had been worn by the Empress Maria Theresia and how it had been kept safe during Napoleon's two occupations of Vienna. Charlie Grew made it his business to learn all that he could of the craftsmanship which had put the Crown together in the sixteenth century. Almost every morning Captain Grew rode in Schönbrunn with Colonel Marchais, and with Major Stern who had the same task as he for the French and Americans respectively. Charlie made up in enthusiasm what he had lacked previously in knowledge.

Having attacked the remoter past, the Captain struck at the present. The last "sighting" of the Crown had been on August 4, 1941, when the director of the Kunsthistorisches Museum had agreed that the treasures of Vienna should be transported to the same secure caverns which were available for the duration of the war for all other works of art in the Third Reich. The Director and members of his council had gone on a last visit to the museum that morning. Eight council members, including Prince Papenlohe, had been present. A luncheon had been held afterwards at the museum. It was wartime, and it had been of modest quality: four courses, not six, as had been usual in pre-war days. Afterwards, the business of packing up the treasures had begun, different council members being responsible for supervising items of their special interest.

As Russians, Americans, English and French were divided over every other matter, they in particular divided over Prince Papenlohe's role in the affair.

Colonel Voronov had no doubts. Papenlohe had been the member of the council of the Kunsthistorisches Museum concerned with supervising the packing of the Crown in 1941. His opportunity was the greatest. As an owner of works of art, as well as an art historian, he knew the significance of the Crown better than did his colleagues on the board. Thirdly, insisted Colonel Voronov, Papenlohe had "an unruly spirit". This was shown by his contesting the nazi regime in many ways. He hid Jews in his house. He "even collaborated with the British". Thus the theft of the Crown was something within the Prince's spectrum of habits. Fourthly, he was an aristocrat, known to have nostalgia for the Habsburgs.

'Men such as he,' argued the Colonel, 'have never been taught a proper lesson till now, never realised that all their flirtings with archdukes are doomed to disappointment.'

Colonel Marchais appeared to have orders to argue a halfway point between the United States and the Russians. Thus the way to "a third force" in world politics could be kept open. The Crown represented for him the soul of Christian Europe as well as of Austria. If such a treasure were lost, more than the sum of its stones would have gone. He could not bring himself to agree that the Prince had done wrong in collaborating with the British; nor could he think helping the Jews a sign of indiscipline; but he did agree that the Prince had consorted with archdukes who were known to want their monarchy back. There was, therefore, a case against the Prince which, had he been alive, would have to be brought against him. In the circumstances, the Prince's house should be "ransacked". Colonel Marchais had been speaking in English. He believed that "to ransack" was just a more thorough method than "to search".

Charlie, doodling his way through these uncharitable reflections, had one advantage over his allies. He had actually met the Prince. Colonel Voronov was impressed by that, and nodded, in an understanding manner, at his every recollection of that memorable meal. All the same, he supported a "ransack". Charlie wished to identify those who had done the packing of the cases before they went to the Salzkammergut. That was not easy, for the foreman had been seen last in the battle of Breslau and had to be presumed dead. One of his two assistants was a prisoner of war in Russia. Colonel Voronov showed a surprising optimism in his capacity to find this key witness "instantly". The second assistant had vanished. No one knew where he was. He was said to have been in Italy.

'Where may he be?' asked Colonel Voronov with an icy irony rather wasted on his companions, as if in some way they might turn out to be protectors of this accused man, 'at Capri or at Ostia, I presume?'

Charlie wanted too to find the drivers of the vans which had carried these treasures west in 1941, the men who had escorted them, and the unpackers in Alt Aussee. Unfortunately, the drivers had mostly been SS. Two of them had been shot in 1945 by the Americans. The others had vanished. The escorts were soldiers who had not taken in what was within.

'They must have had a good idea of what they were carrying if the vans came from the Museum and went to the Salzkammergut,' he reasonably inferred.

'No, no, they were Croats,' explained Colonol Voronov, with the scorn of a member of the master race. 'Croats do not see things easily.'

'My grandmother was a Croat,' said Major Stern, inconveniently.

'Ah,' said the Russian, as if the comment had taught what he needed to know about the make-up of the population of the United States.

'It is agreed then that, under our direct supervision,' said Colonel Marchais, 'the palace of Prince Papenlohe is elaborately ransacked if not searched.'

'Agreed,' said Colonel Voronov.

'I need convincing that Prince Papenlohe, with whom our OSS as well as the British had contact in the war, could be regarded as being likely to be party to a theft.' That was Major Stern's contribution.

'I should like to trace the route of the convoy and to talk to the Austrians in the Salzkammergut to check whether a theft could have occurred subsequent to the deposit of the treasures.'

'We should all like to have an excuse to go to the Salzkammergut,' the French colonel said, 'but the solution to this question is in Vienna. Further, Prince Papenlohe accompanied the treasures to Bad Aussee, so that he would have other opportunities to do his work there.'

'Are you convicting the Prince without evidence?' asked Captain Grew.

'The best way to find this Crown is to survey the Prince's property. He may have acted from the best of motives. He may have wished to return the Crown to the Habsburg family. Or to give it to his Anglo-Saxon friends.' Colonel Marchais had recently become seized of that useful notion, "Anglo-Saxon" interests.

Major Stern and Captain Grew looked at each other. They could not outvote the anti-Papenlohists. But they could procrastinate. But was that not unsporting?

'Very well,' said Charlie, 'I am prepared to sanction the search of Prince's palace under our supervision.'

Major Stern abstained in his vote, but said that, if a search occurred, he wished the US to be concerned in it.

Colonel Marchais wondered whether that was appropriate, given the US abstention. But Colonel Voronov thought that attitude was going too far. The Americans should be involved. Great powers are happier in the company of other great powers.

The search, it was agreed, would be at nine o'clock the next morning. The Soviet Union, said Colonel Voronov, had experts who had searched some of the grandest palaces of Vienna in April 1945. One did not want to leave this in the hand of amateurs. The Russians' search of Lehar's house in Hohe Warte had been successful, Charlie Grew remembered being told by Alois Acht. Nothing had been left in it at all.

This meeting of the Allies adjourned with a snapping of briefcases, squeaking of boots, exchange of bonhomous handshakes, bearhugs, and cheerful "until tomorrows" in several languages, including German.

As they walked out from the main entrance of Schönbrunn to their cars, two Americans approached Major Stern.

'Just a moment, Major. You're the United States representative on the committee investigating the loss of the Crown of Charles the Fifth. Could you talk to the *New York Post*? Are you optimistic of getting the Crown back by Christmas, Major? No, Major, we can't take "no" for an answer, we've been waiting since three.'

Grew and the two colonels succeeded in getting to their cars and away. But Stern believed that one of the tasks of government is to give information, and knew that the press in New York is more important than the government in Washington. He told the two newspapermen the story as he knew it, leaving out no detail and even elaborating on the *entente* which seemed to be forming between the French and the Russians.

At the end, he said: 'Well that's it. But tell me, how did you guys know where to find us? Smart piece of intelligence on someone's part.'

The newspaperman of *The New York Post* put a finger to his lips. But his colleague, an amateur journalist as much as Major Stern was an amateur soldier, explained that a friend in the British Mission had tipped them off.

'Won't tell you his name. But he's tall.'

Major Stern did not take long to place the responsibility in his mind upon Colonel Livingstone.

XXVIII

*I*N A SHORT TIME, KAMO ESTABLISHED HIMSELF AS AN invaluable member of the staff at the Opera, with the mixture of ruthlessness and competence which had ensured his success in so many ways. Not only did he work hard at scene-shifting but he had an extraordinary memory for everything he was told, about the recent past history of the opera house. This memory as well as that quality of being able to charm people soon made Kamo, despite his mysterious origins, an indispensable person.

Kamo began to realise, however, that his movements were shadowed: in his opinion, not only by Russians. By Americans. Was the British intelligence service also interested? At all events, he could not go into a café without becoming aware that somebody was studiously reading a newspaper next to him. He could not walk away from the theatre without his movements being observed. He was aware that he could be picked up at any time. Why did "they" not act? Presumably because "they'" wished him to lead them to unknown accomplices or, perhaps, to be caught in the act of conspiracy; or both.

He explained again to Alice, when he visited her, to tell her that he was learning the art of living in the West.

'I've told you to go before,' she said. 'You are mad to have stayed so long, mad to come here. You must leave immediately, don't even go back now to the theatre to say goodbye. Abandon us. Instantly.'

Kamo had been long enough in Vienna for sentiment to have cast a shadow over his alert mind. He not only returned to his room to pack a few objects – a few months before he would never have had a suitcase – but went also to the theatre to say goodbye to his astonished Director, who could not believe that one of his best workers was leaving the Opera. No one ever left the Opera until they were dismissed as a result of an intrigue. Kamo told the Director that he was going to Australia.

'Australia? Well, some of their women have good voices. Used to. I do not know of any modern Melba. But perhaps you will find her. If you do not like it in Sydney, you can return. There will always be room for you here. Perhaps when you return, we shall be at the real Opera House. The Russians have given twenty million schillings for the new roof. It is propaganda but it is good propaganda. I am seduced by it. I shall personally miss you. Goodbye.'

Kamo left the theatre by the little entrance reserved for the singers. Just as well since, at that moment, a number of senior Russian police officers had arrived at the front door looking for a Russian fascist being sought in connection with reported attempts to re-found a nazi party. The man concerned was believed to be the nerve of a plot to blow up the Russian war memorial in the Schwarzenbergplatz. The Director was surprised to hear of such suggestions, but allowed the Russians to make a minute examination of the building. That was followed by an investigation of the employees. At the end of it, there was nobody at the theatre under any illusion: Kamo, despite his beguiling ways, had been a dangerous individual. Innocent or not, it was as well that he had left. To blow up the war memorial! What an idea! Conversation in the Theater an der Wien consisted of little else. Then Kamo's suitcase was discovered in the porter's alcove at the back entrance and people speculated more as to what had happened. Had it been too heavy for him to carry and had he abandoned it? Had someone arrested him and forced him to leave it? The Director told those who asked that Kamo was assuredly halfway to Australia. Perhaps already in Mexico.

Kamo remained in Vienna. As was his custom, he walked a long way circuitously, sometimes underground, sometimes over roofs, until he believed that he had thrown off all pursuers. He believed himself held by his undertaking to remain in Vienna until Rüdiger returned. His visit to Alice, to his flat and to the Theater had been observed, but there a different police had taken over − one which included a member of the Soviet Repatriation Committee, the organisation concerned to ensure the return of all Russians to their homeland. There were other bodies represented on the command which had arrived at the theatre. One of them was the secret police. The other was headed by Colonel Voronov, the officer in charge of the search for the Crown of Charles V.

Kamo was soon walking into the Imperial Hotel, the headquarters of the Russian High Command, in the uniform of an American officer.

The old reception hall, its gilt tarnished but still astonishing, was full of people. In the heavy leather armchairs, the remains of Vienna's *demi-monde*, elderly *Mitzis* of the street, sat waiting for Russian officers. At writing desks, Austrians sat pretending to be dealing with important correspondence, but were glad to find an empty chair in a warm room. Around the reception desk, ancient concierges with whiskers, men who looked as if they had belonged to the Vienna City Council in the days of Schöner Karl at the turn of the century, tried unsuccessfully to deal with the demand for rooms from American businessmen, international fixers of all sorts, and women with uncertain reputations. A few Russian officers stalked grandly past, slowly, discussing some new refinement of the repatriation rules, so that they might get their hands more easily on "displaced persons" in Austrian camps born in Russian territory. Peacetime Russia was short of labour. Kamo went to the desk and, skilfully making his way to the front of the line to the astonishment of those whom he had overtaken, asked to be announced to Dr Börne – in Room 404. The concierge raised his telephone, asked for Dr Börne, asked Kamo his name, bade him go up to the fourth floor: Dr Börne was waiting for him. Kamo gave his name as Captain Jones. Dr Börne, the concierge explained, in a tone which seemed strange from a man of his gentle manners, was one of the returned Jews: the hotel accordingly was charging him an extra ten per cent more than they were allied officers.

Kamo went to the fourth floor of the Grand Hotel by the stairs. He distrusted lifts and went in them as rarely as he could. All the way up there were nineteenth-century portraits, landscapes in the style of Schindler, and photographs of forgotten hotel owners in elaborate gilded frames. On arrival at Room 404, the door was open. Inside there was standing not Dr Börne but Count Gmunden, the chief adviser on racecourse rehabilitation to the British Mission.

'Please come in. Any friend of Dr Börne is welcome.'

'But this is his room?'

'Precisely, but he is at the Volksoper. Do you know what he is seeing? *The Merry Widow!* The first production in Vienna since the war. I only wish I could have gone. Come in!'

Kamo did not do so.

'Then –'

'Then, why am I here? Dr Börne asked me to receive his guests.'

'Are there others?'

'Who knows? It appears that he asked several people to call on him. He always does. So far no others have done so. Yet I live in hope. Do please come in and have a glass of champagne. Dr Börne would like it. I know exactly who you are. Your costume does not fool me. You are the Georgian protégé, is that not right? He has talked of you, your intense cleverness, your promise, your imagination, your gifts of mimicry. Dr Börne has fine taste in friends. In women too. He is a real connoisseur. We Aryans only marvel that a Jew of his age can be so successful. Of course, I am in no way anti-semitic, I assure you I never was, but I have to say I am surprised at Dr Börne's achievements in these departments.'

Count Gmunden seemed friendly, his moustaches elegant, his suit neat, his cuffs white, his smile genuine: he seemed the real aristocrat. Kamo's education in the Wehrmacht had told him that it is of this kind of charming person that one must be particularly wary. "Beware the man to whom one is attracted" is an old proverb of the Caucasus. Under no circumstances should one enter a small room with such a man, especially if he has the key.

'Thank you. At the Volksoper. I will join him there.'

With a bow such as he had learned to perform in the first week of his service for Rüdiger Acht on the Eastern front, Kamo backed away to the stairs.

As Kamo began to walk down, he saw three Russian policemen going up in the lift. He heard the lift stop at Börne's floor. Doubtless some of the "friends" for whom Count Gmunden at all events, if not Dr Börne, was waiting. Kamo felt that once again his luck had held. Had he remained in Dr Börne's room, it would not have been long before his journey back to Moscow would have begun.

By this time, Kamo had realised that he might not be able to maintain his determination to remain in Vienna until Rüdiger's return. He did not know if he were even alive. Perhaps he could do best by going to America. Before he could leave Vienna he wished, however, to see Dr Börne. He knew that a career in America would require someone's introduction. He set off for the Volksoper. It was a cold night, though the rain expected by the evening newspapers had not begun. From the Grand Hotel to the Volksoper, it is perhaps two miles. Kamo could manage it in half an hour. He arrived just before the interval. The great waltz was just finishing. It enchanted an audience still too hungry to be easily captured. No matter that it was Hitler's favourite: it had been that of Edward VII. Other famous songs had reminded the Viennese in the audience that their speciality was not blood and anti-semitism, but romance and waltzes.

'*Where are you going?*' Kamo heard Sonia saying to Danilo.

'*I go back to Maxim's,*' said he, violins flashing. The curtain came down, to the usual applause.

Aunt Thekla was present. On this first visit to the Volksoper since the war, she was alone. Alice, her usual companion, had gone to visit Cousin Father George, to talk about her soul, as Thekla put it – no doubt to find that that priest would want to talk first about his. So Aunt Thekla was free to look at the audience without even the pretence of having to make conversation.

She observed a discussion in the distance, in the orchestra box, between Ludwig Börne and what appeared to be an American officer. But on closer scrutiny, the figure seemed familiar. Surely he was the same young man who had been with Börne in a box during the evening at the Musikverein? Their conversation was animated. Kamo was gesticulating. Börne was waving his fingers in a circular fashion. Had Thekla been nearer, she would have heard a remarkable exchange.

Kamo had found Börne immediately. The entrepreneur was accompanied by a fair-haired actress, Fraulein Elisabeth, who towered above him. When Kamo appeared, Börne waved her away.

'You should leave Vienna immediately,' said Börne, 'or hide in a better way than this. You are being looked for. All the Allies are looking for you. You are pursued by the Russians as a refugee: the French believe you to be the man who stole the Emperor Charles's Crown; the British have been convinced by the Russians that you are involved in a plot to blow up their war memorial; even the Americans think you are concerned with a group to refound the nazi movement. I do not know what to suggest. But here is the address of an uninhabited house in Leopoldstadt. It belongs to an ex-nazi being looked for by the police. His name is Heinrich Ried. One of the worst. His house is guarded by the police, but only loosely since there is no one in it. The back door is always open, because the locks don't work. Hide there for a few days. It is curiously safe: the police don't believe anyone would hide in such an obvious place. After that, we'll go to Munich. Things will be easier in the American zone there. You can make your way to the United States. There is no time to lose. Ried is alive, incidentally, but he won't come back. You may need this' – Börne gave him two hundred schillings – 'wait till the lights dim, then go quickly. You are noticeable. You will have been followed here. How, incidentally, did you find me?'

Kamo explained that he had met Count Gmunden in Ludwig Börne's room in the Grand Hotel.

'How interesting! It does not surprise me. I never leave anything of the slightest value in such places. Gmunden is an inquisitive man. He has the room next to mine. I assume he works for the Russians. Perhaps the British as well. An interesting phenomenon. I remember him on March 12, 1938. He was at the head of a column of nazis in the Kärtnerstrasse. He is clever, otherwise he would be in prison. Now, there is the second bell. Please leave. Your presence makes me nervous. The curtain will go up soon and Elisabeth will be lonely. Goodbye. I do not need to wish you good luck, for you always have it.'

Kamo left for Leopoldstadt. As usual, he made a circuitous route, walking along the canal. He arrived at Ried's house, entered by the back door as advised, and fell asleep on the sofa in a large upstairs drawing room from which the pictures had been removed from the walls, the curtains from the windows, the carpets from the floor, the books from the bookcases and the bath plugs from the baths.

XXIX

*T*HE SEARCH AT THE LATE PRINCE PAPENLOHE'S HOUSE BY the four Allies occurred with publicity, since the Viennese papers carried reports of what had been published in *The New York Post*.

While the search was going on, the street was crowded with photographers and newspapermen. Each of the Allies brought two cars, one with the political supervisors, the other with searchers: in the British case with rather innocent searchers, in the Russian case with experienced ones. Major Stern looked bashful but he could not keep a smile from his face. His searchers were military policemen who, it seemed to the other Allies, must have been chosen for their height: not a bad principle, perhaps, when dealing with Russians. The French searchers were small and competent. As for Colonel Voronov's men, it was hard to detect their character beneath their overcoats. Perhaps they were automatons. It was obvious that they were armed.

The press in the street bustled around Major Stern as if they smelled him as the good source that he was.

'No, boys, no, I can't tell you anything. This is the beginning of the investigation,' he kept saying.

The searchers strolled around the house and into the garden, marvelling that such space should be found in the centre of such a city. In the course of four hours, they had turned the house upside down and were seen carrying away many boxes for, as they explained to the press, "further examination". This was how Prince Papenlohe's silver was lost, his collection of snuff boxes decimated, and the diaries in his hatbox passed into Soviet hands, so enabling Colonel Voronov to know with whom in those various English agencies without proper names off Victoria Street the Prince had been in touch during the war.

PART 3

DECEMBER 1946– FEBRUARY 1947

XXX

MONTHS PASSED. MONTHS OF ENDLESS WORK, OF BECOMING used to the unacceptable, of clearing the ruins, mending the sewers, restoring the electricity, reviving the schools, opening blocked streets – and beginning, slowly, to build. At Christmas, Otto felt able to invite some of his family to stay. His children decided to put on a play. Hansie and Franzie had always loved the stage, Jean Marie was good at producing, Theresia loved costumes, and the dressing-up cupboard at Besselberg was famous. The play on which they decided was Schiller's *Don Carlos*.

Nothing is more upsetting to the normal balance of life than amateur dramatics. Jean Marie, usually quiet and self-effacing, became dictatorial. Two of Betty Acht's cousins who were staying, and who were usually condescending, were roped in to play some of the minor parts. Of course, everyone remembered that Cousin Klara had been better at acting than any of them, she had taken the lead in Jean Marie's production of *Maria Stuart* two years before, but no one mentioned it. No one wanted to remember unpleasant things at Christmas. The Russian garrison now well established, with the wives of the senior officers present, watched the actors preparing with good humour. General Krivoshein promised to attend the first night with his staff. Otto spent a long time deciding where they would sit.

The play was held in a dilapidated barn next to the house. It was not an ideal place because there was no heating. They would be lucky if they could keep the snow out. Still, that could be said of nearly all the rooms in the Schloss. Everyone would have to wear overcoats. But they were doing that, Jean Marie knew, in the Burgtheater too. The first night was to be on Christmas Day. There would be at least one other performance, probably on December 27th.

On Christmas Eve, the Achts were joined by Captain Charlie Grew and Tatiana Bezhukov. Tatiana was pleased to show off her Austrian connections in a Schloss. Christmas would be more festive for the Achts with the plum pudding and crackers that Charlie and Tatiana would bring. For all of them, the arrangements promised a revival, even under Russian eyes, of that real sense of international, European identity which the old upper classes had breathed and which the world wars had seemed to have sundered. The English pair drove in after a journey which they seemed to be sorry was uneventful. They had had to travel through the Russian zone. Charlie described how he was held up by Russians who wanted a lift, not to see his papers. A corporal with a basket, and a colonel with a captured Mauser pistol on his hip, shared their journey. They in return offered cigarettes which seemed to have little tobacco in them. They talked amicably most of the time, charmed by the fact that Tatiana could speak Russian.

Betty's crippled aunt Zita saw no advantage in having two guests from the British Mission spending Christmas Eve, which was usually only for close family.

'They ought to feel at home,' she said, however, to Otto, 'considering the horrible cabbage roses which your grandmother insisted on putting on every sofa.'

It was true. Besselberg had been decorated in 1910 at a time when the English style was the rage. There was much chintz around, as well as comfortable sofas from Maples in London, and photographs in silver frames.

'You'd better get used to this decoration,' Aunt Zita had told the Russian general's wife tartly. 'When you conquer Scotland, you'll find yourself surrounded by this sort of thing.'

The Russian lady knew a little German but not enough to distinguish a joke from a truth. She coughed, which she always did when unsure of herself, and returned to her favourite task of telling Otto how he ought to treat the servants. Mrs Krivoshein believed that people who lived in castles ought to behave as such: "beat your serfs" was her motto. She berated Betty for dressing badly: 'I'll show you how to dress,' she told her. 'Give me name of good dressmaker in Vienna.'

At midnight mass, the players all seemed to be sitting together and it seemed possible that their lips were moving more to the words of Schiller than in prayer.

Unfortunately, Betty was in bed with influenza at Christmas but the play was performed all the same. It had been cut but, all the same, each performer had to carry out a formidable feat of memory. Cousin Karly played the Marquis de Posa, Jean Marie the King, Franzie Don Carlos, and Theresia the Princess of Eboli. This irritated Cousin Antoinette, for she fancied herself with a black patch on her eye, even though she was playing the more important role of the Queen. Hansie was stage manager. Next day, Christmas Day, the excitement was such that no one even noticed how small the pieces were of the single thin, Christmas goose that year. Everyone thought only of the evening and of the play.

All went well in the early scenes. The complaint of the confessor that

Don Carlos "dared to think" passed unremarked. The cousins had to be reminded many times by Aunt Zita, the prompter, a fact which pleased the Achts; Antoinette only faltered once and recovered herself. The Russian general showed his enthusiasm and clapped, his lead followed by the corporals and female orderlies who stood at the back of the room. Otto had offered to send for chairs for them but the general had said 'no, no, they second rate, they stand'. The General had an interpreter with him whom everyone knew to be a policeman. The British delegation sat at the other side of the room, though Charlie Grew had greeted General Krivoshein with a good rendering of the then usual remarks about the great allies.

The play then reached the scene in Act III, well remembered by most of those present. It went thus:

King: . . . 'ask me some favour'.

Marquis (and Karly shook his head vigorously): 'No, I enjoy the laws.'

King: 'That right every murderer has.'

At that point, General Krivoshein gave his first cough. The interpreter must have been imaginative in the rendering, they afterwards thought.

The scene continued. Other difficult moments followed. Karly almost forgot his cue after the King's 'the Crown shall have a servant new in Spain – a liberal', but rallied, even if the line came out oddly: instead of 'Sire, I see how very meanly you conceive of men' he said 'I see how you conceive of mean men.' This led to tittering among the cousins in the improvised green room at the edge of the stage.

The Marquis' speech followed about Flanders and Brabant – that territory through which, 'Not long, Sire, I chanced to pass,' as the Marquis said:

'So many rich and flourishing provinces. A great, a mighty people and still more an honest people! And this people's father, that, thought I, must be divine; so thinking, I stumbled on a pile of bones.'

That exchange pleased General Krivoshein. He smiled benignly. But a few minutes later a speech came which he definitely did not like:

'This world of yours! How narrow and how poor! The rustling of a leaf alarms the lord of Christendom. You quake at every virtue. He . . . not to mar the glorious sight of freedom suffers that hideous hosts of evil should run riot in his fair creation.'

At this point General Krivoshein left the room, ostentatiously followed by his staff. No one knew to what he had taken exception, nor how the interpreter had put these points: "hideous hosts of evil", were surely not to be inevitably associated with Russia?

The play continued to its splendid conclusion, the children were cheered, and cheered each other. Jean Marie, who had put so much into the production, took three curtain calls.

'No, no, Jean Marie,' Aunt Zita said, 'you must become a professional. It's too much to waste all this talent down here in Besselberg.'

'People could come from all over Austria to Besselberg,' said Jean Marie dreamily, 'we could build a proper theatre in this shed. The stables could become dressing rooms. It would be like Bayreuth.'

'What upset the Russian general, though?' asked Henrietta.

They tried to remember exactly at what point the Russians had left.

'At the very mention of liberty, the Russian general left the room,' improvised Jean Marie.

'It was just where you were talking of a pile of bones.'

'No, you could see he liked that, it reminded him of home,' trilled Henrietta.

'Ssh, child,' said Aunt Zita, 'your father would prefer you not to talk in that way.'

'How do you know, and where is he?'

'He left after the Russians. 'Spect he wanted to tell them where to get sick,' laughed Hansie. 'Let's have some wine, Aunt Zita, it's still Christmas.'

'Everyone thinks that's a good idea,' said Jean Marie, who had begun to feel friendly to his previously disliked cousins.

Charlie Grew, who had been listening to these exchanges without understanding all of them, had some wine in his car and went to get it. It had been his New Year present – an unnecessary present for the proprietor of a Schloss in the Wachau in normal times.

'An Englishman bringing wine is like a Russian bringing peace,' shouted Jean Marie, whom the success of the play was making (as he supposed) specially brilliant. 'It's so unusual that it is doubly welcome!'

'Well, that promises well, since he has some in his boot,' said Tatiana Bezhukov. 'He put it in there with his sword of honour.'

Tatiana, through her mother, was a distant cousin of Betty von Acht. This was her first visit to the kind of household in which her ancestors must have lived in Russia. Despite the continuing shortage of hot water and the glassless windows, she was enchanted, and contrasted unfavourably the spacious life, the vast kitchens, the splendid cellars and the huge dogs, with the life which the exiled Bezhukovs now lived in Notting Hill Gate, an unfashionable part of London. Even the Russian soldiers seemed part of the excitement.

Charlie Grew rushed in just then, his face white.

'They've driven him away in a car!'

'Who, who? Not Papa?'

'Yes, your father. I was just opening my boot . . .'

'Yes, yes, go on.'

'Then the light went on in the hall and Herr von Acht came down the stairs with three or four Russian soldiers. They led him to one of their black cars, they must have had a driver waiting and drove off instantly.'

'Why didn't you question them?'

'Of course, I should have done. But it happened so fast. One moment there was no one there. Next moment there was the light, the marching figures, the car doors opening, slamming and they were gone. In less than a minute.' Charlie Grew had had another chapter of education. He sounded apologetic.

Everyone ran out into the courtyard. There was the light on in the hall at the top of the stairs leading to the wing in which the Achts lived. There was otherwise no sound. The night was not cold, but there was no moon.

Charlie Grew, Hansie, and Jean Marie hurried into the house. Soon after them, her wheelchair travelling like an express train, was Aunt Zita. The others helped her up the stairs. They went up to the Russian guard, at his post by the main staircase.

'Where is General Krivoshein?'

The guard smiled and pointed up the stairs.

'I'm sorry, General Krivoshein asleep.'

'You must wake him, man,' said Aunt Zita.

The guard shook his head and put his finger to his lips.

'General Krivoshein says no interruption, no interruption at all. He tired. He has tiring day tomorrow.'

'A tiring day tomorrow is a threat,' declared Aunt Zita.

Captain Grew went down the hall and demanded of another Russian if he, a British officer, could use the telephone to ring Vienna.

'Sorry. This telephone not work at night.'

'It had a tiring day, do you think?' exploded Captain Grew.

The Russian sagely nodded, 'and will have tiring day tomorrow too,' he added.

The Captain returned to the others.

'There's no chance of getting *anything* going here,' he said, 'and there's only one thing to be done. I shall follow to see where they take him. There were four men in the car as well as Herr Acht. We'd stand no chance if we tried to stop them by force. I'll just follow.'

'You're realistic,' said Aunt Zita drily.

'Realistic,' agreed Charlie. 'It may be that all is well but, still, terrible mistakes are sometimes made in these circumstances.'

They returned to the courtyard. Charlie's car stood by the entrance to the stables. A number of Soviet soldiers had arrived from nowhere and were surrounding it, one of them waving a small torch, pointing to the left hand front wheel. In the darkness, it was impossible to see what had happened. As Charlie Grew approached, the soldiers stood back. A flat tyre was plain to see. The Russians offered to mend it. Charlie accepted the suggestion. Obviously, their delaying instructions did not end with puncturing the tyre. Fifteen more minutes passed before the work was done. When they had come down into the courtyard, it might have been possible to have set off in pursuit of Otto Acht, for there was only one obvious road from Besselberg to Vienna. The chances now were slim. Doubtless the Russians timed it carefully. Charlie went back into the barn where people were still standing about in the cold, without knowing what to do. The audience was still also present, what there was of it. The Captain told Tatiana Bezhukov that they were returning to Vienna instantly. He thought it essential to advise his general of Herr Acht's arrest, as soon as possible. He and Tatiana went upstairs to pack.

When they came down, the family were standing by his car. The Russian soldiers had vanished.

'What will become of *us*?' Franzie asked Charlie.

Before he could answer, Aunt Zita, who seemed from the beginning of this drama to assume the worst, and to quite enjoy it, had replied:

'You, Franzie, will for the time being direct the Schloss just as Jean Marie directed the play. Life is not so different from Schiller as to make it difficult for you. Your turn,' she said imperiously to Hansie, 'has come. You will conduct yourself in this house as your ancestors did, maintaining a shining light in a dark land. And from time to time, messages of hope will come from the British High Command.' She smiled brilliantly at Charlie.

As she spoke a tall figure in a long white dressing gown had approached. It was Betty. She looked pale but not ill. Tatiana wondered whether she had taken to her bed because she did not like Schiller.

'They have taken Otto? Well, at least, he speaks their dreadful language. I don't think we should be too worried. Don't think me ridiculous, of course it's disquieting but there've been all sorts of alarms before.'

Her calm reaction steadied them all. Some of the cousins began to laugh, out of nervousness. They had begun to fear that they might have to leave also. The Captain decided to delay till morning.

All the same, Christmas time at Besselberg had been transformed. The sixteen year old Franzie was sitting in his father's study, fearing that he might soon have to work at his father's papers. Charlie Grew was drinking the whisky, which he himself had brought, with Tatiana and Aunt Zita in the latter's room. The younger children were in their beds praying for the morning to come soon and to bring more excitements. Betty was writing letters to people who might help in Vienna, and the light rain which had begun to fall was turning to sleet.

XXXI

OTTO ACHT WAS DRIVEN INTO VIENNA FROM BESSELBERG AT A fast pace. It would have been hard for Charlie Grew to have caught up with him, even had his car been ready.

The journey had begun with a show of politeness. The Russian colonel had asked Otto whether he would care to go into Vienna to assist in some enquiries relating to the re-establishment of a nazi movement in the Wachau. It probably would not take long.

'Now?' asked Otto, 'it's after eleven, and I was hoping you would join us for a post-Christmas celebration.'

'No, no,' the Colonel said. 'I should prefer to go now, since at night the roads are emptier.' A curious comment, thought Otto, since Austrian roads were then empty at all times.

While the black car sped towards Vienna, Otto attempted conversation with the Colonel and the two other officers sitting left and right of him on the back seat: 'Did you enjoy our little production?' he asked. The Colonel said that it had been wrong to show a work of Schiller in present circumstances. Whatever its intrinsic merits, the nazis had made use of Schiller's dramas, so that even an amateur production was likely to cause trouble. General Krivoshein was not prepared to have his men subjected to "such misguidances" as were provided by the later scenes of *Don Carlos*.

Otto suggested that a knowledge of that play was necessary for those who aspire to administer central Europe. Don Carlos was a Habsburg by blood. The Russian brushed this aside.

It became obvious to Otto that the play had been the occasion of, not the cause of, his unexpected arrest. Perhaps that would have occurred that night even if the play had not been shown, even if the children had not invited General Krivoshein and his staff.

The Colonel sat beside the driver, and never turned to look at Otto during their conversation. The officers to the left and right of him never spoke. Otto sought to offer some *rapport* with them in Russian. They were either forbidden to talk or did not understand. There had been talk of the Soviet Union sending their Asiatic soldiers to the west. In the

153

dark, Otto could not see the colour of their faces. They might be yellow.

The journey from Besselberg to Vienna took three hours. There were delays at the makeshift Krems bridge, put up to make up for the one destroyed, the roads were bad, and even a Russian car could be stopped and searched at the border between the Russian zone of Vienna and their zone of Lower Austria. Otto slept in the last stage of the journey. He was not surprised on arrival in Vienna to find himself in the dark building between the museums and the parliament which had been taken over by the Russians as their "security headquarters". It was the only ugly building in the Ring.

Otto was placed in a small room on the third floor which had once been a waiting room outside a senior official's office. It was not a bad room, with traditional mouldings around a high ceiling. There was a sofa, two chairs and a table, and a picture of a lady, done about 1800, with dogs at her feet and a window out into a sunny garden. The picture gave Otto a feeling of pessimism, since it reminded him of how far removed he, and the country, were from the serene scene depicted. How much had been attained a hundred and fifty years ago but had been thrown away by folly during his own generation by people like himself! How could it be that he, a landowner, member of a well-known family, with a lifetime's record of unsensational service, should now be waiting, in the middle of the night, for some Russian to put invented charges devised to frighten him and people like him into acquiescence to Soviet demands throughout Austria? Otto remembered how Prince Schwarzenberg had known that it would be a bad precedent when, in 1849, he and the Emperor had invited the Russians in to help to put down the Hungarian revolt. But the idea of Russian soldiers in the Ringstrasse, and of himself waiting for interrogation there, seemed all the same unbelievable.

He waited in that room many days.

XXXII

BROOKS SHEAY COULD NOT REALLY REKINDLE HIS OLD LOVE for Austria. His memories of the old Austrians were also vanishing. He found the survivors unapologetic but resilient. They did not seem particularly to resent their new plight. His ADC told him that the reason was that they had discovered that the Allies had no more hot water than they did.

In January 1947, he returned to Washington. His wife, Penelope, and the four children, came down from Connecticut. They spent Christmas in a rented house at the corner of 34th and Q Streets. Christmas in Washington was cold, sharp, beautiful. There were parties for the young and old alike, given in grey houses in Massachusetts Avenue. There were brisk walks along the Potomac and conversations about Soviet intentions in the Executive Office building and over the brandy, in drawing-rooms which seemed more English than England.

'The Soviets need to feel secure.'

'So do we.'

'They are paranoid.'

'So do we give them everything they need?'

'If they won't feel secure until they've got Iran, what do we do?'

'If they need the Balkans, give it to them. Those countries were never much good.'

'What if they need France and Italy to make them feel really happy?'

'You can't trust the British. They're bankrupt.'

'Brooks, what's going on in Austria?'

So the talk went on. The impression Brooks gained, from his friends in the Department of State, was that no one knew what to do. America wanted to go to sleep again. She did not want to be an empire. America liked to have vacations between spells of hard work, and now was the time.

'I don't know what's eating them. They've won the war.'

'They've won the war.'

'They didn't win the war alone.'

'What the hell *do* they want?'

'Averell says Stalin's reasonable. The people behind him are the thugs. Evil men.'

'Stalin's putty in their hands.'

'That's what Averell says.'

'Brooks, please tell us what's the score in Vienna.'

Brooks talked to friends who were dealing with the "score" in Iran, in Turkey, in Germany, in China. The pattern seemed everywhere the same.

'No. I wouldn't say they're on the march,' said an old friend who had been in the OSS during the war, 'but the pattern's the same everywhere. They steal all the equipment they can. They kidnap the scientists. They put whole factories on their trains and run them home. And they say they're doing it in the name of the proletariat. Devilish.'

Sheay sat in the G Street Club with two members of his old staff in the Third Army. They were still in uniform, worked in the War Department, longed to return to Harvard.

'The trouble is that the American army thinks its job is done. The army wants to go home. I want to go home. But then the Secretary of State will have no backing. And our information is: the Russian understands one thing. Force. If he sees that we've demobilised —'

'If he sees Dick's back at Harvard —'

'Right, if he sees I'm back at Harvard — then he'll be uncontrollable.'

Sheay saw every official that he could find in Washington: 'Our guess is that the Russians are going to take over their zone in Austria and make it a satellite, just as they are doing in Poland, Hungary, Romania and the others — it's not as if Austria as an independent state had any meaning,' said a serious major in the office of the Secretary for Air. 'Our guess is that they won't find it too difficult. It's not just the power they've got. It's that they've got friends in so many unexpected places. God knows how many agents they have in Britain. As for here —,' Major McDonald raised his creased brow, 'we're up against a world conspiracy. Austria, we know from our own sources, is a prime target. They've begun already. Trying to frighten it into submission. Keep the Austrians jumpy. Classic technique. We had a signal in this morning about a man in the Russian Kommandatura. Pushed out of a second-floor window. Found in the snow. Fellow called Acht. Dead, of course. Russians say he had been called in for "routine investigation" and jumped out. Court gave suicide. Everyone in Vienna knows he was pushed. Classic technique. Man hadn't done anything. Russians didn't particularly dislike him. All they wanted was to frighten his family, his friends, public opinion generally.'

'Acht? What was his first name?'

'Otto Acht. See the signal yourself.'

Major McDonald pushed a typed signal in capital letters on a flimsy piece of paper across the desk to Sheay. He read it disbelievingly. He had not seen Otto since the war. He had known him in the 1920s.

'I knew him. A fine man. I didn't know he was in Vienna. I'd heard he was holed up in his property in the Russian zone. A beautiful house in the Wachau.'

Pictures of pre-war shoots and summer tennis parties came to Sheay's memory. Otto had been proud of his house. One could hear him telling its history over and over again and never tiring of it. How old were his children? The eldest couldn't be more than sixteen.

'That's interesting that you knew him. That's important. Was he suicidal? Could he have thrown himself out of the window? Classic technique.'

'I'd doubt it. Of course, I haven't seen him for twenty years. Also it depends what happened beforehand. Had he been beaten? Torture?'

'Doesn't say in the telegram. Perhaps you ought to have a talk with the Secretary. How long will you be in town?'

'Till Tuesday? Fine. Where you staying?'

Sheay met the Secretary. Medium height, neat, impeccably dressed, a good athlete, a rich banker before the war, Smithson was good-looking, intense, controlled. 'Walks like a successful gangster in a classy movie,' a mutual friend had described him, and added, 'He's nervy. But he's right.' Sheay had worked with him in the past.

Sheay saw him at his house in Massachusetts Avenue. Outside, the snow lay over fine gardens. The statues were half-covered by snow. Inside he was shown into a library. The room was panelled. A fire crackled in an old fireplace. Books were piled high on the tables. The Secretary stood up as Sheay entered the room and didn't sit down, but started pacing up and down. He smoked continuously.

'We've reached a turning point in history, Brooks,' said Smithson. 'The Russians are behaving as badly as Hitler. In some ways worse. It's them or us. No one else counts. The British are exhausted. They don't count. It's them and us. One of us will win in the end. It won't be the richest, the most intelligent, the quickest. The side which will win is the one with the will to win. Sooner or later the nerves of one side or the other will crack. I don't know whose nerve it will be. It won't be ours while I'm here. Who can say what will happen in future?'

He looked out through french windows into the wintry garden, the snow appearing blue, as darkness gathered.

'The trouble is we're unprepared, Brooks. We're demobilising. Those left in uniform are angry that they're at the back of the line. What sort of impression does that leave on an expanding empire? A friendly impression. We have no intelligence service. The President understands the principle of taking a firm line but he's still new. He doesn't see that it's one thing to decide a policy. It's another thing to get it carried out, even if officials are convinced that the policy is right. Which, in this case, they aren't. What odds would you give on us in Austria?'

'I've never formulated it like that.'

'No. No one has.'

He looked out at the snowy garden and then continued:

'I'm afraid our lives are going to have to change, Brooks. Any chance, incidentally, that this Acht fellow *might* have been involved in a revived nazi movement?'

'Not likely, as he wasn't a nazi beforehand.'

'So how do you interpret this?'

'They want to organise fear, I suppose. Perhaps he didn't answer their questions. Anyway, I don't know much. I've read the newspapers. *The Times* says it could have been suicide.'

'Of course he was pushed. No question about it.' Smithson had sat down now but immediately got up again. He was not a man who found it easy to sit down. 'So what do we do, Brooks?' Sheay was going to speak but Smithson answered himself. 'I tell you what we do. We have to prepare the American people for a fight. I'd say the sooner we have a showdown the better. We could win now. In twenty years, it's not at all certain. The nation will be slack.'

No one expected Smithson to be slack: not at any time.

Sheay left Smithson's house with more foreboding than he could remember since the months before Pearl Harbor. He was driven past the Russian embassy. A vast block of a mansion, a guard outside, the hammer and sickle hanging loosely, no lights save in the top storey. The driver said:

'Wonderful people in there, aren't they, Sir. Wonderful fighters. Very glad we're allies of the Soviet Union, Sir, aren't you? Wouldn't like it at all if they weren't on our side, would you, Sir?'

'It might be difficult.'

'Right, Sir. Very right. I agree with all you say.'

XXXIII

CHARLIE GREW WAS IN SUFFOLK IN JANUARY 1947: GREAT oaks, broad skies, evasive countrymen, forgotten moated houses. It was the first holiday that the Captain had had since he had dropped into the Wienerwald in March 1945. Mildenham was so deep in the country that the villagers' English was almost incomprehensible to outsiders. All the reminders of Charlie's childhood lay around him, as well as his father's commanding presence: a General of the First War. There were his sisters' jokes, novels of Buchan and Sapper beside his bed, rooks in the elms. Charlie's fluency was more marked than when he had last been there, as was his self-confidence. He did not make so many silly jokes, his sisters noticed, displeased. His mother, preoccupied by new sweet peas and old roses, secateurs and raffles, seemed to him not to have changed: outspoken, impulsive, vague, kind but shackled by commitments. His father, on the other hand, treated him seriously for the first time – too much so, his sisters decided – for he talked almost as if he were one of Charlie's junior officers simply because Charlie had been in action – action too of which they were not supposed to talk: resistance fighting was not discussable. On several occasions, Charlie would say to his father 'I'd rather not go into that, Sir.' His father proudly had nodded understandingly. None of his family knew the name of Charlie's wartime organisation. Occasionally, after dinner, the port would go round and Lady Grew and her daughters would leave and Sir Monty would tell his son with iron impatience:

'Say what you like, Charlie, the Russian is not a fighter,' or 'Take it or leave it, your average American is a home bird. He's a summer visitor, nothing more,' or again,

'Europe's finished. The next war will be for the Pacific.'

At this moment, Lady Grew would come in to indicate that, though the serving women were patient, they were old and would like to go to bed; at which, with a humility which Charlie could not previously remember in his father, they would "adjourn to the library", his father saying, 'well, well, victory leads to a few modest discomforts.'

Sir Monty had two obsessions, which usually made their appearance at that stage of the evening. The first was that the Prime Minister was an Armenian – hence the two "e"s at the end of the name Attlee: the second, the fear that the country was shot through with Russian agents – 'everywhere you'll find 'em: in the Tank Corps! In the Marines!'

'Well, Charlie,' he said on New Year's Eve, 'I expect you're thinking of the future. Don't suppose after all this you'll want to go to the University.'

'Not sure of that, Sir.'

'Sensible man. Only means you start life later than the rest of them. Thinking of staying where you are?'

'Well, I don't suppose I'd stay in Austria for ever.'

'No, of course not – but there'll be a lot of soldiering. Malaya, Egypt, Palestine, India. Shouldn't wonder if there'll be a lot of soldiering there. A lot of empire to lose,' he remarked, 'though I'd try to get to Germany. That's the first class game, I'd say. Austria is the minor country, *par excellence*. I'd never trust an Austrian further than I can see him. The Germans are a great nation. They'll be up again one day. You'll see.'

The General's only connection with Austria, Charlie believed, was his presence at the first night in London of *The Merry Widow*: 'the 8th of June 1907', he would sometimes intone, long before Charlie had known that he would go to Vienna, 'the climax of my musical life'. The conclusion too, Charlie thought.

'I like the Austrians, Sir,' Charlie said, 'they've been through hell.'

'So they have. Sounds as if they're still going through it. Heard the news tonight?' The question was superfluous since the General had the only wireless in the house.

'No, Sir,' said Charlie nevertheless.

'Fellow called Acht pushed out of a top floor by the Russians. BBC say he was a landowner. Know the name?'

'My God, I knew him. Was with him at Christmas.'

'Well, he's dead. Quite a to-do over there, it seems. Pity you're here. You'll be missing a lot of the show.'

Charlie had talked a good deal about his new friend, Tatiana. His sisters giggled.

Charlie returned to "the show" two days later. He drove back across a ruined winter landscape. The cities of Germany were still rubble. The concentration camps were refilled with refugees from the empires of Austria, Germany and Russia. His education in history had revolved round the question of "Bismarck and the reunification of Germany". Other titles for new essays rumbled through his brain: "Hitler and the disintegration of Europe". He crossed icy roads in the American zone of Germany to join a line of thirty vehicles at the Enns Bridge over the Danube between the Russian and American zones. The patient faces of waiting drivers were the faces of the twentieth century, he reflected. The scowls on the faces of the Russian police could be those of the twenty-first, if he and his friends were not careful. The delay could have a political purpose, he knew. In Vienna, the papers were full of pictures of Otto Acht lying face down in the snow in Vienna outside the Russian Kommandatura. The question 'Did he fall? Or was he pushed?' was never put, out of deference to Soviet feelings.

Meanwhile, back at Mildenham, General Sir Monty Grew was affording his daughters a new glimpse of the military mind:

'Lehár himself conducted,' he was saying, 'with all the discipline of the Kapelmeister which his father had been.'

There was no one to tell him that, in later life, Lehár had a dog trained to yawn whenever he heard the waltz from *The Merry Widow*.

XXXIV

COLONEL JEAN GEORGES MARCHAIS HEARD THE NEWS OF OTTO von Acht's death in the *Dépêche du Midi*, which he bought at the railway station of Biarritz Négresse on a bright cold morning at about seven o'clock as he descended from the Paris–Irún train. The *Dépêche* carried a long article, in which it said that 'an elderly right wing landowner Otto Echt [sic] had killed himself while awaiting interrogation in the Russian Kommandatura in Vienna. The Russian Colonel Voronov, on behalf of the Russian High Command, stated yesterday that Herr Echt was known to have been involved in a wide ranging plot to re-establish nazism in Austria.' Further arrests were expected throughout the country. Colonel Voronov added that that was a matter where he and his colleagues were working closely with the Western Allies who had a common interest in the uprooting of the nazi movement in Austria. The article added that Herr Echt was the son of the late Max Echt, author of *The Final Solution*, a book which had given Hitler his ideas for the destruction of the Jews. Max Echt had recently died in poverty in Vienna, the paper added. It could be guessed that, with the death of Otto, all that was left of this particular dynasty of Austrian nazis was Gottfried, now in prison: though a cousin of Otto Echt, Alois, was a Minister for Planning, in the government of Dr Leopold Figl.

Colonel Jean Georges Marchais, a long overcoat flapping, counted his luggage and took a taxi to his family home a few miles outside the town. It was the house where he had been brought up, where his father still lived and where one of his brothers, Etienne, an inmate of Auschwitz during part of the war, had just returned. There was also in the Château, his beautiful wife, Hélène, and their four children. Jean Georges had not seen Hélène since February 1946. He looked forward to the prospect with apprehension. He was fond of her but had treated her badly. His infidelities in Paris were too well-known not to have reached her and he would have been able to have visited the Château more often had he really tried. He worried also about his father, a man of strength in the past, who had suffered during the war from shortage of food and who was now beginning to show the marks of his age. His brother Etienne had, before the war, been the problem child of the family. Now he was the hero.

Hélène greeted him affectionately as if they had not been parted for more than a week. She seemed unchanged if, possibly, more stately. Perhaps fatter. She told him she had something to tell him 'very urgent even before you embrace the children'. He went to a drawing room unused and unheated. Heavy chairs, ancient frayed tapestries, a view to the Pyrenees, the smell of neglect.

'No,' said Hélène, 'this is inadequate.'

They went into the library where they would be secluded. The smell of neglect was more marked.

'I am sorry, Jean Georges – goodness it's cold,' remarked Hélène, 'but I have to have a divorce. I am going to marry Julián Onaindía.'

Onaindía was a Basque refugee of a well-known family which lived nearby.

'Is it not a little drastic?'

'No, it is essential. It is overdue.'

'How is it possible to arrange?'

'It is expensive, but it can be done.'

'Don't you find the idea of divorce unsavoury?'

'Perhaps, but it is tidy.'

'Who will pay?'

'I suggest we halve the cost. Julián has money. My father can give money. *Evidemment*, he sends you his regards.'

'Please return mine to him. What would be the technical arrangements?'

'The marriage would be annulled.'

'What, with four children?'

'A marriage can be annulled if a member of the immediate family at the wedding carries a weapon. My father had a paperknife on him.'

'Oh, I see. How are the children?'

'Superb, the four of them. They long to see you.'

'How will they take this?'

'Wonderfully. I have alerted them.'

'Alerted?'

'I have told them that it will happen. They have seemed excited. To have two fathers, it's unusual. And Julián adores children.'

'When do you want it?'

'Today. We have the lawyer here at noon. I gambled on your train being on time.'

'Well, it is certainly fast.' The Colonel looked tired.

'When one has decided a thing, it is best to act fast. You always say that.'

'Weren't the children surprised?'

'Not in the least. They had seen me with Julián.'

'What does Julián's family think? They are Catholic, I remember.'

'I am to them a "scarlet woman". Think of it, me, Hélène! I enjoy the reputation. It is at least new, is it not?'

'Certainly. You have told my father?'

'Naturally.'

'And –'

'He did not seem surprised. He said it was your fault.'

'My fault?'

'For neglecting your duties for so long. Think of it, it is eleven months since we even met.'

'I wrote.'

'Yes, but what letters! All about the Austrian economy. I ask you, Jean Georges, I ask you.'

'Wasn't there one about the art treasures?'

'I believe there was. But Jean Georges, we must prepare dossiers.'

'I had better see my father.'

'Of course you should. Do that. But remember, the lawyer at noon. Then sleep. You look tired. The night train from Paris is tiring. Not that I remember well. Think of it, I have not been to Paris since 1939.'

In the circumstances, the Colonel was not displeased to receive a telegram two days later from his general ordering him to return 'with all due haste, since important developments are shortly expected'.

Returning *via* Paris, the Colonel had a chance of seeing that, where the war had left the buildings standing, the shortages made his own capital not so different from Vienna: the two axles of nineteenth century Europe lay in mud.

XXXV

'*W*ELL?'
Colonel Livingstone and Charlie Grew had achieved a mild coup: a real step forward in their careers. Livingstone would soon return, no doubt, to London and the art world. But just as well to leave when things were going well. A patrol car had brought in a disreputable-looking youth who had tried to break into the officer's club in the Kinskypalais. The sergeant's description had aroused the interest of the Colonel. It sounded like the youth whom they had been looking for in connection with the disappearance of the Crown of Charles V. The sergeant had had the youth fed, washed and brought in to see them.

'You are under arrest for an attempt to break into the Kinskypalais,' said Colonel Livingstone, 'but we know quite well some of your other crimes.'

'Indeed,' Kamo said.

They were in Schönbrunn again. Charlie Grew tried a different tactic: 'Of course, you know, if you come clean we would be able to help you. But silence will get you nowhere.'

'I understand.'

'In the Soviet zone you could be accused of assisting a neo-nazi movement.'

Kamo raised his eyebrows.

'If you do not talk, we would ask the Russians to collaborate in our investigation,' said Harry Mercer, who had joined his two colleagues, sitting on the desk, at which Charlie and Livingstone were sitting.

Kamo was silent.

'Well then there is nothing for it,' Colonel Livingstone said.

'What about the French? Shouldn't we have them in?' Charlie asked, hoping to spread the responsibility if not delay matters. He did not like what he was doing, yet Kamo's silence gave him few alternatives.

'Very well.' Livingstone had no doubt that Marchais would support him in everything where this sort of thing was concerned.

'Shouldn't you like to get an American view?' Kamo spoke sardonically.

'Damn you, why the hell should we?' shouted Mercer. 'We Europeans can handle things.' Kamo was asked to wait under guard in an ante-room.

'Perhaps an American would be good,' Charlie said to his two colleagues, 'they often have helpful ideas.'

'Helpful ideas,' Mercer sneered. 'What you mean is that they'd find a way to let this fascist bastard off the hook. Isn't that it, Grew? But people like this man have got to be dealt with by their Soviet compatriots. Otherwise, our entire post-war policy may as well go out of the window.'

'It's not doing very well, is it, anyway?' Charlie said, stoutly.

'Up to us to try and make it function,' said Mercer. Livingstone muttered: 'Hear hear.'

'I suppose you all know that, if we bring the Russians in, the boy will be as good as dead.'

'It really isn't for us to dictate the pattern of Soviet justice,' Mercer was insistent.

'I think I need to consult my General,' Grew said.

'It's a civilian issue primarily,' Mercer said. 'Anyway Whitelegge would be bound to let him off. He's completely unrealistic about these people.'

They went off to the mess for a drink, where, half an hour later, Colonel Marchais joined them. He listened to their account without saying anything.

'Let's go and see him,' said he after a while. They did so. Kamo was as reticent to talk to to as ever.

'You do know, don't you,' asked Colonel Jean Georges, gently, 'that you're making things difficult for us?'

'Tell us everything and we can help you,' Grew repeated.

'There's nothing to tell.'

'Where were you born?'

'In Völkermarkt, on the Drau.'

'Why do you speak with an accent?'

'I have Croat blood.'

'Name and address?'

The interrogation continued. Kamo had a reasonable story but he convinced nobody. Even Charlie Grew became irritated.

'You must talk to us if you want to save yourself,' he said, while the others were arguing among themselves. But Kamo only smiled. Charlie was not susceptible to such charms.

At half-past-eight in the evening, therefore, after five hours of discussion, Kamo was told that he would be taken to the police station in the Inner City to be charged with seeking unlawful entry into the club. The communist police officers would make certain that Colonel Voronov was able to present his own charges, which they knew would include such delicate matters as conspiring to destroy the Soviet war memorial and helping the re-foundation of a nazi movement. He still smiled.

'Have you anything to say?' asked Charlie Grew.

'Yes,' Kamo said, 'it is that one day I shall see that you regret this.'

'It is our duty,' said Charlie.

'It is a word to cover many things.'

Kamo was despatched to the Inner City in a British army jeep. He was handcuffed. A guard sat next to him in the back of the uncomfortable vehicle. Otherwise, there was just the driver.

'Make it fast,' said Harry Mercer as he slammed the door. 'Justice can't always wait.' The four officers watched the jeep drive to the gate of Schönbrunn, pass through the checkpoint and disappear on the other side. They returned to the mess for another drink. Only Charlie Grew was unhappy at what was happening.

The driver drove fast, as instructed, without looking round till he reached the Karlsplatz. They stopped once or twice for traffic lights. At the Karlsplatz, he turned round and began to say 'not much longer'. But his voice tailed off. He found himself looking into the barrel of a revolver.

'Drive to the Westbahnhof,' Kamo said, 'but unlock these handcuffs first.' The accompanying guard was lying back on the back seat apparently senseless.

The driver was not a hero. He expected to be in Vienna for only a few more weeks. He did as he was bid. He never could make out how it was that Kamo had so silently knocked out his companion and taken his gun. But he did not feel like arguing about it at that moment.

At the Westbahnhof, Kamo opened the door of the jeep and said: 'now drive back fast to Schönbrunn and – don't look round. I shall keep this –' he tossed the gun from one hand to another and back again – 'and will be watching. You understand don't you?' The driver did. Kamo vanished into the night.

Later that week Charlie Grew was explaining what had happened in a conversation with Alois, at a reception at the French High Commission.

'I couldn't help being rather glad, you know,' he said, 'though it doesn't put us in a very good light. What do you do in those circumstances?'

Alois was about to explain that he did not think that Austrian law provided for such circumstances, and how he himself sympathised with Charlie, when a waiter came up to him with a message from Poldi Moser, written in the form of a telegram:

DELIGHTED TELL YOU YOUR DAUGHTER KLARA RETURNS TODAY CLEARING STATION WIENER NEUSTADT AND WILL PROCEED YOUR HOUSE HEILIGENSTADT

HEARTIEST GREETINGS   POLDI MOSER

PART 4

FEBRUARY 1947–
MARCH 1948

XXXVI

*T*HERE WAS ONE THING WHICH EVERYONE AGREED ABOUT
Klara after she had returned to Vienna: that she was more beautiful
than she had been when she vanished. Before the attack on Vienna,
she had been charming, delightful, and pretty. Now no one would have
used the word "pretty" to describe her; she had become beautiful and,
when she allowed her deep violet eyes to rest on anyone, women as
well as men, they were transfixed: it was Klara's attention which would
move away to something else. Where she had been laughing and
friendly in the past, flirtatious in an innocent way, now she seemed to
place a regal distance between others and herself. In other ways too she
had changed: she had been always interested in what was happening to
people, what they were feeling. Now she seemed seldom concerned. She
still played the violin well but where she had been a promising musician,
with a future in performing music, if she wanted it, there was now a
certain stately quality rather than humility about her performances. She
did not seem unhappy but content in a rather grand way, as if she were
much older. But the changes did not suggest the word "tragedy" as
might have been supposed to be the case, considering what she must
have gone through; it was as if a certain remoteness had descended over
her.

And what *had* she gone through? That question interested everyone.
Klara herself was, both in public conversation with journalists and in private
conversation with the family, uninformative. She told precisely nothing.
She had gone; she had returned twenty months later. She was in good
health. What happened in the meantime, was, no doubt, interesting but
of no importance to her future in Austria. Naturally, at the beginning,
no one pressed her. Terrible events, assuredly, had occurred. One would
not press anyone about such things. But when days became weeks, weeks
months, and still no one had an idea of what Klara had done, or undergone, when in Russian hands, the silence seemed odd. No one insisted:
but her relations, her old school friends, her colleagues at the College of
Music, were baffled. They gossiped about her, they invented things,
either romantic, or horrible. When they were with her they felt as if they

were in the presence of a serene priestess who had returned to home altars after a successful mission in pagan territory.

The vexing aspect of the matter was that Klara did not seem distressed, by anything: by whatever had happened to her, by the Vienna to which she had returned or even by the death of her mother which she had indirectly caused. Yet she seemed good, philanthropic, patient; even, in a way, saintly: but if she had emotions, they were not to be seen.

In all these things, Klara was a contrast with others who came back in those days "from the East", either as refugees walking across forbidden frontiers, or hidden in trucks or in goods trains; or as genuine deportees returned to Vienna. These people arrived exhausted, sometimes cheerful, customarily broken by terrible experiences, but always talkative. When Klara arrived at Wiener Neustadt, she had not looked exhausted. When asked who she was and how she felt, she had given her name, smiled and said, like a film star, that she felt "a little sleepy".

Had her aloofness been contrasted less with the usual behaviour of an Austrian young woman, interest in Klara would soon have died away. After all, the struggle for survival, even in those days, was considerable. People were still dying of cold, even old ladies went to collect firewood in the Wienerwald. Where they could, parents sent their children away. For example, Alice had been able to get Heini and Anna away to England, where they were looked after in a village outside Cambridge by a clergyman's wife. The black market, in ration coupons as in food and clothes, was the only lively part of the economy.

After a while, people began to ask questions about Klara (not to her face, they would not have dared) in a malicious manner. Perhaps she had never left Vienna? Perhaps she had become the mistress of a Russian marshal who had taken her to Berlin? Could one not now detect a Berlin inflection in her accent? Perhaps she had been Zhukov's mistress? Perhaps even, she was really not Klara but a skilfully contrived double?

Alois Acht did not speak to his daughter except about trivialities. He was so grateful to have her back, apparently unharmed. He was proud of the strength with which she accepted her mother's death. He respected her reticence. He was delighted by her radiant appearance. Only once he said:

'Klara, if you want to tell me what happened, I am prepared.'

She answered: 'But *I* am not prepared: not yet.'

There it had ended. Admittedly in that "yet" there was expectation. But, as the weeks passed, it became evident that the fulfilment of that expectation would be deferred. Alois accepted that. Everyone else continued to gossip.

Considering that Alois's change of attitude towards the Russians derived from the circumstances of his daughter's abduction, it might have been supposed that he would change his mind or, at least, modify it on account of her return. He was not so logical; if anything he became more determined. Alois dedicated himself to thinking of ways whereby the Russians could be thwarted in what he took to be a plan to make Vienna a provincial capital in their world empire. He combined these views with a socialist domestic policy. The consequence was that, though a minor minister in a lesser department of state, Alois was sought at meetings all over the country by people whose own views had undergone a similar trajectory.

One reason for Alois's popularity was the fact that he was Otto's brother.

The mystery following Otto's death had not been resolved. The Soviet High Command kept to their story that Otto had jumped to his doom in order to avoid interrogation about a neo-nazi conspiracy in Lower Austria. There was, however, in discussion of the event, both with Austrians and with Allies, a hint of intimidation, as if to imply that the sooner people realised that the Soviet Union could do what it wanted, when it wanted, the better. 'Suicide or murder, it is the same,' Colonel Voronov said, at a reception at the French Mission, in conversation with Brooks Sheay on his return from Washington. If intimidation, not interrogation, had been intended, perhaps the Colonel was right.

The Austrian police charged with investigation of Otto's death had supported the Russians: that he had jumped to avoid interrogation, and therefore that he must have had *something* to hide. There may have been some illegal goings-on in that property of his in the Wachau that only the Russians could have known about.

The British were divided in their interpretations. General Whitelegge, along with Charlie Grew and Tatiana Bezhukov took for granted that the case was one of murder: though they differed as to whether Otto had been pushed out alive or, more likely in the General's view, killed before hand, and pushed out of the Kommandatura dead:

'My dear fellow, if one wishes to do someone in, one does not leave it to chance. A fit man, pushed down two storeys into light snow, could easily have survived.' He explained this to Alois at dinner.

But while the General was clear, his subordinates disputed. For Charlie, the death of Otto marked a turning point. He allowed the event to dictate his views on every subject. On the other hand, the political adviser, "rosy-cheeked Harry Mercer", "laughing Harry, dirty Harry" or "red Harry", as he appeared in letters of his colleagues, insisted that Otto, "an aristocrat of counter-revolutionary leanings" "had flirted with neo-nazism" and "killed himself out of an uneasy conscience". That view was also held by Colonel Livingstone, now "amused but not surprised" by the army's failure to find the Crown of Charles V. Had the question been handled by someone "sensitive to matters of art", the Colonel believed that the Crown would be back in the Kunsthistorisches Museum.

Colonel Livingstone dismissed the claim that the Russians had anything to do with Otto's death "except by being there". Otherwise, Otto, "a brother of the notorious Gottfried", and "nephew to that terrible old Max, who should have been shot at the Liberation", was "just the sort of landowner who would try his luck with the neo-nazi crew". Colonel Livingstone was affected in his judgements by another Acht family connection. He "hated turncoats", he told the General. Whatever they might originally stand for, he liked people of a piece. People who were socialists should remain so. For Alois – another of Otto's brothers – to change from revolutionary socialism to "ultra-Bevinism" was "obscene".

'Would you regard me as an ultra-Bevinist?' General Whitelegge asked, amused.

'General, I do not permit myself speculation about colleagues. But I don't think you've changed much.'

The French and Americans saw eye to eye for the first time since the war about Otto. Both were convinced that he had been murdered: Brigadier Sheay followed Secretary Smithson in thinking that the Russians had embarked on "general intimidation throughout Europe". Colonel Jean Georges knew that central Europeans were often murdered by the ancient method of "defenestration".

'If it happens again,' he was heard announcing, at a dinner in the Allied Club at the Kinskypalais, 'I shall start forming an alliance between France and the United States. I do not like it, I do not like them, they do not like us, but it may be necessary.'

Ludwig Börne left Vienna the day of Otto's death. A certain Countess Orsova who lived above Thekla Acht, and with no Russians in her comfortable flat, told that keen concert-goer the news. Immediately Börne heard of the death of Otto, he sent for his bill at the hotel – it was early in the morning – and left for the American airport at Tulln, where he bribed his way onto the first aircraft leaving:

'Just in time, I should say, that Börne cleared out,' said Countess Orsova, 'because no one wants publishing to be again in the hands of people like him. People like him never show either moral or physical courage. And our new Austria must have that if it is going to have a chance.'

The possibility that Ludwig Börne's corpse might just be found one day in the Danube, lower down than Vienna, perhaps on the way to Pressburg was discussed. People talked of it clinically as if discussing fish in the river.

'Ludwig Börne will outlive everyone,' Aunt Thekla declared. 'He's not the type to be found in the Danube. He's just not the type. He'll survive.'

Another who disappeared after the death of Otto was Count Gmunden. He had been expected to be part of a luncheon *à quatre* at the Kinskypalais the next day. But he did not appear. Only at a quarter to two did a message reach his hosts that he had had to "run down for a day or two" to Carinthia to tidy up some shooting problems. But he did not return. Those who frequented the Grand Hotel heard rumours that he had not paid his bill: could it be that he had been working for neither the Russians nor the English but was just a confidence trickster? Yet the Gmundens were a well-known family, and the Count an identifiable personality with a known past. Also his clothes were still in the room. He had left with only an overnight case.

A further depressing development that winter was that the Inter-Allied Mission for the recuperation of the Crown of Charles V had, as Colonel Livingstone discovered, to confess that it had run into the sand. The four Allied enquirers agreed on their candidate for the theft: the young assistant stage-manager of the Opera House who had fled from the Theater an der Wien. The man was also, according to Colonel Voronov, implicated in a conspiracy covering all Austria to revive the nazi movement, as well as in a plot to destroy the Russian war memorial, of which Otto had been the chief organiser.

Voronov thought that this suspect belonged to that "rabble of half-breeds" who had attached themselves to the Wehrmacht in the Caucasus in 1943 and had retreated with them committing legendary crimes. Colonel Voronov seemed to know more about this individual than anyone else. He kept these things secret from his colleagues because all Soviet leaders realise that, while news is silver, secrets are golden and one never knows in modern times when a secret might be useful.

XXXVII

*A*NOTHER MARK OF KLARA'S BEHAVIOUR WHICH DISPLEASED
her old friends was that she behaved normally, as if she had never
been away: or as if she had just been away for a week in the
Tyrol, as if nothing disagreeable had happened. She made visits to old
friends who had been with her on the occasion in the Wienerwald. She
saw the parents of those killed, visited their graves. But she reminded
those who so welcomed her of a Royal visitor: 'thank you ma'am so much
for coming here today,' the friends almost thought of saying after her
visits. 'Klara von Acht seems so extraordinarily untouchable', said Countess Orsova one Thursday to those gathered in the drawing room of Aunt
Thekla.

Klara carried on with her music from the point at which she had left
it. She went on with such social activities as occurred. Indeed, she went
out a lot. People who criticised her were the most curious about her.
They invited her in order to have another look at her, and to be able to
discuss her afterwards. Klara seemed to accept all invitations, so long as
they were in a group. If any young man suggested a *tête-à-tête* at the
Splendide Bar, she would refuse.

In the summer, there was a dance in the house of the Kuttenbergs, an
old family distantly connected with the Achts through Rüdiger's wife
Alice, whose mother had been a Kuttenberg. The Princess Kuttenberg
had explained that her children, tall, fair, plain girls in their late 'teens,
would be asking only cousins: "family only" had for years been the best
excuse for not inviting everyone one knew. The definition of cousins
could stretch far. This time, for instance, it included Tatiana Bezhukov
(another remote connection of the Kuttenbergs) and several of her friends
in the British Mission, such as Charlie Grew. 'No Americans though,'
said the Princess. 'You'll find they get drunk and become unamusing.' In
the end, Brooks Sheay did get an invitation. One astonishing invitation
was made. It was Willy Svoboda.

Countess Orsova never stopped talking about it. 'I can't understand it,'
she said – to Aunt Thekla on a Thursday afternoon – 'and, even if the
invitation had to be made, perhaps to pay off something, I can't see why

a young man of his sort would want to come. Of course, I know you like him but that's different.'

For Tatiana Bezhukov, and for all the foreigners, this dance was the first of its sort which they had attended: the first private party given by Austrians in a private house. Quite unlike the parties given by the Allies in what the Austrians called "stolen property": the Hofburg, Schönbrunn and so on.

'My dear Mama,' Tatiana wrote home to London, 'it was an entirely Austrian party and, do you know, never have I seen such a collection of good-looking tall and charming young men. The Austrian aristocrats *are* fascinating – I couldn't have enjoyed myself more waltzing madly till 4.15 in the morning and didn't want to go at all but was dragged away by Charlie and Mark – another officer in the Mission – who, though they enjoyed themselves, were not *quite* so fascinated as I, because the girls, though very nice, were, with one or at most two spectacular exceptions, not beautiful or at all sophisticated. It was a lovely party, so wonderful to be in a *home* again, with everyone in proper evening clothes – all the men in excellently cut dinner jackets, but the girls in rather made over evening dresses ... There was lots of food and plenty to drink and masses of Wienerwaltzer and a "cotillon": I fell madly in love with nearly all the young men,' she added.

There is no doubt that it was an excellent party. One of the Kuttenberg girls, for example, met for the first time the young Zriny whom she would marry four years later when he, penniless at the time of the dance, because of losing all his property, had made himself a fortune from making toast racks. Toast racks! For a Zriny! Well, strange things happened in those days. But many girls who had gone to the dance with the hope of catching a husband or, at least, of catching some admirers – and for many it was the first such opportunity since the war – found their evening ruined by the evident success of Klara. They did all have rather "made over" dresses, as Tatiana had told her mother, but many of them had taken a pleasure in the "making". Klara on the other hand had a marvellous dress in dark blue taffeta which she said she had taken from her mother's wardrobe: 'Surely you remember it,' she said with apparent innocence to Countess Orsova. 'Mummy was always wearing it before the war.' But Countess Orsova did not remember it and said so. She did not add, though she felt it, that one should not wear the dresses of a recent suicide and, if that suicide was one's mother, it would be as well not to go out at all.

From the moment that Klara glided into the room on the arm of one of Count Sapieha's sons – a schoolboy – she was the centre of attention. She danced with everyone and nobody felt happy unless they had secured the promise of another dance. But she refused: 'We shall see,' she would say with a marvellous smile and the poor young man concerned would stagger back to the bar, or to the arm of a less mysterious girl who would be unable to hold his attention. One girl, Polly Rutzendorf, fat, with a twisted face, with a sense of humour, said later that she had offered to Klara to auction her dances, in exchange for food coupons which they could split. Klara merely laughed.

Aunt Thekla had done her best to avoid sitting with Countess Orsova. She had known the latter all her life, never well, but in recent weeks she had seen her every day: too much. So she sat with the hostess, Princess Kuttenberg, who confided:

'Many people tell me it was bad taste to have this party. There are so many people away. Rüdiger, for example. But I say, if they were still alive – and I don't think Rüdiger *could* be, I wouldn't dare say so to Alice, who is so brave, but I don't think he can be alive – if they are, though, they will be thinking "if only we were in Vienna and could be dancing waltzes with the Kuttenberg girls". That's what they're thinking up in the lumber camps. They'd be disappointed if they thought we were *not* waltzing. Don't you agree, Thekla darling?'

Thekla did agree. 'Of course we could ask Alois's girl what they're thinking up in the lumber camps,' went on the Princess tartly, as she watched Klara on the arm of an eligible princelet while none of her own daughters seemed to be dancing with anyone.

'No one in the family knows where Klara was.'

'Well she was certainly somewhere,' the Princess said, 'and you should ask where.'

'I will, one day.'

'You should ask her now. I'll get her.'

Princess Kuttenberg was a small, round, determined woman like a ripe apple. In a cloud of pink ruffles, she fluttered over to Klara, who was leaving the floor followed by an infatuated remote relation named Hans Kuttenberg-Teppisch.

'Darling Klara, Aunt Thekla and I would so like it if you could spare a minute for us.'

Klara came with her. Her pale skin was flushed from the last waltz. Thekla thought she had rarely seen anyone so radiant. She leant forward and said to her something quite different to what Princess Kuttenberg expected.

'This is your moment, Klara. Whatever happened to you in Russia, I don't care a fiddlestick about it. All I know is, you must take the tide at its flood. Life will never again be so good for you.'

Klara gave her a dazzling smile. It is true, thought Thekla, one does not at all know what goes on behind those eyes which have such an extraordinary violet. That must come from her mother: not from *us*.

'When I was away,' Klara said, 'I did think of evenings like this.'

Neither Aunt Thekla nor Princess Kuttenberg were aware of how remarkable a statement this was, since it was Klara's first reference to having been away at all.

The band had embarked on the cotillon mentioned by Tatiana in her letter.

'In the past it was danced only at the end,' Aunt Thekla complained. The music was to a waltz, by Johann Strauss the Second. The charm of the dance is that it can be danced by any number, who all have to imitate a leading couple, who have a large number of alternative figures to choose from. By the end, everyone has been able to dance with everyone else.

'I know you'll be dancing this,' Klara said to Aunt Thekla. 'You love a cotillon.' Princess Kuttenberg was already on the floor.

Thekla protested but Klara had only to give her a gentle pull and she was on her feet. At eighty-seven her erect figure blended in well with all the others, most of whom were under twenty-five. Many of them were still in their 'teens. A few girls had to dance with each other, because there was a shortage of men.

Tatiana found herself dancing with Hans Kuttenberg-Teppisch.

'Do you speak German?' he asked her in English as they made their way to the middle of the room.

'No. I thought of learning it. But I have been learning the piano instead,' she artlessly said, with a directness that Hans found rude. His upbringing had been odd, as he hastened to tell Tatiana, with some pride.

'Of course, we're surrounded here by enemies, you know. Even the teenagers fought in the Wehrmacht at the end. I'm almost the only one here who didn't.'

'Really, why is that? Were you ill?' Tatiana fixed him with a harsh stare as they began to waltz. She did not approve of ill people.

'No, no, my father was anti-nazi and took us off to Brazil for the war.'

'How disgraceful!' said Tatiana, sympathising, 'I'd have hated to have missed the war, on whatever side I fought.'

With that, she twirled away to dance with another partner, a certain Count Bözendorff, as tall and as fair as Hans and a real war hero Tatiana thought, since he had volunteered at sixteen and had killed several Frenchmen at Bregenz: he was now just nineteen years old.

Hans assumed that Tatiana had misunderstood what he had said. The idea of an English girl being unimpressed by an Austrian who had not fought against her country was too outlandish to be imagined. At twenty-four, rich, with properties in Minas Gerães – that had enabled the family to go to Brazil in 1938 – and no attachments, Hans believed himself one of Vienna's most eligible men.

Klara floated from partner to partner in the cotillon. She held the attention of all not dancing. She glowed with pleasure at her success. As she swirled round with her admirers again, she was able to tell them – 'you see, I told you we might dance again' – before changing partners. At the end of the cotillon she found herself with a young man whom she had never met before, and whose dark hair and shiny pale face, with shadowed black eyes, proclaimed him to be different from the young aristocrats whom she had been effortlessly teasing. He danced clumsily. He was also silent, not prepared with any compliments or witty anecdotes. It was Willy Svoboda. Like everyone else in the room, he had been fascinated by Klara all the evening. Was it to shock or to excite trouble or out of genuine interest that Klara then danced three times with him? Nobody knew.

Charlie Grew, now a temporary Major, was also one of those unable to take his eyes off Klara throughout the evening. He had drunk too heavily of the Wachau white wine and confided to Brooks Sheay: 'That's the sort of person one goes abroad to see. One would never see anyone like that at home.' Brooks, amused, explained that she was Alois von Acht's daughter. He told Grew of her eclipse and reappearance.

'Did you talk to her?'

'I couldn't do that,' said Charlie humbly.

'Why not?'

'Not sure where fraternisation would end,' was the tipsy reply.

'Self-control's one of your national characteristics, surely?'

'Finished.' Charlie Grew said decisively, 'Churchill finished all that.'

'Churchill?'

'You wait and see. Churchill told the Englishmen that they could weep like Frenchmen, as they did in the eighteenth century. Told us that we could drink and say what we think. Wait and see. Churchill finished Victorian values for good and all. Wait and see. The braces are off.'

'In that case,' said Sheay, 'I should pursue Klara. If you can remember to tell me what she says, so much the better,' he added. 'She's a mysterious character.'

'I'm not allowed to take out Austrian ladies,' Charlie Grew insisted.

'Not for work?'

'Not without my General's permission.'

'Get it then.' Sheay was rather insistent.

Two minutes later, Charlie Grew did dance with Klara a haunting waltz by Waldteufel called *The Maidens of Marsbach*. The music was a little slower than the others, the evening had been long and, was it his imagination, but Charlie felt afterwards that Klara had purposely for a second rested her cheek against his.

'You're quite good-looking for an Englishman,' Klara said to him afterwards, 'though I do wonder if you have any sense of humour.'

How the marvellous evening ended remained vague in the minds of most of those present. That it was not so in the memory of Klara Acht was certain. With what fortunate young man did she return to Heiligenstadt was a question for the next day. In those days, after all, taxis were not ubiquitous companions and practically nobody had a car. But return she did – in the company, someone said, of Brooks Sheay, in his Cadillac, driven by a sergeant of the marines. If that was true, it was, presumably, all right.

XXXVIII

*A*T THE CORNER OF THE GRABEN AND THE SAMMLERGASSE, there was a café which had opened its doors two days after the Russian occupation. This was the Café Teller, kept by an energetic couple of that name, then in their sixties. No one would have said that the Café Teller was a good substitute for the Café Grienstadl or the Café Zentral of the old days, but it was still a café, which, as in the past, remained open all hours. The place breathed, from the moment one entered it, the spirit of Vienna, as it believed itself to be. There were hatstands, newspapers in their wooden holders, and energetic waiters pouring boiling milk and *ersatz* coffee enthusiastically into cups, calculating instinctively the force and height at which the product far below would turn the desired shade. When there was no coffee to be had, there was milk which Frau Teller dressed up to look as if there were coffee in it by means of a delicately administered drop of juniper berries, mixed with root of chicory. Upstairs, there was a restaurant which could seat a private dinner for a hundred; on the second floor, there were a few shabby private rooms, needing paint, like other things which survived the Third Reich.

In this café on Tuesday evenings at about eight o'clock, three men would meet. These were Poldi Moser, Karl Reinhardt and Alois von Acht.

Poldi Moser was by now not only a minister and ex-hero of the resistance but a glutton: a rare being in Austria in those days. It was said that Poldi had entered politics in order to eat official lunches, a view which overlooked the fact that even ministers were rationed.

Karl Reinhardt, the resistance leader from the Salzkammergut, had refused all offers to stand for parliament, and was director general of the Tyrolische Bank in Vienna. His youth, good looks and heroism in the war had made him much sought after before the elections but he had eschewed all offers, with the claim that, before he entered politics, he wanted to own a newspaper; and, before he could buy a newspaper, he needed money. Like most other people now in public life, Reinhardt's youth had included some disagreeable passages: where had *he* been on

March 12, 1938? But youth has to be forgiven, and the events between 1940 and 1945 had drawn a curtain over more than the life of Reinhardt. As he once said, when questioned by a communist journalist, 'Well these things are complicated. But I give you my word of honour that I was never half so friendly with the nazis as Stalin was.'

Reinhardt was known in the press as "the first Austrian to be able to buy a new suit": an allusion to a mission which he had led a few months before to America to discuss the future status of the Austrian debt. A year or two later he had become famous by suing a tailor in Gmunden for refusing to make him a pair of lederhosen because he did not own property in the Tyrol.

The custom of these three men was to discuss frankly how they would deal with the "Asiatic cloak" – Reinhardt's words – which they felt was being laid over *Mitteleuropa*. On an evening in January 1948, Moser and Reinhardt were sitting at eight o'clock drinking the "cold war coffee" served to them by Frau Teller and waiting for Alois. Reinhardt and Poldi Moser realised that Alois might be late since, on that day, his brother Gottfried had been condemned to fifteen years' imprisonment: a sentence which Gottfried was not going to challenge but the justice of which the Viennese middle class disputed while thinking not only "there but for the grace of God go I", but also, "many people who did worse things than poor Gottfried are walking about scot free".

Alois was ready, when he arrived, to discuss his brother's fate: 'He was younger than I. Always a dreamer. He wanted to prove himself different to me. I suppose I am responsible in some ways. Yet every man is the master of his own life. I cannot find it in me to reproach myself. For other things perhaps. But not for Gottfried. I hardly saw him after he went to the university. I had left long before that. Do you know I am forty-five? Forty-five!'

'At least it is just a long sentence. I had been increasingly afraid it would be worse. Gottfried will not serve the whole time. He will have books. He will be out before he is forty. These sentences are unlikely to stand.' He laughed. 'Perhaps he will even write a book. His memoirs.'

'You have a family for our time,' Reinhardt said, 'what with Max and yourself and Otto. And now Gottfried.'

'You should not forget Rüdiger. Rüdiger is the person to think of now. Max and Otto are dead, Gottfried is in prison, I am in the Café Teller. But where is Rüdiger? Alice doesn't know. Someone thought he saw him, in a train crossing the Ukraine. But there is no evidence. Even if he were alive then, there is every chance he was killed the next day. Even if he is not dead, he must be north of the Arctic circle. Dark all the winter. In summer only sun. That is not life. There I *do* feel some guilt.'

'You? But Rüdiger was against the Bolsheviks.'

'Yet I did encourage people to feel that Russia could provide an alternative to nazism. I believed it myself. A society organised according to Reason. Where the workers have shown effectively that they could govern better than the people of the past. I do not understand how I was so blind. So. We are not here to weep. We must work. My impression is that things are getting worse every day. We are hemmed in. The Russians have set out to terrify us into submission. They murder innocents like Otto – not because there is a crime to punish – but just to worry people. They treat us, the elected government of Austria, as if we were innkeepers while they are guests who are going to stay as long as they choose without payment. Above all there is control, domination, of the police in Vienna. Through our communists, of course. But that is effective. At the start of the occupation they established their men throughout the police. So even a change of minister makes no difference. Well, what are we going to do? Our western friends do not see it like this. They still think they can all remain jolly Allies if they behave well. "Forged in war, friendships last in peace." And so on. The Americans are ignorant, the British interested in Bangalore rather than Budapest, the French exhausted. Of the three, I place most hope in the French. The French are continental Europeans. They need a good sleep and then, who knows, they will wake up. Anyway I have spoken too much. I always do. You must interrupt me. Poldi – you think I exaggerate.'

'You always did,' said Poldi Moser kindly. 'But it is true, I am not so pessimistic. I agree that the Russians are testing us. But we are resisting, Could you have thought three years ago that we should have here in Vienna a free government with no communists –'

'And no power,' intervened Reinhardt.

'With less power than we should like,' went on Poldi, 'but, all the same, a government with theoretical control over all Austria? Three years ago Schirach was still here, Goebbels was coming to see us with horrible regularity, and no one knew what would happen in the battle for Austria –'

'So we only lost the Stefansdom, the Opera House, the bridges of the Danube, the castles of Burgenland and half the country,' said Reinhardt.

'Yes, but all the same. Now we have the Russians. I think we are being cleverer with them than you say –'

'We have allowed them to carry off nearly all the industries which had not been bombed. They control our oil fields. They have the best agricultural land in Austria and they take what they want of it to feed their troops throughout eastern Europe.'

'Yes, but all the same –'

'That is your slogan, Poldi, today.'

'It is not a bad slogan. "All the same with Leopold Moser!" Last night, I went to a party at the Russian Kommandatura –'

'Again?'

'I always go. I am a minister. I go to every party to which I am invited. The civil servants insist on it. If ministers did not go to parties, civil servants would have no time to themselves in offices. I go to meet the Russians. I do so whenever I can. It's essential. At all events, I met the Russian general. We drank together. He's intelligent. One can communicate with him. Do you know what I told him? "Sooner or later, you Russians will leave us. Why? Because you will see that we do not want to join either the Americans or the Russians. We want to be Austrians. *Na zdravie!* [good health]." I said, and we drank down our vodkas! They filled our glasses instantly, so I said it again. I said exactly the same as I said before. "We want to be Austrians, in the middle." And then I said for the third time, "*Na zdravie!*" We both drank. Just to rub it in. "General," I then said, "Lenin said something interesting which has a meaning for me." "What's that?" he asked, quite alive. I replied: "Lenin says you must repeat everything three times if you want to make any impact in politics!" I'm not sure he did put it like that, mind you, but something like that. And I said to Konev: "Don't you think we've moved on a bit from Lenin. Don't you think, now it's twenty-eight years since the Revolution we might just say things twice, not three times?" He laughed. You know he laughed? And we drank again. Extraordinary, isn't it?' Poldi Moser laughed too.

'*Na zdravie!*, once more, that's my technique. It's the Chancellor's technique. We're going to drink the Russians out of Austria. We'll keep telling them that they've got nothing to fear from us. We'll ask them to our parties. We'll drink them under the conference table if you like. "Vodka very good. Better than whisky." That's what I shall say. We'll survive.'

'You're encouraging,' said Alois, 'but how do we stop them doing what's on their mind, to hang on to half the country till the Americans get bored and they take the rest? It's a nice redoubt to have, Vienna. It has been a redoubt before. Only, in the seventeenth and eighteenth centuries, it was a redoubt of the West. Why not have it as one of the East instead?'

'The Russians are more nervy than you think, Alois, you see.'

'Nervous conquerors make awkward occupiers,' Alois replied, 'and what makes you think the Americans are going to make a fight for it? Do you know any Americans who are going to do anything, except complain about the bars which they themselves have stopped getting enough to drink at and which they aren't supposed to frequent?'

'We have some excellent Americans in the Salzkammergut,' said Reinhardt, 'admirable types. They have already given all power to us. Occasionally they ask us to dine. They are polite, ask us serious questions and speak excellent German. I have no complaints save one: they do not know how to drink wine. So, Poldi, after you have taught the Russians how to drink vodka, you must come and teach the Americans how to drink wine. But surely you underestimate the power play? Your thoughts are admirable. In a normal situation, they would lead to sensible politics. But the Russians are not a normal power. They are Asiatic conquerors. They are not nomads but all the same they want to spread as far as they can. What worries me about your plan, Poldi, is that it relies on personal contact. Fundamentally, that's what it is. Good men meet, drink, agree. Russians aren't like that. I have seen them fighting. They have souls but not inquisitive souls. A personal understanding cannot lead to a political one. Neither with Konev nor with Stalin. Neither with a corporal nor with a prostitute. They – they are different.' He paused and then said, 'A Russian once said to me: "We Russians are all potential spies. We would all betray our country if we had an opportunity. Any of us. Stalin downwards. Provided you make it a matter of honour. But don't offer us money. That would make it an insult."' Karl puffed at a cigarette, one of the few left in Vienna, it seemed, which were used for smoking rather than for currency. 'Something in that perhaps?' Again a pause. 'Of course, I am a Catholic banker. That's all. I am an example of Leo XIII's instructions to Catholics to make their peace with capitalism. I am doing that all the time. Peace-making, I mean, between Catholics and businessmen.'

While Reinhardt was speaking, a certain commotion was going on in the hall of the Café Teller. Frau Teller, the fattest woman in central Europe, had stationed herself by the door. Old Heini, the waiter for tables 5 to 9 inclusive, had adjusted the revolving door so that people should be able to carry in large objects. Expectation had been generated near the bar. After a few seconds, a number of British soldiers came in, carrying cases of whisky which they took upstairs. Even more interesting, two large Highlanders, with red faces, wearing kilts made their way in carrying bagpipes. They too went upstairs.

Poldi beckoned over Frau Teller. 'What's going on upstairs?'

'"Burns night,"' she muttered. 'I haven't the slightest idea what it means, but they've hired the big room upstairs for a hundred and want service till two in the morning. A big night for us.'

'Burns –?'

'Something like a festival. Something to do with Scotland. They needed a piano. We moved one in. Mostly English and Scotsmen. But one or two others, we were told.'

During the next fifteen minutes a large number of British officers came in, many in full Highland dress, and finally General Whitelegge arrived, also in Highland dress. He shook hands with Frau Teller, appeared to salute Alois and Poldi but continued upstairs. Five minutes later, General Konev and several Russian officers made their appearance. They too went up, with many a backward look. Brigadier Sheay came in, followed by the French General, General Epernay, with a number of officers, among them Colonel Marchais.

'I see you have everyone in Vienna,' Poldi called to Frau Teller.

'It is just "Burns night,"' said she, flushed with pleasure.

Bagpipes began to play in the upper room. Latecomers in British uniform ran into the café. Some civilians followed. The evening, whatever it signified, was beginning. Someone upstairs, no doubt a young officer, gave vent to one of those strange northern yelps, which often characterise upper-class Highland celebrations.

'Our liberators seem happy,' said Reinhardt.

'Konev will drink a lot of whisky and put himself in the right mood to talk to Poldi,' put in Alois.

'They will be drunk tonight,' Frau Teller said, seating herself at their table heavily. 'General Whitelegge's ADC says that there may be officers who will need assistance on their way downstairs and through the café. I had requests to put one bottle of whisky – supplied by them – by every place.'

'One bottle!' The idea seemed a mythical dimension.

'The General also asked, through the same ADC, that an open bottle of red wine should be ready for him but hidden.'

'Well, we have heard the Celts are brave. Perhaps it is that they are drunk.'

'Was it a Scot or an Irishman who killed Wallenstein?' Poldi was a student of Schiller, rather than of history.

'Butler was Irish,' said Fritz Hoyt, the political editor of *Das Tagesblatt* who had entered the café and sat down at the table, uninvited but welcome, between Alois and Poldi.

'Well Fritz, what shall we see tomorrow to disturb us in your paper? More about the new nazi movement? Or just the plan to blow up the war memorial again?' said Alois in a sardonic voice.

'Come to think of it, there's something more interesting or anyway something new,' Fritz said, leaning on the café table. 'We are going to tell the Viennese that the waltz was invented by a Russian. Yes, yes, a certain Volzinsky – hence the word. Of course it's a joke. But one of my young men has written a charming article for us, tongue in cheek, which makes it quite believable. The Russian Kommandatura passed it through their censorship and the Colonel in charge told me on the telephone this evening that he liked it. I suppose tomorrow we'll have trouble. But we are going to enjoy today. That's the motto of *Das Tagesblatt* these days.'

Not only *Das Tagesblatt*, it seemed, since the editor's last words were drowned by a gale of laughter which swept down the staircase from the restaurant.

'The Scotsmen enjoy a joke,' Frau Teller said, as she waddled about the restaurant.

'What do you think the Scots think of us?' asked Fritz.

'I don't believe that they give the slightest thought to that question,' said Frau Teller, 'they are too busy. We are just objects to be managed well or badly as the case may be.'

'They think of us as we used to think of Hungarians, as Hungarians used to think of Croats, and as Croats of Serbs. Probably as Serbs thought of Montenegrins and as Montenegrins of Armenians. Need one explain?' Alois's knowledge of racial tensions was second to none.

'It's not the same. The Scots have that special dependence on England who conquered them and whom they subsequently overwhelmed. The Scots made the British Empire. Many of my Americans are Scots.' Reinhardt's study of Scotland started from an exclusive Salzburg root.

Possibly the conversation would have taken a regionalist turn if the door of the café had not opened sharply and the dishevelled figure of Kamo ran in. He gave a look to left and right and, with his usual dexterity, inserted himself under the table cloth of the table at which Alois and his friends were sitting. Frau Teller alone of café proprietors in Vienna had table cloths, clean and crisp, reaching the floor. The newcomer was thus concealed. The speed which which this happened was remarkable. Poldi Moser did not notice that anything had happened at all.

The uncertainty was removed by the entrance into the café of four armed Russian military policemen. At finding themselves the cynosure of all eyes in the suddenly silent café they stopped, uncertain as to what to do. Frau Teller caught the eye of the leader of this group. Slowly, she raised her hand and pointed up the staircase, from which, at that moment, there came not the sound of laughter but the first notes, on the pipes, of a Lament.

"Burns night", as all who have experienced that occasion, whether in Sydney, Buenos Aires or Glasgow, is a combination of glory and gluttony. This celebration, in the capital of central Europe, three years after that territory had exploded its last ammunition dump in the face of west and east, and begun to settle down to comfortable anonymity, was a good example of these contrasts. The Russian policemen in search of Kamo were bewitched by the Lament. It was music which they had never before heard. They froze where they were and took off their caps. This disciplined response impressed the other frequenters of the café, shivering in overcoats which they kept buttoned up even inside the restaurant. Some of them had sat over a single cup of Frau Teller's coffeeless coffee for two hours or even more. They let their conversation dwindle into a whisper. Kamo sneezed. No one took any notice: not even the prophets of modern Austria who sat round his table. The Lament continued, its high-sounding calls trickling like Highland streams into the souls of all present. At the end there was a silence, shattered by a wave of applause from above and appreciative enthusiasm from the café below, including stamping of feet, which showed that, once again, Vienna was capable of high spirits.

The Russians put on their caps and, following Frau Teller's brave directions, walked up the stairs without the swagger which had marked them when they entered the room five minutes before. For Kamo the five minutes had been an eternity beneath the table cloth but an eternity well spent. The staircase up which the Russians walked to the restaurant above was fully in the sight of those in the room below – one could see the khaki-clad legs disappearing, slowly, one by one. Immediately they had gone three-quarters of the way up the staircase, and so only one quarter could be seen, Kamo emerged on the side of the table facing the door, between Alois and Poldi. Alois recognised him. There had been correspondence for months between the Austrian government and the High Command of all four occupying nations about Kamo. Alois knew him to be a scapegoat for all of them. He believed that Kamo might know something of the whereabouts of the Crown of Charles V. He was curious to talk to him. Therefore during the Lament, unobserved, he had taken out a card with his name and address on it from his wallet, and scribbled on it the words 'Go to my house in Heiligenstadt. Here is the address. Tell Klara to hide you. Await me.'

On receipt of this message, Kamo got up, gave his now famous but every time more disturbing smile at Alois and, with a gesture of thanks to Frau Teller, walked gracefully but firmly across the room, not to the door: he was too knowledgeable to leave by the front door of any building where he knew that there would be a back door. He set off to leave through the kitchen. One more nod by Frau Teller helped the waiters to avert their glances when Kamo reached the swing door which led the way to those quarters.

The Russians, at the top of the stairs, had met the Pipe Major of the 11th Scots Guards, decked out in full dress uniform. They stepped aside overawed by such an apparition. Inter-Allied disputes might be intense. Majors from Tula and Kharkov, however remarkable their survival from the wars of the century might be, could not prevent such a figure from doing what he wanted. He descended the stairs with the majesty of a Khan, bowed to the coffee house guests and to Frau Teller, and majestically walked out through the door into the Viennese night where, leaning against a lamp post where police had been hanged, at least in the imagination of Viennese intellectuals, throughout the nineteenth century, and in practice more often students, he was sick: not, as it later appeared, from the enquiry into these events, written in the best military prose, from over-consumption of "the right stuff", but from nerves as a result of his brilliantly played Lament.

The dinner upstairs had now reached a stage where, temporarily, the waiters had left the guests to carry through their rites insulated from Austrian surveillance. They had closed the door. The Russian police, having recovered from the stupefaction induced by the tall piper, continued their search for Kamo, certain that they would find their prey within. Excited by the music which they had heard, they stood back on the landing and jointly hurled themselves against the door of the upstairs restaurant. They burst in to the gathering and found themselves surrounded by Scots officers, flanked by their own commander in chief, a guest of honour. For a second, there was a silence among the lovers of Burns. But only for a second. The next moment there came a spontaneous cry from fifty well-whiskied throats of "Out, Out". Though the Russians knew no English, and had never heard the Scottish accent before, they realised what was being asked of them. They left, hurried downstairs and, for that evening, abandoned, not for the first time, the quest for Kamo. General Konev did nothing.

Thereafter an escape in Café Teller such as Kamo had managed would have been more difficult since the supplies of soap, which were provided to Frau Teller to enable her to have clean table cloths, were cut. The insistence of the world gypsy community that the stocks of that commodity in the warehouses of Vienna had been obtained by the nazis by boiling down human fat, secured from Eichenwald, a concentration camp near Linz, made that inevitable. All traceable supplies were buried in a ceremony in the Wienerwald at which the four Allies each were represented.

XXXIX

KAMO'S ROUTE FROM THE GRABEN TO HEILIGENSTADT WAS as usual of a convoluted kind: the famous suburb being north of the inner city, Kamo set off from the Graben in a south-westerly direction, down Weihburggasse and Rauhensteingasse. Kamo moved through these old streets to emerge in the Ring close to the fatal building of the Russian Kommandatura where Otto von Acht had ended his life in the snow and where, even now, a few lights shone on the top floor, a lighthouse surely to warn against rocks, rather than to guide a path. At that, Kamo left the Ring and approached Heiligenstadt through Ottakring. Guided by his unerring sense of direction, and now an expert in the small streets of Vienna, he found himself among the risky streets of Oberdöbling; dangerous since there were large houses there, spacious gardens and few people. The snow had been brushed aside in the same spirit as in the old days. There was no difficulty in walking along the pavements beneath the almond trees. When Döbling or Hauptstrasse turned into the Hohe Warte, the houses became finer but, there, there were signs of war-destruction: Alma Mahler's mother's house had been ruined. Such arcane identifications were, of course, not possible for Kamo, for whom Vienna as a whole, Hohe Warte and Josefstadt alike, was the first bazaar of the west, and the gateway to liberty.

Kamo had no hesitation in accepting Alois's suggestion to go to his house. He knew who he was: a socialist deputy dazzled by the Russians in the past but one who had seen the light during the Red Army's sweep into Vienna. He knew Alois's relation to Rüdiger. He believed him to be a man who could be helpful.

Alois's house was a nineteenth century one of two storeys, set in a fine garden. Part of the building had been destroyed by an artillery shell and was boarded up, and the rain came in. The kitchen had been re-established in what had once been the hall and one entered it immediately. Kamo knocked at the door to hear a voice asking who it was.

'A message from Herr von Acht.'

The door was carefully opened by a boy taller and younger than Kamo. It was Karl, Alois's son, who at sixteen was six feet and whose chief emotion had been fury that he had not been old enough to fight in the war. Many boys younger than he had fought, even Austrians, by falsifying their ages or by conscription in forward areas – neither of which opportunity had been possible for Karl: Achts did not falsify documents.

'Well?'

Kamo showed the card which Alois had given him. Karl read it, and stood aside to let Kamo in. Around a kitchen table there was Karl's younger brother, Poldo, and Klara, who had just returned from a concert, and was dressed smartly.

'This is a friend of father's; here's a note for you, Klara,' said Karl.

'How do you do? Please be seated,' said Klara rather formally. 'We are having soup. Would you like some?'

Kamo thanked them, sat down and began to eat.

'I do not know what time father will be here. It should not be too much later,' Klara said. 'If he is not here before we go to bed – and we shall do that soon for we are tired, are we not Karl? – you must wait for him. But – will you tell us your name? Where do you come from? You are not from Vienna, I suspect.'

Kamo considered. His instinct was not to answer such questions. People from the Caucasus, including Stalin, know that information should never be given except in return for something. So he said:

'You know, I am only passing through, so there is no need to trouble yourselves with my name. You would forget it tomorrow. As to where I come from, I am, it is true, from a distance. I did not start from home at daybreak, of that you can be sure.'

'You are mysterious,' said Klara, 'but this house is full of fairy stories – you seem to be out of a fairy story – so we shall forgive you for the moment.'

'I can tell where he comes from,' said Poldo, guessing. 'He is a Russian.'

Kamo started.

'Ha, I was right, he must be Russian, he has a guilty conscience,' Poldo continued, delighted.

'He is probably one of those Russians who don't want to go home,' Karl said to Poldo, 'so it's tactless to go on.'

Kamo listened to the unhelpful conversation with incredulous imperturbability. While enjoying the potato soup, someone who had outwitted the Russians, the Americans, the English and the French for a long time was not going to be upset by Austrian schoolboys still studying for their baccalaureat. But Klara was a different matter. He had never seen such a lovely woman. She was looking at him expectantly. Even for him it was not possible to refuse those eyes. So he said:

'Where I have come from? It no longer matters. It's where I am going that counts.'

'That goes for all of us,' said Poldo who was ambitious to be an engineer. He wanted to build bridges across the Danube, across the Rhine, even across the English Channel; bridges without number, 'but all the same . . .'

'It would be interesting to know,' Karl finished his sentence.

'It is not important,' jumped in Klara, suddenly. She smiled at him.

'Boys,' she said, 'I'm surprised at you. Don't you have exams next month? Why aren't you working?'

'We were before you returned,' said Karl.

'Well, you should go back to it.'

'But we are working *here*. Have you tried the lights in any other room? You have an electric bulb in your room. We haven't had any for months. We have to work here.'

Karl was firm. Nobody else in Vienna spoke to Klara in that way since she had returned. People gave way to her. It seemed easier.

Klara considered.

'Our friend and I will sit in the salon,' she said grandly.

'Klara, there's certainly no light there.'

'There are candles.'

'You can't be thinking of using the special reserve?'

'I think father would like us to entertain his friend,' Klara said decisively. She was already at the drawer in the white dresser where the candles were packed. 'Come along,' she said to Kamo, 'we must leave the boys to their work.'

Kamo, with a candle in hand, followed her into the drawing room. One felt that one was entering the nineteenth century. The walls were heavy with pictures, there was a clutter of possessions, and a few photographs in silver frames. Klara put two candles on the writing desk. Kamo placed his on a strong cabinet. It was dark and cold.

In a corner one could dimly make out an Austrian white porcelain stove. But it had not been used that winter.

'Fuel is so scarce,' said Klara, 'that we have given up proper use of the house. We just have our bedrooms, and the room you saw.'

For Kamo, who had lived far more roughly, such apologies were inappropriate. But he smiled.

'We used to have wonderful parties here in the old days,' Klara went on, 'those windows open onto the garden. Mother had them altered like that – so you could go to and fro from the garden as you liked. Think of it! Outside, there would be the young people; here, the old ones. Not separated artificially, but naturally. Some grand people too. I've seen Richard Strauss in this room. And his wife. He did everything she said. Outside, people might be dancing. A summer night. Think of it. We have owls here, you know. We are really in the Wienerwald here.'

Kamo smiled his approval of such pacific activities.

Klara got up. She pointed out the photographs.

'That's my mother. Did you meet her? No, I just thought you might have. She died only recently. She was beautiful when she was young. That's her too over the fireplace. By Roller. I don't like it. Rather, I didn't like it when I was a child. I thought she looked too distant. I quite like it now. Perhaps because she is so distant.' She crossed the room and brought over a silver-framed photograph. 'That's Grandma Acht. A strange woman. She had visions. She even saw John the Baptist in the Wienerwald. Think of it!' Klara laughed. She did not laugh as a rule. Kamo thought this woman odd, showing him pictures of people in whom he was not at all interested.

'But I forgot. You'd like something to drink? Russians are drinkers. We have apricot brandy. Even in the worst days of the war, we had apricot brandy. Father used to get it from the Baloghs in Budapest who made it. Would you like it now?' She was already half out of the room.

'No, soup is enough.'

Kamo was ill at ease, which was rare for him. Why was this girl, so beautiful, so fascinating, taking such an interest in him. He was rough, dirty, unshaven. A groom, now a fugitive. He thought – I must keep her in sight. She is beautiful but she may be a witch.

'Soup is enough.' She echoed him. 'Well, I suppose all over Europe these past years people have been saying that. But' – she laughed again – 'they are also saying "brandy is better".'

She sat down again on the rather small sofa next to Kamo. Still he said nothing. He smiled at Klara in his usual fashion and hoped that it would suffice as it had in the past. He was determined not to talk unless he had to. Was she probing? Possibly. He had not been all this time in Vienna to be drawn into conversation with a girl who, he could see, slid across the world as a fine skater over ice, dazzling the eye, extracting secrets, but leaving neither sound nor mark behind.

Klara apparently did not mind not having an answer and went on: 'It is almost the first time I have sat in this room since I came home.' She looked at him and still he did not speak. Kamo noticed with surprise that she seemed encouraged rather than annoyed by his silence.

'I had a difficult time after the war,' Klara said. 'I think one day I might tell you. It would take too long now. And I don't want to tell you anything less than the whole story.'

'Were you here in this house?' He could not resist asking, intrigued. After all, she was not talking about him, but about herself.

'Here? No. Not exactly. There, more,' she said nodding eastwards. 'There I would say.' She paused. 'You must miss your home. People from there always do.'

Kamo was quick to see the suggestion. Klara had implied explicitly that he was Russian.

'Where is your father? I do not want to keep you up.'

'It is nothing. One sees so few new people.' That was, perhaps, not an accurate picture of the life that Klara then lived. That winter following the Kuttenberg dance, people had started going out all the time. It was a gay time. People danced madly. To keep warm, among other things.

'My father is never late,' she went on. 'He always comes home in a government car now. Lucky man, he has joined the new aristocracy. You know him, so I needn't tell you about that, need I? Where did you meet him? Well, you needn't answer since I see you don't like talking. You absolutely needn't answer. Perhaps you even shouldn't answer. I like people who don't talk all the time.'

'I met your father in the Café Teller in the Graben.'

Kamo felt that this piece of informaton could do no harm. After all, Alois had sent him to his daughter from there. But Kamo meant to ensure that that confidence was a concession.

'The Teller! He's so old-fashioned, my father. He goes to these places which were famous in his youth. He wants to show that nothing's changed. Whereas' – she made a gesture with her hands – 'whereas everything is changed.' Perhaps she was about to continue, even to launch into a confidence. She had not even checked herself. But somebody knocked.

It was Karl. He did not understand some paragraphs in Schiller. A question about the notion of loyalty in the sixteenth century. *Don Carlos* once more. In purporting to be – briefly – the King's prime minister when he was still the friend of the Prince – was not the Marquis conducting himself falsely? How could he justify that by his own code of honour?

Karl would have preferred to have discussed it with Alois who had interesting views on honour. But he had decided to ask Klara, for whose intelligence he had a respect, though he knew nothing of her opinion of honour.

She looked at Karl. Kamo, watching her, thought that she suddenly seemed gentle. It was true that Karl, though tall, looked small there, quivering with cold, talking of honour in this large drawing room, one of the few that had survived the Russian attack.

'You should put on your overcoat before you come to this room. Honour!' She turned to Kamo, 'Honour? An interesting dish, isn't it? What do you make of it?' But she did not allow him to talk. 'A strange dish certainly,' she said almost to herself. 'I've always thought it more important than religion for most of those I know. Why is it people hesitate to betray others? Because they have a sense of honour.'

'Do you think the Marquis could behave dishonourably to the King and honourably to the Prince?' Karl did not want to abandon the texts.

'The Marquis could renounce his honour to the King and feel that he had it only towards the Prince,' Klara said.

'But then he was dishonourable in even seeing the King?'

'That was tactics,' Klara said decidedly.

'Tactics are dishonourable,' said Karl.

'No, not always. No. No I don't think that can be so,' Klara said. 'There are mitigating circumstances.'

'I do not agree, Klara. If you worked for the Allies in the war, it was dishonourable unless you renounced your oath,' Karl said.

'Don't be rigid, Karl, you can't mean you should have gone to the Führer – suppose you were a field marshal – and said "I'm sorry, Führer, I must renounce my oath. Henceforth, I shall work for your enemies!" That's silly.'

'You could have a private ceremony surely, confess to be untrue to yourself. You could have gone to a priest, to Cousin George.'

'I suppose you could,' Klara said, deflated, but then added, 'But things are simpler nowadays. It's clearer. You can have only one centre of loyalty. Either Russia or the Allies. You can't chop and change any more.'

'Isn't Russia an ally?' Karl sounded shocked.

'Not in that sense.' Klara was silent.

Kamo had listened carefully to these exchanges. Klara turned to him, her enormous eyes plainly asking for an opinion. Kamo knew Verdi's version of *Don Carlos*, not Schiller's, he knew that the last performance of it at the Opera House had been in 1935 when Felix Weingartner had been director but he did not feel that he could add much. Besides, he preferred to listen. He thought Klara to be as interesting in talk as she was in looks. Although, he suspected, she was trying to give away as little about herself as possible, Kamo believed that he had detected a lot.

The silence was interrupted by a door slamming elsewhere. Evidently Alois had returned. Klara and Karl went to welcome him, leaving Kamo in the drawing room, amid the pictures and photographs. Alois was in the kitchen, talking to Poldo. He was describing his evening: the pipes, the Lament, the Highland costumes.

'Yes,' he was saying, 'I felt that I was in the Highlands of Scotland tonight. Those people have a special quality, those Scots, I do believe. What kind of Celtic blood do we have left, Karl? Don't they tell you that at school? They should, they should.'

'Of course they don't, father, any more than your school told you such things.'

'And, Klara darling, how was the Zemlinsky?' (Klara had been to a concert performance of *The Infanta's Daughter*).

'Father, your Russian friend is in the drawing room,' Klara said.

'Oh. Oh yes, of course. I know who you mean. But is he – is he indeed a Russian? Did he say so? A strange man. Well, I'll go to him in a minute. Let me get my bearings. The ministry will need me early tomorrow. Eight o'clock. We won't rebuild our Austria by lying in bed.' He was aware that his speech sounded like a pompous stage politician's. Well, one was victim of circumstances.

'No, father.'

'Well, I'll go and see our friend. I may let him stay here some days. I think he's moving to the west. Perhaps even to the United States. One day, perhaps he'll come back rich and successful; we'll need men like that to help us, just as we're now going to help him.'

Alois kissed his children, put his overcoat on again with Klara's help, and went along the darkened passage, the boys went to bed, and Klara hummed the aria from *Don Carlos* to friendship and began to tidy the plates on the kitchen table. Alois returned.

'In the drawing room, did you say? He's certainly not there – perhaps he's gone upstairs –'

'Not there?' Klara looked determined. 'Of course he's there. Come, I'll show you. He wouldn't wander upstairs uninvited. He's polite. He's probably asleep in the corner. Come, let's have a look.'

They returned to the drawing room. Alois was shown to be correct. There was no Kamo. Alois went to the window. It was open. A cold wind blew.

'Well then he's gone,' he said. 'I hoped to help him. Perhaps that wasn't possible. Goodnight dear child. I must go to bed. Will you lock up?'

Next morning, Klara threw open her shutters to breathe the icy air looking west towards the hills and the woods. The morning was clear, cold and fine. Looking out she saw Kamo below in the chicken run. He was feeding the chickens. As she looked out, Kamo, noticing the sound of the shutters opening, looked up, waved and smiled. It is true, thought Klara, he does have a charming smile.

She watched him doing expertly what she had as a child often done with a bad will. In the clear air, sounds carried. She could hear his strange voice talking to the chickens. She went back to dress.

Then five minutes later, rather against her good judgement – who looks twice out of a window to see a refugee feeding chickens? – she gave a quick glance outside again. Alois – his car waiting to take him to his ministry – was in the chicken run with the mysterious Russian. She was startled by the sight. She could not hear what was being said but as she leant out of her window, something fell out of the ivy – a stick, a bird? – and she caught Kamo's attention. She had not intended to. Kamo turned and waved. He turned back to Alois. *Conversation in the Chicken Run*, thought Klara: a Vermeer for our day. But by the time, five minutes later, she had gone downstairs, the rural scene had vanished. Alois was in his car moving up Grinzingstrasse before turning down the Hohe Warte – he always went that way now, to avoid passing Karlmarxhof in Heiligenstadtstrasse, with its unacceptable memories of the socialist revolution whose message he now rejected – and Kamo was not to be seen.

XL

THE CONVERSATION BETWEEN ALOIS AND KAMO HAD BEEN along interesting lines. Alois had assisted Kamo the previous night for good reasons. He wished to question him.

'Well then. I hope you slept well? Where did you sleep?' he asked when he arrived in the chicken run. It was the first time that he had been there for years. 'With the chickens,' said Kamo. 'It must have been cold,' Alois said, 'but perhaps it reminded you of Russia? No, no, I didn't want to laugh at you, believe me. I really wondered.' There was a silence. 'Listen,' Alois said, 'I know who you are. Exactly. And most of your moves over the last year.'

'I'm glad. I'm not always sure of either of those things myself.'

'That I doubt. But perhaps we should just say for the present that you are Rüdiger's groom.'

'Correct.'

'And you've talked often to Alice?'

'I cannot deny it.'

'You went from her to Prince Papenlohe.'

'You remind me of things I had forgotten.'

'That is also not true. But let it pass. When you left the Prince you got various jobs, such as being a waiter at the Allied Club and an assistant at the Opera.'

'That sounds correct.'

'You became friendly with the famous Herr Börne.'

'I had not known he was more famous than anyone else. But·yes.'

'You fled from the Opera House and hid for months. I do not know where.'

'I shall tell you. I was in the Hofburg.'

'You were caught at the Kinskypalais and arrested. You escaped. You came to the Café Teller, but your purpose was discovered.'

'Tell me.'

'You were going to murder General Konev.'

Kamo laughed.

'In addition, the satchel with which you left Prince Papenlohe's

199

house – and on that occasion I saw you myself – contained a certain object much sought by the Allied authorities, and by the Austrian people, who consider it a symbol of their success in holding back the Turks.'

'I do not know what you mean, Herr von Acht.'

'You have hidden the treasure somewhere. Tell me where it is and I shall ensure you escape from this country. If you do not leave soon, you are lost. Your picture is in every police station. You are known as a dangerous war criminal, involved in a major neo-nazi movement. The signal for action will be the explosion of the bomb which you yourself have planted by the Russian war memorial. Is all this true by the way?'

'Why do you want to help me?'

'I want to be assured.'

'Any brother of Captain Rüdiger's can count on me.'

'In addition, more practically, I fear that, if you are killed by the Russians or taken home by them you will carry the secret of where you have buried the Crown to your grave, or give it to them.'

'I see.'

'You must realise your danger. You are resilient, clever, imaginative. But by now there are thousands of police and soldiers looking for you. You need my help. I am risking my career, perhaps my life, in offering to do so. The Russians killed my brother, Otto, you know, for no purpose. Tell me is there a conspiracy or isn't there?'

Kamo laughed.

'Herr Alois,' he said, 'dear Herr Alois, I am grateful to you. But why, since you are Rüdiger's brother, do you not make your offer without conditions?'

'Because I am an Austrian and need to know the answer to these questions.'

'Ah.' Kamo walked backwards and forwards. There was no room to do so in the chicken run. Then he said, 'Herr Alois, I shall consider what you have offered. We are slow-witted in the Caucasus. We live long, sometimes over a hundred years, but we need time to think. I shall tell you here. Tomorrow morning.'

Kamo made a quick leap over the chicken wire and walked to the end of the garden. Before Alois could say anything, he had vanished over the wall. Alois drove to his office saying goodbye neither to his beautiful daughter nor to his promising sons.

XLI

*W*ILLY SVOBODA WAS WAITING IN THE AMERICAN MISSION TO see an official to enable him to import a quantity of paper from Sweden. He needed a permit. When he had the American one he would have to go to the Russians, since the material had to cross the Russian zone.

Willy Svoboda had been through many jobs now since the "liberation". He had started on his present undertaking when he realised that people clearing the rubble in the inner city might like to buy a newspaper on the way home. Within three months, he had three newspaper kiosks and, within six, a shop as well. Now, as well as keeping the kiosks and two shops, he had started publishing: nothing ambitious: out-of-print classics in cheap format, and translations of English or French books, published during the war and which Austria had missed. George Acht, father no longer, "von" no more, was his adviser. It was he who advised against an edition of Goethe's conversations with Eckermann, for instance; against Hemingway's *Farewell to Arms*; but in favour of Vercors as well as Kleist. For these schemes Willy needed paper, as well as good advice.

The American colonel with whom Willy Svoboda dealt was James Macdonald who had been in OSS. He spoke reasonable German. He went through the papers quickly, giving his stamp and his signature without difficulty. When he had finished he stood up and said to Willy, stretching out his hand, 'Good, then. Good luck. It's a pleasure to help a man like you. You seem young for a successful businessman. Let me see, only about twenty-four?'

'I am twenty-one, Sir,' said Willy.

'Only twenty-one. Two shops and a publishing house. That's something. Wish there were more enterprising men like you. Like to introduce you to my commanding officer. Do you have time to meet Brigadier Sheay? Stay here, I'll see if he's free.'

Willy Svoboda rose to his feet when the Colonel did and, while he was out of the room, looked out of the window. These offices looked into the square in front of the Votivkirche. There was much activity of people waiting for, and clambering into, overcrowded trams. There was the sight of a troop of French mounted policemen riding down the Ringstrasse. Willy looked on all these people as potential customers.

Sheay came in, excusing himself as he walked quickly towards Willy. He was busy, he was in a hurry, he had been summoned to an emergency meeting of the Control Commission and he had to lead the American Mission. But he clasped Willy's hand warmly with both of his and said:

'You and I know each other. I was at Max von Acht's funeral. You're certainly the sort of man we need to encourage. How can we do it? What do you want from us?'

Willy Svoboda considered only a moment. It was, after all, what he hoped to be asked – by everyone.

'Well?'

'We need – Austria needs – you, the United States, not to give us up. That you'll never settle for western Austria alone. We need to know that you'll stay with us till the Russians leave. We don't need much else.'

'We've said all that.'

'We don't doubt your good intentions. We do doubt your staying power. You might get bored. Might get interested in some other part of the world. China, for instance. Or South America.'

'Oh hell, how can we learn what you ask of us as well as attend meetings? I've got to go now. I'll drive you into town. Go on talking.'

'A few gestures would be appreciated. You know the Russians have given us a new Opera House. Give us something new too. Give us more music. We Austrians like it. Perhaps the President could visit us.'

'Right, I'll remember. It's a help to know these things. Go on. Let's go down now, my driver's waiting.'

Sheay was easy-going about giving Austrians lifts in his official car. Other people shook their heads but Sheay took Austrians to where they wanted to go, even if it meant passing from one zone to another, which was against the rules.

'Driver,' he said, 'we're going to the meeting but first let's drive this gentleman to where he wants to go. Where's that?'

'The Russian Kommandatura.'

'Really?'

'I have to get these papers countersigned.'

'You may have a long afternoon ahead of you?'

'If you're an Austrian, you have to be patient.'

Sheay quoted a line of Grillparzer about Patience being the chambermaid of the virtues but it was not evident that Willy quite understood. The young publisher of the classics was not himself a man of letters, though his time spent with Max von Acht had instilled in him a respect for literature.

The official black car, the stars and stripes on the bonnet attracting waves of enthusiasm from passers-by, brought Willy Svoboda to the glum headquarters of the Russian Control Commission. Salutes, men at attention. Willy got out. Sheay, watching, lit a cigar which he waved at the Russians. The doors of the building opened and Willy vanished within. Sheay drove on to the meeting, casting a glance at the spot where he presumed that Otto von Acht had fallen. The snow lay there again but it was dirty: it did not have the crispness which, by all accounts, characterised the night of Otto's death. That affair had never been cleared up.

Willy found himself in a file of waiting men and women of all ages, who desired a pass with which to travel to the western zones, or who wished their merchandise to do so. All Austria was there, he told himself, the real Austria which desired to move freely, not just to go but to come back too. Willy embarked on a conversation with a short individual, obviously of military background but too old, probably, for the recent war, who wished to go to Steyr where he had been left a property by an aunt, but whose lawyers had ceased to answer letters. Another couple wanted to go to Lienz for the spring, for no good reason other than that they liked it. They were hesitating, unwisely Willy thought, as to what word to put down in that section on the form which described "motives for travel". A woman journalist of thirty wanted to go to Ischl to interview Lehár; he had returned there from Switzerland. Willy thought that he was the only entrepreneur in the file of people but then soon he saw a certain Herr Vlasovic, who had lost his land in Yugoslavia and was trying to start an antique business which had, to begin with, merely consisted of the memorabilia that he and his friends had been able to hide among their clothes when fleeing.

Willy Svoboda reached the official window. He described his business and he was ordered to go to the second floor, Room 202.

'Up the stairs, not the lift.'

'Why not the lift?' he asked innocently.

'The lift hasn't worked since 1945,' said the Russian tartly.

Willy walked up to the second floor, becoming part of a tide of persons of all nationalities, but mostly Russians in uniform, in such numbers that, for a second, he half supposed that it was part of some uprising. Various posters in Russian increased this impression.

When Willy reached Room 202, it was an ordinary office, with secretaries talking over typewriters. A small square Russian girl looked at the form which Willy had filled in, muttered "*da*" several times and took it to a colleague. That one, the same shape but slightly taller – or was it the uniform? – looked doubtfully at Willy and, after consultation with the first girl, told him, in German, that he had applied for paper which, being above a certain sum's worth, should be dealt with on the next floor up. What room? Room 302. This girl said that it was necessary for her also to stamp the form since, without that stamp, he would not even be able to get into Room 302. He would thus have in the end two stamps: one for the principle of the shipment, one for the quantity. Willy left the room and made his way back to the staircase. When he got there, he saw that the staircase upwards had been closed. There was a notice in German and Russian saying "Please use lift from this floor". Willy went to the lift-shaft. But there was no lift working. He returned to Room 202. By that time, the staff of the room had gathered together over the form brought in by Herr Vlasovic. They did not understand what "antiques" meant and, though Herr Vlasovic spoke every language under the sun, including Russian, the arguments were endless.

Eventually Willy got the attention of the second girl who had earlier helped him. How did one get to the third floor? Room 302. Ah, how foolish of her, the girl admitted, the numbers of the rooms had been changed since access to the next floor had been banned. Willy should go to Room 203. 203 not 302, did he see, an easy mistake? Where was 203? Next door, of course. Further, one could go in by an inner door. He need not go by the passage. She would show him through. Wait, she should see whether anyone was there! She went to the door, opened it a crack, and disappeared within. Time passed. The girl came out and said kindly: 'Where is your form?' Willy showed it to her. She took it. She disappeared again. More time passed. Herr Vlasovic left seemingly happy. A group of old Russian women came in, and started chattering to the secretaries. It was difficult to tell if they were travellers or relatives. The girl came back in and beckoned Willy, the impression in her gesture being that here was a real opportunity for him. He followed her, and the door closed behind him.

The room was immense, with portraits everywhere of emperors and archdukes long dead. A portrait of Maria Theresia was hanging over the fireplace. Standing behind a desk, in the distance, as it seemed, was Colonel Voronov. He peered across the room inquisitively, his vision interrupted by the mist which, in the large cold place, seeped in from the Ringstrasse. Willy Svoboda saw no alternative to walking forward.

'I did not know,' said the Colonel, 'that you were so young.' Willy came closer. 'Nor so small,' he added.

Willy smiled. He had never heard of Voronov; and, though he did know that Rüdiger Acht's wife Alice had a Russian officer staying with her, he did not connect the two.

'However,' the Colonel went on, 'I am glad to meet you. Austrian capitalists are welcome here with me. My duty is to help the Austrians help themselves. Herr Svoboda, I wish you well.'

'Doubtless you want my signature on your little piece of paper. There! Well, well, you are ambitious, Herr Svoboda. The paper you ask for would satisfy the Red Army for six months – and we need, you know, a lot of paper. It is our incurable weakness, we Russians, to write things down – I suppose, to cover ourselves from subsequent investigation. The archives may be closed, Herr Svoboda, but, you know, the archives are full.' Voronov smiled. There was a pause. Voronov got up and walked towards a window where he stood looking out, his back to Willy. A long pause.

'I understand,' said Willy after a while, lamely.

There was another pause.

Willy coughed. Voronov finally returned to his desk. He pressed a bell. A waiter in white coat and dark trousers appeared. An Austrian probably, thought Willy.

'I hope you are in no hurry? I would appreciate a talk.' In a hurry, thought Willy, would it count if I were? He's had me standing here already for ten minutes. 'You will have noticed, Herr Svoboda,' Voronov continued, 'that we Russians are never really in a hurry. We have time, you know. It comes of being great conquerors. No other nation, not even the British, have beaten so many other nations into the ground. Into the mud of Asia. Think of it. It is the reason for our timelessness as well as our self-confidence. Our mistake was to have abandoned Alaska to President Johnson eighty years ago. There would have been a jumping off place indeed. Think of the border incidents we could have manufactured. Cynical, I suppose you consider me. No, realistic. A Russian realist.'

While he was talking, a table, laid with glasses and silver on a white cloth, was carried in. Two chairs were placed by it. Waiters were coming in with bottles and dishes under covers of silver plate. Without fully realising what was happening, Willy found himself sitting down opposite Voronov at this inviting table. Before him there was a yellow glass, a blue glass, and a red glass, as well as a small vodka glass.

'Ah, you notice my glasses. The glasses of the Allies I call them. They are for the United States, for England and for Russia. The little vodka glass, the most important of all, is for Austria. As for France, I have forgotten her. Comrade Stalin does not always consider France a power any more. Drink your vodka, little Svoboda! It will do you good. After you have made your fortune in paper, you might turn over to wines and spirits. Even more compelling for the bureaucrats of the future than paper. By then, the Austrian phoenix will have been re-born and will require much sustaining in my style. I am an excellent prophet, you know.'

The Colonel raised his vodka glass to Willy and drained it: it was instantly refilled by one of the waiters.

'I know you are not at ease here with me,' went on Colonel Voronov. 'That is to be expected. But do let me tell you that I am prepared to help you in every way that you need. There, take my card. It has my telephone extension on it. Direct to me. Any time.'

'Do you entertain many people here?' said Willy at last, feeling that he should say something.

'Only those with large vision,' said Voronov, liberally helping himself to caviar which he then ate with a spoon.

Waiters were filling the coloured glasses with different wines, including pink champagne, in the yellow glass of America.

Willy Svoboda was unused to wine. The difficulty was that the slightest sip led to replenishment.

'How long do you think the Allied occupation will last, Herr Svoboda?' enquired the Colonel. 'After all, we Russians –'

Willy was learning to distrust this phrase.

'After all, we Russians have our own business at home; we cannot wait about here looking after you for ever.'

'I thought you said your business was conquest,' said Willy.

'Oh, but Herr Svoboda, not in Austria surely?'

'Many people suppose it is so.'

'How very interesting! They think we are here for ever? How curious! But what about you – you represent the new generation. I have never met a man so clearly of the next generation as you. Indeed, I cannot imagine anybody more new than you. What do you think?'

'I think – well I think for some time –'

'Yes, yes, but what is some time?'

'Five years?'

'Five years. I think that is an underestimate. But perhaps we can cut it a little. Perhaps we can cut it to five years: you and I.'

'I and you!' Willy Svoboda was frightened at the thought that he might have any such role. 'You, certainly, but what have I to do with it?'

'Look, Herr Svoboda, this will not be the last time you will need a permit to carry your paper across our lines. Forget my candour –'

'What has that to do with it?'

In his confusion Willy was drinking several glasses too many.

'We need to collaborate closely, you and I,' said Voronov in a voice of empire. 'For you to get your permits, we shall have to talk often. We must examine everything. Leave nothing unconsidered. You will make money. I can see that. Everything about you shows that. There are people in Russia, too, who are like you, even though we have abolished capitalism. But to make money involves a social responsibility. In the context of Austria today, that means you must talk to me. There is an advantage. I can open every door to you. Fast. And in return –'

'Yes, in return what?'

'In return, everything: you will tell me, little Svoboda, everything. Everything that's in your mind. You know who I am I suppose? No? I am chief of our intelligence in Austria. All I need from you is conversation. Regularly. Brandy? No? I see that you are abstemious. The champagne is foul. It is Georgian. The brandy is passable, little Svoboda. It is French. Go on now, talk a little! Tell me things. I am all ears.'

Willy Svoboda considered.

'The food, for example. How is it? Can one survive on these rations? What do people think of us? Is it all hatred? Don't be frightened, I can understand if it is. But I must know. What are the Americans trying to do here? Are *they* getting bored? You went some weeks ago to a big aristocratic party. I know it. It was in the Kuttenbergpalais. You stayed at a party till three in the morning. Are you, perhaps, comtemplating exogamy?'

'Exogamy?'

'Marriage, with someone who can bring you status. How do you enjoy the company of the beautiful Klara? You have seen her since, I know that too.'

'If you know so many rather unimportant things, why do you need to talk to me?'

'I have to know *more*. My appetite for information is extraordinary. Cigar?' Voronov leant back. 'Please do not make any confusions. You are talking to a Russian – a Russian imperialist if you like – not a communist. I, at least, can make the distinction. The poor western Allies spend their time puzzling over which part of us is using the other. We know that because we have our eyes everywhere. We see their despatches and telegrams on the subject as soon as they are written because we have friends among them. Do I make myself clear? I use every means – communism, capitalism – even you, small though you are, Herr Svoboda – to advance Russian power. You think I am teasing you with my candour? I assure you I am not. It is my technique. Others have other techniques. Now, dear Herr Svoboda, do not panic. You will not jump out of the window, like poor Herr von Acht. He was a bad choice. You have ambition. He did not. You are not like that anyway, are you? You are a new man, while poor Herr von Acht belonged to the past. The future is for us. Our co-existence. *A nous maintenant!*' Voronov raised his glass.

Willy understood most of what Voronov was saying. He was being recruited: not exactly as an agent. But as an informant, in return for services. And what exactly, if anything, was Voronov telling him about Otto von Acht? Had he been working for them? If only he had not drunk so much wine! Now his only aim was to leave the Kommandatura as quickly as possible. He would accept whatever was asked of him. Perhaps he would go to the west. He might talk to Mr Sheay. But he had to get out of where he was. That was essential. He looked at his watch.

'Excuse me but I am late.' he said. 'The lunch was delightful but I have to go, and I have never eaten so well. All the same, I have to go, I have timetables.'

'Of course, Herr Svoboda.' Voronov rose, extinguished his cigar, looked up at the Empress Maria Theresia in her portrait, said 'I wonder what she would say to a divided Austria,' and started to walk Willy across the large room to the door.

'Next time, Herr Svoboda, you will invite me. Shall we say a week today? No – a fortnight – to give you time to get your paper. You will telephone my staff to tell me precisely where. You do not need to go to any trouble. A café would do. The Café Teller on the Graben is a good choice, isn't it? Upstairs? A table by the window? We will talk again, Herr Svoboda. Until then.'

He stretched out his hand. Willy felt that that imperial Russian hand was about to possess him, but he shook it. The Empress Maria Theresia, whatever the difficulties even in 1742 (Willy remembered from Max von Acht's lessons), had always shaken hands in order to observe the niceties. He expected Voronov would walk along the passage with him but he did not. He stood by the door of his room – was it his room? – and watched while Willy, slowly, not without dignity, made his way to where he knew the head of the stairs to be. He had half thought of turning and waving when he got there, but he did not, and anyway he would have been unseen by Voronov – at least, by any ordinary method of vision – for he was quickly swallowed up amidst the crowds of applicants, both humble men and grand, who desired a pass to cross the line of the zones.

Willy had to admit, when he reached the Ring, that he was pleased to hear the sounds of an English military band in the Volksgarten.

XLII

THE FOUR ALLIED DELEGATIONS SAT AROUND A SERIES OF tables so arranged that each of them were at right angles to one another. In the centre, there was an open space. The Russian and American delegations were both large, the first the larger by half: 'That's because they need so many security people to watch those doing the watching,' Sheay always said. The room in the Hofburg, famous in the old days, was white and gold with mirrors set into the panelling, and a fine chandelier had recently been re-established there after spending the war in a cave.

Many such meetings had already taken place. They were long and drawn out. The need for everything that was said to be translated into two other languages slowed the pace. What folly it had been in 1945 to allow the French to proclaim themselves a great power! That delayed everything!

As a rule, the western Allies had the habit of meeting beforehand. There were also some parties at which the western leaders met – those, too, usually led to discussion as to how to deal with their Soviet allies.

'When you invite the Russians, either they don't come,' said General Whitelegge one day, ill-advisedly, to the correspondent of the *Daily Herald* (who published the comment), 'or they come with a team of people whom you can't feed. Sometimes they say they must bring their wives, who turn out to be Austrian tarts. Makes it difficult.'

The accurate reporting of these remarks created less of a scandal than might have been supposed: possibly because the English word "tarts" had been translated in the German press as "sweet dishes" which irritated the Austrians but pleased the Russians.

No one, except the Russian commander-in-chief who had called for this meeting knew why the wartime Allies had once more been gathered around the green tables of peace. Perhaps the commander-in-chief would not know what he had to say till he had read the speech provided for him. Both he and his staff had seemed to constitute the spirit of bonhomie to all who saw them arriving, taking off their coats and hats, and shaking hands with their acquaintances on the Allied Missions: in exchange for

'Ah, Mr Bykov, how good to see you,' there would be a friendly 'Miss Mackenzie, good afternoon, good afternoon,' or *'Cher monsieur le colonel, I hope you have good news from Paris.'*

On this occasion, the French General was the chairman. He had the merit of pace. He brought the meeting to order on this Wednesday afternoon with an elegant tap of a gavel which he had had brought with him from Paris. No central European gavels for a general of France!

'Le représentant de la Union Soviétique, ayant demandé la session, tient la parole.' The General of France glared at the Soviet commander-in-chief while the Russian interpreter translated. The Soviet General read from a document placed in front of him by a dark bespectacled gentleman sitting behind him. Sheay did not remember seeing that individual before. Perhaps there had been a change in the police's representation in Vienna?

The Russians seemed now plainly to be making a bid to extend their zones so as to cut off their parts of Austria completely from the rest of it. Russian Austria would be tied to the rest of the countries of the east. Doubtless close links with the tottering economies of those nations would be established. Sheay knew his Russians. The inconvenience, so far as they were concerned, was Vienna. The western Allies had their place there. Perhaps the Soviets believed that they could be hounded out. Terrified out. Just as their colleagues were trying in Berlin.

General Popolaev did not say all this in so many words. On the contrary, he was concerned about the further extension of the new nazi movement, its tentacles throughout the American zone, the many sinister meetings which had been held in the British zone in deserted farmhouses – meetings often held under the noses of the British and American commands. One would not like, General Popolaev commented, to suppose that those commands were consequently in connivance. But if they were not, the commands were more lax than they had permitted themselves to be in the Great Patriotic War. Now, as during the war, vigilance was essential. Perhaps it was even more important in peace than in war! Now, what was to be done?

The first thing, said the Russian, was to take no risks with meetings in farmhouses in Styria. One might have to increase one's forces if the current levels had been allowed to drop below a certain figure. For its part, the Soviet Union had cut its forces since the war. But it would always ensure that it had enough men to carry out its international duty. The second thing was to study innocent organisations. For example, "everyone knew" that there had been formed a society of friends of the Russian fatherland in Salzburg. What could sound more attractive? But that society was not a society in the normal sense. It was a skeleton for an anti-Soviet, monarchist, White Russian army. It was being staffed by ex-nazis, fascists, black arrows, iron guardists and so on from all of eastern

Europe. All the riff-raff of the east was converging on Salzburg. He, General Popolaev, was convinced that Brigadier Sheay knew nothing of this. But there were Americans in Salzburg who certainly knew what was being prepared. Of course, such "pygmy operations" could not cause a pin-prick in the side of the Soviet Union. The Soviet Union, generous to its friends, was tough to its enemies. A neo-counter-revolutionary White Guard in Salzburg was a laughable development in many ways. All the same, it was bad for Austria. Bad for the United States for turning a blind eye.

Certain measures were necessary. One had to be "vigilant". All the crossing points between the zones would have to be manned with double strength. No one, no one at all would be allowed to pass the zonal frontiers unless they had all the appropriate documents. There would be no exceptions. That would apply to western soldiers in uniform as to Russian. There would be no more Pöchlarn incidents (a reference to what had happened on the Schubert express when an American soldier challenged by Russians had shot two of them dead). Sometimes, kind-hearted Russian officials had allowed people to pass without papers. That fatal tolerance would stop. All consignments of merchandise would have to be examined to ensure that there were no arms and no persons hidden within. General Popolaev was aware that this would cause hardship. Delays usually did. He was known to his staff as an impatient man. Nevertheless, in this instance, delay was essential.

Finally, the search for war criminals had to be intensified. It was no use pleading lack of staff. All Austria should be enrolled in a crusade against those who between 1938 and 1945 had taken the whole world on a journey to the edge of Hell. As a good communist, General Popolaev said he did not believe in the Christian hell. But he did believe in Hell on earth. The nazis had taken Austria along that path! One had to be alert. There were criminals everywhere. One should be ruthless. Austrians should be encouraged to inform on their families, if necessary.

There were three important things to note, the General continued. First, though many people found the Austrians charming, they had been enemies only a short time ago. The Russians knew this better than anyone since they had captured many Austrians at Stalingrad. These included twelve Austrian generals. One should be on one's guard against charm. The battle against charm was the first engagement of the new awareness. Second, one had to guard against injustice. Many Austrians had become nazis in order to save their skins. They might be bad men but they were not necessarily so. Those who were not might be reintegrated in the body politic easily ("into the communist party", whispered an adviser in the American delegation, Stephen Sparks, new enough in Vienna to believe in old jokes). Thirdly, and this was the most important, there were war criminals of other nationalities "loose" in the country. These included vipers who had been born in the Soviet Union but ensnared by the nazi gangsters. Some could be found in the camps for displaced persons in the west. Some of them had been "spirited away" to play a part in neo-nazi revivals. These included the most dangerous swine in the world. One had to be on one's guard against them. There was no crime of which they were incapable, in their insane desire for destruction. They might even seek to blow up the war memorial to the Soviet Union in Schwarzenbergplatz.

Having spoken, General Popolaev sat down heavily, tired by his rhetorical exertions. After wiping his forehead with a handkerchief, he looked round hopefully. The French General, however, had concerted his tactics with the Americans and English, much as he might in principle dislike it, and merely said in a quiet voice:

'At the request of the leader of the delegation of the United States, I propose a half-hour adjournment. Is that acceptable?' It was.

The three western Allies retired to a small waiting room on the floor below the conference hall. General Whitelegge, Brooks Sheay and the French General huddled round a table with their political advisers leaning over them, while other delegations stood around aimlessly, there being not enough chairs to seat them or any attempt to draw them into the discussion. Tatiana had her two hundredth argument with Harry Mercer, her still inexplicably pro-Soviet colleague – a conversation which had all the characteristics of a stroll through familiar country, since each of them knew how the other would respond: Tatiana was anti-Soviet, so much so that Harry Mercer had once (unknown to her) complained to his then superior that she was inappropriate to translate the Russian of the present Soviet leaders since the Russian language had changed since the Revolution. Major Stern, of the American delegation, was wondering why the question of the Crown of Charles V had not been brought up by General Popolaev, along with all the other material which he had heard before. Then, he thought, the Bolshies have perhaps got it themselves! Colonel Jean Georges Marchais, now doing everything for the French delegation, politics as well as art, was at the only telephone in the room, his gauloises cigarette at an angle more raffish than normal. He knew that his general wanted him to be available to discuss what had been said: so he had to delay a call which he had arranged on that charming old lady, Thekla von Acht, who had invited him to tea with her that afternoon. But the telephone did not function.

In a few minutes' time, the western principals agreed that the best thing to do was to leave the task of replying to General Popolaev to another occasion. That necessitated a return to the conference room: and that in itself took half an hour. The threat to the West in Austria might

not be so serious as it was in Germany. But, all the same, General Popolaev agreed, after a consultation over his shoulder, with his new dark-
haired assistant. So the peacemakers were at last able to get to their cars
for the journey over the pockmarked roads of Vienna to their offices. As
they drove off, they could observe a column of overcoated communists,
of all ages and heights, and of both sexes, marching along the Ringstrasse
towards them carrying banners which they could identify as calling for
new action against old fascists as for many of the other things which, by
an amazing coincidence, had been spoken of in the meeting by General
Popolaev.

'You can just see how on the ball the Russians are,' said Harry Mercer
to Tatiana Bezhukov. His tone of voice did not make clear whether he
was intending to be ironic. She rather thought that he was not.

XLIII

AUNT THEKLA, SPIRIT OF SURVIVAL, HAD PEOPLE TO TEA ONCE a week. That day she had spent a longer time than usual preparing it. It was the first time that Colonel Marchais would be coming to the house. She was keen to make it a success. She knew that, for the French, a meeting at that hour had no gastronomic significance. It was the talk which counted. Tea was the only English invention tolerated by the French. So she found a packet of Chinese tea and dusted the stand for cakes which she knew the English used. Her mother had brought it back from England in King Edward's day. The sight of it brought back memories of the days when her family used to go to England every autumn. But Aunt Thekla was not sentimental, so she did not indulge herself much in that way. (England, she had heard, had changed for the worse even before the war. She had no desire to return.) Unfortunately, she had little to offer the French colonel to eat. She had black bread made in the country. She cut the bread so thin that it seemed as if it were an English tea in those old cucumber days that she had enjoyed as a girl.

All these things prepared, she sat down to wait. Her book was the autobiography of Goethe's youth, a volume which she was not enjoying but thought that she ought to read before she died. It did not seem impossible that, in the next world, she might encounter the Great One. She would feel better if she were able to say that she had read his entire work. But she had no sooner sat down and opened the book when she heard the door of her apartment open, and shut. That could only be her Russian lodger, who had taken over her own bedroom where he slept with her ex-maid, the odious Gisela. (Gisela's equally odious child had gone to live in the countryside with his grandmother.) "The Russian", Major Golunsky, had been a silent guest, like Alice's Colonel Voronov; though even more quiet and reserved. Once, she knew, he had taken Gisela to an Inter-Allied party, and had introduced her as his "wife" – a phrase which had done the girl no good, since she was assumed to be a prostitute from Mariahilferstrasse. Aunt Thekla preferred Major Golunsky to Gisela. Once, two months ago, she had seen the suspicion of a smile on his heavy, not unhandsome face: and once, only recently, she believed she had heard a sigh, not unlike a human sigh, emanating from his be-ribboned, khaki-covered chest. His unexpected re-appearance at this house, when she was expecting Colonel Marchais, was inconvenient, but not completely disagreeable.

But there was more to it: the Major had not only returned. Thekla could hear strange sounds. Could the Major be weeping?

Out went Aunt Thekla into the hallway, a forceful Teuton, to observe the splendid (if not unprecedented) scene of a Slav in tears. The Major was in the passage, sunk into, more than seated on, one of her chairs, his hands clasped over his face. His head shook and his whole body heaved with emotion.

'Well, well,' she said to draw attention to the fact that she was there.

The weeping continued.

'Well, well,' she said again, kindly. 'What is the matter, poor man?'

Privately she thought, if Gisela has left, I shall not weep with you, thought she doubted Gisela's capacity to inspire emotion. Major Golunsky went on crying.

'Come on, man,' Thekla said, 'it doesn't do much good and it's embarrassing.'

These solid words reminiscent of the English nanny had no effect, though the Major knew German and though Aunt Thekla had spoken slowly.

'What's the matter?' she asked again.

The Major straightened up.

'I have to go home to Russia,' he said simply.

'Well, that's nice, you'll see your family.'

'No,' said the Major, 'all of us who have been in the West have to serve two years in a camp north of the Arctic Circle.'

'Why?'

'For having been in the West. I shall never come to the West again. It is over.' Although the Major had ceased to weep, he looked the picture of desolation.

'Stay in the west! Go to America! Go to Australia! There are steppes unlimited there for the traveller.' Aunt Thekla was on uncertain ground since her knowledge of that continent derived from Rolf Boldrewood's *Robbery under Arms*.

'I can't. I have to go back.'

Aunt Thekla knew he was right. Children of the East could not survive in western pastures.

'Well then,' she said, 'have some tea.'

The instruction, for such it was, awoke the Russian to courtesy. He accepted. Aunt Thekla and Major Golunsky went into the sitting room and sat opposite each other.

'Very kind,' he said.

He looked round the room in a wondering way, almost as if he had never been there before.

'Very beautiful,' he added. He ate a sandwich.

That was not strictly true. Aunt Thekla had a few good pieces of furniture left but the room, dimly lit by a single bulb, gave the impression of a storage depôt, as she knew: the natural consequence of having, late in life, to collect in a flat the best products of two houses which her parents had had before 1914.

'Major Golunsky,' she said, 'you would like to take back something to remind you of Vienna. Choose what you would like. I have too much. Take a picture, or one of those boxes. What about a china egg? Perhaps not a photograph,' she added harshly as the Major looked acquisitively at a picture of her father in military uniform in the Austro-Prussian war.

'I should like – a box,' said the Major, after a time.

'Of course, which?'

'That one.'

He pointed at a papier-maché Russian box, whose cover depicted a sleigh with two figures dressed in a murky green. It was something in which she had no interest.

'Please take it,' she said. She was a little disappointed in his taste.

'Thank you,' he said, eyes shining.

A knock came at the door, and Aunt Thekla went to open it. Late, the gallant Colonel Marchais was apologetic. He explained the hastily convened meeting, the crowds of communists who had protested, and said that, even then, there was a meeting in the Schwarzenbergplatz, in front of the war memorial. Aunt Thekla put her finger to her lips:

'My Russian,' said she, 'has eaten your sandwich.'

The way she whispered this, the hint of conspiracy, the impression of discomfort, moved Colonel Marchais to merriment. Aunt Thekla, remembering that two minutes before she had been trying to stop a major of another occupying power from weeping, saw a different joke and began to laugh also. The Russian Major, hearing the noise, emerged into the hallway, clasping his box. He could not prevent himself from joining in: laughter was as rare with him as tears. Thus Aunt Thekla's tea party which now moved to the drawing room took a different turn to that which she had anticipated.

The two officers sat in silence. Colonel Marchais made polite conversation with Aunt Thekla. Major Golunsky said nothing, though; by now his face was as inscrutable as it had previously been glum. Little by little, however, he began to join in. Aunt Thekla turned from French to German, which Colonel Marchais managed adequately, though with a bad accent. Golunsky had never been in Paris, but he knew of its pleasures. He recited the names of streets of which he had heard as if they were verses in a prayer: Champs Elysées! Place de la Concorde! Rue de Rivoli! after each name he gave a sad, understanding smile, as if indicating the regret of the Orient that it did not yet stretch as far as the Occident.

Colonel Marchais, moved by the recital of these names, sat back in his chair. He wondered where the litany would end and at what point it would reach the Impasse de la Visitation (6e) where he had those "*quelques pouces carrés*" without which he would feel naked but with which he could face any future, however dark. Major Golunsky's list reached the Avenue Foch. Suddenly he stopped and, with his face once again anxious, begged a private word with his colleague. Marchais and Golunsky retreated to the hallway. Aunt Thekla shrugged her shoulders. Tea was not what she had planned but why should she be surprised? There was nothing more to eat.

Thekla turned to the sage's autobiography and picked up the story, at the point where Marie Antoinette, not yet fifteen years old, is described passing through Strasbourg on the way to Paris.

In the hallway, Golunsky made an astonishing statement to Marchais. He was, as he assumed Colonel Marchais was aware, a major in intelligence. Colonel Marchais nodded. He did not know, and had not heard of Golunsky beforehand. But he believed that an appearance of omniscience is wise to leave behind. The Major continued. He had received instructions to return to Russia. He believed that he had much to contribute to the west. In short, if it could be arranged, he would like to go to France. Precisely to Paris. The Champs Elysées! Or the Avenue Foch, for example.

'Yes, yes,' said Colonel Marchais, horrified at the prospect of another geographical tour of the same dimension such as had occurred before. Then he said, in a matter of fact tone, as if such things happened daily, 'You want to come over?'

'Come over?'

'Join us. Come across. Yes. Well, one can arrange it. Whether Paris would be right at first, I'm not sure. Perhaps a provincial town?'

'That doesn't matter.' Golunsky's eyes now gleamed. 'I shall bring material. A great deal of material. I have access to identities of all the Soviet agents in Vienna. For that perhaps I could live – in the Avenue Foch?'

'It is possible. When are you supposed to return to Russia?'

'A week tomorrow.'

'I see. Of course. Then – should we say the Café Teller on Saturday?'

'Too obvious. I'd like a suburb.'

Colonel Marchais considered.

'Could it be then in Neuwaldegg? Just before you reach the Wiener-wald. There is a tram, No. 42. The last stop. On the left as you get off there is a restaurant, the Restaurant Päiva. It is an appropriate name. It is open on Saturdays. Be there with your list.'

'Shall I bring the list of agents within the Allied Missions? That could also be.'

'Within the Allied Missions?' Colonel Marchais hid the excitement in his voice.

'Yes, of course. We have laid eggs there too. Good eggs, long ago.'

'Bring the lists. France will be ready to receive you. At the Päiva.'

He stood up and saluted.

'I salute a brave man,' he said, though that was not what he was thinking. He wondered whether it was true that under every Russian there lurks a traitor; or whether it was only those who allowed themselves to be invited to tea, or to the Avenue Foch, who might be so suborned.

XLIV

*K*AMO SPENT THE DAY IN THE CENTRE OF VIENNA. WHEN IT was disputed later where he had been, he gave various versions each more fantastical than the one before. Photographs subsequently shown by the Soviet High Command to the western Allies suggested that a figure resembling Kamo was seen close to the Soviet war memorial: but these photographs were not of much quality. It was unclear whether they had been touched up. But, between morning and evening, he had not been in Heiligenstadt and he was observed by a neighbour returning with a satchel just about dusk – a short time after Klara left the house, attracting the attention of everyone, to go to dine in the city.

When Kamo returned to Heiligenstadt there were only the two boys there, who again were settling to their homework. Kamo assumed the task of feeding the chickens as he had done that morning.

At a quarter to eleven o'clock Klara returned from the Opera, driven by Captain Hudson of the British Mission. Roger Hudson escorted Klara to the door but was not encouraged by her to follow into the house: 'My brothers are studying; I have to see if I can help. Thank you for an enjoyable evening.' Klara smiled but her eyes had grown cold as she easily disengaged herself from the Captain's embrace. She shut the door in his face and went to her room. About a quarter past eleven, Alois returned from his fourteen-hour day at the ministry. That day he had read several briefs on the Russian demands to take over tracts of farmland in lower Austria which suggested that they wanted to ensure a source of food for their armies. Alois had fallen alseep almost as soon as he had left the office. He awoke to get out of his ministerial car and say goodnight to his driver. He went to bed and back to sleep instantly.

At midnight Klara left her room silently. The house was asleep. She was still dressed, but over her clothes she flung a fur coat that belonged to her mother. Her dark hair fell in ringlets over its collar. She looked radiant. She made her way, mostly by memory, since the night was dark, to the ivy-covered summerhouse where, in her now scarcely remembered childhood, before the Anschluss, she and her brothers used to read, or to pretend to be in, fairy tales. There she had first met the dog with eyes like saucers, the wise Soforina, of the Italian story, and the boy whose parents had wished to dispose of him in the forest. There too she now found Kamo. There was a candle.

He did not seem surprised to see her. A man who had survived as a hunted being in a civilised capital did not permit himself the luxury of astonishment.

'So,' he merely said. 'You.'

Klara said nothing but spread her coat over a dilapidated bench and sat down.

'You have a message for me? From your father?'

'I do not have a message from my father.'

'If you do not have a message from your father, from whom do you have a message?'

'From no one.' She hesitated. 'Is it true that you are going to America?'

Kamo considered. 'I am trying to,' he said in the end. 'It is not going to be easy but I will probably get there. Earlier I thought I should stay until the return of Major Rüdiger. I have now heard that he is dead. So my obligation is dead too. I have,' he confessed uncharacteristically, 'just one thing left of which to assure myself. That depends on a conversation with your father. Tomorrow morning. Here.'

'Here?'

'In the chicken run, actually.'

'I see.'

Kamo continued doing what he had been doing before she had entered: which appeared to be sharpening pencils. Klara looked at him curiously. Pencils were not easy to come by. He smiled; that strange smile which had carried him from Stavropol to Vienna and which had so easily charmed Klara.

'Take me with you.'

Kamo turned to her, startled.

'You want to leave Vienna? But you are happy here? So sought after. I know you are admired by everyone. Loved, I should say.'

'All the same, I have to leave. I cannot now explain why. But I must leave because, because I am caught. I am in a trap. I must escape. I am not on the run like you. But I am also in danger all the time. So I must go to America. There is no other place. No other way.' She knew that she was not quite clear in what she was saying but she had not spoken so openly since her return to Vienna.

'But you need not go to America as I am going. I am an outlaw. So I must take the outlaw's route. But you are the daughter of a minister. He is part of the future here. He can get you to America. It would be easy for you to have a musical scholarship. I know how to get there. There are more routes to capitalism than there are to socialism.'

'I would not be allowed to go like that,' said Klara simply.

Kamo never argued with, nor questioned, people. He allowed them to make statements without challenge. He was too wily to take anything at face-value. He realised that Klara had made her proposal seriously, but had no idea why she had done so. He did not permit himself speculation about her motives. Of course, he distrusted her. To a man from Stavropol, a proposal such as Klara had made was open to several interpretations. The most obscure explanation was the most likely. The most simple – that she merely wished to go to America to escape from the poverty of postwar Vienna – was the most improbable. He was not insensitive to Klara's beauty. It was impossible to be so. But she belonged to the future so far as he was concerned. The future was for him an unknown valley. He had many passes to cross even to see it.

So he said (and he had never said anything so open to sentimental interpretation), 'It is better that I go and come back for you. Later.'

'That is impossible,' Klara said, 'I must go now.'

'Why?'

'They – they are following me. I cannot do anything without them. They – terrify me.'

'Oh,' said Kamo.

He knew whom she meant. "They" were – they had to be – the horsemen of the east.

'Then you must escape certainly. But you cannot escape with me.'

'You are sure of it? I might help, to forge – the – link.'

'There is no need for forgery. It is already made.'

Klara felt defeated. She began slowly to cry. Kamo had no experience to let him cope with such a state of affairs. He sat down beside her and patted her head, as if she were a child. He knew that his survival depended on restraint. Survival depended on suspicion, not sentiment, certainly not on compassion. Human beings were less reliable than horses. Much less reliable than dogs.

He moved away from Klara and stood up. She did not move and sat, vulnerable, looking into her lap, her beautiful face curtained by her hair.

'You were in Russia?' Kamo finally asked, the master of his emotion again.

'Yes.'

'Where?'

'Many places. How can I remember?'

'What happened?'

She was not often asked directly.

'I still can't talk of it. On the journey to America, I could tell you. I could have told you.'

He said nothing. Curiosity for its own sake was not one of his virtues.

'Do you miss Russia?' she feebly asked, surprised at his refusal to follow up his own questions.

'Of Russia I know nothing. I only know my village.'

'Where?' she asked tonelessly.

'Near Stavropol.'

'Is your family there?'

'No. The village was murdered after I left.'

'Who by?'

'By their own people, for God's sake.'

'Why?'

'We were a religious village. So we greeted the Germans as liberators. We expected to be free. We carried ikons. My father was among the leaders of the procession. All my brothers were there.'

'How many?'

'Seven brothers. I had three sisters.'

'Had? They were all killed?'

'Yes. By the Red Army. The village had to be punished for its treachery to the Soviet Union. It's understandable. We *were* traitors to *them*. Not to ourselves.'

'The Germans had treated the village well?'

'Honourably.'

'That was not always so, I think?'

'It was so with us. In other places they killed everyone too. With us it was different. I was lucky. I was found by Major Rüdiger, your uncle. I was with him for two years. It was – an education.'

'How? The fighting?'

'No. What I learned from Major Rüdiger. About life, about people, about right and wrong. I shall avenge him.'

'Are you sure he is dead?'

'I have heard it said. As my village is dead. I was told that it was singled out for "exemplary treatment". Not only were the inhabitants shot. The livestock were killed too. The houses were set on fire. Afterwards, tractors were sent there to destroy the debris and to extinguish any suspicion that there had ever been a village there. I – I didn't believe it. But then the war came back and we re-occupied the place where it had been. There was nothing there. So. I have told you my story. It is a short story. But' – he came forward, leant over her, and there was excitement in his eyes – 'it is going to be longer. In America I shall become rich. Wait and see. Then I shall come back. For you.'

Klara had to smile.

'Would that not be a long time? Won't you be old?'

222

'I don't think it will be long,' Kamo said.

There was a prolonged silence.

Klara made a last attempt to alter the course of events. Her mind was confused. The complex fate which had led her to where she now stood, next to this both primitive and subtle Asiatic, in the ivy-covered summerhouse, obliged her to do so. She had never previously, in Vienna at least, been refused what she asked. She leant forward so that the candle-light lit her face and laid her tapering fingers on his hand.

'What actually is your name?'

'People call me Kamo.'

'But what is it really?'

'I am what people call me.'

'Kamo, then. It would be good for you as well as for me if you took me with you. I could make people like me. I am strong. Our struggle would bind us. I could make you love me.'

'But you do not know, cannot realise, how I go,' said Kamo angrily. 'I move as dogs do and live worse than they do. I cannot – you could not – no one could – live as I am able to. You would die of cold or exhaustion. You – you are too beautiful to travel so. You *are* Vienna. However often you ask, I shall say "no", "no", "no" again.'

Klara straightened, her face calm, her eyes once more distant. She picked up her coat, turned and left the summerhouse without a backward glance. On returning to the house, she went to the kitchen. There was no one there. Schoolbooks and saucers. She took the telephone and dialled. Someone answered instantly. She spoke in a low voice two or three words. She went to bed and slept soundly.

XLV

THE MORNING WAS BEAUTIFUL, COLD AND CLEAR. KLARA awoke at first light. She looked out at the garden covered with frost. There was frost on the lime trees and on the walnuts; on the refugee's cottage in the garden of their neighbours: on the houses leading west to the Wienerwald; on the roof of the ivy-covered summerhouse.

In the street outside, a large black motor car slid quietly to a stop, so discreetly driven that one hardly noticed the intrusion. Such cars were a common sight at that time, anywhere between Vladivostok and Berlin: an essential part in the way that human nature was controlled. Such things were, however, not usually seen so early in the pre-dawn of Heiligenstadt. Klara pulled a shawl round her shoulders, trembled, but did not move. A second car followed, equally discreet. When, in the misty morning with just a hint of pink to be seen, but no more, in the east, she observed the doors of the black cars silently opening, she herself gently closed the shutters. She even slept again, without dreams.

Klara awoke to knocking on the door.

'Yes, yes, who is it? Father? Wait, I'll come.'

She rose, found her dressing gown, opened the door to Alois, already dressed and ready for another fourteen hours' work in the ministry: a countless chain of minor actions which make up the life of democratic man in a place of responsibility.

'He did not appear.'

'He did not appear,' Klara echoed, innocently, since she was still drugged with sleep.

'Kamo had arranged to meet me in the garden. He did not come.'

'He suspected a trap?'

'Why should he? I was going to help him get away.'

'Perhaps he got away first and didn't need you.'

'It is incredible. I knew what he was going to do. I had it worked out. I do not understand.'

Klara did not speak.

'It's strange.' Alois seemed lost in thought.

There was a noise below:

'Herr Alois, Herr Alois!'

It was the housekeeper, Theresia, an elderly woman who came in the mornings to clean for the Achts. Alois went down. Klara dressed and followed. Alois, the two boys and the housekeeper were in the kitchen.

'Klara,' said Alois, 'Theresia says that when she came early this morning she saw them take Kamo away.'

'Who? Who is "they"?'

'The State Police! Not the Russians!'

'But isn't it better that it should be the State Police?'

'Not much. The State Police is full of communists. He won't stand a chance.'

'Can't you do something? Father, you are powerful. You can do something.' It was Karl, not Klara who spoke.

'I can only try. Theresia, once more. Please tell us what you saw.'

'I came especially early,' said she, 'to bake bread, and I saw it. They came and took him with no difficulty. The young man who was helping with the chickens. It was a surprise, I suppose. Whoever he was, one doesn't like to see a man caught like that. Not even if he'd been a murderer, one doesn't like that. It must have been at daybreak. Before the sun rose. Yes, certainly, before the sun.'

By now, the sun was up. The blue of the sky was clear. The frost was beginning to melt but it would not go far. There was a scent of winter sharpness, even in the kitchen.

Alois put on his coat.

'You will do something for him, Father,' Karl pleaded.

'Certainly. What I can.'

'Should I come with you to Vienna?'

'No, Karl. Your school is the most important thing that any of us is doing today.'

XLVI

*P*OLDI MOSER HAD RETURNED FROM ANOTHER DRINKING session with the Russian commandant. He enjoyed the national drinks of all the Allies: it was no hardship for him to have to test the brandies to be found at the French Mission; the bourbons of America; the drambuies of the British. He was not specially covetous of the vodka, slivovitz, or obstlers to be found with the Russians. But he drank a great deal. As a result, his body was in disrepair. Diplomacy meant drink and repetition of one's remarks: a repetition that the Allies would, in the end, leave Austria to itself; that Austria could be safely left alone; neither Russia nor the Americans need worry. Austria might be useful as a neutral. Think of Switzerland.

At all events, Poldi was back in his ministry by six that evening. One of his secretaries, Dr Wertheim, had been to the British Mission to try and wheedle some extra food ration coupons for the Moser family. Many of the windows were cracked, the new glazing for the office had not come, and it was draughty. Poldi settled down to an uncomfortable evening of paperwork. The snow was falling steadily. There were no snow ploughs – the Russians had taken them the previous year: a theft which inconvenienced the Soviet Mission in Vienna more than anyone. The streets would soon be impassable. Poldi expected to sleep in his office though his house was only twenty minutes away, in the Strohgasse. Alois came in unannounced.

'Well, this is a surprise. A real pleasure.' Poldi Moser liked Alois. Before 1946, he had looked on him as just another of those silly upper-class socialists who had no idea what life was like and had helped to lead their country into a mess. But things had changed.

'I have a request,' said Alois.

'Go ahead.'

Alois described how, early that morning, his brother Rüdiger's groom, Kamo, had been caught by the Austrian State Police in his own, Alois's, garden: how that corps, being run by communist officers, had handed him over to the Russians; how at the moment he was in a transit prison which the Russians had in Leopoldstadt; how the Russians were accusing

him of seeking to blow up the Russian war memorial in the Schwarzenbergplatz, associating him in the same conspiracy which had led to the
suicide of Otto von Acht; and that he was likely to be transferred to the
Kommendatura in the Ring the next day.

'Looks as if he has a choice of being shot behind the neck in Russia or
pushed out of a window in Vienna,' Poldi said.

'Not necessarily. He is a Russian. In normal circumstances we could
do nothing for him. But because of all these extra charges, they may just
have overstepped the mark.'

'Are they all trumped up?'

'I am convinced of it. The accusation of neo-nazism is just an idea to
get opinion to side with them over some new dishonourable action.'

'You've come a long way, Alois.'

'We can talk of that later,' said Alois. 'All the charges are trumped up
except for one which they seem to have forgotten about. Probably keeping
it for tomorrow.'

'What is it?'

'Kamo is the man who either stole the Crown of Charles V or knows
where it is.'

'Really!' Poldi was interested.

'That's why we need to catch him. Save him from Russia and so save
the Crown for Austria.'

'What do you want me to do?'

'Come with me now. Claim him personally as a criminal against Austria. Say we are shocked at the plan to blow up the war memorial. Pretend
we accept the possibility of it. Then, insist on investigating. The accusations will be seen to be worthless. We shall have a substantial moral
victory. It will be the turning point.'

'Why do you need me?'

'Because you are the Minister responsible. You have the confidence of
the Russians. Because as a matter of fact, you like Russians, you talk to
them, you drink with them.'

'Right,' said Poldi Moser, 'your car or mine?'

'Both,' said Alois decisively.

'What about the Allies?'

'We need not worry about the English and the French. I have told
Brooks Sheay what I'm doing.'

'What did he say?'

'He wished me good luck.'

'On the telephone?'

'On the telephone.'

'It's listened into. I suppose you know that.'

'Of course. But by the time that call is interpreted, we'll have succeeded or failed. The benefits of bureaucracy are always with us.'

The two Ministers, accompanied by secretaries, drove to Leopoldstadt. Alois and Poldi Moser sat at the back of the first car, Poldi's secretary in front: Alois's secretary sat in the second car. Two Austrian police, on Poldi's insistence, drove in a third car: Poldi Moser knew that if things of this sort are going to be done at all, they have to be done on a substantial scale. These cars were old if large, and made their way over the rough and pitted streets with difficulty.

'What exactly did Sheay say to you?' Poldi asked Alois to repeat himself.

'He wished me luck.'

'Nothing else? He could have done more than that. We may need more.' Poldi said gloomily, as the two cars came to a halt at the traffic control point on entering the Russian zone.

'Nothing,' said Alois.

'I can see that we might need to go to Leopoldstadt. But *tonight*? Is it necessary to go tonight? We might get there and not be able to get back,' Poldi worried. But he did not stop the car.

Nervously, he brushed the window pane as clear as he could. The snow was falling heavily.

They eventually arrived at the grey cement building which the Russians had set up as a transit prison.

The cars drew up at the Russian building. Two corporals, from deep in Soviet Asia by the look of them, gazed in surprise at the Austrians. They had not seen such a delegation before. They were accustomed to seeing Austrians arriving in the back of Soviet vans. The sight of ancient motor cars in which the Emperor Franz Josef might have travelled caused them to salute the men who got out.

'They're saluting the cars, not us, you know that, Alois, don't you?'

Poldi was in the habit of making jokes when nervous. Alois was not. He frowned.

Alois asked to see the commandant. He spoke with determination. He and his friends were shown to a waiting room on the right of the passage. A door stood open as they passed. He observed men of the Soviet military bureaucracy in a brightly lit room, busy placing papers in one basket and taking them out again. It was seven o'clock. But Russians work late.

Two officers came in unexpectedly soon. They were intelligent. They spoke excellent German. They announced it to be an honour to have two Ministers with them. They desired to help. They listened to Alois's questions attentively. Yes, it was true that the neo-nazi, Kamo, was in the building. It was also true that he was going to be transferred to the Kommendatura: when, precisely, they did not know. Certainly, he was going to be charged with the crime of planning to blow up the Russian

228

war memorial. Fortunately, there was no difficulty about securing the evidence: he had been arrested with a sufficient supply of dynamite to blow up a barracks, much less a delicate piece of modern sculpture. Did the ministers care for a cigarette? Coffee? No, well, they need only ask. Now, as to their suggestion that Kamo should be tried by the Austrian courts. That was an original suggestion. The matter would certainly have to be considered. Perhaps the ministers would like to discuss the matter with Colonel Voronov. As it happened, the prisoner Kamo would be taken to Colonel Voronov shortly. If he were going to constitute a *cause célèbre*, as appeared likely, it would be better to place him in more salubrious circumstances, such as the Kommendatura, where he could be easily seen by the world press. The two Soviet officers saw no difficulty in the ministers accompanying Kamo. Not, of course, in the same vehicle. Kamo would have to be guarded – protected from attempts by his movement to free him. But all the same, they could go in a cortège.

Alois said that he would like to see Kamo. The two Russians looked at each other. Why not? It would be arranged immediately. They apologised for the condition of the prison. After all, they had inherited it from the Germans. They had not built it to measure.

'In the Soviet Union, you have better prison architects?' asked Poldi Moser.

'Outstanding. Quite excellent.'

One of the officers left to summon a corporal. In a few minutes, the corporal re-entered to explain that Kamo was in a nearby office. The two Austrians were free to see him for a few minutes. But afterwards he would be transferred to the Kommendatura.

Alois and Poldi were led to another room out of which an internal window led into a further room. The Russian corporal knocked on this and pulled it aside. The head of Kamo appeared.

The conversation was brief.

'You betrayed me,' Kamo said, 'therefore we have no more to say to one another.'

'I? Of course not. How could I?' Alois expostulated.

'Who else knew that I was on your property? Never mind, I shall soon be free and, before I leave Austria for America, I will know on whom to take vengeance.'

'This man is your best friend,' Poldi Moser interpolated.

'If that were true, I should be lost,' said Kamo. 'The arrangements which you mentioned are now no longer a matter of treaty between us,' he added, 'and now there is nothing more to say.'

'Don't you realise that you are about to be transferred to the Kommendatura? We will follow you there –'

'That must be an excellent drive on a night like this,' Kamo said, with a flicker of his old smile.

'Even if you do not wish it, we are determined to save you,' Alois said. 'We can deal with responsibilities afterwards.'

'Forgive me if I do not accept your remedies as promptly in the future as in the past,' Kamo commented.

At this point the corporal intervened. Kamo's escort was ready and, if the ministers would permit it, would now set off.

The journey began across snow-bound Vienna. Two Russian cars led. Kamo was in the second of two vehicles. The other car, as it would seem, was full of corporals and policemen. The three Austrian cars followed. The main road was open but every side street seemed blocked by snow. From time to time, people were seen seeking to move stranded motor cars which were held by the snow as if they were nuts in a cake.

It was Poldi Moser who first spoke.

'Do not be in any way discomfited by that conversation,' he told Alois. 'It was to be expected. Russians always make their prisoners behave unpredictably.'

'There was no sign of maltreatment.'

'No. I agree. But they must have sown that doubt in his mind. That is the kind of thing the Russian imaginative genius has gone into since the Revolution.'

Alois remained silent, shocked.

'You are sure of it?'

'Certain. When we reach the Kommendatura, I shall take the lead,' said Poldi. 'As the responsible minister, I shall insist that he is an Austrian prisoner to be tried by Austrian courts. We shall alert the press. We shall see. We, not they, will make of it the *cause célèbre* that they do not want.'

Unfortunately, the *cortège* of cars became separated in the Opernring. The consequence was that, when the slower Austrian cars reached the Kommendatura, the Soviet vehicles which had preceded them had already arrived. Kamo and his escorts had gone. Poldi Moser and Alois made their presence known. But it took an hour of repetitious explanation, to different groups of officials, before they reached Colonel Voronov. He received them in the room in which he had only a short time before entertained Willy Svoboda.

'Very well,' said he, 'how can I assist? The prisoner in whom you are so interested is being well looked after and is at this moment dining. Few Austrians can be enjoying tonight so good a dinner as he is having. Legally, that is.' The Colonel smiled.

'It is hospitable,' said Poldi Moser 'for the Soviet High Command to take such care of an Austrian prisoner.'

'How, "Austrian"?' asked Colonel Voronov. 'I think it is clear that the subject was born in the Soviet Union.'

'But his crime is the Austrian one of seeking to explode the Soviet war memorial in the Schwarzenbergplatz. Hence he must be an Austrian prisoner, since not only is the war memorial a Soviet gift to Austria, but it is in Austrian territory.'

'Yes and no,' said Colonel Voronov, warming to the discussion. 'It is true that the land is Austrian. Yet the memorial commemorates Soviet heroism and the nobility of Soviet soldiers. An offence against it is one against the Soviet Union – and it is action against the cause of international peace.'

'It is also an Austrian case,' said Poldi, 'and I shall explain why.' He then began an intricate argument which confused Alois but to which Colonel Voronov listened with attention.

'Even if it were as you say,' he said, 'we should bring the prisoner to justice, because of his war crimes in the Soviet Union. It is an immutable law of Soviet justice that the most serious crime is considered first, before the less serious ones.'

'In Austrian law, there are many rules which consider in what circumstances an accused charged with several crimes is to be tried. Very often, it is not the order of committing the crimes which determines what should be done: it is the order in which a man is indicted. Thus if you kill a man, rob an old woman in the street and buy foreign currency illegally, it could be that you could first be tried for the currency offence if that were the crime for which you were first charged.'

'Still,' contested Voronov, 'Kamo is a Russian. The crimes he committed in Russian territory were committed during the war. If Russian law is like Austrian law – I am unfortunately not a lawyer – he should be tried in Russia first for he committed the crimes there first. Thereafter he would serve his sentence in Russia. Then he could return to Austria to be tried here. He could receive further sentences. You laugh, Herr Minister. Surely this is not a laughing matter?'

'The thought of returning to Austria after a death penalty in the Soviet Union is ridiculous.'

'That is not a laughing matter,' said Voronov, 'but as I understand it, your view is that the prisoner should be charged here before he is charged in the Soviet Union. It would be as well of course that the Austrian public know of the attempts on the war memorial. Incidentally, they will be informed in general terms in tomorrow morning's press. We have already given an ample press release.'

Alois and Poldi began to feel that there was nothing which they could achieve. At every point, Colonel Voronov held trump cards. Above all, he had possession. Poldi intimated that they would leave, consult, and return the following day at eleven in the morning.

Voronov bowed: 'Always at your disposal, Herr Minister. I have tomorrow morning a hundred appointments. They will, naturally, be pushed aside to make possible the continuance of our discussion. Herr Doktor von Acht,' he said to Alois, 'it is once again a pleasure to see you. I shall accompany you down. No, I insist.'

And the Colonel escorted them to the front hall of the Kommendatura: an action which he had not been known to have taken before.

XLVII

THAT NIGHT, GENERAL WHITELEGGE WAS GIVING A RECEPTION at Schönbrunn for his Allied partners. The Austrian Cabinet had been asked, and all the members, despite the hardship of seeing the Union Jack flying there, had accepted. But the heavy snow, and the fact of Schönbrunn being on the outskirts of Vienna, seemed likely to make the party less successful than the gatherings at the Hofburg given by the Russians, the garden parties given by the Americans or even the enjoyable receptions, on a smaller scale, but with good bands and excellent champagne, given by the French. Further, though General Whitelegge's Olympian dignity and reputation as a combat soldier gave every assembly which he attended a sense of occasion, his quartermaster had a unique gift of turning everything which he organised into, as Harry Mercer put it to Tatiana, "the last night of the voyage on the Queen Mary, cabin class". There were benefits: although the same *dramatis personae* which had graced other parties in liberated Vienna were expected, and, though a band continuously played waltzes by the Strausses, people felt less on parade than in those other places.

Colonel Marchais, after consulting his general, had decided to tell the English about his conversation with the Russian major, Golunsky. France made a habit of passing on such information at social occasions. French policemen thought that noisy parties were more secure than offices; the spoken word more discreet than the memorandum. Marchais accordingly arrived more punctually than was his custom. He found most of the British Mission in the centre of the ballroom at Schönbrunn preparing themselves for the ordeal of meeting two hundred non-Englishmen by toasting each other in gin and water. Tatiana, present in some administrative capacity, came up to ask the Colonel what he needed, to whom he would like to speak, and so on.

The Colonel said that he had to talk with General Whitelegge and hoped that it could be arranged quietly. But, he said, he would be grateful if he could also talk with Colonel Livingstone. He had some point of art history to discuss.

'Oh, what a pity,' said Tatiana Bezhukov, 'but that isn't possible.'

'Really. Is he ill?'

'No, no, he's returning to London. Got a wonderful job. Director of the Worthington Gallery.'

'Really?'

'He was pleased.'

'Not a person I admire.'

'Excuse me, Colonel Marchais?'

'It's a complicated affair. So we shan't see him again?'

'Well, not as a Colonel I don't suppose. And that's not the only change there is. You've heard about Brigadier Sheay?'

'I hadn't, actually.'

'Yes, well, he's going back to Washington.'

'Is he indeed? Why?'

'They say he's going to work with the new American intelligence service. Interesting, isn't it?'

'Intelligence? Well that is rather curious, I agree.'

'So not many of the old guard will be left here, Colonel Marchais.'

'Quite, quite.' His eyes were abstracted.

'What about you, Colonel? Will you return to Paris?'

'I do not know. But, surely, is that not Colonel Livingstone over there?'

'Couldn't be. I'm sure he was leaving for London tonight.'

But it was. Aircraft had been grounded in Vienna because of fog.

Colonel Marchais was unable to resist a conversation with the future director which afterwards, sitting in his room overlooking the great courtyard in the Louvre, he had some reason to regret.

'I hear I have to congratulate you,' he began.

'Yes, yes, it is very cheering,' said Colonel Livingstone. 'I personally had no idea,' he said, 'but my work here is done. We have set in train the restoration of all that needs restoring. As for the rest –'

'You will be happy in London, of course?'

The tall colonel looked down with surprise. Small talk was unusual with the French, especially with Colonel Jean Georges Marchais. There must be something more to the enquiry than there seemed.

'I think London perfectly frightful,' said Livingstone, 'but I don't mind admitting that I like the Worthington. You too will return soon, I imagine.'

'Possibly. Meantime, it's a tragedy the Crown still remains lost. I thought we were onto something a few months ago.'

'It *is* a tragedy. But I'm sure we'll find it. *You'll* find it. It must be your, *French*, mission to do so.'

The conversation continued in this vein till Colonel Marchais said:

'I must be off. We have news of a member of our staff who's gone over to the Russians. Terrible thing. Most embarrassing. Just as well General de Gaulle is no longer Prime Minister –' He wished to observe how Livingstone would react.

'Embarrassing. Clever of you to find him out. Caught him red-handed, did you, handing over documents in the street?'

'No,' said Marchais confidentially, 'it was more complicated than that.' He made as if to look round the room in a discreet way and he said, in an undertone, 'Betrayed. By a Russian boy. One of those distasteful sexual matters.'

'Oh quite: one of those distasteful sexual matters. Boys, you said. Oh dear! Do I know the man?'

'I don't think so. But, you, Colonel, heard no rumour of this?'

'None at all.'

'That's a relief. We certainly don't need the press.'

'The last thing you need,' heartily agreed Colonel Livingstone, of whom *The Times* correspondent in Vienna was a close friend: he had seen him across the room only two minutes ago.

'Still, we have to work now on the assumption that the Russians have their antennae everywhere, I suppose.'

'Of course we do,' said Livingstone. 'You know I'm very friendly with the Russian command here. Always going to their parties. Drinking with them. Looked on it as part of my job. I like them too.'

'Of course.'

'But one must be careful. One can't talk to them beyond a certain point,' said Livingstone, and looking the colonel straight in the eye, so much so as to shake his confidence in what he was going to say to the general.

At this point, the indefatigable drinker of toasts, Poldi Moser, approached. Colonel Marchais made his excuses, and sought out Tatiana. Poldi, his visit to Leopoldstadt notwithstanding, was raising his glass high to Livingstone.

'Could you get me to speak with General Whitelegge now?' Marchais spoke so urgently that Tatiana, in conversation with Captain Hudson, choked on her gin and orange.

'Of course,' said she and fled, reappearing quickly to beckon Marchais forward.

Poldi Moser had nothing to say to Colonel Livingstone and, having said 'Cheers' and 'How are you?' several times, without any hint of an interrogative or any obvious wish for an answer, was about to move away, when Livingstone drew him aside.

'Shouldn't tell you this. But there's something you'd like to know, Herr Moser.'

'Yes, Herr Colonel, there are many things I'd like to know from you.

Where is our famous Crown for one thing? Then, where shall we have our Bruckner concert next year? It has to be in Vienna. You would give good advice.'

'Good advice, I can give you. You know, Herr Moser, I leave for London tomorrow?'

'Not for long, I hope?'

'Yes, for good. I am to take over our greatest gallery. It is a great challenge. The Worthington Gallery. I shall enjoy it. I shall be the director.'

'Many congratulations, Herr Direktor, it is a great honour. One which will bring you back to Vienna often, I know.'

'I hope so too.'

Poldi Moser, exhausted, tipsy, but vigorous, had seen two Russian generals at the corner of the room. It was his job to salute them, to drink with them, to *Na Zdravie!* them, to reassure them. He was about to make for them when he felt Colonel Livingstone's arresting hand firmly on his arm.

'Herr Moser. You are interested, as I am, in the fate of the Crown of Charles V?'

'Quite right. All Austrians are.'

'The first suspect is the mysterious boy who was Rüdiger Acht's groom, is that not so?'

'I believe it is so, yes, I believe so,' he said, by now waving at the Russians.

'You have been interested in the boy, I think?' He now had Moser's attention.

'You seem to know a lot, Colonel, but the answer is yes. How do you know?'

'Well, we are a global power, you know,' sententiously said Colonel Livingstone.

'I understand,' said Poldi Moser, who did not, but one born under the Habsburgs did not question the claims of others to empire.

'You might like to understand something else. If I were not leaving for London tomorrow, I might not be able to tell you, but the information I have is this. Your man will be taken to Russia by the train leaving the Franz Josef station at five in the morning. He will be alone in the second carriage, or box car. It will be nailed up so he can't escape if the train stops. I'd get your friends to have something on the railway near Klosterneuberg if I were you. There ought to be a lot of snow about.'

'Thank you, Herr Direktor. How did you manage to learn all this?'

'Oh, just something I picked up. Oh! Good evening, Count Gmunden. Nice to see you back among us. I need not introduce you, I'm sure, to Herr Moser.'

Poldi Moser shook hands politely with the elusive nobleman before going to a telephone to talk with Alois.

Colonel Marchais had his conversation with General Whitelegge.

'A grave accusation, Colonel,' said General Whitelegge. He drummed his fingers on the little console table where they sat. The band was playing a mazurka. 'A grave accusation. Particularly since, as you know, Colonel Livingstone has not only had artistic functions here. He has always had a broad series of responsibilities.'

'Including intelligence?'

'Not excluding intelligence,' said General Whitelegge. 'He has already formally left us. I am no longer his chief. I do not think that at the moment he has a chief. Or will have one. I shall have to consider what you say most carefully.' He had to speak loudly because the strains of the mazurka made it difficult to hear otherwise: 'Which day did you say that you would receive the Russian? Six days from now? Well, take care about that. That could go wrong. You should have a lot of men there. There's nothing like numbers when you're in a tight corner.'

XLVIII

AT DAWN, IN THE SNOW ALONG THE RAILWAY LINE TO MOSCOW, the train took a long time to arrive. A small oak wood separated the line from the road which runs from the little town of Wagram east towards Gänserndorf and the Hungarian border. Wrapped in heavy overcoats and feeling both foolish and apprehensive, Alois and Poldi sat in a black car on that road. The snow was falling. Poldi's chauffeur kept the engine running to avoid freezing. The loneliness seemed so absolute they might have been in Russia itself. No difference of culture could distinguish that wood from the thousands of such woods which began less than four hundred miles away to the east, in what was now Russia, at Lemberg. If there were farmers in this neighbourhood at Gänserndorf, they were asleep, for to sally out at first light from their houses on a day such as this would have been pointless.

Four members of Poldi's ministry had cut down a tree in the heart of the wood. It lay neatly across the railway track. The ministerial woodcutters had taken trouble to deform the ends of the trunk so as to disguise the fresh cuts, and snow had covered the stump. Ten Austrian policemen had followed Alois and Poldi, in a small black maria, such as is used for carrying criminals to gaol. These police had been chosen from the American zone of Vienna and screened to exclude any communists. They were stationed one hundred yards down the track where they believed the second carriage might stop.

They had precise instructions. They were to attack the box car with axes the moment the train stopped. Two men would leap into the carriage, seize Kamo, hand him to two others who would hurry him to Poldi's car and put him into the back seat between the two ministers. The driver, who would have his engine running, would set off instantly – all this before the presumably sleepy Russian military establishment in the first carriage would know that anything was amiss. On the way into Vienna, Poldi and Alois would extract from Kamo the information about the Crown which they needed, and arrange for him to be taken to the British zone whence he would travel to America. The police would return to their bus and go to their Vienna headquarters along the same road by which they had come. Alois, Poldi, Kamo and the bus would be in Vienna before any alarm could be given. Trains such as the one which they were going to attack never had telephones, while the nearest village, Gänserndorf, was too far for swift communications.

All these preparations depended for their success on the accuracy of Colonel Livingstone's information which Poldi and Alois had no reason to doubt but which could either have been designed to mislead or been based on a misunderstanding. To the Russians, Poldi would claim that the attack had been made by "bandits". Who exactly the "bandits" were would be investigated. Of course, no one would be fooled but honour would be satisfied. Afterwards, Poldi would use the illegal transfer of Kamo to the Russians by the state police as a pretext both for dismissing the communist chief of the State Police and for carrying out a thorough, long-overdue purge there, dismissing all the communists in that body. The stakes were thus high.

Events so elaborately prepared as these do not ordinarily occur without dislocation. It was so with the assault on the 0505 Vienna to Moscow train that morning.

The train was late leaving Vienna. When first sighted, a distant spot along the snowy track, it was ten minutes behind time. A message about its approach was taken back to Alois and Poldi by one of the policemen. The chauffeur prepared to start. Alois opened the door, ready to leap out and have Kamo thrust in. They waited. Both ministers knew that their careers in politics might depend on the success of this enterprise which suddenly appeared to them both as foolhardy. They heard the train, they heard it slow down, they heard it stop. It seemed that there followed a long moment of absolute silence.

Then Kamo did come out of the wood. Wearing only a shirt and trousers, he ran out like a deer: but alone, with no policemen escorting him. He was making for the road somewhere behind Alois and Poldi, and he was moving fast. Poldi leapt from the car and followed Alois, already running after Kamo, calling. Kamo continued on his way, the space between him and his pursuers widening. He reached the main road, and set off at a loping pace, more like an animal than a human being, for the village of Wagram. Poldi called, Alois called, to no avail. It was as if Kamo had not seen them. No doubt the sight of a black car filled him with disagreeable memories. Poldi jumped back into the vehicle and ordered the chauffeur to give chase. They started well enough but the snow held them up for several minutes. As the chauffeur struggled, a hapless victim of new technology in a central European winter, the wood suddenly seemed alive with men. Not just the police and Russian guards, there were others: a motley crew of civilians and, judging from

239

the behaviour of the police and guards, it became obvious that Kamo was far from being the only prisoner on board the 0505 train.

What happened when the train stopped was only heard by Alois later. The policemen were in position near the second carriage although further removed from it than they had hoped. They did not need to break in, since, before the train had even come to a halt, a heave by the men from within broke open the wood of the box car. Instead of there being only one man in that carriage, forty, maybe sixty men, all Russian, or Ukrainian, or Georgian, or Lithuanian, all, as the Russians claimed, Soviet citizens, who, in a last effort, had seized this chance, like Kamo, to avoid shipment home, tumbled out and into the snow. They had been "displaced people" but had been found, registered and were being dispatched by the Soviet repatriation commission. But here was a chance of liberty. They took it. Out they fell into the snow, Kamo only the fastest among them. Soon ten or so desperate men furious but silent were descending on Alois and Poldi. Their energy was endless, they seemed to symbolise life itself. Behind them were Austrian police and Russian guards. But what did that matter, here was a car which they might steal, here even was a chauffeur whom they might force to drive away, here were two solemn-looking gentlemen who might even help.

Poldi Moser had to act. He commanded that his car should be pushed out of the snow.

'And, you know, it is surprising,' said Poldi later, recounting the story, 'even a refugee Russian finds orders irresist-ible! Irresist-ible! They all gathered round, prisoners, police, Russians, Austrians, heaved and moved the car back onto the road.'

Having united the men in the labour Poldi declared himself the minister that he was. He proclaimed the displaced Russians "his" prisoners. While he was speaking, a number escaped. How many, one never knew. Probably the police didn't know either. Those who remained were marched to Wagram. Poldi wished to hold them there. But he, an Austrian, had no rights over Russians unless they had committed crimes in Austrian territory. At least he had given some of these persons a chance. What more could one do? Nothing really. It was all underhand, but that surely is what politics is like. All one has is just a chance of giving people another chance.

'And Kamo?' Brooks Sheay (to whom this story was told) was asking.

'Disappeared.'

'The devil!'

'I wonder if he is.'

'How did you know he was on the train?'

Poldi explained. Brooks Sheay said nothing. The tale had ambiguities. Poldi then said that he and Alois proposed to make a public complaint over the way the police had behaved, to insist on a purge of that police and to disperse its senior officers to new appointments, in other parts of the country. He regarded this as a test of the government. The communists had to be shown to have over-reached themselves this time. The question was, could the Austrian government count on support by the United States? That was fundamental. If the Russians thought that the United States would turn a blind eye, they would not listen to Poldi nor to any other Austrian. He, Poldi, had to have assurances.

'We'll send the boys round the town with a band, sure,' said Sheay.

'No, with tanks.'

'Well.'

'It's essential.'

'I'll see. I'll contact Washington,' he said, 'I think it will be alright. Washington ought to know.'

'*Tell* Washington,' Poldi said, 'that this time it's essential.'

Sheay's next visitor was General Whitelegge. It was General Whitelegge's habit to discuss major troubles with the Americans on Tuesdays. This was a Friday. Something had clearly happened.

'You know,' said the General, 'my training in matters of security has been shattered.'

'Really?'

'My training has been based on one maxim: don't trust the French. Now, what would you do with a Frenchman who came to see you and told you that a member of your own staff was working for the other side?'

'My inclination would be to throw him out of the window,' said Brooks pleasantly.

'Certainly. And then?'

'I'd examine him and see what his interest was in telling me. I'd like to have some backing, of course, for the tale. Not just gossip.'

'Exactly. So you'd do nothing immediate?'

'Not sure. I suppose it isn't the tall intelligence colonel with an artistic cover?'

'How did you guess?'

'Something occurred to me. Tell me the story.'

Whitelegge did so. He had not come across such an accusation before and was distressed. He had not told London; and, indeed, was thinking of not doing so. After all, the man concerned had gone back there. He had been only a temporary officer. An artistic gentleman, a wartime soldier. There was no proof against him. There were only accusations.

'Did the Frenchman say anything else?'

'No, not especially,' said General Whitelegge, 'except that his source was coming over in a day or two with a list of others who are working for the Russians.'

'Let's hope our names aren't on it.'

'Indeed,' said General Whitelegge. 'It would make things most confusing.'

'I've just had Leopold Moser here,' said Sheay.

'The hard drinking conservative?'

'Precisely. Although, General, there are times when a capacity to drink has importance.'

'I haven't served forty years in the British army to have to learn that in Austria, Brigadier.'

'Anyway, Moser was here. But he and his socialist chum, Alois Acht, got some useful information from your chap.'

'Livingstone?'

'Yeah.'

'Well?'

'Real information. Hard fact. The truth. What do we make of that, General?'

Sheay gave General Whitelegge an account of what happened at Wagram.

'Just as confusing as Napoleon's battle of Wagram,' remarked General Whitelegge. 'I could never decide who really won that battle.'

'It's a pity that Livingstone went.' Sheay considered. 'What about Marchais? What's he doing?'

'He thinks his informant is genuine. He's proud of him. The French are finding a flat for him in Paris, I believe.'

Again Sheay considered. 'When does his man come over?' he asked.

'Saturday at 2100 hours,' said General Whitelegge.

'Well I think we must just wait. Whatever happens then will determine events.'

'If he comes over in a fit state,' said General Whitelegge, 'perhaps he'll tell us more about Livingstone.'

'If he's genuine, Livingstone's a dud. Is that right? But how about this? We know Livingstone gave Moser information which turned out to be mostly true. And useful. So what light does that shed on Marchais' man?'

'A murky light, indeed,' said General Whitelegge.

'Of course, the information given by Livingstone just might have been genuine because they wanted to confuse us. Because they knew Marchais' man was coming over. That's why they filled up Kamo's carriage with other returnees. Of whom one or two were probably working for them.'

'In that case will the Russian come over?' asked the General.

'Not unless he was caught since the time he had tea with Marchais. And turned.'

'In which case, the list he will bring will be a different list to what he would have brought before.' The General was entering the spirit of the thing. 'Will Livingstone's name be on it?'

'Certainly. Now he's leaving the British army he's disposable.'

'But the Worthington Gallery's not a bad job for a spy. Quite a useful headquarters I should think. Better than some of the nightclubs they run.'

'Not bad. All the same, the price of pictures does not quite equal in value the British draft for an Austrian peace treaty.'

'I don't see that we can do anything else but wait and see. If Marchais' man comes over, will we see him? You, me? Our people? Or will he be whisked to France?'

'I don't know, but I imagine they'll be in a hurry. And whether the man's a fraud or not, they'll do all they can to get him to France quickly.'

'So the situation is this: if he comes over, he may be right or wrong. If he doesn't come over, he's right, and probably dead, and Livingstone's wrong. Therefore Livingstone's information, even if right, came to us for the wrong motive. That motive could be to discredit Marchais' man. It could be something else. We just don't know yet. But we probably will next week.'

'Next week.'

The two officers took a deep breath.

'I think we've cleared things up nicely,' said Sheay, smiling.

'I don't ever remember a more confusing conversation,' said General Whitelegge.

Sheay went to show the General out of his office. They walked to the head of the staircase. Sheay became aware of the figure of his secretary hovering in the background. When he turned from saying goodbye to the General, she came forward:

'Sorry to interrupt you, Brigadier.'

'You're not.'

'There was some bad news this morning.'

'More of it? Well?'

'Gottfried von Acht escaped from the prisoner's room in the law-courts.'

XLIX

NEUWALDEGG USED TO BE A PRETTY VILLAGE AT THE FOOT of the Wienerwald. At the beginning of the century, it was linked to Vienna by tram line 42. Driving along the road to Neuwaldegg in the 1930s one had the sensation of being in Vienna, whereas in truth one was on a long finger of houses, pointing to the woods. Colonel Marchais sat at the Restaurant Päiva at nine in the evening. He was alone. Outside in the garden, a platoon of French paratroops were swearing in the icy evening. Golunsky was late. It was ten past nine.

Colonel Marchais had not shared in the discussion by his fellow western Allies of the significance of Golunsky's defection. For him, Golunsky was a French success. Or would be, provided he came. Marchais himself would play a minor part in Golunsky's interrogation. He would receive him and take him to a French residence prepared in Mariahilferstrasse. Arrangements would be made for his transfer to Paris. Such a thing might take time. Marchais would talk to him, since a prisoner in those circumstances would be given to gloom, even attempts at suicide. He would need, while waiting in Mariahilferstrasse, to be treated gently.

Marchais had made arrangements to ensure that the Russian would receive an excellent reception in France once he arrived. He would tell as much or as little as he liked and then he would go into retirement as Georges Dupont, advising on the genuineness of other defectors. France was not the US, which now had so many intelligence officers that they did not need the member of the mission concerned with artistic questions to stray into this area of operations. Thus Marchais had done all the work. A French officer had then to be a jack of all trades. Doubtless, Colonel Marchais thought, working himself up into a temper, if he had been an American, it would not have been he who was sitting in this ill-appointed tavern waiting for a lachrymose Slav.

'Colonel Marchais?' A cheerful waitress, with pretty eyes and a figure like a turnip, approached his table.

'Yes, it is me.'

'You are wanted on the telephone.'

Marchais went to the squat instrument which stood on the bar.

'Oui, je vous écoute.'

A strained voice – was it Golunsky's? – told Marchais that its owner would be late. He could come – but at ten. The receiver was put down. Marchais returned to his table and ordered another *viertel* of white wine.

Up till then the restaurant had been empty, save for himself and an elderly Austrian sitting in the corner talking to the barman. Now the corner table was taken by two lively and laughing young men, who evidently had had much to drink, though they were in command of themselves. From time to time, they burst into song: a local Neuwaldegg air, Colonel Marchais told himself (others would have considered the music to be American.) One of the barmen, who plainly knew these two characters, played music on a battered accordion. The laughing Neuwaldeggers danced with each other and then with Gretchen, as the Colonel supposed every Austrian waitress to be called. The Colonel looked at his watch. Three-quarters of an hour before Golunsky could arrive.

He smoked a cigarette. He went outside to tell the paratroops of the delay. He instructed them to tell the drivers. The colonel wondered why Golunsky had to be late. Surely for an appointment like this he could have been on time? After his failure to find the Crown of Charles V, the colonel had invested much of his remaining prestige within the French mission into delivering Golunsky to the West. He could not afford another failure. He had another cigarette.

At five minutes to ten, the colonel's equanimity had vanished. He was beside himself with nerves. He ordered a third *viertel*. He had smoked a packet of cigarettes. Here was the turning point, he told himself, in great power relations. It was a French moment. France needed victories. Here was the chance of one. How could anything go wrong?

At exactly ten o'clock, Major Golunsky entered the restaurant. He looked neither nervous nor disturbed. Colonel Marchais might resemble a bicyclist at the end of the Tour de France, but Major Golunsky looked like a man who had ensured a lifetime of happiness in the 16th arrondissement.

'Colonel Marchais, you waited for me. How nice.'

Colonel Marchais made a bow, and tried to hide his irritation. Golunsky was behaving as if he and Marchais had been lifelong friends meeting for coffee.

'I have news. Plans have changed.'

'What plans?' expostulated Marchais. '*Einmal, noch ein Viertel. Nein, ein halb. Nein, vodka, für zwei.*'

'Well, Major, what plans have changed?'

'My transfer to Russia has been delayed one week. So I believe I must delay my journey to the West one week also.'

'Major,' said Marchais running his hands through his hair, 'it is whatever seems best to you. But each day is a risk.'

'How so, Colonel?'

'Someone on your side could get wind of your movements. Anything could go wrong.'

'Someone on *your* side too, Colonel?'

'Certainly, someone on our side whom you know to be on your side.'

'Uh-huh.'

'It would be better if you maintained your original plan, Major, and came over tonight. We have the arrangements for your reception. Paris would be disconcerted.'

'I see.'

Colonel Marchais believed that he was making some headway.

Perhaps he would have clinched matters there and then had the door not opened and a group of young Austrians come in laughing, teasing one another and stamping their feet to warm themselves. They were from a different *milieu* to the first two young men but they sat at the next table to them and, in a second or two, seemed to have drawn them into their merriment. There were eight or nine of these newcomers. Marchais recognised them – or rather the kind of people that they were – children of the old rich, or children who had been too young for the war and saw no reason why, whatever their parents had done or not done between 1938 and 1945 (or 1934 and 1938, come to that) they should not enjoy their youth. The girls all seemed to be wearing their mothers' furs, the young men had the bearing of officers in a Schnitzler play. They all seemed charming, thought Colonel Marchais and, from the *hauteur* of his experience as a man of forty, he half envied them. The centre of the party was a beautiful girl of about twenty. Marchais seemed to have seen her before. There were three other pretty girls and five young men who all seemed to convulse with laughter whenever any of the girls said anything.

'Do say it again, Klara, I didn't hear you properly,' shouted one of the young men, a pale fair youth. 'These idiots are laughing so much that they drown you out.'

Klara, for it was she, obliged. Pointing to the dirty list of fare on the table she said:

'It's really not at all interesting, Georgie, I simply said, anyone who wants to be a real musician must be able to set a menu to music.' Such peals of laughter followed that the waitress (and a waiter hitherto unseen) came immediately. 'And I didn't even say it first, I promise,' Klara said. 'Richard Strauss said it.'

'But you say it divinely,' said the fair youth, who was presumably Georgie.

'I'm sure Klara says it better than Richard Strauss.'

'Than anyone!' shouted another boy.

'See if you can sing it, Georgie,' Klara said to the pale boy.

'Sing it, sing it, do sing it, Georgie,' the girls cried.

'Wait a minute. Of course I can sing it. But do be quiet for a moment. Let me think of a tune. No, stop making me laugh, everyone. Just a *moment*.'

The waiter had set down two half *carafes* of white wine on the table.

'You see we have two halves not just one,' shouted another of the boys. 'I ask you, when do two halves not make one? When they are two half bottles of white wine in Neuwaldegg!'

Further laughter followed. Georgie was clearing his throat.

'No, please, silence for a new composition,' said Klara. 'I know it's going to be good.'

'Of course it's going to be good.'

Georgie sang in a pleasing tenor:

'He who would truly be a music man, must the very menu put to so-o-song.'

Everyone in the restaurant clapped. Colonel Marchais feared that Major Golunsky might cry again. He did not. He looked quite earnest.

'There!' said Marchais, 'That's the West for you. Just like Schubert and his friends, don't you think? Laughter. The innocence of youth. Games. Carefree. Singing. You'll find it in Paris too. Even in this devil of a cold winter. The right people can make a song out of anything.'

'It is true,' said the Russian, 'yet I have to tell you something. Something serious.' He lent down over the table and said *sotto voce*:

'You should know something about that girl in the middle. The girl in the astrakhan. She is not innocent.'

Colonel Marchais laughed.

'Well,' he said, 'in these days –'

'No, that is not what I mean – I mean you should beware of her. She is not what she seems. She is, I assure you, one of the special friends of Colonel Voronov. She is on my list.'

'I cannot believe it. I know who she is. She is the daughter of a well-known socialist. A man who will be the next socialist leader probably. Well-known family here –'

'Acht.'

'Exactly. Acht. She couldn't be. She had some terrible experience at the time of the liberation of Vienna.'

'Perhaps. But has anyone ever asked her what happened at that time? I know. One day I will tell you.'

'When might that be?'

'In Paris! The Avenue Foch!' Golunsky raised his glass.

'So you will come?'

'Yes, I will come. But not thanks to the singing children. Thanks to you, Colonel Marchais. Thanks to the Avenue Foch! That girl frightens me, you know, Colonel, I think I would like to leave.'

'To Paris!' Colonel Marchais raised his glass.

'Paris!'

Colonel Marchais rose. The young Austrians were still laughing, now being in the middle of some game. Klara had said something else which had delighted them all.

'The loser drinks from Klara's shoe. As a punishment.' Georgie sounded very appealing.

'Certainly not, it would punish my shoe more than the loser! Put them on the table if you like,' Klara said. 'We can all analyse my shoes. Where have they been, how sure is my step? Franzie, you are a scientist.'

'Do you know,' Major Golunsky said to Colonel Marchais with awe, 'that boy they called Franzie! I believe he's a Hohenheim!'

'May well be, Major,' said Marchais briskly, 'shall we go?'

'Let us go.'

The Colonel left the restaurant with a twinge of regret. His own youth had been spent on his doctorate. He had had plenty of enjoyable days since. But those days of earliest youth, when nothing seemed to matter, those he had missed. The words of a Chinese poet came to his mind: 'As we grow older, a moment of joy is harder to get.' Should he take seriously Golunsky's remarks about Klara? He thought not. She had not even glanced at them. If there had been anything in Golunsky's accusations, at least one of the two of them would have been of interest. As he reached his car, he looked back to the restaurant. Through the windows he could see that now Klara herself was singing, and everyone in the restaurant – including the two waiters and Gretchen, as well as the first comers – was standing round her. No, surely Golunsky was seeing a spy in every corner, in order to make himself more interesting.

Marchais' driver opened the doors. Both Golunsky and Marchais sat in the back. As the engine started, Marchais offered Golunsky a rug, and a cigarette. He said to the driver:

'Well then, Mariahilferstrasse.'

They drove off preceded by one car full of paratroops and followed by another.

The cars were driving at a great pace when, turning into the Gürtel, Marchais suddenly noticed that the black car driving closely behind was no longer one of his own. It was not a French car. He told the driver to hurry. But to do so, the driver overtook the car carrying the paratroops. Marchais then gave an order to slow down. The instruction caused the unknown car following them to drive hard into the rear of Marchais' car.

Marchais leapt out.

'Fool!' he shouted in German.

They were on a dark corner – near Urban Loritz Platz. The driver got out, too, to survey the damage.

'No, please remain inside,' said Marchais to Golunsky who had opened the door. Marchais was relieved to see one of his own cars of paratroops draw up and halt beside the black car, which had no lights, probably smashed on impact.

'Control that car,' Marchais ordered his men. But before they could do anything, the car leapt into reverse, knocking several of them to the ground, and, without lights, disappeared backwards into the darkness.

Marchais rushed back to his own car. The back door onto the pavement was open. Golunsky had gone. Whether sucked out by force into the ruin which meets all those who tempt fate, or by his own volition, Colonel Marchais was not to know.

L

A WEEK AFTER THE RESCUE OF KAMO, POLDI MOSER TOOK
his courage in his hands and dismissed all the communists in the State
Police, headed by their commander Major Durkheim. He sent him to
Salzburg, and assured him it was promotion. Poldi Moser, and Vienna,
held their breath. So did the Western commanders. Sheay told Washington
to alert its overseas divisions: it did, all three of them. General Whitelegge
sent the Argyll and Sutherland Highlanders to play rousing tunes in the
Ringstrasse – not quite what Aunt Thekla would have expected to hear in
that street, but she said it was "none the less elevating". Alois, with other
socialist ministers, spent several nights in their offices, waiting for a
communist insurrection. Colonel Marchais, his star in eclipse after his
unfortunate loss of Golunsky, had gone to Salzburg, with Madame
Charpentier. But his colleagues supported the Anglo–Saxons, flew the *tricolore* on official cars, and a singer from Nantes gave a marvellous rendering of the *Marseillaise* in the Stadtpark, on the invitation of the mayor.

The first hint that the Russians were going to decline this challenge
was when the Russian Command and their 'wives' appeared at a party
given by the mysterious Count Gmunden in the Sacher hotel. No one
quite knew why he had reappeared in Vienna just then. Of course, Count
Gmunden was not a reliable indicator of anything but he had his ear
close to the ground and, if he were holding a reception – to which half
the Allied Commands had also been invited – then his sources of information were optimistic. During the reception, Brigadier Sheay, who
had only a week left before he returned to Washington, was accosted by
Colonel Voronov.

'So, Brigadier, you are joining us.'

Sheay started.

Voronov laughed.

'I did not mean literally joining the Soviet services. I meant you are
attaching yourself to that part of your nation's bureaucracy which concerns itself with analysis. Like mine. Now let us join our wine glasses.
We have much in common. Perhaps in time we shall work on something
in common.'

The Brigadier knew from this that his term in Vienna would not be concluded by a Soviet *coup* or takeover.

Count Gmunden's party was memorable for some other occurrences too: for example, Major Grew's intemperate suggestion to Tatiana Bezhukov – who was also about to leave Vienna for London – that they marry. Another noticeable happening was the host's particular attention to Klara von Acht; and her surprising tolerance of this not wholly reputable admirer. Most unexpected of all was General Whitelegge's remark to Alois Acht that he thought the Austrian peace treaty could be signed by Christmas.

But none of these things so commented upon at the time seemed to lead to much. Thus Tatiana turned down Charlie Grew, even though the British Mission had assumed them to have been engaged long ago. It came as a shock to the gallant Captain when Tatiana laughed kindly at his suggestion: 'Dear Charlie of course I adore you,' she said, 'but really, not at all like that. You need a proper wife. A fulltime wife. I'm not good enough to sit in the country and knit for the General whom you will soon be. As for me, I want to go to Paris next.'

As to Count Gmunden and Klara: her cheeks were flushed, her eyes shone, she smiled radiantly but disdain could be easily lurking beneath.

And General Whitelegge: the peace treaty could be signed by Christmas? '*Could be*, I said,' he would say over the next few years when reporters motored down to see him in his retirement near Shaftesbury: 'Could be, I said.' He kept monkeys dancing in cages outside his house. The original pair were a gift from the Sultan of A – whom he had assisted to win back his throne before 1939. 'Just observe those cousins of ours outside,' he would say. 'Their activities show what we are capable of. We could spend our lives leaping about a gymnasium. We could sign the Austrian treaty draft. But we don't always live up to our opportunities.'

PART 5

MAY
1948

the Germans caught them in the barbed wire or

LI

AFTER BEING REFUSED BY TATIANA BEZHUKOV, CHARLIE GREW decided that he needed a change of scene. He volunteered, in the late spring of 1948, to take charge of a mission to check the Soviet accusations that, in the southern part of the British zone, there were concentrations of neo-nazi sympathisers. The Russians had also said that "white" troops headed by Tsarist officers were gathered in parts of the British zone notably, again, in Carinthia. Someone had to make clear that these rumours were false, in order that General Whitelegge could rebuff his Soviet colleagues. There were British troops in Klagenfurt, and in Graz. There were civilian commissioners everywhere. But a personal visit to confirm the facts seemed a good idea. General Whitelegge, like everyone else in Vienna, knew that these accusations were as fanciful as those put round about the now half-forgotten Kamo.

The major left Vienna with two cars – he, with a driver, in one; three corporals in the other. They drove south out of Vienna on the main Graz road and stopped for lunch by arrangement at the mess of the 14th Royal Signals at Bruck. Here the officer in charge, Major Evans, seemed preoccupied, and conversation between him and Grew was stilted.

'Is anything wrong?' the latter asked afterwards, as the two officers sat over bad *ersatz* coffee served in beautiful china.

'So you noticed? Well, yes it's most upsetting. We spent all last week negotiating with the Soviets over the return to Russia of about twenty-four DPs: Soviet citizens born all over the place. Same old story. The Soviet repatriation mission has been buzzing round everywhere. We sat down with them and spent hours negotiating. Can't tell you how difficult it was. They wanted to know everything these men had been doing, since the Germans caught them in 1941. Wanted us to find it all out. All right?'

'I understand.'

'Well, we fixed it all up. Papers worked out. We assembled the men. They were to be handed over at six this evening. We had an NCO go down and tell them they were being taken to Italy.'

'To Italy?'

'Yes, a ruse. To get them into the van. Otherwise, they'd never go. Couldn't have done it myself. Hate having to tell lies to people. Besides, it isn't my job. Anyway,' Major Evans gulped and took a sip of his *ersatz* coffee as if it had been a rare cognac: 'Anyway, do you know what happened?'

'Tell me. But I must warn you. It's a familiar story.'

'I daresay. Hasn't happened to me before. Anyway. The NCO! Corporal Watling. Lives in Bungay, Suffolk. Know where I mean? A chicken farmer in civilian life. He couldn't do it either. So he arranged with the mess chef to give these fellows a slap-up breakfast and then goes sick. I ask you! Leaves the chaps sitting there. They get into conversation with the mess chef. A Pole. Fellow of the name of Rataj. Used to live in Poland, captured by the Russians at the beginning of the war, came back through Persia, joined up with Anders' army, fought at Arnhem. Now an English citizen. Salt of the earth. Guess what he told these Russian boys?'

'I expect he said that if they didn't watch out they'd be sent back to Russia and kept in a concentration camp.'

'How did you know?'

'Oh I put two and two together.'

'Know what happened? The twenty-four boys had a real breakfast, two helpings of sausages and scrambled egg. Tomatoes. Potatoes. Officers' breakfast, grade one. They said thanks very much to the chef, rolled him up in the mess carpet so he couldn't cry out and skedaddled. All twenty-four. No sign of them. The chef, nearly smothered, unrolled himself at 9.30 and himself went sick. What the hell am I going to tell Colonel Satchikov?'

'Tell him you've sent out a mission hunting them. Have you, incidentally? Or are all your men sick like Corporal Watling?'

'They are, you know, Grew. They are all sick.'

The major and his cortège drove on and, despite bad roads, reached Klagenfurt at dusk. They were to stay the night there put up by the 8th Northants Yeomanry. Grew arranged to dine with Colonel Rogers at his mess in the Malevolti-Durkheim palace in the square.

'Can't say we do badly,' he told Grew, as they sat down to dine with ten other British officers. 'Occupying Austria is a difficult job but it has compensations. The red wine is quite good here, for example. Then there's a good start-me-off called an Obstler. Fruity. Kind of Pimms's brandy, I suppose. The natives drink it after dinner. I like it before *and* after dinner.'

'What are the inconveniences?'

'No hangmen.'

'What?'

'When we want to hang a man, we have to get a hangman specially out from England. Damned bore, isn't it. Takes forever. Requests have to be in triplicate and reach the Judge Advocate General after trundling for bloody weeks through the foothills of Whitehall. That's our number one complaint down here in Klagenfurt. Had a man called Demmer waiting for the hangman six bloody months. Not very fair, is it? I ask you!'

'Demmer the butcher of Auschwitz?'

'Right.'

'Deserves all the bad treatment he can get. What else?'

'Well, if you want me to be honest, the Austrians shoot all the roebuck.'

'You can't be serious.'

'Of course I am. Then the Austrian municipal people are no good. Don't speak English. No war guilt. Just want to get back to normal and make money. Crazy, isn't it?'

'Don't we want them to get back to normal?'

'Yes, but at our pace. Pass the port, Grew.'

Colonel Rogers was not typical of the British officer overseas. He was irascible but he was also efficient: if a man were going to be hanged, he wanted him hanged quickly. In the American zone there were some more liberated souls, such as Colonel Myron Turner, who lived in Schmalk-aldig, carrying a riding whip wherever he went and who, when a vet did not come immediately to tend his sick alsatian dog, ordered him to walk naked into the town hall.

The next few days were occupied by the Major in peaceful excursions into the countryside. He was soon able to report the south shore of the Worthersee free of nazis.

Grew drove into deserted farmhouses and ancient barns, he disturbed rats in empty shooting huts, and he engaged Carinthian peasants in discussion about next year's harvest in the hope of finding, by accident, what they knew of one or other of a number of missing nazis believed to be in the area: for example, the hated leader Ried.

After two uneventful days in empty country, Charlie decided that it was ridiculous to be making his so-called secret "sweeps" in convoy and decided to drive himself alone along the Drau valley and beyond, almost into the Tyrol. It would give him a chance to think, to review his last two years, and replan his future, now that it was not going to include Tatiana Bezhukov. At the same time, there were a few places there that he should have a look at: one in particular, Damberg, a castle near the Italian border, had cropped up twice in intelligence reports as a place from which nazis were said to be able to escape into Italy and thence to Spain or South America. Colonel Rogers had reported everything calm there, the owner unchanged since before the war, but the proximity to both the Italian and the Yugoslav border meant that it was in a key position. The castle, so Grew's references told him, had been in the hands of the same Austro-Italian family since long before Austria and Italy existed as nations.

Grew found the village of Damberg easily. But when he asked for the Schloss, no one much wanted to help him. People pointed vaguely up towards the mountains and hurried on. He stopped at a gasthaus, and ordered a sandwich – black bread, bad sausage and a *viertel* of red wine – and then drove along a small road which he found at the back of the village leading south towards Italy. It was not paved. His car was strong but not too high off the ground. At one moment he saw a tower, though far off, a mile or so above him. That showed, so he told himself, that he was on the right route. But the tower seemed to vanish. He drove on. The road improved, worsened, dipped and rose. Finally he reached large gates which lay open, seeming to invite him up a still steeper road heading for the sun. He hesitated for a moment and drove in.

After ten minutes of driving upwards through sparkling air, Charlie, no genius at the wheel, came to a dead stop just beneath a small shrine. The low car had hit the ground. It would go neither forwards nor backwards. Charlie was stuck. He blamed himself for advancing without escort. Still, he was an intelligence officer, not an infantryman, and he was not to be deterred. He would continue on foot. The Major removed his service pistol from the map compartment and slipped it into his pocket, picked up his briefcase containing a few personal possessions and, in the calm morning, began to walk upwards.

The road, though bad for cars, had been clearly used by mules or horses for many generations, for old cypresses had been well-established up the left of it, on the windward side. On the right, where the path hugged the hillside, the earth had been held in by a skilful patchwork of stones and mud. That he was on a well-tended property was obvious since, when the road crossed a grove of pine trees, there were piles of logs well arranged on the edge of the path. What would the citizens of Vienna give for such fuel! On the other hand, the ground under the pines was rough: crumbling slate like stone. There was no sign of the castle nor of any habitation. Looking back, the cypresses and scrub oak screened the valley, whence sometimes an indistinct noise rose of distant cattle bells.

Though the road bore traces of some recent use by wheeled vehicles, here and there a rock jabbed outwards, presenting a hazard to any motorist, and surely having been looked upon as a landmark for countless generations of horsemen.

After he had been walking for about twenty minutes Grew noticed that he was under Spanish chestnuts, large noble trees struggling out of the undergrowth, themselves looking like lost travellers, their roots exposed on the hillside. To an English eye, it was comforting to see such familiar sights as heather, and the ends of bracken. Wisps of broom, dead ends of thyme hung raggedly downwards. Grew was left in no doubt that he was still in civilised territory by the sight of another small shrine: more elaborate than the one before. It must once have been painted. The remains of a Pompeian design on the surround were visible. A plainly carved Mary and Child stood within, guarded by a clutch of artificial flowers, against a background of a painted pale blue sky with clouds. Beneath on a marble plaque were the Italian words VERGINE MARIA MADRE DI DIO PREGATE JESU PER ME. ANNO MDCCCLV.

A little beyond this, still with no castle in sight, Charlie Grew sat down on a mossy wall which perhaps had once been part of a bridge over a torrent, now dry. Two elderly women dressed in black came down the hill walking at a good pace. As they passed, he put to them the single question 'Schloss?' Without bothering to pause, or even to look at him, they answered '*Ja, ja, Schloss hierüber,*' and continued on their way.

A golden pheasant walked down towards him in a dandyish way. Grew's appearance scared him into an escape into the brushwood.

Occupied by vague attempts to guess what, symbolically, two witches and a gold pheasant might portend, Grew did not notice at exactly what point the road became level and when the landscape opened up. Though the rough mud wall on the right continued, the gaps between the trees on the left showed, beyond a drop, some open meadows. Suddenly the castle appeared again, with light behind it, a scalloped half Italian tower seeming to emerge from over the top of the trees like a swan resting on its nest. Still perhaps a mile or more, as the crow flies, a combination of the grim and the beautiful, the tower seemed to Grew to possess a magical quality.

The road became broader. There were two rows of chestnuts, one on each side. A strong breeze blew, for now, but for the *allée*, there was no protection, the road lying along a ridge from which wooded hillsides swept down, after an infinite number of gradations, to the distant valley.

By this time the placing of the trees proclaimed that they had been planted to please the eye. One or two oaks stood as if determined to prove their resistance to the demands of felling and thinning, for the benefit of the Imperial navy, over many generations. Grew became conscious of noises of animals in the undergrowth – perhaps a snake, certainly a squirrel, and a hen pheasant. A group of tall pines left the view clear and the needles beneath them on the ground smelled sweetly. He observed a rabbit. Not far below on the left, and hidden until then, Grew saw a prosperous peasant's house. In a paddock beside it, pale horses tossed their tails.

The road curved sharply, a wall of cyclopean rocks rose fifty feet or more, a group of farm houses with arches appeared on the left. Grew found himself before a wrought-iron gate, topped by balls of stone. Above him the castle loomed. Between him and it there was only a long slope of stairs flanked by a well-tended formal garden of low box hedges, a few wallflowers, geraniums, and gravel paths. On one side there was a fountain. From the distance, a panel of stone gods and goddesses surveyed him. It would be easy to have supposed oneself in Italy. Perhaps, thought Charlie for a moment, he was. The frontier was close.

The castle seemed of two dates – the tower probably an ancient watch-tower; the body of the building, eighteenth century. The tower rose two hundred feet, twice as high as the rest. It was built of stone, though plastered many years before, for the stone peeped out at the corners. The lantern of the tower, as frequently in northern Italy but rarely in Austria, was of embrasures surmounted by what looked like a walkway, covered by a tiled roof. The tower had irregularly-placed small windows on the front, and Charlie noticed that three of them were open, though covered by blinds. Near the window of the first floor, a faded sundial sought to proclaim the hour.

To the left of the house a broad, open archway led to what seemed to be a courtyard. The main body of the house also had embrasures along its roof, though these were less deep than those on the tower. Along the eaves there was a walkway which apparently served as a home for doves judging from the many birds strutting there.

The iron gate was locked. A little to the side of it there was a small wooden door held by a clasp which was only too easy to open. Being resourceful, in uniform, armed, and confident that he could talk himself out of any difficulty by a mixture of arrogance and fluent if incorrect German, Charlie pushed through and found himself, not, as he had expected, among the petunias of the forecourt, but at the beginning of a pergola supported by curved bricks placed on low stone walls. Across the top, around weathered wooden struts, twisted the arms of a colossal vine, now cut carefully back and showing no sign of life. This walk was some forty or fifty yards long. On one side, roses grew on an old wall. On the other, south side, one could just see a kitchen garden and a few fruit trees. There was a scent of herbs and the noise not far off of the trickle of water. A black and white kitten rubbed itself against Charlie's legs and purred.

Halfway along the pergola two stone flights of shallow steps descended to the vegetable garden. Between them stood a stone basin in which water dripped from a satyr's head. Though delighted with the place and his journey from the valley, Charlie was tired and thirsty. He leant down for a drink. He became aware of a small window in the wall behind the stone basin at the level of the ground. Perhaps it was an air vent to some part of the cavernous cellars which places of this sort usually had. Charlie bent down further. As he did so, he saw that something like a knuckle, a human knuckle, was grasping the base of the window from within. He caught his breath, a sudden chill of excitement passed through him, and the hand vanished.

Charlie stood back and wondered. Had it really been a hand or had his imagination taken wings, heightened by the beauty of the scene and of the evening, by the vision of the golden pheasant and the sombre women in black? Perhaps he had merely seen an early lizard? Looking through a gap in the chestnuts, all seemed tranquil, the dying sun invested the stone with gold, the bells of sheep and of cattle quietly rang out from far below. A vast panorama of wooded hills and long leonine mountains lay in the distance. In the south there were the mountains of Italy; in the north, the Alps of Austria.

'*Che fà?*'

Grew turned to see standing above him in the pergola a big black-bearded man, over six feet tall and broad as well, wearing a worn leather apron. He spoke softly, in Italian, but with determination.

'*Venga, venga,*' he beckoned, '*al castello.*'

In half a minute Charlie had ceased to be the free soldier of the Alps and had become either their guest, or their prisoner.

LII

*T*HE GIANT LED GREW THROUGH A SMALL IRON GATE INTO the orchard and into the castle itself through a side door. They passed into a courtyard, sparse and empty save for a well in the centre, and up some outside steps which brought them into a large dark, though comfortable, drawing room.

'*Aspetti,*' said the gardener. He left the Major and went back downstairs, where he must have disappeared into one of the rooms leading off the courtyard. Though Grew could not see him, he could hear voices.

The drawing room was only lit by the glass doors leading into the courtyard and a small window which looked onto the terrace, bounded by another wall. Beyond lay the cypresses and the forests.

He waited for ten minutes. His eyes became accustomed to the dark. He observed the usual furniture of an Austrian drawing room: thick if faded damask curtains, a few books of architecture and painting, heavy pictures in ornate gold frames on the walls, photographs on the grand piano, one of which bore the likeness of a smiling, young, handsome German in nazi uniform whom he believed to be Schirach. Another photograph had no such ambiguity. There was the unmistakable jaw of Il Duce, Benito Mussolini, with his neat handwriting beneath it; dedicated to UBALDO CONTE MALEVOLTI, SALUTI CORDIALE, IL 5 GENNAIO, ANNO XI.

The doors of the drawing room were suddenly flung open and a thin, tall, powerful man of about fifty strode in wearing a white jacket. He had bushy eyebrows, blue eyes, dark hair flecked with grey, and a fine carriage.

'*Grüss Gott, grüss Gott, lieber Gottfried,*' he said with enthusiasm, holding out both hands towards Charlie, but as his eyes became accustomed to the dark he stood back surprised, went to open wider the shutters screening the windows so that he could see more clearly. Having done so, he returned to Charlie and looked at him with much attention, his smile never leaving his face.

'I – am – so – sorry,' he said in English, 'I was confused. We were expecting a good friend and in the shadow I had mistaken you for him. You are, I take it, an English officer? Welcome, welcome! I am Ubaldo

Malevolti, I welcome you to our house. It is many many weeks since we had an English visitor.'

'Is this lovely place Damberg?' asked Grew.

'No, no. You are at Tremamondo, Schloss Tremamondo.'

'Oh so I am in Italy?'

'No, not yet. The border is on the side of the hill. We are the last inhabited building in Austria before you get to Italy. We are half Italian here. Half Austrian. But wholly European! Well, well, an English officer! Where is your car, your escort, the rest of your mission? How can we help? Here we are so remote that the help we can offer is modest. But, such as it is, we are at your service.'

Charlie was charmed. He thought the Count – as he assumed him to be – delightful. He explained what had happened.

'Of course, we shall get your vehicle,' said Malevolti, 'my men will draw it up by horsecart and they will have it repaired in no time. May I invite you to dine? We are short of company. My wife will be pleased to meet an Englishman again. We are so isolated. You will drink something?'

Malevolti pressed the bell, and an aged butler appeared, in pink livery, through a door which previously Charlie had taken to be part of the bookcase.

'Allow me to offer you a *vermut* made here. It is all we have. It will remind you of the Savoy vermouths, but it is sharper.'

Charlie enthusiastically accepted.

'It is wonderful to have you here. Are you sure there is nothing I can get you?'

'Do you have a telephone?'

'Alas, no, I am afraid, no longer. There was a wire here before the war. But the Americans bombed it and it has never been repaired. No doubt one day we shall get a new one. Peace will bring back civilisation eventually, will it not? We dine, incidentally, at eight, in an hour. By then we shall have a report on your car. Probably it will be mended. May I leave you, to make the arrangements? No, wait, first I shall show you the sights of my house, such as they are. I shall give you time to prepare for dinner – which you will realise, in these days, and in these remote places, has to be of a primitiveness barely believable. May I lead the way?'

He gave Charlie a warm smile and opened the book-lined door out of the drawing room into a small, high library, with books stretching up twenty feet or more.

'You would be surprised how giddy it is up there,' he said, pointing to a pair of library steps which might have enabled a tall man, such as he, to reach the top row of books, 'and with the political changes of these days,

I have to go up there often. You see, I banish those writers who are not fashionable to the top shelves!' Once again, a very disconcerting warm smile.

The library was square, with a large central desk on which were piled papers, letters, newspapers, open books, paper weights. A dark green sofa and some well-worn armchairs stood beneath the window.

'You see a certain disorder. Alas, I do not have the instinctive sense of arrangement, the determination to conclude something once begun which is the characteristic of the Anglo-Saxon.'

'Are you perhaps writing a book?'

'I am editing my diaries.' He sighed. 'It is not easy. I have experienced interesting things. But many of the people with whom I shared them are still, in one way or another, living. Strange, we have had this terrible war, millions have died, yet my friends are mostly alive. Odd, is it not? Then, there is a problem of one's wives.'

'Wives?'

'Obviously in diaries, one's wives appear, sooner or later. But what to say of them? In a published version, I mean. The truth? Or lies?' He gave another terrible smile.

Charlie examined another photograph, in sepia, leaning against an old *Brockhaus* on one of the book shelves. It showed a bathing party before the war – perhaps of the 1920s. The women had the quick eager smiles of old snapshots. Their mouths were darkened by what looked like, in the over-exposed pictures, almost black lipstick, their bodies encased by old-fashioned bathing suits. Several of the men had their arms folded as if in a team photograph. Some straw-hatted men were making a pose standing with one leg crossed over the other. A few waiters, carrying trays, the only ones fully clothed, hovered on the sides of the pictures.

'You recognise me?' asked Malevolti. 'I am the one arm-in-arm with Ciano.'

'I – I hadn't recognised. Which is Ciano?'

'He was thinner then. There! A clever man. Too anxious to please, possibly. So, would you like perhaps to see the tower?' asked the count. He opened another book-lined door without waiting for an answer.

They mounted an iron spiral staircase which led into a rough attic. Brick stairs, two more flights, led further up. They came out under the eaves of the tower.

'That's all eighteenth century,' said Malevolti pointing downwards vaguely. 'My ancestors then destroyed the rest of the castle. Unfortunately, they were rich at the time. One of them married an Istanbul silk merchant's daughter. The marriage was criticised at the time, his father disowned him, but it was the only good marriage that the Malevolti made. We used to pretend that she was a Venetian but what is the point of such self-deception nowadays? Who knows, even Jewish blood may one day seem useful.' Another affable smile. 'Now, is that not a fine view? Or are you perhaps afraid of being shown the cities of the world?'

'But you, Sir, are not the devil, nor I Christ!' ventured Charlie.

'I suppose that is so,' said Malevolti gravely.

The view was certainly fine. To the north, a vast perspective embraced villages and rivers, farmsteads and roads. Not only could one see the valley of the Drau and more distantly the Carinthian Alps but, from another angle, one looked south to Italy. There the mountains stretched more savagely than picturesquely. Huge gorges interrupted the forests. There was not a habitation to be seen. Only an occasional vulture reminded one that life continued.

'The last bear in the Alps was killed four kilometres away, over there,' said Malevolti, pointing, 'and, as for the last wolf, it has yet to die. I saw one in the winter of, was it, '44.'

Charlie looked down not into the valley but into the vegetable garden where he had been surprised by the giant gardener who spoke Italian. It seemed even better laid out from above than from ground level. His eye travelled along the top of the pergola to find the steps and the tap.

'Is there anything that specially concerns you in our poor kitchen garden?' asked Malevolti, the smile gone from his fine face for an instant. His tone was, however, the same, interested, anxious to impart information if necessary, and courteous.

'That's in some way the best view of all,' Charlie said, pointing down to the courtyard which showed itself not to be a rectangle but an irregular polygon.

'Yes, you are right and yet it is not regular,' said Malevolti. 'It is meant to ward off the evil eye.'

'Has it succeeded?'

'Who can tell?'

He placed his hand on Charlie's shoulder. Charlie started violently.

'Forgive me. We Latins – and I am three-quarters Latin – we are rather demonstrative.'

The roof of the living quarters of the castle was covered by alternately curved and flat tiles. On it were set a number of agreeably castellated chimneys. Swallows and pigeons, an occasional bat, swooped. In the courtyard below, the gardener was standing talking to a servant carrying a tray.

'My ancestors used those to pour boiling oil on unwelcome visitors,' said Malevolti, pointing to the shafts beneath the embrasures of the lantern.

They went downstairs, walked in the formal garden, over the croquet lawn, and along the pergola. Then Malevolti showed Charlie a pleasant bedroom, with grilles over the windows, facing south. In an adjacent bathroom, there were toiletries including shaving soap and a new brush. Charlie washed, hesitated whether to take his gun with him to dinner, thought that he had better not, placed it in the drawer of the dressing table, then changed his mind and moved to put it under the mattress. Turning, he saw, standing in the half-opened door, a maid. Irritated at being observed, he left the gun on the dressing table and returned to the drawing room, where the Count was waiting. He had changed into a green smoking jacket. Another change had occurred. The photograph of Mussolini had been replaced by one of an elderly professorial gentleman, with thinning hair. This picture, like the other one which had preceded it, also read "SALUTE CORDIALE". But it was signed ALCIDE DE GASPERI.

A few minutes later, the Countess Malevolti joined them. She was much younger than her husband. She was tall and fair with the auburn gold hair associated with paintings by Titian. She had piercing black eyes. She managed to move both languidly and quickly which Charlie attributed to the effect of her low cut black silk dress and her very long elegant legs. Unlike her husband, she did not judge it worthwhile to make herself friendly. Malevolti's remark that she would welcome company seemed the reverse of the truth. Indeed, her face seemed continuously suffused by fury – a fury which apparently had little to do with the presence of Charlie, since she barely looked at him. But she watched her husband from the moment that she entered the room, as if one of them were intending something that the other would try to prevent. Nor was her German perfect. Fluent but imperfect. Perhaps she was Hungarian. Charlie had been long enough in Austria to know that the best-looking Austrian women usually have Hungarian blood.

An unnerving event occurred before dinner. They were standing in front of the fireplace. Count Malevolti pointed out an interesting detail on the eighteenth-century chimney place. Suddenly the door leading to the library opened and a very old woman dressed in night clothes with a mass of long, loose snow-white hair thrust herself into the room. She was rapidly followed by a nurse holding a hairbrush. Both Malevolti and his wife made for her and, with the nurse tugging from the other side, pushed her forcefully back out through the door. Out of breath, Malevolti returned, brushing his hands as if to rid himself of some disagreeable dust, and commented: 'My aunt. I am afraid she has quite lost her reason.'

Charlie ventured a sympathetic word.

'No, no, we never talk of it. Incidentally, I have good news. They have found your car. It is already here. During dinner we shall be told what is wrong with it. Then, if anyone can treat it, Gonzalo will. He is a genius with vehicles of all sorts.'

'Gonzalo?'

'The gardener whom you encountered. A man of immense ingenuity.'

'He is an executioner in his spare time,' remarked Countess Malevolti with a glance at her husband, who frowned.

They went in to dinner along a broad passageway hung with rough tapestries made in Flanders in the early eighteenth century. The passage, and its length, made Charlie conscious that, despite his host's expressed desire to show him his house, 'Such as it is,' he had only seen a twentieth of the castle which, in its rambling construction, was more like a village.

Before reaching the dining room, they were joined in the passage by a thin, pale ageless man, who came out of one of the many doors which they passed. He was wearing a dark suit and blue tie, and was introduced as Herr Doktor Alessandri.

'The Herr Doktor is as useful to me with my diaries,' said Malevolti, 'as he is invaluable for all sorts of useful information.'

'Such as the climate in Uruguay,' spat out Countess Malevolti.

'Precisely,' Malevolti said, but did not laugh.

The Herr Doktor spoke little during dinner. His grave face mildly reassured Charlie. There could surely be nothing wrong in a castle where he was present. He seemed to treat Malevolti as he would a clever boy. They sat at dinner at a very long table in the style of a refectory, the Count at the head, the Countess opposite, the doctor and Charlie between them, all their chairs a long way from each other. As Charlie had expected, Malevolti's disclaimer about the quality of the food was misleading. They ate well: spinach soup with barley; some birds which Grew took to be quail, but perhaps were crows; dried mushrooms explained to him as a local delicacy – so sought after that people risked even Malevolti's dogs in order to steal them from the brushwood; some hard, goat cheese; and some good local red wine grown by Malevolti in the valley. The dinner was served by the butler who had brought the vermouth. Franz, as his name turned out to be, shook continuously and made the sign of the cross before putting down a plate. He too had an amiable face. Malevolti told Charlie that he had been gassed fighting against the Italians on the Isonzo in the First War.

During dinner, Charlie learnt that his host regarded the break up of the Austro-Hungarian empire as the principal cause of mankind's troubles; that he, himself, had fought in the First War and had been wounded in the Brusilov offensive – hence his bad leg; and that he had regarded the nazi movement as a socialist conspiracy.

These views were put by Malevolti in the course of a monologue. Neither the Herr Doktor nor the Countess interrupted. They looked at their plates. Charlie's mind began to wander. He was, however, awakened to the present by the arrival of Gonzalo, who whispered something to Malevolti which, from the gesticulations, affected Charlie.

'Alas,' said Malevolti, smiling yet again, 'it seems that your vehicle is not such an easy matter, after all. There appears to be a break in an essential.'

'A break in an essential – what on earth?–'

'No, no, do not be disturbed. It is easy to stay the night. In the morning, you could either go down with the farrier – or he will go for you and find the missing part in Lienz. An easy matter, I assure you, even nowadays. You would not be badly missed tonight, would you?'

Charlie Grew, his doubts about the real business of the castle lulled by the wine, agreed to spend the night. The conversation resumed. Soon after they returned to the drawing room for coffee, the Herr Doktor withdrew. So did the Countess who, having begun dinner hissing and tossing her head, had become quiet, lost in her own thoughts. Malevolti took Charlie outside. He showed him a nearly full moon over the mountains to the south. The silence was absolute. The beauty of the evening extinguished the fear which Charlie had intermittently felt before dinner. Malevolti showed him to the same room in which he had been before. It was large, the ceiling painted, there was a stone chimney piece, a table for writing, on which two lamps burned weakly. There was an armchair and a large bed with painted wooden bedposts, on which some English-looking blue pyjamas had been laid out for him. The single small window has been closed by shutters.

'I bid you good night,' said Malevolti. 'Gonzalo does not leave till eight.'

Tired, Charlie went instantly to sleep. But he was awoken by a terrible storm. Shutters and doors slammed, the thunder cracked overhead and, through the window which had blown open, Charlie observed the forest lit by lightning. The dogs which he remembered having been discussed at dinner did a good deal of barking. Charlie only fell asleep again at four.

He awoke still feeling tired. Franz, the pink coated butler, was opening the shutters. He had placed a tray of coffee, hot milk and some bread and jam on the writing table with the lamps. He chattered a great deal to himself. But the time, the time! Charlie looked at his watch, it was after nine o'clock. The farrier might have left. He shouted the question to Franz, who knocked his head, shook it and waved his finger. All the same, Charlie dressed hastily and ran out into the courtyard. He saw Doktor Alessandri in a white suit by the well. He was busy tying the laces of his neat shoes.

'Aha,' said the Doktor, 'the farrier has gone. The Count Malevolti wanted to wake you, but I said let him sleep, he can go down after luncheon and the Count agreed. The farrier will fetch the missing part, incidentally.'

268

Charlie spent the morning reading, sitting on a wall on the far side of the croquet lawn, looking over the dense vegetation of the valley. The storm had left behind mud. At noon, Alessandri appeared again. He explained that the farrier had been unable to get to the valley since two trees had fallen across the drive – yes, the drive up which Charlie had walked. Men were at work shifting them. But they might not be successful by luncheon. Could not Charlie make the best of an embarrassing situation, as embarrassing for Count Malevolti as it was for him, and remain another night? A runner could take any necessary message to the village of Damberg. A cable could also be sent to Vienna explaining the situation. The Count, said the lawyer, had formed a special liking for Major Grew and would dearly like to have further conversation with him over dinner. What about over lunch, asked Charlie? Unfortunately Count Malevolti was detained for lunch. Not in the valley presumably, asked Grew? No, not in the valley but an old friend had arrived in the course of the night and, since he needed to rest in bed, Malevolti believed that he should lunch by his side. But the Countess and he, Alessandri, would await him with pleasure.

'Quite a thoroughfare, this castle, isn't it? remarked Charlie.

'Would you like to give me the message then?'

'The message?'

'For the runner to take to the village.'

'Oh yes certainly.'

Charlie scribbled a message to Vienna announcing his delay, attributing it to mechanical breakdown, and promising a telephonic report the next day.

'That will do for now.' Charlie had no expectation that the message would arrive.

The Doktor still lingered. 'One can almost see summer from here today,' he said.

'I feel it myself,' returned Charlie and added, 'Incidentally, Doktor, who is that man watching from the tower?'

He had seen someone observing them through field glasses. The figure moved away as soon as it met Charlie's glance.

'Excuse me, I see no one. But it could be anyone. One of the servants.'

'With binoculars?'

'No, no, of course not, servants do not have binoculars. It could not be anyone with binoculars.'

'I saw binoculars, Herr Doktor.'

'The Major has a wide imagination; I expect that explains why the English won the war.' Doktor Alessandri bowed and went into the house.

LIII

THERE WAS AN HOUR BEFORE LUNCH. CHARLIE TOOK A leisurely stroll through the gardens and the orchard, and even the vegetable garden. It was warm. How different from the menacing beauty of the evening! The storm had been followed by sun. The stones had become really warm. Looking back to the tower to ascertain that nobody was watching from there, Charlie made his way to the grating where the previous day he had seen the clenched knuckle. There was no sign of life. He tipped in a pebble through the bars. He heard it fall on a stone floor below. Relieved, he went back to the castle. Malevolti greeted him in the courtyard.

'Ah, *cher ami!* Alessandri has explained! A million apologies! But how grateful I am to you that you will stay another night! We shall talk over dinner. It will be an enjoyment for us to have again such company.'

Charlie went to lunch. The Countess was there. She was as uncommunicative as ever. Her proud black eyes kept as ever to her plate. Dressed in a linen suit, in lime green, she seemed even more agitated than at her previous appearance. The Doktor, however, maintained a stream of conversation. More disturbing news had come in during the morning.

'Have you ever heard, Major, of the monster of Damberg?'

'I have not.'

'No. Well, there has long been a tale that this stretch of the Alps is the habitat of a land reptile. You have your Loch Ness monster. We have our Damberg monster. It comes out after storms such as we had last night. Then, for many years, no one hears anything of it. Perhaps we even forget that it exists. It is looked upon as a myth. Suddenly it reappears. Like this morning. There was a sighting this morning.'

'Oh, where?'

'In the undergrowth below the croquet lawn. Very high up. I do not think there has been a sighting so high before. Of course one cannot be sure of anything.'

'Really? And presumably you dismiss this tale as a ridiculous one, just like our Loch Ness story?'

'Major Grew, I would agree were it not for something too unpleasant to mention before the Countess.'

'Oh for God's sake, Alessandri,' said the Countess. 'As you know very well, after the horrors I have seen in Budapest nothing can shock me!'

'Well then, the men on the estate saw the ground heaving. They knew what it was, they armed themselves and gave chase. He – one rashly assumes it is the male of the species – vanished. But he left behind the remains of what he had been eating. I do not wish to say what it was.'

'Do not keep us in suspense,' laughed the Countess.

'Well, forgive me? Near where the animal was found a child had been collecting pine cones. You know the seeds are used here for pesto. The child, a son of Bauer, chief gamekeeper, was found dead. His head had been bitten off.'

'Good God, how appalling,' said Charlie. 'You must send for help to find this beast. Our troops in Lienz, for example, could search the woods.'

'I don't think that would be sensible. The animal is believed to enjoy only one or two days of violence. By the time that the English get here – no reproach to your troops, but we know how slowly even the greatest armies move in days of peace – by the time the English reach us, the day after tomorrow, surely, at earliest, the beast will have vanished again, perhaps for many years.'

Charlie Grew considered. They were trying to frighten him; to prevent him from going to the valley on foot. All the same, he was glad to have his pistol with him.

'Well, the moral, Major Grew,' said the Countess, 'is that, if you do not want to be eaten by anyone out of Teutonic myths, it would be best to stay put till Sunday. As a Hungarian, I know how vile these German stories are. We have suffered from them for centuries.'

This was the first time that the Countess had addressed him. Her large dark eyes seemed suddenly less angry. Charlie Grew fancied she could not have been more than twenty-eight. If the Count were, say, fifty-five, that made quite a difference.

'When did you leave Hungary, Countess?' Charlie asked, hoping to continue the conversation.

'Centuries ago,' answered the Countess tersely and got up, signalling that both their talk and lunch were over. Doktor Alessandri walked with Charlie to his room.

'I forgot to say, Major, there is good news of your car. They say it is in working order now. Once the trees are clear, you will be able to drive off tomorrow morning! You will return to Vienna and leave behind our slightly anachronistic way of life.'

The lawyer seemed so genuine that Charlie began to wonder whether he had imagined the untoward doings in the castle. But that would mean that he had dreamed about both the knuckle in the kitchen garden and the man with the binoculars.

In his room Charlie found that a pale blue suit had been laid out on the bed, along with white shirts, blue cotton underclothes, dark blue socks and white handkerchiefs. Even a pair of canvas shoes in his size had been placed by the armchair. He lay down on the bed. He was nearly in that deep oblivion so characteristic of sleep in afternoons in hot countries, when he heard voices outside the window. He rose to close the shutter. When, however, he reached the window, he heard his hostess. He looked out. To his left and beneath him, with her back to him but close enough for him to have stretched out and stroked her golden hair through the grill, the Countess Malevolti was talking to the gardener. She had changed from the linen suit and was wearing jodhpurs for riding.

'Take him out at dusk, on a chain, of course,' she was saying, 'and before it's properly dark.'

Was it a horse of which she was speaking? A dog? Or, a man!

Charlie tiptoed back to his bed, looked for the reassurance of his pistol. It was not there. It had gone. He suddenly became overcome by fear. He determined to leave instantly. He packed his few belongings into the briefcase and went into the courtyard. It was still not four o'clock. The shutters of the windows were closed, the gate open. He went through it. He reached the croquet lawn without, he believed, being seen, and dropped over the wall. He did wonder whether he was not making a silly mistake – whether he had not exaggerated the significance of all the proceedings. But then he had to concentrate on his route through the bushes. In no time, he passed out of the sight of the castle and was in the depths of a dark forest where every clearing which looked as if it might lead to a path ended in a track which went up not down, and where the brambles and sloe bushes made descent so slow as to be scarcely perceptible. Monster or no monster, this journey was going to be difficult. After a while, he adopted the technique of walking backwards, so that the thorny bushes lost their impact against his battle dress. But that caused great confusion of route. Nor was it possible to go on downhill since the hillside did not, after all, decline with regularity. The sun should have been a guide but, in the afternoon, it lay hidden behind the castle. Of course Charlie had a compass, but to walk to a compass line was impossible. After an hour and a half he hit upon a bridle path. It did not seem to him to be going down, but at least it was a path going east. Hoping that he would not land inadvertently in Italy, he found two things: first, a view of the castle which revealed how short a distance he had travelled; second, horses' hooves recently marked. Possibly, he thought, even since lunch. He was still observing these when he heard the sound of a horse coming towards him – away from the castle. His instinct was to hide in the brambles but then he saw the foolishness of such a thing. After all, he needed help himself from whoever might give it. So he stood at the side waiting for the rider to draw level with him.

The rider was the Countess.

'*Grüss Gott, Grüss Gott*,' he managed to stammer, 'I'm taking a stroll. I needed a walk. I wanted exercise.'

'And so,' said the Countess, 'did I!' She laughed expansively and recklessly. She looked excited, flushed, happy. What had happened? She read his thoughts. 'You wonder why I am so different? Well, I can tell you. It has been decided; I am leaving tonight. At eleven I leave Europe forever. I shall never see this ugly, lonely house again. This is my last ride in Europe. My last ride till I get to Uruguay. After these months of waiting, hiding and concealing, I must say it aloud: to-night I leave for Italy! Now nothing can stop me! We shall drive through the night. Long before daybreak, we shall be in Venice. A boat is waiting. We shall set off instantly. We shall embark by the time the breakfast is being served in the Danieli. I should not be telling you but I cannot help myself.'

'But – it is lovely here – why do you want to go?'

'Why?' asked the Countess. She smiled down on him, her horse becoming restless. 'Because I am a war criminal. I am on all sorts of lists. I am wanted in Budapest for murder. It is a reasonable charge. I personally killed ten Russians and four Hungarian communists during the siege. I do not apologise – I would do it again – I only wish I had killed more, even though they were unarmed at the time. So, British officer, now you know but you can't stop me. There is no one you can get into touch with. Say what you like at dinner. I shall deny it all and pretend I have never seen you except at meals. Certainly never talked to you.'

With that she reached down and ruffled Charlie's hair, as if he were a small boy, and gave her horse a switch and trotted on. Then a thought seemed to strike her, and she called back to him.

'You know where this path leads? To the top of the Damberg. It goes nowhere else. The ride is fine, the walk less so. There's a pretty path which leads back to the castle eventually. And –' She looked seriously suddenly. 'Now, let me tell you something. This is to show you I don't hate the whole world. Only a few million! The rest, including the English, I quite like. But that's of no importance. Don't, Major, fail to do one thing before you leave the castle.'

'But I may not return to it,' Charlie feebly said.

'May not return, fiddlesticks. If you go either way along this path, you cannot leave the mountainside without returning to the castle. The thing I want to tell you is this.' She had turned her horse and ridden back towards him. 'There's an English officer in the prison beneath the castle.

He's been there for four years. He dropped into Italy, and was making his way to Austria to make friends with the so-called resistance – it didn't exist that I know of – and came through here just as you did. Malevolti entertained him as he has been entertaining you for two or three days and then popped him inside. Kept him there ever since.'

'Good God, why? What an outrage!'

'Malevolti *is* an outrage. Don't underestimate him. He kept him there because he thinks one day he might be useful. I don't believe that even now the Englishman knows that the war is at an end.'

'I do not believe it. And anyway why do you tell me all this? Are you not after all Malevolti's wife?'

'I am telling you because I want not only to be free, but to feel free. I am telling you because I hate Malevolti. It is true I am at the moment his wife. But I am a war criminal. He is letting me go – at a price. A large price incidentally. It's after all his profession now. He has smuggled many wanted men and women out of the country for money. Mostly Germans. And, I am travelling with my lover. With Heinrich Ried!'

'Heinrich Ried! The nazi! Surely he is dead?'

'He is not dead! He too has been here for months. But we leave tonight. I had been afraid for Heinrich. Malevolti wanted to keep him indefinitely –'

'Why on earth?'

'Well, you see, he likes having prisoners. He collects men. He told me once that he wants to found a human zoo. Other people, he explained, collect rare animals. He collects rare humans. So he arranges border crossings for those that don't interest him. The others, he keeps. He had a wonderful collection last year. A Frenchman, a Canadian, many Russians. How he teased them! They're all dead now. Original, isn't it?'

'Why is he giving up Ried then?'

'Oh he's got several other nazis. Better specimens in some ways. Gottfried von Acht, for example. He came last night during the storm. He thinks he's on his way to Buenos Aires. He may be. He may never leave here. You never know with Malevolti. The prisoners don't really know that they are prisoners at the beginning. I don't really know. Perhaps Malevolti doesn't know either. And, from today, I don't care.'

'Your story is so fantastic that it is hard to believe.'

'I heard the English were unimaginative.'

'What would your husband say if I told him what I know?'

'What a question, Major Grew! Your body would never be found. It's terribly easy to stage accidents in the mountains, you know. Oh, and there's somebody else you ought to know about. He's only been here a few weeks. But he's giving a lot of trouble. Probably Malevolti will kill him in some way because he's so difficult. First and foremost, because so many people are looking for him. Second, because he's a Georgian. The Russians are looking for him. The Americans too. He blew up the Russian war memorial in Vienna, or wanted to.'

'I know his name.'

'Probably you do. Perhaps you too are here looking for him? Most people are. I told you he was famous.'

'Why is he here?'

'Why? Because the Schloss is a staging point on the way to freedom. Many people do get away through Malevolti. As I and Heinrich will. Goodbye, Major. I have some packing still to do. I believe we shall meet at dinner.' She cantered off along the path. Her head was high. She turned once.

'What are you carrying in your briefcase? Guns?'

LIV

CHARLIE HAD A SENSE OF DUTY. HE COULD NOT LEAVE THE castle without discovering whether it was true that there was an English prisoner. The question of Kamo – obviously, it was Kamo – was separate, but equally important, since the military police of all four occupying powers, including his own, were looking for him. (It had been assumed that, by now, six months after being seen in Wagram, Kamo had got away.) He was not convinced that the Countess was telling the truth. Like the Count's aunt, she might be mad but the things which she said were too serious to be neglected. It did occur to Charlie that his safety, and that of the prisoners, if they existed, might be guaranteed were he to go back to the valley and return with a platoon. But he knew that General Whitelegge would take some persuading to allow him troops for such a mission, on the basis of a story told by a Hungarian countess on a horse in the woods. He would have to have harder evidence. Charlie could imagine how his story would be greeted in the mess in Klagenfurt. Colonel Rogers would require facts. So would Charlie had he been in Rogers' place.

Charlie reached his room in Schloss Tremamondo at seven, giving him an hour in which to prepare for dinner. On the dressing table there was a note: Charlie's car had been mended. The part had been repaired, not replaced. The trees had been removed from the drive. Nothing could interfere with the Major's return to the valley, although Malevolti personally hoped that he would remain until the morning. The views on the way down were spectacular and, of course, could only be seen in daylight.

The normality of this letter was equalled by the conventionality of the dinner. Malevolti was in a lively mood, talked continuously and often entertainingly. The Countess, who acknowledged Charlie with a smile, seemed calmer than before, although she appeared flushed. She was dressed in a full black satin evening dress, with a white ruffle at the neck. Her blonde hair was tightly drawn back from her face and arranged in a knot: sensible for travelling? She had also a pair of black pearl earrings. Doktor Alessandri again had little to say. His bland appearance seemed benign. Charlie wondered, as often before, from the moment that he entered the drawing room, whether he had imagined everything. The truth might be ascertained by further conversation with the Countess, alone. But the possibility of that seemed remote, if the previous evening were any guide.

After dinner they adjourned to the drawing room. The evening was thus more drawn out than the previous one. The Countess sat at the piano and played a Chopin Mazurka, expertly. Count Malevolti adopted a melancholy pose. Doktor Alessandri began leafing through an album of old photographs. Charlie, intensely puzzled, wondered whether he would ever know the truth about the castle and its denizens. He was relieved not to be in the valley trying to explain his hallucinations to Colonel Rogers. Charlie walked over to the piano determined to engage the Countess in talk for a time even if it meant interrupting her playing.

'Do you go often to Vienna, Countess?' he asked a little feebly.

'In November and in May,' she replied, without lifting her hands off the keys.

'I did not believe all you said,' said Charlie, his eyes on Malevolti who oblivious seemed transported by the music into another world.

'Why should any woman tell the truth?' she asked loudly and began to play.

About half an hour later Franz, the butler, came in and engaged Malevolti in a whispered conversation. Malevolti then withdrew into the library, and Franz followed. The Countess stopped playing.

She stood up and walked over to Charlie. He was conscious of always looking up at her, and even now her eyes were a fraction higher than his. She was very near to him.

'You will never know really the truth,' she said, 'I hope for your sake at least,' she smiled – in contempt? In pity? She left the room.

'There are difficulties,' the Doktor said to Charlie, 'I think I should tell you. The Count has been looking after some friends who have needed rest. You know he is, among other things, a student of psychiatry and friends under stress often turn to him. Quite unofficially, of course. These friends are not responding to his treatment. It is sad. Naturally it is an unfortunate interruption for him to have to worry about such things, with the work of editing his diaries already far advanced. But the Count has always placed friendship first. He is certain to be back in a minute. I know that he has two or three things that he wanted to say to you. He did so hope it might be possible.'

'I have no other engagements this evening,' said Charlie, pompously.

'Please help yourself. This is our own brandy. It is good. Unchanged since the distilling process was invented in the valley beneath us just a thousand years ago. One of Austria's many unappreciated innovations.'

When Malevolti was not in the room, his acolyte, Charlie noticed, tended to talk like him. The Doktor poured brandy out for him.

'As for me, unfortunately, I too must leave you. Like you, I have an early start tomorrow. The Count may also have to undertake a journey.'

The Doktor left the room, leaving Charlie again alone in the drawing room, as he had been when he had first come to the castle. He helped himself to brandy. He must be either entirely deceived by Malevolti, as the Countess implied; or she was insane and, seeing his discomposure, had seized on him to be a recipient of her mad confidences. Unable to decide which of the two judgements was correct, the Major sat down on the sofa, and began leafing through the album of photographs which had been the object of the Doktor's attention. An hour passed. On two occasions Franz returned, pottered about, crossed himself and withdrew. The house was silent. Was Malevolti, Charlie at last wondered, still in the library. He knew that there was another way out of that daunting room. Charlie decided to see. The book-covered door was firmly locked. Yet Malevolti had left that way.

At about a quarter to twelve, Charlie gave up the evening for lost. Whatever, good or evil, had delayed Malevolti, he was not going to return. He left the drawing room by the door leading to the courtyard and made for his room. It was a fine evening. One could scarcely believe that there had been a storm. The air was fresh. The summer was almost upon them. He walked through the courtyard, past the kitchens where some servants, including old Franz, were at work and singing in their incomprehensible dialect. He decided to stroll on the terrace. Charlie found himself outside and began to walk along the pergola towards the grill where he had seen the mysterious knuckle. There was a moon but no stars. Across the moon, clouds sped fast, as if drawn by some magnet.

There it was, an innocent air vent. He bent down. There was no knuckle. No light from within. He clasped the vent.

'Is there perhaps something about that grill which especially interests you? I had not noticed the design is out of the ordinary?' Malevolti's voice echoed from above, by the door in the orchard. Charlie started.

'No, no,' he said, 'it was just that when I passed here first I sat down and – I thought I dropped something. But it couldn't have been here.'

'Of course, it could be anywhere,' said Malevolti, 'what was it?'

'Ur. A pencil. A gold pencil. I thought it might show up in the moonlight. It is of little value. But should you find it, after I have gone, perhaps you could send it to me? I'll leave you the address.'

'Surely,' said Malevolti. 'A gold pencil? Not a thing to lose lightly.' A pause. 'Would you perhaps care to look into the cellar whose grill you have been studying? Perhaps the gold pencil fell inside? We have colossal cellars here – I should have thought of showing them to you – once used for wine – now for all sorts of things.'

'Farm goods of all sorts, I imagine,' Charlie said.

'Of course, farm goods. Apples, wines, hay even. Shall we go?'

'Certainly, if you have the time?'

'Time? I have all the time in the world. Now,' he added.

They returned through the courtyard. Through the open door of the kitchen, Charlie could see the Countess, dressed in a long brown leather coat, of the sort used for motoring in the 1920s, apparently saying goodbye to the servants. Malevolti followed Charlie's eyes.

'My wife is taking a journey tomorrow, just as you are. Not far. But she needs to get away. We all do sometimes. She leaves early. She wants to say goodbye to the staff. She is Hungarian, you know. A wonderful people. But restless.'

Malevolti went to a door in the courtyard and unlocked it. He turned a switch, and motioned Charlie to go on. He hesitated but ruefully thought that this was not the time for hanging back. He walked down the first steps leading into the cellar and waited at the corner of the staircase for Malevolti to follow him. As he did so, a small, fair man came running up the steps and pushed past him. He turned to look at Charlie as he passed and smiled. A charming smile. There could be no doubt of it, it was the endlessly sought after fugitive, the mysterious groom, the Georgian, Kamo.

Charlie started back, to Malevolti who was, to his relief, following him down the stairs.

'Who was that?'

'One of the stable boys. A delightful lad. I think his name is Dietrich. Why?'

'I don't believe you.'

'My dear Major Grew! What can you mean.'

'Get the boy back.'

'Certainly.' Malevolti called back into the courtyard: 'Dietrich! There is a gentleman who wants to speak to you.'

The boy returned, not smiling. Charlie looked at him carefully.

'Surely you are Kamo? You are the man who escaped from the Russian train. You are Georgian.'

The boy looked him in the eyes: 'I am sorry I do not know what you are talking about. I am Dietrich. I have lived here all my life. I am an Austrian.'

Charlie considered.

'Forgive me, Count, I have made a mistake. I could have sworn – but perhaps I am wrong.'

'We all make mistakes,' said Malevolti easily, 'do not preoccupy yourself. You have finished with Dietrich? Or Kamo, as you call him?'

'Yes, I have finished.' Dietrich bowed, and Charlie and Malevolti proceeded on a tour of the cellars. They were immense. Room after vaulted room, lit by bare bulbs. It seemed as if the house had not only been built upon them, but that they stretched far into the gardens. He saw vats of wine, corridors full of apples, rooms full of grain. There seemed to be no shortage of food.

'And here,' said Malevolti, 'we come to the room in which you were interested. Forgive me if I go first.'

Charlie was relieved that Malevolti should go first. All the same, his expectation of being shut in was renewed. There was certainly a grill. It might be the grill which led to the terrace. Or, again, it might not be. In darkness, all grills are alike. The room was one which could have served as a cell. It would not have been agreeable.

'My wife used to say that these cellars have been built in the shape of a cathedral. Well, they are remarkable. For a hilltop, unique. I suppose my ancestors anticipated long sieges. Even I have never entered all the rooms. Who knows what secrets may be hidden here for centuries! There are places comparable in Italy. None here in Austria. The great cellars of Göttweig and Melk are puny in comparison.'

They looked on the floor of the cell for the golden pencil without success. Malevolti promised to return it if it was discovered outside.

They returned to the courtyard. Malevolti escorted Charlie to his room.

'I wish you a good night. Shall I ask for you to be called at eight? Very good. What a pity that we have talked so little. Major Grew, I do hope that we can look forward to this being the beginning of a friendship. Our two nations, yours still a mighty empire, mine now a poor truncated limb, still have something to offer the world. We can benefit from conversation. Good night, and please do me the favour of sleeping *really* well.' Malevolti left him.

Charlie felt more confused than ever. He believed himself still on treacherous ground, indeed he could not see the firm ground at all. The only thing was that somehow he knew himself to have been out-manoeuvred. He looked at the books in the shelf on the dressing table, at the pictures and sat for a moment at the table.

There was a knock at the door.

'Come in.'

It was the Countess Malevolti.

'Didn't you want something more?' she asked. In his memory he could not decide whether she had spoken this provocatively. At the time, he thought she did.

He took a step forward. A flame unexpectedly kindled.

'No,' she said, stepping back, 'I did not mean what is crossing your mind. I meant this –' With that she drew out his revolver from her pocket.

'You may need it,' she laughed, 'here we think of such things as the poor Romanovs thought of Fabergé eggs.'

It had been well polished. The Countess left the room while he was examining it.

LV

CHARLIE FOLLOWED HIS HOST'S INSTRUCTIONS. HE SLEPT well, heavily, and late. He awoke with a start, after eight. There had been no call and no breakfast. But today, he remembered, was Sunday. Even so, he felt angry for having permitted himself the indulgence of a late sleep. He opened the shutters. Sun streamed in. He dressed. He had an acute sense of having acted foolishly the preceding day. He thought of Malevolti and the Doktor with appreciation. He pitied the Count that he had such a disturbed wife. But if she were indeed Hungarian, she had lost her country; so perhaps it was understandable that she had lost her reason too.

He went to the dining room. Silence. There was no sign of servants. Nor of breakfast. He went to the drawing room. Nothing had changed from the previous night. The photograph album lay on the sofa where he had left it. The brandy stood on the table. The signed photograph of De Gasperi stood on the piano. The door into the library was locked. The windows were closed, the curtains drawn. He went out, down to the courtyard. The kitchen doors were shut and locked. So were the doors of the cellars. The door of the castle was open. Everything else was closed. The throng of maids whom he had seen last night saying goodbye to the Countess had vanished. Franz in his pink coat was gone. He walked through room after room, calling into some that he had never seen. He returned to the court-yard of the castle. Only echoes answered him. He ran into the kitchen garden. There was no gardener. There was no knuckle at the grill. The building was deserted. Nor was there any sign of his, or of any other car. He returned to his room, picked up his revolver and briefcase, and set off down the drive beyond the gate – the little gate through which he had first come was open – in search of the small farmstead outside which he had observed on his way up.

The farmer's wife was at home. She was friendly but non-committal. She had had an idea that the Count and Countess would be leaving with some guests one of those days. She had no idea how long they would be away. The Count used to be away in the old days for weeks, even months on end. Vienna certainly, also Venice. So far as she knew, there were no cars to be seen in the neighbourhood. There had been a black car there the previous day, quite true. But she thought the Countess might have taken it. The Countess loved cars, she drove like the wind. She also rode a lot. Yes, her horses were there, her husband looked after them. As to the servants, well it was Sunday and often on Sundays there would be only a few people at the castle. No, she had never heard of a stable boy called Dietrich. They did not have such a person, her son Pepi helped out when he was needed. But one could never tell nowadays. As to guests, she could not say. There was a great coming and going. She knew Doktor Alessandri. A stern man, she thought.

That was that. Charlie walked down the drive up which he had come. There was no sign of his car. Nor of fallen trees. At the bottom, he did see the same two women in black whom he had met before. They were walking up, not down. They did not look at him and this time he said nothing to them. It was four hours before he found himself in a village with a telephone.

Charlie did not tell anyone in detail about this journey when he returned to Vienna. He did not know what to make of it all. He had to confess himself out of his depth. He filed a dull report. He had a lot of trouble about the missing motor car. The Major told the quartermaster that it had been stolen when he was lunching in the König von Ungarn Hotel in Klagenfurt. The quartermaster raised his eyebrows. The occurrence seemed to risk a setback in his career, hitherto brilliant. Then people forgot. When, two years later, a car similar to his was found in a ruined condition in a ravine in the Val Popena in the South Tyrol the matter was deemed to have been cleared up. It had evidently been stolen.

Charlie did ask about Heinrich Ried. Everyone assumed that he had got away, probably to "somewhere in South America". In the early 1950s, he was reported in the Pampa. But after that he vanished. Charlie never made any enquiries about the fate of the castles in southern Carinthia. They were becoming too big to be lived in without servants and many were allowed to go to ruin: including, probably, Schloss Tremamondo. The decomposed body of a British officer lost in the war was one day found in a ravine on the Italian side of the Alps in the region of Damberg. His papers suggested 1944 as a date of death although one of the pathologists thought it could not have been earlier than 1948. His views were discounted.

As the years passed, Charlie's conviction grew that the story told by the Countess on the bridle path was substantially correct. He never referred to it. Kamo, Malevolti, the Countess, Doktor Alessandri, Heinrich Ried, Gottfried von Acht, and even Franz remained in his memory as if they had been disagreeable hobgoblins in a nightmare. But they were hidden, beneath the carapace of professionalism which carried him upwards in his career. In intelligence operations, after all, a capacity to forget is as important as one to remember.

283

PART 6

1955–1956

LVI

YEARS PASSED. THE AUSTRIANS PERSUADED THE RUSSIANS that they would remain a no-man's land in the centre of Europe. *Na Zdravie!* proved the most successful policy towards the Russians. Poldi Moser ruined his health in drinking the Russians' health. Alois von Acht's persistence carried him to the top of Austrian politics. If that peak turned out less high than it was when first glimpsed through Habsburg windows, it was a pretty high one all the same. A treaty was signed. The Allied Missions including the Russians withdrew. General Whitelegge, when he became a peer in the 1960s, adopted under his new coat of arms the motto *Serio sed ad tempo*: late but in time. Many prisoners came home, even from Russia. The Austrians could begin to think again of Lower Austria and the Burgenland as a part of civilisation, while the Achts from Vienna could drive out to visit the Achts in Besselberg. The Opera was reopened.

The first production was *Fidelio*. The evening was remembered, not only by all present, but by those who had not managed to be present, as the beginning of an era. Thekla – was she ninety-six or more? – with two generations of nephews and nieces in her box, was critical. The decoration seemed dull, not grand enough: only two thousand could be there, not three thousand. Two thousand! When the need was for more seats, not less, considering how people were enriching themselves. Though many of the stars of the past were there, some who had gone to America – "the new Austro–Hungarian Empire", Thekla called it – had not even been invited. Maria Jeritza, the greatest singer of them all, for example, was not there.

The Austrian cabinet, of course, were there including Alois von Acht sitting beside Poldi Moser, the latter suffering from the cirrhosis which would send him to an early grave. The Viennese saw through their opera glasses that their old friend Brooks Sheay was with the American ambassador. Sheay was known as the Americans' chief of intelligence in Europe. In one of the English boxes sat Colonel Grew, who had come back to the British Embassy as a security attaché. The always popular Tatiana was by his side. Despite a record number of refusals, she had finally married him. The Trustee of the Louvre, Maître Marchais, had flown in specially, with his new wife known in Vienna as Madame Charpentier. An astonishing number of Viennese seemed able to afford the expensive tickets. But there were many nouveaux riches. Thus Willy Svoboda – he remained a rich bachelor – had some of the good seats. There were also many Americans in the best boxes, a thing which outraged those Viennese who had found it hard to find tickets.

Next to Thekla was a bald individual, with a melancholy cast of face, whose age was difficult to judge. It was, as old friends discovered in the interval (and did not know what to say), Rüdiger von Acht, who had returned, two weeks before, after eleven years in prisons and camps in Russia. Whenever anyone commiserated with him and said "ten years!" he would say, "well, it could have been worse". It was not in any way a recognisable Rüdiger von Acht. The wild young man who would have set his cap at any vain cause, provided Kleist had a line justifying it, had died somewhere in the lumber farms of Karaganda. Rüdiger had turned into a hesitant, thoughtful, troubled man who wanted "to give the Russians their due".

'Mind you,' he would say, after recalling some anecdote of mediaeval horror, 'mind you, I learnt a lot in Russia. It was an education. One could never have it in ordinary circumstances. You know, when you see Prussian field marshals playing dominoes in captivity – well, then, you learn something, don't you?'

'What do you learn?' someone asked him.

'Oh well,' he would say, 'you learn. You really do.'

Hearing this balanced approach, Alice would sob. She had slaved for the children all these years, cleaned for Russians in her house and had seethed with rage at the iniquity of the thing, until her quiet personality developed an unyielding fury. Rüdiger would be sympathetic – as he had not been at the sight of tears in the 1930s. But he would observe her, rather as if Alice's conduct was just one more aspect of human life with which, with all his experiences, he would one day learn to cope.

Next to Rüdiger and Alice were their cousins from Besselberg, Otto's children, now grown up and doing well: Jean Marie, a theatrical producer, married and living in Munich; Theresia just married to one of the Moldens; Franzie was still at the university but had been left by Jean Marie in control of Besselberg. The Achts were adapting. Thus Alice's children were establishing themselves: Heini was now an engineer, while Anna, who had eschewed the university, was in a firm concerned with pharmaceutical goods.

In the first interval of *Fidelio*, Vienna and her guests flooded through the bars and saloons, bowing to and studying each other, noticing among other things that the once controversial Moritz Schwind paintings were undamaged in the old foyer.

'All I can see is that they've created room for a thousand new drinkers and taken away a thousand seats,' Aunt Thekla commented.

Jean Marie and his young English wife had not expected to see so many of their cousins. He had scarcely ever seen his cousin Antoinette since that unhappy Christmas Day of 1946. She was now looking mature and grand: she had married a Sudeten German who had arrived in Vienna with nothing in 1947, after a year in a Czech prison. He now was a millionaire.

'You know, Jean Marie,' Antoinette said to him at the opera bar, taking up a great deal of space with her new creation by Dior, 'I've always thought that Austria would be all right after the war when I remember your wonderful performance of *Maria Stuart* that Christmas.'

'It was *Don Carlos*,' he said smiling, 'but I know what you mean.'

'Don't you think Irmgard Seefried is the equal of any singer in the past?' asked Antoinette Bender.

'Anyone, anyone,' answered Countess Orsova without listening.

'I don't like the Pizarro, though, do you?'

'Not at all, not at all,' the Countess replied, 'but surely that must be Ludwig Börne? What an extraordinary thing. I was sure he was dead. He must be well over eighty. He was old even when we used to see him before the war.'

The great publisher was bearing down on them. He looked at the Countess with unseeing eyes. A stroke had injured his reflexes. He spoke more slowly than in the past. But he looked even more imperial than he had before. One of the Dalmatian emperors perhaps. He was in the company of a blonde American actress, Lana Gerhart, also born in Vienna. They were making as fast as they could across the room to greet Minister Alois von Acht.

Alois's hair was now white. He looked more like Beethoven than he had ten years before. He had now been in power in one way or another for over ten years. He was still young, still only in his 'fifties, but the earnestness, and the partisanship of his youth had gone. He seemed even mellow. He had never married after Lise's death: there had been no liaison that anyone knew of. The friendship which people talked of with the English secretary, Pat Mackenzie, had never amounted to anything. Perhaps his daughter Klara, and her dramas, compensated for the absence of a new marriage.

Herr Börne descended upon him. Greetings, embraces, handshakes. Börne had not been in Vienna for years. In fact, not since the first winter after the war. How things had changed since then! Of course, things were still shabby but Herr Börne detected a real rebirth. Yes, he was staying at Sacher's. Nothing had changed there. Strange that his father would never have dreamt of even going there. The Opera? Oh excellent. Seefried was every bit as good as Jeritza. Dermota made a remarkable Florestan. A master. The Opera House? Cleaner lines, one might say. Incidentally, did Herr von Acht know Lana Gerhart? He would present her. Such a talent. A real discovery. How was Herr Acht's family? That ravishing daughter? Married? Excellent! But what a pity no grandchildren. That would come. And the other children? Building bridges? Across autobahns, not rivers, how strange! Very good. Herr Doktor von Acht would excuse him. There was Herr Moser. He had to salute Herr Moser. And so must Lana Gerhart. 'She too is Austrian, you know,' he was saying. Not Viennese, Eisenstadt! Born under the shadow of that horrible yellow palace. But now, and for many years, an American citizen of course. America? Well, it was a whole world. People who thought it a country made a great error there. He, Börne, now had publishing houses and newspapers which sold everywhere from California to Florida, from the Rio Grande to Grand Central Station. It was a different thing. In a way, perhaps, yes, America did resemble the old *Kaiserliches und königliches Reich*. But on how much bigger a scale! Far more open. Herr Börne moved on, pressing hands. The bell for the end of the interval rang.

During the next act there was criticism of the way that the new production had been mounted: re-arrangements, new decor, new 'business' and so on. An undercurrent of complaint was evident in the President's box. On an occasion like this, one had to keep one's critical facilities active. So there was even more talk in the second interval.

Once again, the crowd of bejewelled women and white-tied men swept out to tour the lobbies. One saw jewels believed lost or sold, and people believed dead, as well as a new generation of jewel-seekers and treasure hunters.

Princess Kuttenberg, her now even rounder figure still swathed in pink, anchored to her by dusty diamonds, sat contentedly with Countess Orsova, whose appearance had become that of a bird of prey.

'We are the survivors,' the latter said. 'We may be eighty, but we have seen more than these people. Incidentally,' she added, 'what do you do when you see the Countess Gmunden?'

'I try and catch her eye as she approaches. But I do so coldly – so – and bow – so – but not smile. If she comes too near, she could give me a kiss. I should prefer not. Fortunately, I did not see her in the first interval.'

'Nor I. But now she is coming our way.'

It was true. The still wonderful-looking Countess was making her way through the throng, rustling in black taffeta, a smile, a kiss here, even a sentence there.

'She must be thirty at least now,' said the Countess Orsova. 'Mind you, I never admired her looks. Too theatrical. Look at that ridiculous waist, no wonder she has no children.'

The two old ladies sat wondering how the younger woman would greet them. It could be anything: cold; or gushing. But, as it happened, she did not come their way. She had seen the burly figure of the famous American friend of Austria, Brooks Sheay, and made for him instead.

'Very rude of her, I would say,' said Countess Orsova. 'She should have greeted us.'

'Of course, she should,' said Princess Kuttenberg.

'She knows nothing,' said the two ladies together.

A pale young American man in a dinner jacket was standing by them.

'Excuse me,' he said in excellent German, 'would you know who is that magnificent-looking lady in black who has just passed over there?'

'That? Oh that,' said Countess Orsova, who had never before spoken to anyone to whom she had not been introduced, 'is Countess Gmunden. One of the great beauties of our time, don't you think? A daughter of State Minister Alois von Acht. A very intelligent person too, is that not so, Hélène?'

'Utterly so.'

'Thank you. Forgive me for asking.'

The young American turned back to his party of four men, two women. Rich young Americans, without a care in the world. He seemed to be reporting what he had learned to a slightly older, balding man – who still only in his 'thirties, seemed to be the central character in the group.

'Do tell me who that is?' Countess Orsova put her question to Willy Svoboda who, all courtesy as usual, had come, in his white tie, to greet them.

'Do you know, that's George Grenville. One of the richest men in America, and hence the world. He always travels with a team of assistants. All of them young. He owns airlines, hotels, film companies. We had it in the paper yesterday that he was coming here. No one in Vienna has seen him in the flesh before. It's worth being here if only to see him.'

'But Willy, you too have done so well.' The Countess Orsova was flattering.

'Yes, but only here in Austria. George Grenville operates on a world scale. The Pacific. Japan. South America. He's really somebody.'

'Then why is he here?' snapped Aunt Thekla. Bored with observations through her lorgnette, she had persuaded Alice to take her into the bar. 'In Vienna, I mean. Austria's a backwater. Nothing is going to happen here again.'

'The new Europe will recover,' said a man of about sixty standing next to her.

'Rubbish. The new Europe will never recover. We shall take turns in seeing how we can get to Washington quickest. Austria is what Europe will be.'

'Aunt Thekla, you are certainly being Uncle Max's sister tonight and no mistake,' said Alice.

'What's wrong with that?' snapped the old lady 'Mark my words. We're finished. With any luck, we'll be dull. So we'll be happy. It was in Frederick III's time that they coined the phrase "Happy is the country with no history". Frederick III. I suppose no one remembers who he was.'

'Of course they remember! You shouldn't sound so cross Aunt Thekla,' Franzie von Acht had joined them.

'You only know because you read, Franzie, but no one learns that sort of thing any more,' Aunt Thekla went on, 'and more's the pity. Who was Charlemagne's second wife? I can tell you: Desiderata, it was, and a very pretty name too. That's the only history which counts. No one learns it.'

'None of my children knows who Desiderata was,' said Alice stoutly, 'but they're happy, good Austrians. They'll be all right. They'll do well.'

'Won't be the same. They won't be Austrians.'

It was just as well, perhaps, that the bell for the end of the second interval rang. They returned for the last act.

Countess Orsova found herself searching the auditorium for the rich Mr George Grenville. She swivelled her binoculars furiously. She saw the President, she saw old actresses and singers, old critics and old editors, she saw many members of the Gotha, she saw Habsburgs, ambassadors and ministers, but she could not find the American and his party. She gave up. Suddenly she realised that he was sitting in the next box to her. That was the reason why she could not see them. She craned over and tried to listen to their savage conversation, in its horrible English but, though she had had an English governess, like many in her generation, she could not understand a word.

'Such a charming group of Americans,' she said to the Princess Kuttenberg and sat back in her chair as the curtain went up.

At the end of the opera, there was much cheering and many encores – "for what, all things considered, was a fairly indifferent production". The rich Americans slipped away without being seen. No one saw them again in Vienna save Willy Svoboda, who had some business to do with them: and even he only met one of Mr Grenville's assistants. It was well known in business circles that Mr Grenville scarcely talked to anyone except occasionally on the telephone; and, even on the telephone, it was believed that he talked only to New York or Chicago.

LVII

*T*HREE MONTHS AFTER RÜDIGER HAD GOT BACK TO AUSTRIA there had been no Acht family reunion to welcome him. Alice did not feel it was for her to do anything formal. She thought that Alois should do so, as a minister. But he was busy. The Besselberg Achts were so preoccupied with what to do about their property that they never seemed to talk about anything else. A great house can be a great burden. George Acht, now married, lived in America and had broken with the family. Aunt Thekla was too poor, though game.

Alice had been pondering this and wondering how to discuss the matter with Rüdiger. Rüdiger had made no effort as yet to find any employment: understandable, but surely his pride should prevent him from forever living off Alice even if she owned, as well as managed, a bookshop in the Kärtnerstrasse. Of course, the Achts had money, but nothing like enough for Rüdiger to stay idle for the rest of his life. The children were earning but, again, their father would not want, presumably, to live off them. *Presumably* was the word, since Rüdiger was still living in a dreamy manner, apparently independent of reflection about the future. Such an attitude was more that of a pre-war Austrian, not a man of 1956. Alice thought that he half missed Russia; or rather the camps, for he had never seen Russia. Every evening, he would reminisce about people whom he had met in the camps, people of unmatched courage, resilience and imagination, whose company he had loved.

'All nationalities, mark you. One could find a friend from the Italian communists or Japanese officers. Croats. Whatever you like. Amazing people.' Then he would say: 'Mark you, you can't but like the ordinary Russian. They're remarkable people. Such patience. So long suffering. They'd do anything for you. Of course, they hate their government. You can see it. No, they wouldn't say so, too dangerous. But you sense it.'

One morning, the telephone rang. It was half past eight. Alice was about to go to the shop, while Rüdiger was still asleep. Anna had already left for her office; Heini was away.

'Yes, who is it?'

'Aunt Alice?'

'Yes.'

'It's Klara.'

'Klara!' Incredible! Alice had scarcely spoken to Klara for ten years. 'Yes, Klara, how nice to talk to you.'

'Aunt Alice. I was wondering. Shouldn't we have a family party to welcome back Uncle Rüdiger? After all he did have ten years there, didn't he? It's quite a long time.'

'Yes, Klara.'

'Would you think it quite wrong of me to arrange it? I could do it so easily. It would give Kurt such pleasure too.' Kurt was Count Gmunden, cordially loathed by every member of the Acht family – 'and every member of every other family that I have ever heard of,' as Aunt Thekla put it.

'Well, Klara –'

'Do leave it to me, Aunt Alice. I'd love to do it. It would be a way of making up.'

'Making up?'

'Compensating, then. So is it agreed?'

Alice did agree; though she never got to know what Klara meant by 'making up.'

The arrangements were made by Klara. Magnificently. The dinner would be at Klara's house in the ancient square, Am Hof. Count Gmunden had bought an old building there for almost nothing in 1947 and there was ample room for a banquet. Only recently the house had been redecorated – the outside in that Habsburg yellow which all Austria was then, as it were, painting itself, in order to be persuaded that nothing had happened between the fall of the Empire and the present: a necessary piece of historical amnesia.

Few members of the Acht family had been to Klara Gmunden's house. Fewer of the younger members had even been invited to her wedding. None of the older members had accepted the invitations which they had received. Count Gmunden was not acceptable, and that was that. Afterwards, there had never been any move towards a rapprochement by Klara herself, even though she went out a good deal and latterly, more often than not, without Count Gmunden, known to be ill with a "debilitating disease."

Why Count Gmunden should have been quite so reviled was never apparent. He came from a respectable landed family, which used to have estates in Lower Austria – not Gmunden itself, with which delicate city he had no connection. He had worked with the nazis, true, but, on examination, no more enthusiastically than others still well received in Austrian life. He had also been quicker than others in making up to the

Russians. Again, thousands of people had done that: one had had to do it to live. Then he himself was now rich – at least, in Austrian terms. That could only be something to do with the black market. But then other people had profited by that. What disturbed people was that the Count had played an important part with *both* the nazis *and* the Russians. What part, no one could say. Count Gmunden was not only untrustworthy but in some indefinable way the reverse of charming. The fact that he had carried off the wonderful but slightly flawed Klara von Acht added to his reprehensible qualities. Finally, no one knew what he was; a business-man? A public relations man? Moscow's man in Vienna? Or, even, rep-resentative of a group of American banks? All was obscure. Nor did anyone know just how rich he was: perhaps it was façade. Still, a house in Am Hof needed upkeep. There seemed to be any number of servants there. Klara dressed well. It was odd. The oddness upset Klara's relations. Their taste as a family for the unexpected had once been limitless. Think of Max, think of Gottfried. But now they, like other Austrians, wanted a change from such things. Conventionality was *à la mode*.

In practice, Klara's behaviour had been a source of conversation. What would conversation have been during the many dull years, waiting for the signature of the state treaty, if there had not been Klara to talk about?

So it was, with peculiar fascination, and diverse motives, that about sixty people of all ages found themselves accepting Klara's invitation to a dinner in her house on a February day the year after the signature of the state treaty.

'Do you think there will be an empty place for Uncle Gottfried in case he turns up at the last minute?' asked Jean Marie von Acht's English wife Anne when they received the invitation in Munich.

'No, I don't think we can expect empty places. There would have to be rather a number of those.'

'Can they mean that they want us to bring Ralph?' Anne asked. (They had called their son aged seven, Ralph, after Ralph Richardson, whom Anne admired.) 'It's nice of Klara, but I wonder what she thinks such a very young Acht will do there. Perhaps she doesn't realise how young he is.'

'No, perhaps not. I don't think you even know her, quite true. But then I haven't seen her for years. Except in the distance at the Opera.'

Jean Marie walked over to the tall windows of the flat which looked down on the English Garden. Every year there were rumours that Uncle Gottfried was in South America. It was a hard thing to say but he privately hoped he was dead. No one wanted him discovered, and dragged back to be tried again. No one now remembered what he had been guilty of. It was not irony on Anne's part to ask about the extra place. Other family feasts had done exactly that in Germany. Jean Marie had lived long enough in Munich to want to avoid all dramatic scenes. Dramatic producer though he was, he wanted to live in an age of prose. Everything was to be professional. Germans – German Austrians too, if one could still use the term – had had enough rhetoric. Jean Marie was delighted to hear from letters from his sister that even Uncle Rüdiger had forgotten Kleist.

Among other turbulence caused by Klara's dinner was the rumour circulating in the family that Klara had invited Willy Svoboda: and, even more extraordinary, had not invited the Countess Orsova and Princess Kuttenberg.

The two latter ladies made it clear that they did not mind. They both, as it happened, had something to do on the occasion itself. Countess Orsova, neither connected by blood with Rüdiger nor even a friend, was in no way surprised. She did feel, however, for the Princess, a second cousin of Alice von Acht's mother and who had done so much for Alice during 'the difficult days.' The Princess said she did not care either. But she did think it surprising that an outsider and a commoner – one could not put it differently – such as Willy Svoboda should have been invited. Svoboda! Son of a Czech tailor! One would like to talk to Alois about it, but he was so aloof, so *affairé*: indeed, he was so polished that one half preferred him in his old communist days (although many people said that he had never been a real communist, Princess Kuttenberg knew better.) But the real question was, why was Klara asking little Willy Svoboda? One would like to know. Of course, he had looked after Max at the end. So had all Vienna in its day, so that was no reason, and someone such as Willy would never understand just how important Max had been nor how learned. Or did Klara know something that they did not? Had there been talk of the tailor's wife, Willy's mother? They really could not remember. How could one remember every little story about every Czech tailor in Vienna? One feared that Klara had invited Willy because he was now rich. If that was going to be the criteria by which modern Austria was to be judged, and people asked to dinner or not asked to dinner, God save them all!

The dinner was a challenge. It was to be full evening dress. Alice, hurrying back from the bookshop, found Rüdiger complaining bitterly that he had no studs, no clean collars, nothing ready: that, despite years in concentration camps, he had become too fat for his dress coat. Alice had therefore to pay a visit to the little shop on the corner of the Rennweg which was always open, at least till ten o'clock in the evenings – a symbol, so Alice was wont to say, stuffily, as to how Austrians now worked in the evenings, instead of going to political meetings, as their fathers had done in the 1930s.

Rüdiger had spent the day preparing his speech. Alice had begged him to show her what he was going to say. He had refused. Alice was terrified lest he would say something which would offend everyone – such as that they would all be better off for ten years in Russia. She resigned herself to knowing that someone would be hurt – perhaps Klara – but Alice, a kindly woman at heart, did not think that that mattered: Klara was tough. She had to be, to be married to Kurt Gmunden. The two children, Heini and Anna, would be no help about all this. They had embarked on their own careers. They were non-political. Indeed, not only would they not help, but they did not see the reason to do so. Heini had returned only that day from a course at the Massachusetts Institute of Technology, Anna was preparing for another pharmaceutical exam half an hour before they were due to leave for the banquet.

Alice's bedroom was again the one where, for so many years, Colonel Voronov had lived, and smoked, with some of his "wives". She was just finishing dressing – her red velvet was a little tight – and Rüdiger was still groaning with his studs in the next room when the telephone rang.

'Yes?'

'This is Klara.'

'Of course, Klara, we shall be there as we said, early enough, I hope, by 7.30 or at least 7.45. Rüdiger's ready.' She looked across at him, but without confidence, as he stood in the dressing room still fiddling with his tie, complaining with every movement. 'The children will be coming a little later.'

'That doesn't matter, Aunt Alice,' Klara's voice sounded infinitely weary, 'I want you to know something. It will be in the papers tomorrow. We can't stop it.'

'Yes?' Alice, who shared her nephew Jean Marie's feelings about the odiousness of great events, had suddenly a horrible suspicion that the age of drama might be about to begin again, at least in the Acht family.

'It's Kurt. He shot himself this afternoon.'

'Kurt, your husband? Dead?'

'No, unfortunately not. But he's in hospital.'

'Oh Klara, why? How awful for you. Of course we shan't come.'

Had she really said 'unfortunately not'? Surely –

'The dinner goes ahead, Aunt Alice. I have decided. It's essential.'

'Why did he do it? No, no, I don't want to know now.'

'I am telling only you. No one else will know.'

'How terrible!'

'Until 7.30. Goodbye.'

'Goodbye, until 7.30.'

Alice put the telephone down. Rüdiger was at her side.

'What was it?'

Alice was determined not to tell him. She did not want drama under any circumstances. Not in public. Not that night. She wondered whether they *should* go. Not knowing anything of the true relations between Kurt and Klara she could not picture herself in Klara's position. In any case, they were not comparable personalities.

'Well, why don't you say who it was?'

'Klara. Shall we say, for the moment, darling, that she called to say that she has broken a valuable bowl? A very old family relic. But the party will go on.'

Rüdiger hesitated.

'Very odd. Didn't know Klara had any good bowls. Alois and Lise certainly didn't. There were some good figurines at Besselberg but Betty wouldn't have given them away. Not Betty. Suppose it was his family's?'

'I suppose so.'

Rüdiger was oppressed by the prospect of his speech. Now bespectacled when he read anything, Rüdiger was different from the kind of man that his relations remembered. How dashing he had been, how spontaneous, how delightfully preposterous – and how long those amiable youthful characteristics had lasted into his marriage, even till the war. Alas, the confused, bent, friendly, bald man arriving at Klara's beautiful house, did not fit the memory which even Alice had had of her husband in the years before 1945. Rüdiger knew that he had changed too. Still, this was a test for them all. Alice had been looking forward to it. She was grateful to Klara for going ahead with an occasion which anyone else would have abandoned.

As they entered the hall, a quartet of violinists was playing waltzes. Klara received her guests there. She looked calm, beautiful, but not exactly young. Too much paint. Well, that was understandable. Anyway, Alice admired her that night. She kissed her warmly.

'Uncle Rudi!' said Klara, 'it has been a – very long time indeed. You look – well, older, I must say but, just as nice.'

Rudi smiled and Alice wondered for a moment whether he was going to weep.

'Too early in the evening to cry,' said Klara nicely. 'Tell me if you like the table arrangement.'

They went into the white and gold dining room and examined the *place à table*. Klara used the French style of seating, then fashionable in Vienna, in which the host and hostess sat opposite one another in the middle. She had Rudi on her right. On her left, there was Jean Marie. Opposite her, in place of Kurt, she had seated Ralph, Jean Marie's young son.

'I thought I'd have the new generation opposite,' Klara said, 'and then on Ralph's right Thekla, the oldest beside the youngest. How old is Ralph?'

'Oh, about seven,' said Alice laughing.

'Well, then Thekla will do the talking and he'll remember what she says longer than anyone. Then, you know, I must warn you I've asked one or two new friends. Not related. There's a couple, the Grews, at the British Embassy whom I like. She was here after the war – Tatiana Bezhukov, she was then – you know, a relation of the Papenlohes, I think – she's a real person, she's become a great friend. You'll like her enormously. Wonderful eyes, very Russian. Her husband's a typical Englishman – very good-looking but so – well, English! You needn't worry about him. Brave, I believe. Tatiana says he liberated Baden-bei-Wien in 1945 all by himself, and nobody noticed. Doesn't seem likely, does it? Then there's Willy Svoboda. Sorry, Uncle Rudi, all this will seem so tiresome but it's good to get it over. Willy Svoboda now. He's a clever man. So quick. Very kind too. Is it all right, Aunt Alice? I do hope so. Uncle Rudi?'

Klara prattled on and Alice thought how charming she was, but brittle with less 'soul' than she had promised before everything had collapsed, if that was the right way of putting it. The waltzes continued and Alice accepted a slivovitz – unusual for her – from one of the footmen and stood drinking it in front of a warm fire. She thought how extraordinary it was that Klara should have such a burden – a shot husband – and treat it so lightly. Then she thought, 'I don't even know whether he did it on purpose; I assumed so. But perhaps it was an accident. The sort of accident that people had when they went shooting. That must be it.' But that 'unfortunately not' stuck in her mind. Perhaps it was a slip of the tongue.

All of a sudden, and all at once, the guests began to stream in. Handshakes, kisses of hands and of cheeks, dropping of furs and of loden coats onto footmen and maids, as well as of heavy dark overcoats brought on visits to London or New York, straightening of ties, checking of studs, brushing of shoulders, compliments to Klara, on the house, on the music, on the open fire, on the pictures, on herself. In no time at all, fifty people were in the room, their talk drowning the music. Rudi looked happy but confused. He drank two glasses of champagne and started behaving graciously, for once, as if he were at home.

'Yes, they were harsh years,' he could be heard saying to almost every-one, 'really difficult, in some ways. But fascinating times all the same. You know, in Vorkuta, I met a Romanian who gave me a good tip. In a concentration camp above the Arctic Circle, the way to survive is to volunteer to work in the mortuary. Why? Because when people die, there has to be a post mortem. And to have a post mortem, you need to have a warm room. The body can't be frozen. *Ergo* the man who works in the mortuary keeps warm. Keeps alive. You keep alive if you are in the mortuary! That's good, isn't it? You see the point? That's a good fire though, isn't it?' he said pointing to Klara's logs, merrily burning.

Alice heard him telling Klara another tale.

'I was in a transit camp outside Kiev. In a railway waggon. Very hot. Terribly overcrowded. Wouldn't have missed it for the world. You see what human nature is. All these people here tonight. They don't know. I know. I've seen human nature as it is. Not as poets describe it. As it is. A Russian said to me – wonderful man – a bearded man straight out of Dostoevsky I'd say, if only I'd read him then – he said in warm weather, you should volunteer to work in the camp latrines. The nausea will wear off after a week. Then after that, you can be certain you're doing something good. To keep yourself and all the others alive, you need clean, efficient, latrines. Funny how one remembers these things. But one does. One learns.'

Alice remembered that Rudi did not know much about Klara's adventures the other side of the Russian lines, whatever they were. But it was too late to go into that that evening. He just was not interested in other people. It would be doubtful if he would understand.

They went in to dinner. Many servants seemed to be standing about. At one end of the table, the life and soul of the party as she had been ten years before, was Tatiana Grew, née Bezhukov. She was sitting between Max von Acht's son Otto, who had been a prisoner in America for a short time and Besselberg Otto's third son Hans who, at twenty-two, was at the University studying law. Next to him was Alice's Anna, the pharmacist.

'No, not a chemist, an ordinary pharmacist. I'm studying too.'

'Really, in a white coat?' asked Hansie.

'Exactly, in a white coat. I go at eight in the morning. I serve customers on the prescription desk. I tell them things that their doctor would not. I act as their consultant. It's a rewarding day.'

Tatiana laughed. 'I expect you enjoy the gossip with the customers most,' she said.

'You laugh, it is not a grand job, but I get as much satisfaction from it as Uncle Otto got from running his house, or as Jean Marie from producing plays. I am of service. I meet people. Every sort. And, people like me!'

'How often do you go home to Besselberg, Hansie?' Tatiana asked. 'I do remember that wonderful house – the huge chestnuts – the splendid barns.'

'I don't get up so often. I am here in Vienna studying and in the holidays I like to travel, see things. My brother Franzie runs it, you know, with my mother. They have done wonders with the wine. They produce twenty thousand hectalitres a year now. That's good.'

'And the house?'

'Well, that's not so good. I don't know how we will manage to keep it up. It costs hundreds of thousands of schillings a year. I don't think they're extravagant. I wonder what will happen? Mama has been approached by some Americans who want a country house in May, money no object. Want the whole place redecorated to their choice. Perhaps that will pay for this year.'

'You must marry the American's daughter, like the girl in Thomas Mann's *Royal Highness*.'

'No, thank you, I'd prefer not. I'd marry a shop girl from Ottakring before an American.'

'Well then your sister Theresia.'

'Theresia? Yes. She could marry the American's sons. Perhaps that would be a good thing. Our family has certainly done everything except marry an American. But, what about Franzie? He's running the house.'

So the conversation continued, as many such must have in those piping days of the new peace: how could the fine houses, inherited or bought in different circumstances, looted or demolished during the Occupation, be maintained in a time which looked as if it would be colder for the great estate, though warmer for everyone else.

Tatiana's other neighbour, young Otto, was more reserved. She had more difficulty with him. Young Otto had been captured in 1944 by the Americans near the Gothic Line in Italy. He had been Kesselring's ADC. But his short time as a prisoner in Connecticut had passed well enough. Unlike his brother Jakob who had never come back from his captivity in Russia. The family believed that he had died of wounds in 1945, though they only heard of it in 1952! While a prisoner of war, young Otto told Tatiana, he had been asked by his captors to write an essay as to why the Germans had behaved as they did. What was it that had taken Germany to the brink of insanity, if not across it? Young Otto had wanted to discuss the question, he said, methodically with his father, as he had been used to discuss everything with him. But at the time it was impossible and when he came back he was dead. Young Otto had decided, in the end, that it was the Prussian notion of service combined with the Catholic one of obedience which was responsible. The mixture put the nation at Hitler's disposal. Yes, he said, those essays should be published. But it was not up to him to do so. The American army had the rights. And they did not have a need for royalties. One day he would look for those papers in the archives. Now he was a lawyer. Well, one earned a good living, one had to say. It was not like writing for the *Neue Freie Presse*, as his father had done. But then nothing was like it had been. Vienna had changed. It was a prosaic place now. Yes, he was married. His wife, Francesca, was sitting further down the table, the one wearing a blue dress. Yes, they had children. Two little ones. And how did Tatiana now find Vienna? She had known it in the black days. She must see changes. But how had they changed?

Tatiana considered. In retrospect, those black days of 1945 had been the happiest ones of her life. Black for Austrians, no hot water, little food, but so much gaiety, so much dancing! The music too had been wonderful, even if the opera had been in the Theater an der Wien. Although she was happy with her two young Grews, sitting then at that moment in a flat in Traungasse just near the Embassy, she had to admit it was different now. Not as exciting!

'Exciting!' Young Otto laughed mirthlessly. 'Well, I agree with Jean Marie there. We were talking before dinner. The one thing we do not want is excitement. My generation had enough of it. I am older than you, Mrs Grew. I remember it all. I can remember the exciting days after 1919 when the schilling collapsed. There was real poverty then.'

'Are Austrians still rather anti-semitic?' she said blithely.

'Possibly. But I was not. Nor was my father. The fact that he wrote that book! It was an accident. You know, you must know how he suffered from it. *The Final Solution!* What an absurd idea! A typical illusion, I suppose, of the beginning of the century. That one could have final solutions. The Jews are still the same kind of problem in the Middle East as they used to be in *Mitteleuropa*. We shall never get to the end of it. That was Hitler's mistake. My father's also.'

Tatiana did not think from that conversation that Austria had changed as much as she had expected.

The guests had been making their way through a splendid dinner which began with a *bouillon*, continued with crayfish, reached a crossroads with a tender *tafelspitz*, whose sauce was apparently made from apples and horseradish brought by Betty from Besselberg. There followed what Charlie Grew described afterwards as a particularly disgusting mound of cream in which a plum pie had been secreted. In the course of this, new glasses were brought and champagne poured, and Alois, standing at the end of the table, rose to speak.

His speech, everyone felt, was too impersonal. It could have been made by any prominent European social democrat of those days: Spaak, Mollet, Gaitskell or Bevin. It was a public speech, excellent of its kind, but not an appropriate one for the occasion. The diners sat back and listened to a parliamentary oration. Tatiana wondered mischievously whether Alois had been given the wrong speech by his private secretary and whether the electors of Wiener Neustadt would tomorrow hear the real welcome to Rüdiger von Acht. But, no, after a time, Alois came to the point.

'None of us who have lived through the last ten years here in Vienna,' he said, 'have any illusions about the character of our eastern neighbour.

The expectations of many of us in our youth have been shown to have been false. We now live without illusions. Among those who will help us do so is Rudi.

'Some of you – all of you, probably – know that we used to dispute a good deal before the war. We disputed seriously. Rudi will remember how one day we walked from the Kahlenberg all the way to the Sofienalle, without stopping, talking about Dollfuss. We were both wrong. He will admit it. I will admit it. I thought Dollfuss was a fascist opening the way to the nazis. Rudi thought he was the only man who could bar the gate to them. Well, what worlds have crashed since then! Then, Rudi, you may remember a talk we had in 1942. Not so long ago. Just fourteen years! But what years! He was going to the war. I had just left a health resort outside Munich. I was ill. He was wonderfully well. Wonderfully optimistic. I was not. He was going to free the world of communism for ever. There was nothing in common between us. We looked on the world through different lenses. The only thing we had, it seemed, in common was our Acht blood. But the world was the same for both of us. We were both fighting against brutality. Dictatorship. Illegal imprisonment. Then, as now. You were deluded then. So was I, in a different way. Now we meet. In agreement. I think Rüdiger has returned from hell. But he *has* returned. We both, I think, accept that there's not much difference between the nazi tyrant and the communist. Tyrants are much the same. There's far less difference between them than there is between a Sachertorte and a Linzertorte.

'Now what about the future! You know, when I think of the future I think always of that tale of the son of the famous member of our social democratic movement in Germany, at the turn of the century, Otto Braun. He was *de passage* in Paris, with his mother, who worked in the social democratic movement. Little Otto saw a regiment of infantry marching down the Boulevard Saint Germain. His mother explained that the purpose of soldiers was to make war. The child asked: "What is it, war?" "Ah, my boy," she said – and we are talking of 1901, not 1921 or 1951 – "Ah my boy," she said, "so much suffering, so much anguish, so much mourning, so many upheavals! Whole nations collapse into catastrophe. Science turns away from its true purpose. The brutal awakening of barbarian instincts, cruelty, the taste of blood." "Mama, are all men soldiers?" "Yes." "So, when I am grown up, I will also make war?" Little Otto awaited his mother's answer with terror. His hand trembled in hers. She reassured him: "My child, you are only a soldier when you are twenty and you are still young. If, from now on, people like your father, like me, work without respite, without rest, without leisure, then, by the time you are grown up, nations will be reconciled among themselves and there will be no war." A quarter of an hour passed. On their way home,

Frau Braun looked in a shop window. She felt herself tugged by the skirt. It was little Otto, begging her: "Don't stop, mama, work, work!"

'Dear friends, those words are our motto in Austria. "Don't stop, mama, work." We must all work. Prosperity will be our reward. Peace will follow prosperity. And now, dear friends, I ask you to think of dear Rüdiger, and Alice, and their marvellous children, such a pride to our dear Austria, such a wonderful example! *Hoch soll'er leben dreimal hoch.*'

Everyone at the table rose and raised their glasses three times, echoing the word *"hoch"*. The statesman sat down, sweating, knowing that with that simple tale, a favourite of Léon Blum's, he had moved his nephews, nieces and other relations just enough for the evening to be remembered by them for a long time.

Soon Rudi stood up.

'First, of course, I thank my dear niece for this evening. I did not expect it. It is too lavish for the occasion. Hundreds of thousands of Austrians and Germans have suffered as I have done, learned as I have done. It is what half my generation has experienced and it would have been good if the other half had experienced it also. Yes! I mean it. I have told some of you this before. I know that my repeating it upsets my wife. But I have to say it. These are the days of truthfulness. I learned in those years, in those weeks, in those railway carriages. You can't imagine what it's like. Early on, we were waiting outside the station at Tomsk. We waited there for a week. No one knew what was wrong, what our fate would be. We would go into the station to wash. They had wonderful washing basins there, on the platform itself, no delay, you didn't even have to open a door. Then the Russians! Well, I'm sorry, Alois, you are wrong about us agreeing with one another now. You were right, we disagreed in the past. Your memory is excellent. I expect something did happen as you said it did. Probably. But we don't see eye to eye now. We certainly don't. You, Alois, have got to understand the Russians. We can't do without them. They're not ordinary people. They may be at a lower stage of human life. But I admire them. No one would put up with what they do.'

'Now, I realise nobody tonight wants to be lectured to. I'm spoiling things. I know it. I am being rude to Klara. To Alice. To Alois. Well, perhaps not to Alois, he is a statesman. He can put up with it. I must just tell you: all the time in Russia, I was trying to remember one thing. Do you know what it was? It was the name of the Crown Prince Rudolf's driver. In Vienna the day of his death. Today, without looking it up, it came to me. Do you know what it was? Bratfisch. That's what worries you over there. You know you know something. But you can't remember. And you can't look it up. Now I can look anything up, I suppose. If I don't know something, I can just go into Alice's bookshop and ask one of the assistants.

'Now I have to stop. No, one more thing. Very early on the journey to the east. I do not know where we were. I forget the names. Anyway, as you can imagine, I was homesick. I was separated from everyone else. Pannwitz and the other Cossack officers had gone to Moscow. To be tried, I suppose. Probably to be shot. Well, that happens in war. Anyway, there were hundreds of us at a railway station, somewhere in White Russia. We were always, or so it seemed, at railway stations. I was cleaning my boots with a twig that I had found. Another train went by. Very slowly I had a vision. I thought I saw Klara looking out of the window. Just as she was. I had been thinking of Vienna, of Alice and the children, of old days, and quarrelling with Alois and, suddenly, in my mind I saw Alois's daughter leaning out of the window, wind through her hair, cheering. She looked so happy. Klara, you wouldn't believe it. You were not as you are now, a grand lady. You were a girl, passing by framed in a window, waving at the remains of the Wehrmacht. Cheering them! You were new life. Extraordinary, wasn't it? The train moved on. Of course I knew it was a vision. Or perhaps it was someone who looked like Klara. But I remembered it and it helped me. Now one can forget these things.'

'No!' It was Klara, loud and clear, so that the whole table would hear, 'You cannot forget these things. It was me.'

There was a silence.

'I remember the day very well,' she said looking straight in front of her. 'It was a wonderful morning with a wind, but a warm wind. The sky was blue but pale. There were birds – everywhere. We had been up late the night before. We had been dancing. Not with anyone, you understand. But for them. That's what happened most nights. We danced and danced. For our lives, we danced. Then we fell down exhausted and slept where we lay as often as not. I remember the morning. How green it was! So many shades of green. And then the train – and the journey – and the thousands of soldiers. Just sitting there. I waved and waved. I wanted them to know that I, an Austrian girl, was waving to them but I couldn't be sure they could hear. They were human beings, as we were. We all wanted to live. We'd do anything to live.'

There was a long silence. Everyone wanted Klara to go on, yet they felt that it was not the time. But if not now, when would it be?

'How extraordinary,' said Rudi. 'Well, so you know what I mean? About the Russian character. So I am among friends.'

'No, no,' called Alois from the end of the table. 'You have not understood –'

But at that moment, by prearrangement, Klara's musicians, refreshed by a dinner of their own, began again to play, beginning with the waltz from *The Merry Widow*: Alice could not help wondering whether it would soon be specially appropiate.

'I have always thought that music has had a good deal to do with Austria's recovery,' said young Otto, whose enthusiasm for *The Merry Widow* was no greater than that of Franz Lehár's dog. He and Thekla Acht walked into the drawing room.

'Recovery, fiddlesticks,' said Aunt Thekla surveying the scene with some distaste. 'Are you saying that now we've lost everything we can say that we have recovered?'

Aunt Thekla made no bones about her distaste for everything modern.

'It was perhaps a good thing we lost our occupiers,' said young Otto.

'Not sure of that. The Americans gave us protection, the Russians gave us warnings. We need both.'

Such perverse reasonings were too much for Jean Marie, who was standing in the drawing room near a pretty Baroque cupboard filled with eighteenth-century porcelain, talking to Erno Bender, the Sudeten who had married Antoinette, cousin of old Otto's wife Betty.

'Oh, really Aunt Thekla, from our angle in Munich, Austria has done well,' said Jean Marie. 'You are, unlike Germany, in one piece. You are forbidden an *Anschluss* with the Germans, but it will probably happen all the same. Only nobody will notice it. Also, you can pretend you are neutral but, of course, you are western.'

'You, you, you, you keep saying you,' said Aunt Thekla testily. 'Who are you, that you keep referring to Austria as another person? Anyway, you are wrong. Vienna is an eastern city. I have more in common with a Hungarian than I have with a Bavarian. As for the English, I have nothing in common with them. They might be on the moon.'

The conversations after dinner continued in small groups like this for some time in different corners of the pleasant rooms. Anne, Jean Marie's English wife, looked at the paintings and found herself having to introduce herself to everyone, since this was the first occasion that she had met her Austrian relations by marriage.

'You are rather overwhelming to meet in the mass, you know,' she said to Poldo, Klara's brother, the builder of bridges.

'Yes, of course, but then who is not, in the mass? I have not seen them all together like this since – well since Aunt Zita's funeral – she was my great aunt – she used to live at Besselberg with Uncle Otto's family. The funeral was in the Karlskirche. But we didn't meet properly. A few of us only met in Thekla's flat afterwards. It was not very enjoyable. Perhaps this will be the last time we all meet. The next generation will be too big. If so, Klara has done us well. It would anyway be difficult to do better. She is a good hostess, my sister. Ah, here she is –'

Klara, moving graciously between the guests, was bearing down on them.

'You are Anne,' she said, 'I haven't talked to you. You look very pretty. And Ralph! So well brought up. I watched him opposite. Jean Marie is very lucky. One day, I should like to visit England. I feel ashamed that I have not done so yet. One day I will –'

'You are so Viennese. I wonder if you would like it?'

'No, no, I am not Viennese. I am Austrian. Viennese is different. There is a great mixture in Vienna. I – I – am pure.'

She said it with such conviction that Anne started.

'I wanted to introduce myself to you. Now I have to go upstairs. My husband is not well. I must go and see him. I will be down directly.'

As usual, Klara's behaviour caused comment: adverse comment. However ill Count Gmunden might be, it was bad manners to go upstairs in the middle of one's own party. Suppose one wanted to say goodbye. It was inconsiderate.

Willy Svoboda did not want to say goodbye at all. He loved everything about Klara, her family, her house, and he knew more about the Achts than any of them knew themselves. His part in the last days of Max had given him the opportunity of being, he believed, almost an honorary Acht. His own fortunes had prospered so much, he had worked so hard that he was richer than any of them. But they were for him more than a responsibility, they were almost a hobby.

During the evening, he too had heard that Gmunden was ill. It would not have surprised him if the illness had been brought on by nerves. Klara's husband had been involved in many financial deals which could have driven him mad. With the Russians, with the Americans, with people in Stuttgart. He, Willy, found it difficult to keep the balls of his own conjuring tricks in the air at the same time. He could not imagine how Gmunden was able to. He would need four hands to do so as well as one behind his back.

'What's this I hear about Gmunden shooting himself?' It was Erno Bender who put the question.

'I didn't know he had.'

'That's why Klara has temporarily abandoned us.'

'Well you know more than I do,' said Willy coldly.

That was something. Shot himself! Was he dead? Was he alive? And how did Bender know? The servants perhaps. Willy needed to find out. But whom could he ask? Gmunden's death would be no loss but he did not know how Klara would react. The rumours in the last weeks were that Gmunden had been outmanoeuvred by an American company, with some nondescript name like United Manufacturers. No one knew much about them save that they operated on an intercontinental scale. He knew that the discreet American whom he had seen at the opening of the Opera, George Grenville, might be behind United Manufacturers.

'You are Willy Svoboda. I am Tatiana Grew. How do you do?'

Willy had always noticed how English and American women were always introducing themselves in a way that no Austrian would. He admired them for it. Life must be easier for women with no inhibitions about such things.

'Yes, I am Svoboda.'

'You must be Czech?'

'My grandfather came in 1910.'

'And now you feel wholly Austrian?'

'No. Wholly Viennese!'

There was a pause.

'I was here in Vienna ten years ago – in the British Mission. I remember you then. You probably came across my husband? He was only a Major then.'

'It is possible.' Willy smiled warmly. He knew Tatiana to be one of Klara's new friends, but he did not remember her. Klara kept different friends in different boxes. 'Count Gmunden is not well?' he hazarded.

'I don't think very well.'

Tatiana knew little but she never liked to appear uninformed. Klara had muttered something to her about her husband's absence as she came in and that was all. Klara had now come down again, looking composed but pale. People were beginning to say goodbye. There was confusion, not wholly disagreeable in character. Rüdiger appeared to think that his speech had been a success. He looked pleased with himself. People said that they had found what he had to say interesting. He replied that he had expected that it would be interesting, and that he had had plenty of time to practise and prepare for public speeches. He was grateful to Klara, but thought she had unkindly stolen the show a little at the end. Alice had not enjoyed the speeches – any of them – she had contrived not even to listen to what her husband had said. She was anxious to leave, but felt it would be rude to leave before the others. So she waited, and had her hand kissed by all the departing gentlemen. Then she turned back into the drawing room where Klara was alone with Willy Svoboda and Tatiana Grew. Rüdiger was waiting in the hall, his heavy fur coat already on, humming and looking at the naval prints.

Alice knew what had happened from looking at their faces. Kurt Gmunden was obviously dead.

Still, she had to ask. To assume a mortality from a look of pallor would be precipitate.

'How is your husband?'

'I'm afraid he died just after dinner.' Klara spoke in a matter of fact manner.

'Oh! What a tragedy! And it had to be today!'

'Perhaps better today than yesterday,' said Klara, smiling.

'Can I do anything?'

'No. Thank you. Willy will help. He always helps me just as he helped Uncle Max. Tatiana will help.'

'Your father!' Where indeed was Alois?

'Oh he went back to the Parliament immediately after dinner.' Klara looked at ease, and Tatiana looked competent. Alice kissed them both, shook hands with Willy, and took her husband by the arm, who was still looking, wistfully, at naval prints.

'What an extraordinary battle that was at Minorca,' Rüdiger was saying, 'and afterwards the English decided to shoot their own admiral for being over-cautious. Just shows what a wild people they are underneath.'

LVIII

*T*HE DEATH OF COUNT GMUNDEN CREATED ONLY A MILD
sensation at first in Vienna. Clever lawyers found by Willy Svoboda
ensured that it was left a little vague as to whether the Count had died
intentionally or as a result of some accident in a gunroom. After all, the
Count was a well-known shot.

But after a week or two, the event grew in significance. That was
partly because it was soon known that Gmunden had left his widow
nothing, except debts. Had it not been for Willy Svoboda, Klara would
have had to leave the house in Am Hof immediately, and sell the furniture
and the pictures. Interest grew too because of the events leading up to
Count Gmunden's suicide. He had been ruined, apparently in a vindictive
manner, by the sabotaging of his affairs by United Manufacturers of
Chicago. Nobody had much liking for Gmunden. Most people who had
known anything of him had suspected him of being a thief, traitor, bully,
opportunist and so on. But he was a Gmunden and part of an old family,
once respected. Given that, his ruin by Americans caused a flicker of
anti-American sentiment to light the winter scene in Vienna and even to
make several leader writers say to themselves, and even to their readers,
that they were, after all, Europeans. The gossip in the drawing rooms of
the third and fourth Bezirke, now again the most fashionable place to
live, was that Klara was someone bound to live, as it were, against the
grain of events. If Vienna were happy, Klara would be ruined and *vice
versa*.

What added another note to the scandalous affair was that, according
to Willy Svoboda, the American who had taken Besselberg for the
forthcoming summer was that very George Grenville who was President
of United Manufacturers. The argument that they should not have any
dealings with a man who had ruined Klara's husband was put to Betty,
old Otto's widow, and to her son Franzie. Both were insensitive to the
suggestion that they were dealing with a scoundrel.

'Oh well,' Franzie said, 'he has already paid a large sum. So why go
into the details? He comes well-recommended. He will use our staff, who
will be able to control him in the unlikely event of it being necessary.

Anyway, he probably doesn't know what is done in his name. United Manufacturers is a big enterprise, you know. It employs hundreds of people who are themselves millionaires.'

'In schillings?'

'No, in dollars, American dollars,' put in Betty.'

'You sound adamant, Aunt Betty.'

'We are not adamant. We have made arrangements from which we cannot withdraw, even had we wanted to.'

Those "arrangements" went ahead. The Americans – it was known that there would be a large party of them – would move into Besselberg on May 1st.

Klara kept living in Am Hof though, from time to time, there were rumours that she was going to return to Heiligenstadt and live with her father, now alone in his large house. She and Tatiana met one day in April at Sacher's for lunch. The latter was in a state of furious excitement.

During the morning, a member of one of Britain's security services called on Colonel Grew at his office in the British Embassy. Then, instead of asking some routine questions about security in the Embassy, as Charlie had expected, the man had proceeded, almost as if in a court room, to put a series of questions about Charlie's role in 'engineering the escape of certain prominent nazis' in the late 'forties. It had been alleged that he had something to do with the escape of such people as Gottfried von Acht, Heinrich Ried and even a leader of the Hungarian fascists in exile, the Countess Malevolti, all of whom were to be living in Brazil.

'And others – and many others,' cried Tatiana, barely in control of herself. 'How could such accusations be made?'

'Well, Gottfried –'

'No, there's more too. There is talk of a British officer active in the resistance in Italy crossing into Austria and being mysteriously murdered. Charlie's been asked to say what he knows about that.'

'Well, how extraordinary.'

'He's with the ambassador now talking about it all. He said he'd join us here. I do hope you don't mind. Of course, since that odious Harry Mercer did his flit they're all very jumpy. But even so! Charlie!'

This was an allusion to the recent flight of Harry Mercer from his desk in the Treasury in London to Russia, and his admission in Moscow that he had been a Soviet spy for years.

'Well, all of us in trouble should stick together,' said Klara, 'but I'm not sure I'm a good star under which to regroup.'

'You are, though, Klara, that's just what you are.'

It was true that Klara's beauty, even her air of distance, inspired and, when necessary, soothed. Her reverses of fortune did not seem to make any difference to her looks.

A young man, whom neither had noticed before, approached their table, and cleared his throat.

'Countess Gmunden? Do you mind if I interrupt? My name's Ed Pole from the *New York World Gazette*. Could I ask you something?'

Klara looked at him doubtfully. She looked at Tatiana, shrugged her shoulders and smiled at the intruder.

'If you must, very well then.'

'It's about your husband, Countess.'

'I'm afraid my husband's dead.'

'Yes, yes, that's just it. We wouldn't be so interested if he were alive.'

'Charming!' Klara said.

'The question my editor would like to have you answer is : did *you* know, *at the time*, that he was a senior Soviet agent?'

'You must be mad. I must ask, please leave us.'

'If I could press you –'

'I'm sorry. Waiter, waiter!'

'Do you think his death had anything to do with that?'

'Waiter!'

'Did you know about this at the time?'

It was only then that the waiters escorted the American from the dining room.

'How unpleasant!'

'It would never have happened at Sacher's in the old days,' Klara insisted. 'Of course, what he was saying was rubbish.'

'Well, obviously.'

'They ought to devise some way of keeping that sort of person out of a restaurant like this! It must be possible.'

The next moment Charlie Grew came in. The waiter made at first as if to remove him as well.

'No. This man's all right,' Klara said, trying not to laugh.

'You are sure, madame?'

'Yes, yes, he is this lady's husband.'

'You are sure of that, madame?'

Charlie did not, as it happened, look the least like his usual confident self.

'I am afraid I've got bad news, darling,' he said, sinking into the empty chair at the table. 'The ambassador's asked us to return to England pending an enquiry into my mission in Carinthia in 1948. Sorry, Klara, for rushing in and blurting it out so ill-manneredly but I'm upset.'

'Go back to England! Well! What a pity,' said Tatiana.

'You can't go. We shall miss you,' said Klara, 'but you'll come back soon.'

'I don't think either of you understand,' said Charlie Grew, 'I – we – are returning in disgrace. There's to be a full service investigation.'

'You'll be exonerated.'

'It may not be so easy as that. I'm afraid there were various things that occurred in Carinthia which will need a good deal of explanation.' He then began an account of what had happened to him in Carinthia in such detail that the three of them were still at Sacher's at five o'clock. The mention of Kamo especially interested Klara and caused her to ask him many questions.

So busy were the Viennese dealing with their own affairs at that time that few of them noticed in the press that the well-known English art historian, Livingstone, had been persuaded to resign from his directorship of the Worthington in London as a result of blackmail by one of the cloakroom attendants at his club; and, by an extraordinary coincidence, another old Vienna friend, the Trustee of the Louvre, Jean Georges Marchais, was also disgraced: apparently on the proof in America that, for financial profit to himself, he had wrongly authenticated an eighteenth century painting of the Duke of Osuna as having been by Goya. Each of those concerned in these dramas were, like Charlie Grew, and Klara, so preoccupied by their own troubles as not to observe the co-incidences.

LIX

DURING THESE MONTHS, THE FUTURE OF THE VINEYARDS outside Grinzing and Heiligenstadt, which had over the generations made such a contribution to the gaiety of Austria, was threatened by entrepreneurs who wished to do for Vienna what their equivalents in London, Paris, Madrid and elsewhere had already done to their hearts', and pockets', content. In future doctorates the manner whereby this wreck of the suburbs was avoided in Austria will be carefully considered, with appropriate learning, analysis of land holding and use of crops which has characterised Viennese history for hundreds of years. In the streets where Alois von Acht lived, a contrary movement was decided upon by philanthropic householders. They decided not to build on their gardens but to turn them back to vineyards.

The movement to "turn back the clock" gained support from all the forward-looking people who lived in the neighbourhood. Alois did not want to be left out of this movement. That meant the transformation of the Achts' ramshackle chicken yard into the cultivable land which it had been during the early 1800s, when Beethoven used to summer in one or other of the houses in the street beyond. Alois did not see himself as giving up the land himself. He was turning over an acre previously used as private land to a vine growers' cooperative.

The idea was attractive for many reasons. In his recent speeches, as a senior minister, he had not ceased to speak of the need for social collaboration, beginning at the lowest level, for example, with parish councils. Alois argued that the consumer was the Great Elector of the time. He also liked wine. He thought that democratic socialism should concentrate on giving people happy lives, securing for them wine when they were well, not just hospitals when they were ill. Cooperatives, too, had interested him. He told Klara, now his chief confidante, that he had often wondered whether he and his generation had not made a mistake about guild socialism. Thus the local press had difficulty in keeping up with Alois's enthusiasm for the idea.

Klara had been critical of these plans. She was against neither cooperation nor cooperatives. She was not against wine. She had nothing against parish councils. But she had an attachment to the land which Alois possessed in Heiligenstadt and on which she had grown up. This attitude of hers became more marked when she returned to live in Alois's house, after her own house in Am Hof was foreclosed for debt. Her brothers being away during these discussions, she took what she imagined might be their opinion as her own. She argued relentlessly in favour of a traditional view of property. The brothers, when they returned, made it clear that they did not differ much about this from their father. They did not care either way. She became angry. Her father's laughter infuriated her. She believed that her father was fecklessly abandoning one of his most prized possessions – indeed, his only one, since Alois had never had time to make money. He had accumulated nothing. Why did he want to give away his garden?

Alois thought that he was making over part of his property to a good cause, which would benefit them all. His action would guarantee that there would always be a beautiful view from the back of the house – never a bank or chalets, such as had disfigured other outskirts of Vienna: new buildings hurriedly put up to fill gaps caused by the war.

In the end, this discussion in the family was settled by compromise: the interests of Klara were satisfied by retaining a larger garden than Alois had thought right: but the wishes of Alois were fulfilled by giving the lion's share to the cooperative.

There was one untoward event in consequence. The disputes in the Acht family over this piece of land did not reach the national newspapers. Willy Svoboda was able to prevent that. But there was much chat about it in the shops nearby. The location of Achts' chickens, apple loft and croquet lawn came in for minute analysis among the shopkeepers who had provided for the family over the last twenty-five years, who had always looked upon Alois's socialism with ribald disbelief, and who had themselves, since 1945, voted for the People's Party. Their attitude to the shelling in 1934 of the Karlmarxhof two streets away had been to offer their sons as runners to Dollfuss's artillery, to close their shutters, and go to bed.

It was perhaps not surprising, given the neighbourhood's talk, that Alois should come back to his house one Friday evening to discover Klara in tears and the housekeeper distraught. There had been a robbery: an unheard of event in the neighbourhood. What is more, the thieves had stolen the chickens.

'The chickens! But how ridiculous. They are worth nothing.'

'But they were our chickens,' Klara cried. Her usual calm had been shattered. Indeed, Alois thought the breakdown of Klara's serenity over such an insignificant event was more surprising than the act of theft, disquieting though that might be. Opulence often brings brigandage, Alois knew that well.

'It is true, they were our chickens. But when one considers what else they might have done, how fortunate we are.'

'Papa, you are so conciliatory it is painful to hear you speak.'

'I am an Austrian of our time, Klara, I believe in conciliation. I do not believe in perpetual challenges. I have seen what happens.' Alois rose. 'Still, it's silly to have a quarrel over a few old chickens.'

'I am not quarrelling, Papa, I am telling you the facts.'

That is what was always argued in these circumstances, Alois reflected, and said:

'All right, let us go and see what there is to be seen.'

Father and daughter went into the garden, followed by the housekeeper. The thieves had been rumbustious. The chicken run had been destroyed, the chicken hut had fallen in, there seemed to have been digging.

'Well, I do see that it's odd,' Alois conceded.

'Odd! It's an outrage,' Klara insisted, 'Politics is bad for you. Papa, you should choose a new career. It stifles your sensibilities, including your anger. You don't seem to know that there are occasions when you have to be livid in order to maintain the respect of your family, friends, neighbours –'

'We must send for the police, I suppose.'

'Don't be silly, Papa, they've been. They caused half the mess, as a matter of fact.'

'I am certainly angry about that.'

'The wrong time, the wrong time, Papa!'

The events in the garden seemed all the more surprising when, a few days later, nearly all the chickens were returned.

'Someone borrowed them, perhaps they discovered how badly they lay, let's leave it at that,' Alois said.

'Papa, can't you see that you can't have people walking in and borrowing things as they choose. Anyway, what was behind all the digging and vandalism?'

'I thought you said it was the police?'

'Some of it. Not all of it. Not most of it.'

'If I were to go into everything obscure we should spend our time raking up the past. In Austria that's not sensible. Who wants to know about the past now?'

'I'm afraid, Papa,' said Klara, now quite herself again, 'you're a terrible pragmatist. I shall talk to Willy Svoboda about it.'

'Willy. He's a pragmatist too. He's a better one than I. Look at his career. He's made money out of everyone. Austrians, English, French,

Russians. Someone the other day told me he'd even made money out of the Yugoslavs.'

'I'll ask him. I'm seeing him tonight. He's taking me to see *Manon Lescaut*.'

'Well, ask him what he'd have done about the chickens. But then I expect he'll agree with you. He usually does, I know.'

Alois had nothing to say about his daughter's private life. He had never asked her about her marriage. He never questioned her intentions towards Willy Svoboda. This lack of curiosity, he believed, constituted the spirit of conciliation in domestic affairs just as a reluctance to discuss people's political views (if within the law) was his policy in national politics. He had the same view in international matters: live and let live. It was desirable to forget about principles, if one had to negotiate Danube River transport. One should tie down the Russians to western practices in a hundred ways. Gradually, they would become manageable. One had to assume that there was a Tsar.

Some weeks after that Alois received an invitation to the Soviet Embassy. Of course he had to go. That was what co-existence meant: vodka in the Soviet Embassy. Poldi Moser had laid down the policy years ago. These drinkings happened ten times a year. Alois had been so often that he knew the cloakroom attendants by their Christian names. One of them, a Croat, he knew, worked for the United States. In the American Embassy, there was an attendant, also a Croat, who worked for Russia. What a farce, yet at the same time how essential was this business of interlocking systems of espionage! Equally important, because equally meaningless, were the heartfelt enquiries about health, ski-ing holidays, the education of children.

'Yes, yes,' Alois heard himself often say, 'Karl is now quite the engineer. He will be in America next year. Then he will come back and surprise us by his Danube basin plans. But we bureaucrats will defeat him, won't we Ambassador, eh! Can't have anything from America upsetting our plans here, can we?'

At the reception, he knew, there would be, as was inevitable, poor Poldi Moser, dwelling on the past, now minister without portfolio, already tipsy, his life's work complete, shifted to one side, to an unimportant position, but not quite able to detach himself from the world which he had done so much to create. There would be that uncrowned prince of communist intellectuals, Fritz Toblach, of whom Alois had once been so in awe, and who now had no more than the role of demon king in a Christian play: spitting venom, but with a twinkle in his eye as well as a glass in his hand. Toblach, with his great head of silver hair, and lately a stooping presence, was familiar not only at the Soviet Embassy but at every good Vienna dinner table – and not only among people who like to think of themselves as on the left, the *gauche de vigne*, but even with bourgeois hostesses, such as the Benders. (In recent months, Henriette had made a salon in her pretty house in the Cumberlandstrasse.) Once there had been a time when Alois had had to take a deep breath when he saw Fritz moving towards him in a busy room. Now he enjoyed it.

That night, Klara and her father left Heiligenstadt at the same time – in two separate large cars: Willy had sent his driver to pick up Klara to meet him at the opera house – Martinis was singing in Gunther Rennert's production. Alois had never been known, for over ten years now, to go anywhere without his driver who, like Willy, was Czech in origin and, confusingly, also called Svoboda. This tough, big-boned driver always referred to Willy as his cousin. Alois had given up trying to decide whether that was a joke or not. Willy's driver, on the other hand, was an elderly man of melancholy bearing who might have passed for a Furst but was the grandson of a certain Floradora who had been first violin at the Scala in the 1880s. That evening, the two drivers stood by their cars, outside the house, waiting for their charges, with nothing to say to one another. Conversation, much less conspiracy, within the petite bourgeoisie is less to be counted on than Marx imagined.

Klara came out in a long fur coat. It was one of the last possessions left to her after the sale at Am Hof. Alois appeared in his ministerial loden. Klara sat at the back of her car as became a widowed countess. Alois sat in the front, next to the chauffeur, as became a socialist. While Klara sat silent with her own thoughts, Alois talked constantly to his driver who was by now his chief source of information about ordinary life – how people were coping with the winter, the lack of snow for skiing, or the excess of it, the state of housing in what had been the Russian zone, the price of potatoes, the prospects for the harvest.

The reception at the Soviet Embassy was what Alois had expected – even to the extent of Fritz lumbering up to him and telling him that the Americans were planning trouble: this time in Hungary.

'Trouble for *whom*, in Hungary? For the party? For the Hungarian people? For the Hungarian economy?'

'*Total* trouble, Alois,' said Toblach, glinting his gold teeth, 'it will affect them all. Well, greetings,' he added, knocking back a glass of vodka. 'This will be a year of surprises, you'll see. Let us hope we survive them and, if we do, you may again see that monopoly capitalism has failed to give the world security. Fun, yes, I suppose one must admit, you monopoly capitalists *have* given us entertainment. But how long can the world suffer in order to keep these many centres of power on which monopoly capitalism thrives? We want one world. Unless there is one world, we shall die in the nuclear bonfire.'

'That's an old theme of yours, Fritz.'

'Yes, but it is current too. Britain gave up her empire since she got bored with it. Not because she had to. France will destroy herself in Algeria. The United States does not want to rule anything – yet the world needs empire. Who else is there but the Soviet Union? *Na Zdravie!*'

'*Na Zdravie!*'

'I know, Alois, that you wonder what you are doing surrounded by these sycophants. How does an intelligent man like you survive? You know the value of the people you see now, foreigners as well as Austrians! Zero! Half of them. Zero! Yet when we were young, there was *something*. Disagreeable. Horrible. But something!'

'We have no Jews.'

'Yes, but it is not only that. That may account for sixty to seventy per cent – say seventy three per cent – of the inertia. But it does not account for a hundred per cent. Who has heard of any new Austrian poet? Who knows any new composers? Or painters? It is all the same old things, Mozart and Beethoven, Strauss and Lehár, Kokoschka and Mahler. Your new Austria is dull, Alois.'

'It is good that it is dull,' Alois said, this being a favourite theme of his, as it was of Aunt Thekla.

'Ah, I except you, of course, Alois,' said Fritz. 'You are a real *objet d'art*, which previous ages could not approach. A socialist with no socialist ideas at all. A minister in perpetuity, whom no scandal can shake, to whom no problems ever cause a moment's imperturbability. Do you know, Alois, if it had been you in charge of our party in 1934, I might have remained a socialist myself. If you'd been in control, I don't suppose anyone would have noticed that the artillery was being used. Rather a dull noise, eh, those big guns!' Glitter of teeth!

They were joined by Karl Reinhardt. The former resistance leader was now Austrian president of the Kredit Ullstein, one of the largest banks in Germany. Though now in his 'fifties, he appeared if anything more golden than he had been ten years before. He nodded in a friendly way to Fritz who immediately said:

'So, Alois, I will leave you to your *new* friends. I have my *old* friends to see to.' And with another glint of golden teeth, Fritz was gone.

'What a strange character,' Karl Reinhardt said, looking after the departing communist. 'There is no one who is better company. Yet if the revolution were to come, he would hang us both on a lamp post. I can hear him saying, "yes, and start with my friends. Here is a list".'

Alois laughed and said 'I do not know what his future is in his party. Perhaps he will leave if there is a real "thaw" here. I don't think he could personally take another united front.'

'No, a "united front" would cause him trouble. But Alois, that isn't what I want to talk to you about. Have you ever heard of "United Manufacturers of Chicago"?'

'Yes, just. My nephew's house, Besselberg, is being let in the summer to the supposed boss of it. It's causing bad blood in my family.'

'Do you know the man's background?'

'George Grenville? No. I don't. But I could discover something. It sounds a fairly solid name.'

'I wonder if it's really so solid?'

'Do you mean – it's an adopted name?'

'Yes.'

'Jewish?'

'Must be.'

'It is possible. My son Karl was at a university in California with a man called Brown. He was so obviously a Pole that Karl asked him what he had been called before he was "Brown". The reply was intriguing. It was "Jones". But before that it was Schmutchkevitch. Why did he change from Jones to Brown? Because he was tired of being asked how he was named before he was called "Jones"!'

'Very elaborate. Could you find out something about Grenville for me? It would be useful.'

'Do you mean through my Besselberg sister-in-law or nephew? Well, I'm afraid my relations with them are not too good.'

'What about the police?'

'The police? Why should they have anything on an American like him?'

'His passport must say where he was born. He was here in Vienna in the autumn. I would be interested.'

'Of course,' said Alois, 'I could ask the police department.'

'Thank you.'

Alois wrote a note to himself in a little book that he kept for this kind of enquiry.

A senior Soviet official whom Alois knew, whose name was Semenovich, ambled up to him, took his arm and led him to a table, where the usual assortment of Georgian wines, vodkas and caviar stood available.

'*Na Zdravie!*, Herr Doktor!'

'*Na Zdravie!*, comrade!' Alois found it still easy to use that address when talking to communists.

'Comrade minister,' said the Russian, 'to good relations between the Soviet Union and the Austrian Republic!'

'I drink to that too.'

'Comrade Doktor, do you have any plans this year to return to the Soviet Union?'

'None, Mr Semenovich.'

Alois had been to Moscow in 1950, dealing with trade. He had no wish to go again. The buildings of Moscow were bleak, the people so dull-looking, the shops drab: never again. Moscow reminded him of what Vienna might become if his generation failed as the previous one had.

'It could probably be arranged this summer, Herr Doktor. Everything is now easier than it was, you know. With Nikita Sergeyvitch, well, you know, I cannot say too much. But it is different.'

'Better?'

'I think so. Some wine? No, well, you are wise. I am not so wise, so I shall help myself. A pleasure to see you again, Herr Minister. We will telephone your office with a good plan.'

Alois found himself talking next, by chance, to an American. He had met him before but he had forgotten his name. With an American there was less trouble.

'Minister Acht. I'm George Semenov. Yes, it's a Russian name. My grandfather came across in the 1910s. You mean there's a Russian official called Semenovich? No kidding? I've taken over our commercial section. It would be a pleasure to call on you one day to sort out the problem of Danube oil exports. Do you remember, you wrote to us about it last week? No, of course, you don't remember, why should you? You must forgive our free and easy American ways. I believe my French colleague would lose his job if he talked to you as I am doing. Only an ambassador can talk to a cabinet minister. Well, we're the new world and I guess in some ways we're gauche. But it makes things easier.'

'Mr Semenov, you're in the commercial section? Then you must know something about "United Manufacturers of Chicago"?'

'Sure. What do you need to know?'

'Well, I'm interested in the firm. It seems to be doing well.'

'I'll say it is. It's one of the top ten truly great American companies, according to *Fortune* magazine.'

'Is that so? And I believe its chairman is honouring us with a visit this summer.'

'That's so. I was one of the people who helped them choose the right place for his stay.'

'My brother used to live there, my sister-in-law and my nephew still own it. Do you know anything about Mr George Grenville?'

'No, I don't, sir, I have not met him personally, but I know he's a very clever man. Very good with figures. Built up the whole business in a very few years.'

'The name Grenville – is that an American name?'

'One of the great names in our country.'

'He's from an old American family then?'

'Oh definitely. His father was rich before him, I believe. Coal, I think, Sir.'

'I see. I'd heard differently.'

'No, no. The Grenvilles are as American as you are Austrian. I read all about it in *Fortune* magazine last week. George Grenville was cut off by his father when young. Well, he's still quite young – but he made his own fortune and he has doubled it five times over. A reserved man. I doubt whether Austria will see much of him when he comes over. He wanted a quiet place, within two hours of the airport by car, but secluded. He'll have a large private staff with him. And he needs an excellent telephone service. I had to go into that myself. All his calls will go through the United States army line. It has to be really efficient, you see.'

A few moments later, another American official, this time from the legal department, approached Alois. He was tall, distinguished in appearance, and plainly Anglo-Saxon in origin.

'Herr Minister, I do not like to interfere but I couldn't help overhearing your conversation with my colleague, Semenov. Would you forgive me if I corrected what I understood him to tell you. I believe that the story in *Fortune* magazine about Mr Grenville is not correct. Grenville is certainly not his name. Grenville, I assure you, is as Jewish as a seven-branched çandlestick! He is nobody, nobody but a clever calculating machine, and not at all scrupulous with other people's money. I'm sorry to speak like this of a fellow American. "United Manufacturers" is a powerful enterprise, but it is one the SEC is already curious about.'

'Well, it's kind of you to tell me,' said Alois, 'but it is confusing.'

'If you ask me, Herr Minister, that's just about how Mr Grenville would like you to find it.'

A few days later, Alois had a third conversation with an American businessman about Mr Grenville. This man listened to Alois's inquiries for a few minutes and made the following observation:

'Do you know, Herr Minister, I can see you and your friends may want to know about Mr Grenville's past. Well, *we* in the US haven't the time for that; we need to know, urgently, about his future.'

LX

TO BEGIN WITH, MR SEMENOV'S PREDICTION THAT AUSTRIANS would not see much of the multi-millionaire at Besselberg seemed realistic. Mr Grenville visited Besselberg in late March when the snow was still on the ground. He made some demands for redecoration. The arrangements for the telephone, though the most elaborate in Europe, still did not meet with Mr Grenville's expectation. He had, it was understood, to be able to talk instantly, whenever he wished, with Chicago. In consequence, the US army in Frankfurt had to lend him for two weeks their best engineers.

A technological breakthrough followed which enabled instantaneous conversation. It was as well, his associates thought, that the Russians did not choose those days to make a military breakthrough. Others thought that it would have been a good thing had they done so, since Mr Grenville was a keen strategist who had his own ideas as to how the Soviet Union might be beaten on every front.

The first sign that Mr Grenville gave of being in Austria was when he had made a private visit to the Kunsthistorisches Museum. The director, a man of discretion, never spoke about this visit, nor what was said, nor how knowledgeable Mr Grenville seemed to be of these treasures. But he did make a brief statement some weeks later to the press. Mr Grenville had been shocked by the empty case in which, before 1941, the Crown of the Emperor Charles V had stood. Shortly after, the director had issued the statement, United Manufacturers of Chicago made a more startling declaration of their own. Their president, in the interests of assisting the recovery of "precious masterpieces" – yes, that was the quaint formulation – would offer a reward of one million American dollars to anyone who gave information leading to the discovery of the Crown.

The size of this reward brought back to people's minds the extraordinary train of events which led to the Crown's disappearance. The tale which associated the alleged saboteur of the Russian war memorial with the loss of the Crown had been discredited. In the age of prose now unfolding, there was no place for whimsy. It was assumed that the Crown had been stolen when the treasures of the Kunsthistorisches Museum had been removed in 1941, probably by a workman killed on the Russian front.

During the second week of May, another extraordinary announcement was made. The Crown had been found! A peasant near Kirchstetten had found it in an old barn when pitching hay from one side to another. The Crown was wrapped in a piece of canvas. The peasant, Andreas Schmidt, expressed himself baffled by the discovery since it was only last summer that he had put the hay there. He was as certain as he could be that there had been no crown, and no canvas then, in that barn. It had obviously been placed there subsequently. This fact was forgotten in the general celebrations, both in Vienna and in Kirchstetten, and the transformation of Andreas Schmidt into a substantial personage.

Unfortunately, after a brief exhibition to the press, the Crown itself went into the vaults of the Kunsthistorisches Museum for "rehabilitation". It seemed that, though the stones were there, many were loose, and, at one time or another, had been removed. Perhaps whoever had looked after the Crown in its "lost years" had, at one time or another, thought that its safety would be best ensured by dispersal. It was evident that the peasant Schmidt had not held the Crown for long: his simplicity was evident from his short, strained, two-sentence speech made on accepting United Manufacturers' cheque from one of its senior directors at a ceremony in the square at Kirchstetten on a fine day, in front of the Maypole. Afterwards, Herr Schmidt and his family celebrated at Der Goldener Schlüssel, and Herr Schmidt, not for the last time during his era of prosperity, became drunk.

While Austria awaited the return of the Crown to its place in the Museum, the president of United Manufacturers kept to himself. There was a good season at the Opera that year, Karajan had succeeded Karl Böhm as Director. Callas sang superbly in *Lucia di Lammermoor*. Yet although it was known that Mr Grenville enjoyed opera, there was no sign that he visited it, even during those special *Jubelwochen*. This disappointed Countess Orsova and the old Princess Kuttenberg, who saw no good reason for taking a Schloss if you did not want to mix with other castle-owners.

Still, towards the end of July – rather late in the season – a dinner was offered at the American Embassy for Viennese "leaders of opinion" to meet Mr Grenville. The Chancellor and several members of the cabinet were invited, including Alois, and there were also businessmen such as Karl Reinhardt, Willy Svoboda, Erno Bender, and young Otto von Acht (who had just become president of Kredit Humboldt). Much to her surprise, Klara Gmunden had also been asked. To Alois's shock and to the shock of anyone else who knew of the invitation, Klara accepted.

It was obvious by then to Alois that Klara had some kind of an understanding with Willy Svoboda, who had helped her in her financial difficulties. It was also obvious that he adored her. But it was far from obvious what association they had. Vienna speculated. Alois preferred not to and, though he hoped that Klara would marry again, he hoped that she would not marry a Czech. Better an Englishman than a Czech!

Embassy dinners are all very much alike, but this one was especially grand. The ambassador, and ambassadress, stood in the receiving line but there also, with an aide standing by his side, was the mysterious Mr George Grenville: short, well-dressed in a traditional style, cautious, serious. He seemed the reverse of the tycoon. He held no cigar in his hand or mouth nor did he wear a worried frown. One did not feel any urgency in his greeting though a disinclination for friendship could have been sensed in the way that he passed on each handshake fast to his aide. Mr Grenville did not drink. His English sounded fluent, though there were some who afterwards said that, because of his "a's", one could tell that he was from Chicago.

Dinner was announced. It was formal. The ambassador had made a great effort: fifty guests at one long table. A series of exquisite dishes succeeded one another. Outside in the garden, a lovely summer day died behind the roses. At the end of the dinner, the ambassador tapped his glass, in the way which Americans do, and said:

'Ladies and gentlemen, I don't want to make anything in the way of a formal speech but I must say a word tonight about our guest of honour, Mr George Grenville. Mr Grenville has held interests in this country, through United Manufacturers of Chicago, for over a year. His investments began right after we signed the State Treaty and it's clear that they have been the trail-bearer for the new young Austria. UMC has shown dynamic leadership here. It's a real pleasure to have with us tonight UMC's president, Mr George Grenville. He's a personality who's stamped himself on the face of Austria as a result of his munificent reward to the man who found the Emperor Charles's Crown. Welcome to Mr George Grenville!'

Everyone raised their glasses to Grenville, who rose and thanked everyone, said that he was sure that they would have successful future friendships, and that he hoped to be able to welcome many of those present at a house in the Wachau which he had for the summer. He had unfortunately to leave the following day for Tokyo in order to discuss a new UMC textile mill there, but he would be back before the grapes were ripe, as he prettily put it.

At dinner, Mr Grenville – and again one noticed that no alcoholic drink passed his lips – sat between the ambassadress and the wife of the foreign minister. After dinner, the guests went into the adjoining drawing rooms and formed small groups among which George Grenville moved freely. He found himself with Karl Reinhardt on a sofa beneath a portrait of Benjamin Franklin. After initial courtesies, Grenville said:

'Could you tell me, Mr Reinhardt, the origin of this story? Some time in the 1920s, the tree of Act III of Tannhäuser at the Opera began to look tired. The stage manager asked the director if it could be renewed. The director, who was close with his money, replied: "Oh, but it still looks all right if Jeritza stands in front of it." Who was the director who made that remark? I have been searching for the answer ever since I have been in Austria."

Reinhardt, who had expected to be asked something about the Brazilian debt, or local interest rates, was amazed.

'My wife – I do not know – my wife may be able to help – Helena, please – come over here – we have a question – forgive me Mr Grenville, my English is not good – Helena –'

But she could not answer. She did say that Thekla von Acht – an old lady whom Mr Grenville might like to see and who would be certain to know the answer – had always said that if one had never heard Jeritza singing *Glück, das mir verblieb* at the Opera in 1921, one could not be said to have known happiness.

Mr Grenville bowed and moved on to talk to the Chancellor.

'Well, well,' said Reinhardt, 'I suppose the conversation over there is about Metternich. But I have to tell you,' he said to his wife, 'there is something that does not fit. The man can understand German – I watched him while I was talking to you.'

'Is he – a nazi?' Helena asked, exhilarated.

'No sweetheart – a Jew!' was the banker's reply.

'He does not look Jewish.'

'No one could be so rich so young unless he were so.'

Mr Grenville had meantime with his aide Mr James passed on to another fellow guest. It was as if he were a monarch talking to a subject of what he wanted. He spoke to the Archduke Ludwig who had been permitted to return to live in Austria the year before,. Again, it was the American who asked the questions, the Prince who answered. The hovering Austrians were expecting Mr Grenville to make a mistake of manner, address, or at least of protocol: in the event, Mr Grenville was faultless.

'With your experience, and your family's history, I suppose you would say that this is just a brief pause in the thousand year struggle between Slav and Teuton?'

'I would be less dogmatic and a little less pessimistic. Who are the real Teutons? The Prussians? They are half Polish and were looked upon as a

Slav monarchy at the Congress of Vienna. Our family has been above nationality. We were not unsuccessful in the past.'

'In the same way, we financiers in international businesses are above patriotism. I suppose we are your heirs.'

'I believe you are right,' said the Archduke eagerly.

This Archduke, a cousin of the claimant, had once been a possible leader for the monarchist cause in Austria. But he was now like Bonnie Prince Charles in later life. People treated him as they had that prince: obsequiously, and hopefully – attitudes which the Archduke did nothing to foster.

'The Soviet Union has shown by its action in Austria,' said Mr Grenville, 'that it too knows when to retrench. How do you explain the phenomenon?'

The Archduke smiled:

'I think they got tired of being asked to go home by Poldi Moser and others! But Russia had its eye on Germany. A neutral Germany, Mr Grenville, that was the aim! The plan has not worked.'

'Do you see this as a turn in the Bolshevik tide? Will they retreat and retreat? There are many things they could give up once they begin. Even Moscow, for example. It is an old Finnish city – as its name suggests.'

The Archduke looked at Mr Grenville keenly.

'You are a philologist?'

'Only an amateur one.'

Mr Grenville bowed and turned to Alois. The Archduke seemed relieved that the conversation had gone well.

'Mister Acht, I hear much about you. I know about your family. There is hardly a part of Austrian life which your family has, I believe, not adorned – politics, music, literature, the law.'

'Alas, except business, until now,' Alois's English was not good enough for this conversation, but still, he could talk.

'Is that so?'

'Until now. Many of the new generation have gone into business which their parents despised. My cousin Otto over there has just become president of Kredit Humboldt. One of my own sons is now in Baumsteffen products.'

'Ah, really Mister Acht. I believe I have the pleasure of telling you that at this very minute,' he looked at his watch, 'Baumsteffen is a subsidiary of United Manufacturers.'

'Indeed. My other son is an engineer. Do you know, he is at the Massachusetts Institute of Technology.'

'That too is fortunate, since United Manufacturers only last year equipped them with a new laboratory for molecular biology. You have a daughter too?'

'Certainly,' said Alois proudly, 'she is over there, talking to the Foreign Minister.'

Mr Grenville nodded gravely: 'Perhaps we can do something for her! I shall naturally hope to be able to talk to her in a few minutes. I congratulate you, if I may! However, Mister Acht, your achievements have been so remarkable, and your experience so great, stretching back to the pre-war generation, that you must have good advice to offer a mere novice, such as myself, who knows enough to see that to dabble in the economics of central Europe is to risk much, unless he has spent a lifetime learning the nuances. Tell me of what I should beware in the new Austria. I, in return, will tell you why I have been able to accumulate a fortune.'

Alois gulped slightly. There was something disquieting about this man's elaborately formed sentences. Was it a play, he wondered. He spoke rapidly in German:

'My advice is to avoid making up your mind about modern Austria from what you read. We are changing. All the myths are gone. We are no longer satisfied with muddling along. We used to be known for our *schlamperei* – perhaps you know the word.'

Mr Grenville seemed to hesitate. He turned to his aide, Mr James, who had been translating: 'disorder, confusion, sloppiness' – Mr James muttered. Mr Grenville nodded understandingly. All the same, Alois had the same feeling as Reinhardt: he felt Mr Grenville understood more than he allowed himself to admit. But Alois knew that great men like to employ interpreters to give them time, even if they were technically unnecessary.

'We are now workers, you know,' he said. 'We used not to be. Some people think the Germans taught us to work. Perhaps the Americans. After all, you Americans were here longer than the Germans were. Ten years, in place of seven. In the past, the Viennese were characterised by a man sitting in the Café Zentral, sipping endless cups of coffee. Now the Viennese is like any other European, he goes to work. The old café has gone.'

Mr James happily translated. He was fluent.

'You do not speak German?'

'I have some German. But it is rusty. I prefer Mr James's English.'

'May I remind you Mr Grenville, you said that you would tell me how it is that you are rich –'

'Yes, I did.' Mr Grenville raised himself up to his full height. He seemed immensely impressive. He said: 'Avoid the newspapers. Read books. Never listen to the radio. Books make money. Thank you, Mister Acht. I pray that we shall talk again.'

With which, he moved on to address Willy Svoboda.

'We are, of course, of the same generation, Mister Svoboda, so we 'ought to understand one another very well,' Mr Grenville said a trifle wearily.

'We do already,' said Willy, whose English had become excellent. 'I think we have reached a good understanding over the Linzer timber plant.'

'I did not mean that. Indeed, I knew nothing of it. Mr James will know of it. Please make sure,' he said turning to Mr James, 'I have the papers in my aeroplane about Linzer timber. I leave for Tokyo tomorrow, as the ambassador said. I meant that we are likely to see the problems of the present with the same eye, despite our differences of nationality. We shall live to see the problems of prosperity. The rest,' Mr Grenville shrugged his shoulders and looked round the room, 'what can one say? They have weathered the storm. They have survived.'

'We too have weathered the storm,' intervened Willy. 'We had a difficult time. The war, the time after the war –'

'By we – do you mean you and I?'

'We – our generation. The Countess Gmunden, for example,' said Willy, looking at Klara with undisguisable admiration.

'The Countess Gmunden. Ah! Yes, I suppose so. I had hoped to have time to talk to her. But it does not look –'

'I am sure she would like –'

'No. I cannot interrupt the Foreign Secretary. Furthermore it is late. It is eleven.' Yet he did linger a second, looking at Klara.

'You will travel to Besselberg tonight?' asked Willy politely.

Mr Grenville waved the question aside as if it were of no importance. Willy Svoboda felt foolish for having asked it.

'Do you find the economy more buoyant than you had assumed, Mr Grenville?' Willy asked instead.

'Buoyancy is a frame of mind, Mister Svoboda. It is scarcely a commodity.'

'In comparison with Germany, though?'

'There is little comparison.'

'May I ask why?'

'You have here a brilliant piece of parochial architecture. In Germany, you have a metropolis. Austria has an economy which one looks on as a toy.'

'Then why do you invest in Austria, Mr Grenville?'

'A hobby, Mister Svoboda, a hobby.'

At this moment the Foreign Minister detached himself from Klara and Alois, to walk over and take Mr Grenville by the arm and lead him into an embrasure looking out over the gardens.

'I must see that you talk to him,' Willy urgently turned to Klara, 'he has an extraordinary grasp. Wonderful use of language.'

Reinhardt was standing there.

'Did you ever find out where he was born?' he asked Alois.

'No, no, I never did. I meant to. I forgot. I'll do it.' He wrote another note with his little gold pencil.

'That's exactly what you did last time I asked, Alois!' Reinhardt said, 'Tell you what. As a good socialist you should like to make money. I'll bet you a hundred schillings that man was born within two hundred miles of Vienna.'

'Two hundred miles – where does that take me – I suppose nearly to Cracow – Well, I'll take that bet. You're an obsessive man, Karl, but I suppose you always were.'

The Foreign Minister returned with Mr Grenville.

'We were looking to the future,' he was saying. 'Mr Grenville was saying that West Europe will unite, that the history of old Europe is at an end, that Austria should associate herself commercially with the West, even if our freedom is due to the fact that we cannot do so politically. All most interesting.'

For the first time in the evening, Mr Grenville had been talked at rather than respectfully heard. But his imperturbability prevented any indication of discomfort. His Mr James was talking to him – something to do with the departure. The others could not leave before the guest of honour. But he could not leave before the Foreign Minister. Obviously they should leave together. Mr James would ensure it. And so he did! He turned towards the Foreign Minister, who eagerly nodded and the two, Mr Grenville and the Minister, began to make for the door. But before he turned away, Mr Grenville addressed himself to Klara.

'Countess, I had hoped to profit from this evening to make your acquaintance. I have talked to your father. Perhaps one day he – or perhaps Mister Svoboda – could bring you to lunch at Besselberg. You must know it so well. I know it only a little. But I am happy there. It would be a pleasure if you could show me more of it, Countess Gmunden. The climate there is different, I can see, from Vienna. Sharper. But just as beautiful.'

'Since my husband died, I do not go out much.'

'But you could make an exception in the country? After all, it must be a family place for you. Do you not have childhood memories? May my staff be in touch with you?'

Klara hesitated. She was aware that the eyes of several people were upon them, though it was not clear whether their ears could tell what was said.

She spoke rapidly in German: 'I know very well that we have met before.'

'Indeed? Then that is perhaps a reason for renewing our –' and though he had spoken in English the right word seemed to elude him and it was his turn to hesitate, for the first time in the evening.

'Acquaintanceship?' Klara completed the sentence for him, also in English.

'Very well, acquaintanceship.'

'And as you seem to be proficient in German, perhaps *you* might like to be in touch with *my* staff,' Klara said, this time in English.

Mr Grenville did not smile. He kissed her hand, murmured "undoubtedly" and left for Tokyo.

LXI

Several weeks passed. Presumably Mr Grenville had been to and returned from Tokyo. No sign came from Besselberg. Klara was relieved. The summer heat began.

In the third week, Mr Grenville made a move: an oblique one. Willy Svoboda told Klara that he had been asked to lunch the following Sunday at Besselberg. There would be a large party. Perhaps he would like to bring Countess Gmunden? Mr Grenville had anyway thought of inviting her. Klara asked how the invitation had come; who had invited him. It had been a male secretary. Mr James? No, Willy thought not. Anyway, whoever it had been had talked to his secretary. Klara thought that it could have been Mr Grenville himself, but she did not say so. Willy proposed to go. It was a professional responsibility to accept. He would take Klara with pleasure. They would drive. It would make a pleasant Sunday. Perhaps they could walk afterwards by the Danube. Even if he were unable to talk directly to Mr Grenville about UMC (and at the dinner at the American Embassy Mr Grenville had implied that he did not discuss finance at social gatherings), he would gain more knowledge of Mr Grenville's withdrawn character; he might talk with people who might be useful for him. It would be advantageous to go.

Willy was innocent about his social strivings. Willy plainly wanted her to go with him. It meant something to him to walk into the room accompanied by a beautiful even if somewhat notorious countess. Klara did not mind that. She was grateful to Willy for a hundred things. He would do anything she asked. He arranged things for her. She decided to accept, if only for Willy's sake. Besides, she was herself curious. She wanted to see how Besselberg had been reconstructed and how Mr Grenville managed when, even by proxy, he was "at home".

Sunday came. It was already hot, and Willy's ducal chauffeur arrived in Heiligenstadt at the appointed hour. They drove north along the south bank of the Danube through Tulln and other places mentioned in the *Nibelungenlied*. They crossed the Danube by the new Krems bridge built by the Russians. They made their way through the leafy lanes of the Wachau to Besselberg. They noticed, immediately, on crossing the

Danube and arriving in what had been the Soviet zone at Krems, how the agriculture and the villages declined. They felt in a different, more primitive, world. Not less attractive. A horse is more beautiful than a tractor. The past was graceful. But a journey into the Wachau was then still a journey into the nineteenth century.

Precisely at a quarter to one, as invited, Willy's car turned in by the lodge gate to Besselberg. One could see a transformation. In the last months, a fortune had been spent on refurbishment of the park as well as of the house. The white gates had been newly painted, there were horses in the paddock, the gravel by the stables had been raked, the tiles repaired. They drove into the splendid courtyard. The pink roses climbing the façade of the house were in bloom. They made their way into the house up stone steps, whose well-known cracks had been eradicated. Klara had not been to Besselberg since the summer of 1944. She remembered a party there long ago before the war, in Uncle Otto's time, with Uncle Otto's spaniels knocking the glass out of a very proper, tall, fair man's hand and how cross he had been. Then she remembered: the tall, fair man had been Count Gmunden.

Mr Grenville received his guests on the verandah. There were twenty or even thirty people present, a number of them Americans. Several were connected with United Manufacturers. There were also the American ambassador and his daughter, only eighteen years old but sophisticated. The Austrians present did not, for once, include any member of the Acht family apart from Klara and, rather surprisingly, Rüdiger and Alice. A black butler from Barbados mixed strong martinis. Like Mr Grenville's aide, he too was called James.

The conversation in the verandah was about the house. Klara, with her memories of it and knowledge of it in the past, was asked many questions. She found herself telling the life history of Uncle Otto, of his love of the house, and how he had died so strangely, on Christmas Day after the family had put on a play. About 1948.

'Were you yourself in the play, Countess?' asked the Ambassador. Mr Grenville was watching, drinking lemonade.

'No.'

'At that time, I suppose it was difficult to get out here from Vienna?'

'It was not easy. But I was not in Vienna then, actually.'

'Ah, how fortunate. You were in Salzburg perhaps?'

'No,' said Klara easily, 'I was in Moscow that Christmas.'

The American ambassador was surprised. He narrowed his eyes trying to remember.

'I suppose,' he said, 'the first Figl mission to Moscow was about then.'

The black Mr James announced lunch. The dining room had been beautifully repainted in pale green, the curtains were new silk, the needlepoint chairs repaired, the stucco and wooden carving picked out in white. One felt oneself carefully arranged on a stage set.

Mr Grenville had not placed Klara next to him. That distinction was reserved for Alice: a strange choice, it was generally supposed. Klara, however, guessed the reason. The lunch was agreeable. Klara thought, with relief, nothing interesting at all was said. Afterwards, there were suggestions by the ambassador that there should be bridge. Willy Svoboda was keen to play. Two tables were formed in the library where it was cool. The white Mr James, Mr Grenville's aide, led Klara back to the verandah. They began some vapid conversation. Klara complimented Mr James on his excellent German. He explained that he was by origin Swiss, having gone to live in America with his father, a professor of numismatics, in 1936. He wondered if the Countess would like to walk to the lake. Although the day was hot, the breeze was exhilarating. The buttercups were enticing. Klara thought to herself, why not? She had always liked the lake. They began their walk down through the meadow – a path had been carefully mown – when she became aware that Mr Grenville, whom she had supposed to be playing bridge, was about to join them. Some sign, unobserved by Klara, must have passed between him and Mr James, for the latter soon slowed down his pace, turned round and returned to the house; and it was Mr Grenville who continued walking beside Klara to the lake. There was a bench there (newly painted). They sat down and observed the swans.

'So,' he said. It sounded as if his extraordinary endeavours had been directed to the achievement of this moment.

'You are Kamo, of course?' said Klara. It was more a statement than a question.

'No, no,' he said, 'whoever I once might have been, I am now definitely George Grenville. We have to begin with that.'

'If we begin with that, where do we end?'

'That is for you to decide.' He crossed his legs.

'When we last met,' he said, 'you asked to go with me to America. Do you remember?'

'Yes, very well.'

'Naturally, I could not be accompanied on such a journey. One cannot travel fast in such circumstances: with a companion, I mean.'

'I understood at the time.'

'I also said I would come back for you.'

'That I remember.'

'I was at the time penniless. I had nothing. There was nothing in my conduct which could have led you to suppose I could ever, in America or elsewhere, be a thousandth as successful as I have been. You hardly knew me at all so it could not have been a matter of affection. You had

334

everything at your feet. Beauty. The position of daughter to a minister. An accepted place in the society of Vienna. Yet you wanted to leave with someone who had nothing, whose position was below everything, in order to get to America. Why? That is where we must begin.'

Klara said nothing. She continued to observe the swans.

'You said, I remember very well, that you wanted to come to America in order to escape from people. Who were those people?' Klara still remained silent. 'You do not want to answer? I can understand. But there is another question. It may have the same answer. Between the time of our first conversation and the time when I left your garden with the police, someone informed on me. Somebody told the police – or told somebody who told the police. Now it could have been your father, but I think that is improbable. I have made a careful examination of your father's affairs, including his bank statements and I believe him to be innocent. Your brothers? Equally improbable! The maid? I have talked to her at length. I am satisfied that she did nothing. There is only one possibility left. Was it you, Countess? And if, as I think, it was you, why? Did you ask to leave with me after you had betrayed me? Or, was it *just* before the betrayal? If I had said "yes", would your telephone call (if you made it) to the police not have been made? No. Please do not get up. The game of bridge has only just begun. There are some good players there. They are busy. This is our game. It is more interesting than bridge. I need to know these answers. I have waited for them. For years.'

He himself rose and addressed her standing up.

'People who betray me do not as a rule benefit in the long run. I have built an enormous fortune precisely so that I can avenge the slightest affront just as I like. A more serious injury will warrant a proportionately more serious reply. While you are considering your answer, consider some of the other people who injured, or betrayed, me in those months in Vienna. There was an English officer, a Major Grew. It fell to him to pursue me even as far as the Italian frontier. I saw him in a remote castle in Carinthia, he recognised me and he put me and my friends to some inconvenience thereafter. His career, because of the news that he falsified his report over his mission in South Carinthia, which in turn I have leaked to the appropriate authorities, is in ruins. He now faces court martial in England. I had the news only yesterday. His wife, your friend Tatiana, has decided to leave him because it is plain that he lied to her about various things there. Do you recall a French colonel interested in the works of Goya who, at the time, served with the French Mission here? He, with Grew, as it happens, pursued me like a dog through Vienna. He had two months ago to resign in ignominy from the Louvre. A coincidence? Of course, it must seem so. But I was able to ensure that he made a fatal mistake in identifying a picture. He was quite innocent. But we have arranged that it does not look at all like it.'

Klara expostulated: 'What a petty man you have become.' But he went on: 'Then you may not recall an English art historian, also temporarily in Vienna in those far off days. Those "Kamo" days! His name was Livingstone. He recently had to resign from the Worthington Gallery in London. A sudden inflammation of two English viruses, homosexuality and hypocrisy, did for him. Worse may incidentally await Livingstone since he may himself have been worse, but I do not yet know. On that, your father may be able to throw some light. I believe that he was working for the Russians at the very time that he was seeking to defeat them over my case, formally and officially. He made one mistake, however: he told your father and Poldi Moser, or one of them, not of the train on which I had been supposed to travel to Russia, but by error another one into which I had been placed because my own special train had something wrong with it. It is to that error that I owe my life. By giving some nearly good information, Colonel Livingstone (as he then was) hoped, I understand, to be able to give himself credibility which he seriously needed, since he knew himself to be under suspicion due to a Russian defector who had betrayed him and who, in turn, his own friend Mercer would later manage to destroy. It is a complicated story, Countess, and I do not at all wonder that you look confused.'

'I am not confused by your story but by the extent of your cruelty,' she remarked between her teeth. 'I have never known a man so evil.'

'*Never?* Never? Let us come to that. There was Count Gmunden. Deeply involved in the unofficial Soviet network in Vienna, he tried not once but several times to turn me over to the Russians. He did many other things as well, into which I need not go, since you know something of them. Perhaps he thought the Russians were certain to take over Austria in the end because the Americans would get bored. He miscalculated. He also miscalculated when he became concerned with United Manufacturers. I have to say that he took the initiative. I merely used the opportunity offered. I did not even know that he had killed himself.'

'I would like to go back to the house.'

'Certainly, if you wish. But there are some things which I am surprised you would not like to have cleared up. Your own part –'

'They forced me. If you had accepted to take me to America, I should have avoided them. Escaped then.' Thus she had admitted it.

'Very well. But remind me, would you, who are, or were, "they"? We do not know the first chapter of your story, don't you remember? *Your story*.'

'*They?* You, who know everything, know perfectly well.'

'But tell me, it is so interesting. Look, let us clear this up now. Let us walk round the lake. We are in full view of the house. You need not worry that I shall throw you in –'

'The thought had not occurred to me,' said Klara, startled. 'Anyway, I can swim.'

'That is something which I have never yet had time to learn. In Georgia the rivers are used for drowning one's enemies, not for swimming. They say, though, that it is not difficult. To swim, I mean. Listen, let us walk round the lake. You can see that little temple. On the further shore. James is bringing tea there.'

'James, or Mr James?'

'Black James.'

'You had ordered it before! What would have happened if I had gone back to the house when I wanted to?'

'Well, I really don't know. I expect James would have found another use – so shall we go?'

'Very well.'

'Who were *they* then?' asked Mr Grenville again as they began to walk.

'But since you know, why ask?'

'I do not know. Not precisely.'

'Do you know why?' This was the question she had not wished to ask. Yet she had.

Mr Grenville did not answer at first. Then he said:

'I put two and two together. You were abducted by Russians. Yes. Then you spent many months with them. Then you return. You are returned, I should say. You tell nothing about what happened. Why should you be returned? They are not kind-hearted people, my ex-countrymen.'

'Any more than you are!'

'You think I am unkind?'

'The German language does not have a word for your ruthlessness.'

'That is rather strong.'

'It was intended to be.'

'Well then, you are returned. On what conditions? On no conditions? Inconceivable. We are dealing neither with idiots, nor with philanthropists. There must have been conditions for your return. Why deny it? What were those conditions?'

'Very well,' Klara said. 'I agreed to work for them.'

The summer sun bathed them both in light. Had one been watching from the windows of Besselberg one would have thought, perhaps, how romantic: the richest man in the world and the most beautiful woman in Austria are walking around the lake. They were too far away for their expressions to have been observed. But it must have been evident that they were in deep conversation.

'How beautiful it is,' Klara was saying, shading her eyes.

'Did you work for them?'

'For a time. Not very effectively. I didn't know much they wanted to know. They liked to know about people who took me out. Silly things. They hoped I would marry well, and be in a good position to report for years. They were rather like Victorian parents in that respect. They were always afraid I might marry Svoboda. He wasn't good enough for them.'

'Them, them! Who was *them* then?'

Klara hesitated.

'The most important one was called Voronov. He was responsible – responsible for everything. He was personally not without redeeming features.'

'What did they think of Gmunden?'

'They were unenthusiastic. You obviously know all about him. Anyway they thought it a waste to have me and him married. They told me that they had been friendly with Gmunden for a long time. Since before the war, think of it. Even before he was a Heimwehr youth leader. You must say they are thorough. As thorough as you. They thought that would put me off. I became engaged the next day.'

'Why did you marry him?'

'Why should I tell you?'

'Because I find it extraordinarily interesting.'

They had reached the far side of the lake.

'If you walk a little further you find a waterfall. When I was here as a child we used to call it a camp. Jean Marie's camp. My cousin.'

'Shall we walk there then?'

'As you like.'

'You were telling me why you married Gmunden.'

'You were asking.'

Then, looking at the ground, Klara did speak. 'On the surface he was kind. He also seemed rich. Not as rich as you. But rich for Austria, as it was then. Kinder than you, of course. And he seemed to understand the Russians and the Americans equally well. It was helpful to talk to someone like that. Kurt used to argue that, like it or not, one had to deal with the Russians. They were here to stay, he would say. One could not get away from it. I wanted to get married. I wanted to escape from what I was. I thought it was a way. I did not know that he was an agent. Voronov told me that only after we were married.'

'Did you continue to work for him – for Voronov – after your marriage?'

'Not for long. I had nothing interesting to say. Anyway they were getting bored. Voronov had left.'

'Where to?'

'I haven't an idea. Siberia, I suppose. It's the usual posting after Vienna.'

They were now in a remote part of the park. The stream which flowed out of the lake did reach a waterfall. Over the top of it there was a rickety bridge. When children, the Acht cousins would be accustomed to play there. Their nannies – including an English nanny whom Klara remembered, her name was Miss Lillie – had used to shout and say 'careful, careful, one false step and you go to meet your God. So be very careful and stop dancing now. Stop dancing *now*.' It had always been a dramatic spot. The trees were tall. Even in winter one could see little of the sky. Klara remembered picnics in that spot.

'What happened to you after you were kidnapped in the Wienerwald?'

'Do you know no one has asked me that question for years? No one. And when they put it it was always put indirectly. My husband never asked me.'

'He perhaps knew.'

'No, I don't think he did. He – like most other people – unlike you, felt that the past was better forgotten and buried.'

'To face the future one needs truth about the past.'

'I see you are a Freudian. And I am an Austrian not a Viennese. I believe that the past should be left to rot like leaves so that everything becomes in the end indistinguishable from the other leaves, as in a wood like this.'

She walked airily on the rotten bridge and gave a sprightly dance.

'This is the one part of the park that you don't seem to have done up as well as you should,' she said. 'The whole bridge needs rebuilding. The pool looks like hellfire now. What a horrible death!'

'The bridge will be mended before you come again.'

'Shall I answer your question now?'

She was high above him on the rickety bridge and he could not see her, only hear her voice.

'It is not dangerous, I hope?'

'It is rather dangerous. But don't worry Mr Grenville, it always was. In my recollection, which is not always good, what happened was this. We were kidnapped. There was another girl with me. But she rode into Vienna waving on a tank. I, by bad luck, was thrown into a lorry and driven back behind the lines. There was terrible confusion. I thought I might escape. But there was no chance. I saw terrible things. People being killed for no reason. Some, like the mayor of Priedorf, being burned at a stake. He was a nazi, but even so! It was all confused. That is the impression I have above all. There were terrible assaults on peasant women before my eyes. Old women! Why old women? Why should a young man want to rape an old woman? I still think it rather odd. Women were being shaved. Not at all nice, Mr Grenville. I thought my turn was next. I suppose I looked nicer than the others. So there was competition over me. Had it not been for the spirit of competition, I would have been dead. As a capitalist, you would understand. Competition delayed things. We were still somewhere in the Wienerwald – the other side. Near Tulln. My time had come, as I thought, when a colonel came forward. He told the men to stop. They didn't care. They were so drunk. He killed two of them with his revolver. I protested. Do you know what he said? In German. "Don't worry, we've got plenty more where they come from." He took me into his headquarters and talked to me. He was a cultivated man, but had forced himself not to be. He said he was a colonel in intelligence and was looking for girls to help in the Sovietisation of Austria. Would I help? I would have to be trained in Russia. If I said I'd help, I would survive. That's what he said. The conditional case. So I agreed. I was driven to the airport and in no time was in Kiev. Then I was put in a train. There were other girls going to Moscow. We were all going to Russia to be trained. On the way we had to dance for the benefit of the staff of Tolbukhin's army. We said we'd dance well if they fed us the same as them. It was the kind of argument they under-stood. They agreed and gave us huge haunches of beef. That was when I saw Uncle Rudi, I suppose. Or, when he saw me, because of course I could not distinguish who was there. Anyway you know about all that don't you? After about ten days, I arrived in Moscow. After my training, I would be put back into Austria as a bacillus of revolution. They thought I came from a socialist family, of course.'

'Nothing else?'

'Yes. Voronov became my lover.'

He could not see her above him on the bridge.

'In Moscow? Voronov? How can I believe you? Voronov was here anyway.'

'Voronov was a cynic. He said he was a Russian imperialist. He always told me that he would have been a colonel in the Okhrana if the Tsars had lasted. I believed him. He never pretended to be a communist. He was brutally candid. He had a sense of humour. He came back every month or so. Oh – do you know the name of that little bird with the red breast and black head? Could it be a bullfinch? Do you see? There is no need to believe me, if you don't like it. Historical truth is difficult.'

Mr Grenville could not see the bullfinch. He did not care about the bird. Who could be sure of anything any more? He had to see her to believe her. He began to walk up the stone steps to the bridge. They were high, the bridge was rickety, Klara was in the centre of it.

'Why did you return from Moscow looking so well?'

'Did I? I have to say, I did not suffer. Well, I must say that I became fond of Voronov. We used to play chess. I have to tell you this – I did not dislike my experience! That's my crime isn't it? That's why no one will forgive me. So that's my story, Mr Grenville. Not exactly edifying. But still, I survived. That's something. It makes one feel well, survival. Guilt makes one feel distant, perhaps. Do you have any more questions? Because this is the moment, isn't it. Tomorrow, you will be in Chicago. Or where? Valhalla perhaps? There isn't really quite so much time in your Austrian summer as you thought, is there? How did you make your fortune, incidentally? So quickly! Surely I deserve a confidence myself?'

'Would you like to come to Chicago with me?'

The question echoed up to Klara from where Mr Grenville stood on the step next to the top.

'Not much,' Klara said, 'I now rather like it here.'

'Most people do what I suggest.'

'But – I – I am not quite like everybody else, some people would say.'

'If you don't come I should revenge myself on you.'

'Oh, how old-fashioned! Love or vengeance! Is that what we want in our new Austria? Don't we want harmony and affection? That's what Europe needs now.'

'I am not a part of your new Austria,' said Mr Grenville fiercely. 'I am not a European. I belong to the past. I am an Asiatic!'

He reached the top of the steps. Klara had moved to the other end of the bridge. He began, with the delicacy of step that had carried him over so many roofs and through so many scrapes, to walk towards her. The bridge was certainly rotten and dangerous. One needed to walk slowly.

'Did you use the stones in the Crown of the Emperor to start you off? Or was it Ludwig Börne? And incidentally what have you done with him?' she called.

He hesitated.

'Only one stone.'

'Which?'

'The pearl of Saint Agatha of Hungary,' he said simply. 'That I sold – and replaced with a false one. Ludwig Börne helped. But, of course, he knew too much about me.'

'What *do* you mean!'

'He died.'

'You killed him?'

'He had a heart attack in his hotel room last winter in Saint Moritz in the Alps.'

'Are you just a common murderer to kill the man who helped you?'

'I am an *un*common murderer.'

Mr Grenville had reached the middle of the bridge and was moving slowly towards her. Klara was enraged, and frightened at the same time. She stamped her foot heavily, just as she had done when angry as a child, once, twice, a third time. The wood broke, she sprang onto the steps, but

341

there was no such escape for the President of United Manufacturers. He fell, slowly, he tried to fling himself to the side, he nearly arrested his fall on the greenery, but the ivy he skilfully caught gave way and he fell into the horrible dark, disturbed pool below.

'Savage,' he screamed as he went under for the second time.

'I don't know about that. If we can talk of vengeance, I'm avenging Tatiana Grew. How odd that you, who do everything so well, can't swim,' said Klara.

It was true. It was the one thing that he could not do. But he was very strong. The pool was not very large. He pushed himself to the side and heaved himself up. After all he was not old. In the prime of life.

'That was not very sensible,' he said, still out of breath.

There was no reply. Klara had run back to the house. He walked dripping to the summer house where James had laid the tea.

LXII

YET ANOTHER WEEK PASSED.
          The telephone rang in Klara's house at Heiligenstadt. Alois took the call. He passed the receiver to her. It was Grenville.

'I am on my way to finish our conversation,' he said.

'Let me finish it on the telephone,' said Klara. 'Isn't it the modern way?'

'But I told you, I belong to the past.'

'You cannot expect me to remember everything you say, you talk too much.'

'The conversation needs to be continued in person.'

'But we had finished it. Didn't you notice I tried to kill you?' Klara asked lightly.

'I had noticed it. I have something else to say. I want you to come with me to Chicago. It is the most beautiful city in the world. The lake, the buildings, the Opera House. It is like Vienna a hundred years ago.'

'But I do not love you, as perhaps you noticed.'

'That is not what I was offering.'

'But that is what I should like if I am going to go to Chicago with anyone.'

'My car anyway is on its way. I am speaking from the car telephone. I am already in Döbling.'

'By the time that you reach me, I shall have gone. Goodbye.' She put down the telephone. Alois had withdrawn upstairs at some point while she was talking. She took a deep breath and made one more telephone call, much the same sort that she had made in the same house many years ago and to the same destination. After putting down the receiver she shouted to her father:

'I am going to Grinzing.'

'To Grinzing? Where? Why?'

'I am going to the Schuberthaus.'

'Alone?'

'Someone will join me there. If anyone calls, tell them.'

'Calls? Telephones? Visits?'

'Either.' Alois heard the door slamming. He thought, well, Klara never had a proper youth, she must enjoy herself while she can.

343

LXIII

KLARA SAT IN A CORNER TABLE AT THE DOOR OF THE
Schuberthaus. The garden was crowded, the inside empty, but it
was filling up. Grenville came in alone. He seemed to be unescorted.
Klara had known that he would come. She had had experience of obsessed
men.

'Well,' he said.

'It is for you to begin the conversation.'

'I have forgiven your attempt on me. In fact, I respect you for it.'

'Thank you.'

'All the same, my proposal stands.'

'And your threat?'

'And my threat.'

'Withdraw your threat, and I shall consider your proposal.'

'I cannot.'

'You will regret it.'

'I regret nothing.'

'You are playing with fire.'

'I have played with little else.'

'Would you like a drink?'

'I never touch it.'

'I thought all Asiatics drank.'

'You must permit me an idiosyncrasy.'

'Would you mind if I had a slivovitz?'

'I shall order it.' He did.

'For the last time, withdraw your threat.'

'I shall not,' said Grenville.

Klara looked expectantly at the door.

'What are you expecting?'

'Aren't you very foolish to trust yourself to me? I have betrayed you
once and tried to kill you once.'

'I have confidence.'

'Is that always enough?'

'I have luck. Would you make up your mind?'

'Make up my mind? What about?'

'Chicago; or the alternative.'

Klara looked involuntarily again at the door. No one had entered. 'Let us play chess,' she said, suddenly, seeing a set on the next table. 'When we have finished, I shall tell you.'

'Very well.'

Klara did not know exactly what she was doing when she made this proposal. She might have spent three years in Moscow but her chess was not good. Grenville could play very well. The early moves indicated that. Klara's queen's pawn fell very quickly, Grenville made a swift, devastating, if expensive, assault on both sides of her defence preventing her from castling and then, though two bishops down, in the eleventh move forced her king to begin a pilgrimage up the centre of the board, where, with immense elegance, she was check-mated by a pawn. Klara had wanted to play for time. She had chosen the wrong game.

'Well?'

The night was warm. In the distance, there was singing: a sweet, and sickly but all the same charming irresistible Austrian melody such as the land of smiles produces in such generous profusion.

'It is true that songs like that are not sung so often in Chicago,' said Grenville.

'Nor in Georgia, I suppose.'

'Ah, our songs are very good.'

'Why not sing one while you are deciding?'

'Decide what? It is for you to decide.' Klara considered. 'No,' she said, 'you have to decide. Whether to withdraw your threat.'

'I shall sing if you like. My threat cannot be withdrawn.' With that Grenville took a deep breath and began to sing a soft, delicate Georgian lyric. As he did so four tall men in raincoats entered the Schuberthaus. They did not look like Austrians. They glanced round the room in an expert way and, seeing Klara, made for her table. She signed to them to wait till the song was over. They did so but moved to stand behind the singer who, uniquely oblivious to his surroundings, stood up, his chest swelling. The restaurant was too crowded for anyone to notice what was happening. Nearly everyone there except for Klara and Grenville was drunk.

The song finished, the men closed in on him. Mr Grenville (and he became instantly Kamo again) was, as it were, folded away by the men in raincoats. In a second they had gone. Klara could not quite see what had happened. The men in raincoats were after all professionals.

The waiter came up to ask her to pay for the slivovitz. She could not do so and became involved in a long argument. The waiter refused to give her credit. She promised to go and get her father to pay. The waiter refused. The name "Acht" meant nothing to him. She asked to telephone to Willy Svoboda. The Schuberthaus had no telephone. In the end, Klara left her watch with the waiter, and promised to return with the money to redeem it the next day. She never did. It was a reminder of the bleak days of the cold war when in Vienna one's watch often vanished in strange circumstances.

LXIV

*T*WO WEEKS LATER KLARA ANNOUNCED HER ENGAGEMENT TO Willy Svoboda.

'Dull, isn't he,' said Aunt Thekla when she heard.

'Klara wants to be dull. That's the whole point,' Alice Acht answered.

The disappearance of Mr Grenville was never explained. Most uncharacteristically he had gone out by himself that night with no chauffeur. His car was found in Grinzing. The Danube was searched. Could he have disposed of himself from guilt? It seemed improbable. The speculation continued for months. His vice-presidents took over his businesses, announced that they would continue his policies and programmes, but soon fell out. United Manufacturers of Chicago became disunited within a year. Meanwhile a rumour took hold. It suggested that Mr Grenville had been suffering from an incurable disease, and that he had put an end to himself, secretly, with his customary efficiency. The tale appeared in all the newspapers and became gradually believed.

'A better end than he deserved,' said Countess Orsova. Klara was never implicated. As usual, Alois asked no questions. To what good?

A little before Klara's wedding, by an unexpected coincidence, the Crown of Charles V was re-exhibited. It stood in a dark grand room. It was difficult for experts to decide whether the jewels had suffered during their inexplicable exile. One jeweller, Dr Elkhorn, an expert from Amsterdam, drew aside the keeper of the coronation jewels and said:

'The central pearl – the pearl of Saint Agatha. It has a strange colour. Could I examine it closely outside of the glass case? In daylight?'

'I am afraid not,' was the answer.

'Not?'

'Look, my dear Dr Elkhorn, you know modern Europe. You know modern Austria. That pearl glows well. It looks fine. Don't examine anything too carefully. You might get some unpleasant surprises. It's the same with Austria. Please don't look too closely.'

Klara's second wedding took place in the Karlskirche.